ULTIMATE ADVENTURE

ULTIMATE ADVENTURE

Lawrence Essex

The Book Guild Ltd

First published in Great Britain in 2023 by
The Book Guild Ltd
Unit E2 Airfield Business Park,
Harrison Road, Market Harborough,
Leicestershire. LE16 7UL
Tel: 0116 2792299
www.bookguild.co.uk
Email: info@bookguild.co.uk
Twitter: @bookguild

Typeset in 11pt Minion Pro

Printed on FSC accredited paper
Printed and bound in Great Britain by 4edge Limited

ISBN 978 1915853 288

British Library Cataloguing in Publication Data.
A catalogue record for this book is available from the British Library.

To Elliott, who ventured with me through fantastical realms in childhood, may these pages evoke our past adventures and inspire future ones.

*So many of this world's secrets remain hidden to us. We
are wanderers, lost in a dream.
Is it reality that shapes us? Or us who shape reality?
Is any of this real or not?*

PRELUDE

Desperate screams are drowned out by lashing rain. Heavy breath fogs the upstairs window of an English terraced house while sweaty palms beat the glass. Ed Holmes, a lifelong fantasist and comic shop clerk, is in grave peril and all attempts to signal to the girl in the window across the street have failed. The swift motion with which she shuts her curtains kills any hope he had. Plan B then. He scurries into the bathtub of his en-suite, ducks down and listens feverishly to someone or something stumbling around in his dark bedroom – clattering, then a loud thud.

Carefully he peers over the edge of the tub and through the doorway to the Game Station controller lying beside his bed. A long sinewy hand looms from the shadows and grasps it between three gangly fingers. The intruder steps into the light emanating from his upturned television and, whatever it is, it's tall, standing eight or nine feet and hunched over the ransacked bedroom. All he can do is helplessly watch the creature tear his shelves clean off the walls, scattering his pricey collectables everywhere. Its attention turns to his bed. Whipping the duvet off, it tears the pillows apart until feathers blanket everything like snow.

Ed slides down again and struggles to quell his racing

explosion of thoughts. *Piss off! Please piss off! What does it want? To eat me? Kill me? Worse? What's worse?*

A video game case ricochets off the tiled wall and lands on top of him. He picks it up, scanning it with wide eyes. Printed in bold font on the cover are the words 'ULTIMATE ADVENTURE VII'. He quickly flips the case over and notices the customer helpline number on the back. It's worth a shot. He already tried the police, but they dismissed him as merely a prank caller. He holds the case up into the sliver of light coming in through the bathroom window and dials the number with his other hand, then he cups his iPhone to his ear. The droning ring brings only dread, until a voice heralds salvation.

"Good evening and thanks for calling the 4D Games customer helpline." A woman speaks in a dull robotic tone, utterly devoid of humanity.

"Help me! Help me! Help me!" Ed says in a hoarse whisper.

"We are currently experiencing a high number of calls so there may be a wait time. Some calls may be recorded for training purposes," the voice says.

Of course. Of course it's a machine. Ed's chest tightens up as the voice lists menu options.

"… if you are calling for anything to do with billing say 'billing'; if you have a complaint and would like to voice your concerns with a member of our team then say 'complaint'."

"Complaint! Complaint! There's something very wrong with your game!"

"You have selected 'customer satisfaction survey'."

Ed gasps, "That wasn't even an option!"

"Yes it was," the voice replies, with a sudden spark of humanity.

"Wait, you're not a machine?!"

As the realisation that he's the butt of a bored employee's joke dawns, a monstrous black hand tears the shower curtain away and flings it into the air. The intruder casts a foreboding shadow on the wall as it raises two freakishly long arms and cries out in some garbled language. Its booming, guttural voice rumbles like the storm outside and reverberates with electronic sounding pulses that grate Ed's ears. The creature pulls him from the tub by the scruff of his hoodie, silencing his wails of terror. He clings to the rim, kicking violently while the assailant wrestles his legs, and all he can think is that it wouldn't have killed him to do a few push-ups once in a while; a little upper body strength would go a long way right about now.

With growing impatience, the intruder splits the bathtub like a log with one broad swipe and hurls Ed into his bedroom. He skids across the carpet and hits his bookshelf with a thump, and scrambles across the floor for a means of defending himself, landing on his prized replica lightsaber. Taking it in both hands, he ignites it. The intruder emerges from the bathroom and into the blue light cast from the lightsaber's plastic bubble. Ed gets a good look at it now. Its gangly, hunchbacked body is shrouded in tattered black robes and its face is hidden behind an eerie bronze mask adorned with small sculpted faces, twisted and screaming. Everything about it is utterly out of this world, but at the same time, it looks very familiar to him, like something has stepped right out of his video game. Seeing what he's up against, Ed hurls the toy at the creature and bolts into the corridor and towards the stairs. He doesn't make it past the first few steps before the creature grasps a clump of his messy hair and yanks him back through the hallway. He pulls and scratches at the leathery hand, which only encourages the creature to tighten its iron grip until the pressure on his scalp is too painful to bear. Ed gives in, surmising that if he's going to die, he'd rather go out with a full head of hair. His body goes limp, and he's dragged screaming and whimpering into his bedroom again, worrying whether there will be anything left of him for his father to identify when he gets back from his nightshift in the morning. The door slams shut and a booming hum reverberates from behind it. The whole house tremors as the room is engulfed in a blinding light. A moment later it dissipates, and all goes deathly quiet.

The bedroom is empty now. The game case lies open on the floor, illuminated by the glow of the television lying on its side. Its display flickers. The screen reads, 'Game Over', but this is only the beginning.

I

REALITY SUCKS

Thirty-seven hours, two minutes and fifteen seconds earlier, Remy Winters sits lost in a dream – or perhaps a nightmare would be more appropriate. Her sharp eyes fixate on a small brown stain besmearing the cold, white ceiling. She shuffles uncomfortably in her chair and gauges her surroundings. Placed about the drab magnolia walls of her local job centre are patronising posters of people looking overly optimistic about their work prospects, a stark contrast to the expressions of the people actually populating the room. A look of anguish graces her face as cold, hard reality comes crashing down on her. At twenty-seven, the only thing of note she's got to show for her life is a 'Mickey Mouse degree' and a chip on her shoulder. So here she sits, in the funk of her life, trapped in a place no one wants to be.

From behind the desk, her careers adviser, Norma, looks upon Remy with an almost predatory gaze. She shrinks into her raggedy old sweatshirt and Norma's eyes tighten as she reads what's written on it: 'Reality Sucks, Take Me Away'. Not really choice interview attire.

"So Miss… Remy Winters? That sounds like a porn name," Norma chuckles.

Remy's eyebrows shoot up her forehead, and she quietly asks, "Are you allowed to say that?"

Norma looks worried for a split second and her thin lips give way to a false smile, then she quickly turns to her computer monitor to skim Remy's credentials. Her résumé lists a six-month internship at a minuscule television channel and a few work experience placements that promised significant remuneration in 'exposure' – a currency often bartered within creative industries that holds zero monetary value and cannot be exchanged for goods or services, but it sounds like a prelude to success, doesn't it? As Remy knows all too well, it is not.

What her résumé doesn't tell Norma is all the countless job applications and cover letters emailed into the void, all while working long shifts waiting tables in a restaurant she could never afford to eat at. It is said that effort will release its reward only after you refuse to quit, and refuse she did. Eventually, Remy landed herself a pretty little gig as a production assistant at a blossoming production company. Their content didn't exactly have the artistic licence she had hoped, but it paid and she got to travel. She was starting to live the dream – nights out in trendy London clubs, nursing hangovers with the kind of 'I'm going to live forever' attitude a young city creative acquires. Remy could see the next five years sprawled out before her, like a yellow brick road leading to the kind of life people vlog about. Her future was bright, but like a dying star that light was snuffed out.

Oh, how the mighty fall, she grumbles to herself, reflecting on what led her to this special hell.

"I have to say your CV is very 'media-centric'," Norma says, making air quotations with her fingers.

Remy sits up and mumbles, "Oh, well, I—"

"Only there aren't really any media jobs, you see." Her tone is a cocktail of pity and condescension. "Maybe you should try something a little more achievable? Do you have any other skills?"

As what little self-confidence Remy has slips away, she desperately tries to present herself as a capable human being and not succumb to the crippling self-doubt whispering in her ear. *Useless talentless loser ugly pathetic failure.*

"Um, I, uh…" She trails off with a groan and folds into herself.

"Hmm." Norma leans back in her chair, hands clasped. She glances at her monitor again, and after a moment, her eyes light up.

"What about dentistry? Wig making? Taxidermy?" She leans forward, looking eager.

Remy slowly susses that Norma wasn't joking. "Um… no."

Norma sits back again. Her eyes brim with disappointment as she scrawls 'no hoper' on Remy's file.

"What did you write?"

Remy tries to sneak a glance, but Norma hastily covers what she wrote with her hand and brushes Remy off with a smile forced through pursed lips, then her face returns to cold stone.

With a pained sigh, Remy sinks in her chair, and resigns herself to the next twenty-six excruciating minutes of suffering.

*

Free from the mind-numbing fluorescent lights and deprecating company, Remy leans against the graffiti-covered brick wall behind the job centre, closes her eyes and gathers her thoughts.

Please God let this be temporary. She pleads with the universe and meanders towards the bus stop along the high street while her self-pity playlist drowns out the world around her. She's so busy resonating with Noah and the Whale's 'I Have Nothing' that she doesn't notice the dishevelled woman hobbling towards her until the stench of damp mildew permeates the air. Remy

3

edges further across the bench to distance herself from the vagrant, but at a second glance, she notices they're both wearing the same jumper – only the vagrant woman's is in far better condition. It's like Remy is looking at her future self and all her worst fears were realised. The hiss of an approaching bus pulls her out of her emotional spiral into the abyss. She jolts up and holds out her arm to flag it down, but the driver ignores her and the bus whizzes by. She hurls her change after it with a roar and watches the bus trail down the road. Defeated, she stares at the coins scattered across the tarmac like her hopes and dreams. She should pick them up. She doesn't have money to spare right now, but she'd lose face – and what's more important, financial security or the perceived opinion of one stranger she'll never see again?

With a puff, she blows her hair out of her face and as she sweeps it back she meets the gaze of a young man locking up his bicycle across the street. It's her neighbour, Ed. They've never actually spoken before, only exchanged brief eye contact in passing. He smiles at her as he always does, and as usual she rebuffs the gesture. She's not in the mood to deal with people, especially chipper people. No one has anything to be happy about this early in the day.

*

Ed watches her mope down the high street and reasons that she must be having a bad day. He and his dad moved in across the street from her parents' house a little over a decade ago. Although she only moved back in recently, she seems to be sporting a permanent scowl as far as he can tell.

After checking his bike is secure, he enters Limited Edition Comics. Its brightly coloured walls are stocked with figurines and statuettes, and boxes of comic books are arranged in the centre of the shop. Ed takes his place behind the counter and

4

buries his nose in an old issue of *Elf Quest*. He's only four panels in when a huge box lands on the counter in front of him. Peering over his comic, he finds himself facing a large figurine.

"Just this, please," a little voice squeaks.

Ed looks over the box to address the customer behind it, but no one's there. He pushes it aside revealing a boy dwarfed by the toy he is trying to purchase. The kid smoothes down his combed-back hair with one hand and stares up at Ed with an expression too severe for a boy his age.

Ed grins as he lifts the box and eyeballs the toy. "The Dread Knight Grimoirh. You know he's the bad guy, right?"

The boy nods. "Yeah, but he looks awesome."

"There's nothing awesome about evil, kid." Ed imparts wisdom like an old sage.

"I'm not a kid. I'm George."

"Well, George, you sure you wouldn't rather have 'Regis the Good'?" He motions to a shelf stocked with Ultimate Adventure VII merchandise. Amidst monster manuals, guidebooks and trading cards, a large stack of 'Regis the Good' figures sit on top of one another.

George looks over to the toy, and then back to Ed, to whom the figure bears an uncanny resemblance. Messy orange hair, dopey expression and all.

"Uh, no."

Ed shrugs. "The remake launches at midnight, do you want to pre-order a copy?" he asks, while struggling to locate the bar code on the gargantuan box.

"My sister works for the devs, so she's getting me a free one."

"Whoa, for real?"

The kid nods.

"I guess nepotism has its perks. Have to say I'm a little jelly."

George looks uncomfortable. "You're weird."

"That's thirty-nine fifty." Ed tries to downplay that George's comment touched a nerve.

George slaps two twenties on the counter, and Ed wonders how come this child has more walking-around money than he does. He slides the cash towards himself, keeping a shrewd eye on George while he quickly inspects the notes to make sure they're real. By the time he puts the money in the register, George is halfway out of the shop.

"Hey! What about your change?" Ed holds up the money and his receipt.

"Keep it," George says, pushing past other customers and clinging to the box with both arms.

"What a mysterious child," Ed laughs to himself as he drops the coin back in the till, then turns to his colleague Barney, who has been silently leaning on the counter beside him the entire time, with his head buried in a back issue of *Heavy Metal* magazine.

"Can you believe that, Barney? A free copy of the remake."

Barney says nothing, totally unfazed by Ed's presence. He stuffs a sausage roll into his mouth and chews. But Ed reacts as though he can read Barney's thoughts, if he even has any; he does, and they're mostly about sex or sausage rolls. Sometimes both. Don't ask.

"... I know, I bet his sister's cool." Ed watches as George strolls past the window balancing the box on his head.

*

Amidst a sea of people moving in all directions stands Lauren Baker, a girl with the posture of a fish hook, rubbing shoulders with a dozen strangers crammed on the platform at Highgate tube station. Her vacant gaze lingers on the dark tunnel as thunderous clanking echoes louder. The coming train's brakes screech as it grinds to a stop. She pulls her head in cautiously as the doors close aboard the already jam-packed carriage. The sweltering heat makes the journey even more unbearable, but at least it's only a few stops. As soon as the doors open at Camden

6

Town station, she fights her way out and up the escalator. Brisk morning air blasts her awake as she arrives topside, and the yellowish fluorescent light of the underground turns to blue skies.

Her destination: a dilapidated warehouse along the canal which one could easily assume derelict. Inside, though, is a very different aesthetic. The building houses prominent video game developer 4D Games – in its beginnings a humble indie game company known for its *Ultimate Adventure* series. This was a low-poly, 8-bit, tongue-in-cheek fantasy role-playing game that spawned many spinoffs and sequels. However, since the first release over thirty years ago, the market has become oversaturated with sprawling open-world, branching narrative games. Recent releases have seen a slump in sales and ratings, so in a bid to reinvigorate relevance, the company has set about completely remaking its most popular release: the legendary Ultimate Adventure VII. Expectations are impossibly high, development has been long and arduous, and one day from now the game will release. 4D needs a big hit or else it's curtains.

Inside has been converted into a neo-rustic office space. Banks of computers are connected in rows on the bottom level, manned by developers hammering code and building worlds. Lauren scans the office as though she's searching for someone. Her attention lingers on an empty desk at the far side of the room. Her heart sinks, and with a sigh she climbs the stairs to 'The Imaginarium', a room for quiet contemplation sometimes required to stimulate creativity. Crimson light shines outwards through the small glass pane above the handle. Hearing voices from within as she nears, Lauren presses her ear to the door but can't make out much. She goes to knock but hesitates, and after wrestling with herself for a minute or so, takes a deep breath and finally taps the door. Nothing. She hesitates to knock again. The internal debate over whether or not to knock the first time almost tore her apart. Indecision is one of the qualities about herself she loathes, and it's a pretty long list. Eventually she musters the courage to just go in. The door creaks open and she quietly steps into the room.

Inside, on an expensive gaming chair, sits Eric Garland – deep in thought, legs crossed, mind open. He's the lead developer at 4D Games London – confident, self-assured, sometimes ruthless. Time spent demoing games to the roar of adoring fans at expos or being interviewed by high-profile game journalists and YouTubers have cursed him with a bit of a god complex, but he certainly has the Twitter following to back it up. In his early thirties, Eric's heading up the most anticipated game of the year. He relishes the tranquillity of the Imaginarium. Playtesting the remake is a welcome break from the pressures that await him downstairs.

Lauren's intrusion visibly annoys Eric. He doesn't acknowledge her, which only adds to the anxiety crushing her chest. She's been interning for almost eight months, and she's still unsure whether he knows her name.

"Uhh…" she croaks. Eric doesn't so much as flinch in her direction. "… Sorry to disturb you."

With a slow exhale, he sweeps his long sandy hair off his face and puts on a pair of round spectacles. The light from the hallway gleams off them as he turns to her, shrouding his eyes.

She takes this as a cue to continue. "You're alone? I just… I thought I heard someone else."

Eric tilts his head and looks her up and down. She holds her shoulders in tight, as though her body yearns to curl up, like a scared woodlouse.

"I hoped it might be Vincent, 'cause you said he'd be back this week, but I didn't see him downstairs so I'm not really sure what I should be doing—"

"Vincent doesn't work here anymore."

Those five words steal her breath. She stares ahead like a doe in headlights. For the last few months he had told her Vincent was overseeing some work from their Guildford office. *Was that all a lie?*

"But… What?"

Eric leans forward, looking over his glasses. "I know it's sudden, but we both agreed it was for the best. His vision for the remake was at odds with where we wanted to take it."

Her searching eyes fix on Eric for a fleeting second before she looks down at her shoes. "But… but I thought—"

"Of course you'll keep this between us. I thought best not to break the news until after the launch."

She nods. "Oh, of course."

"You're the intern?"

She nods again.

"Report to me from now on—" He gestures, unable to recall her name.

"Oh, it's Lauren."

"Lauren. Right."

Eric pulls a wry smile and they endure a brief but uncomfortable silence. He eyes the door, then her and after a moment she gauges the hint.

"Oh, I'll let you—" She trips over herself as she leaves the room.

"Thank you, Lauren." He watches her like a hawk until the door closes, then turns his attention to the monitor displaying the game and rubs his left palm while stretching his fingers to alleviate the dull ache that's been plaguing him for a while now.

Outside the room, Lauren presses her back against the door, relieved that she survived the encounter. She combs her hands through her hair and counts to five, a trick she uses to soothe her nerves.

*

Remy's scuffed boots trudge towards her house, and she approaches the door as her stepfather exits.

"Morning, Remy." He greets her with a smile on the way to his car.

"Ray," she grunts and pulls the door shut behind her.

Remy's mother, Helen, is sitting in the kitchen, furrow-browed as she pores over the household finances, intricately trying to balance the books to keep the house. Times, after all, are tough and austerity is a bitch. Remy's younger sister, Jessica, perches on the counter, her ash-blonde hair aglow in the morning sunshine beaming through the window behind her. She strums her guitar and pencils chords in a tatty notebook she keeps close for when inspiration strikes. This is until Remy stalks into the room and swipes her guitar as she passes.

"Hey!" Jessica reaches out to snatch it back, but Remy pulls it away.

"Good morning, Remy," her mother says in a sardonic tone. "How was it?"

Remy responds with a groan and leans over the counter opposite Jessica. She pilfers one of the strawberry Pop Tarts that shoot out of the toaster.

"That's mine!" Jessica watches helplessly as Remy chomps half of it in one bite then licks the icing before slapping it into her hand. A bitter glare graces her cherubic face. She desperately tries to recall a time when she could enjoy a morning without her sour shrew of a sister raining misery upon her. "First you take my guitar, then my breakfast. Anything else you want?" She tosses the pastry in the bin.

Remy pours herself a glass of juice and doesn't even do her sister the courtesy of looking at her while she speaks. "Maybe show a little consideration for the other people that live here, and it'll come back around."

Jessica cackles. "Consideration?!"

Helen lets out a loud sigh, but she keeps her head down.

10

She's not getting involved. Not this time.

"You pluck that thing all day and night. It's mind-numbing," Remy says.

"Well, how else am I going to drown out your 'poor me, heartbroken victim of the world' attitude? Sulking in your little box fort like you're homeless, but do you really have to smell like it? Take a bloody shower, I'm begging you."

"How's this for a shower?" Remy thrusts her drink at Jessica, but fortunately Helen grabs her wrist in the nick of time, staying her hand.

"For God's sake, Remy, be nice to your sister," she barks.

"She's not my sister, she's your husband's daughter." Remy pushes past them out of the kitchen.

"Oh, real nice, bitch," Jessica scoffs and takes the remaining Pop Tart from the toaster.

Helen rolls her tired eyes and stalks Remy through the house. "You should be thanking Jessica for sharing her room with you. Lord knows you're not easy to live with."

"Oh thanks, Ma."

"Just act your age, both of you!" She wags a finger back at Jessica, who trails them both down the hall, anticipating what is more than likely the precursor to another argument. "Now tell me, how did it go? Did they find you anything?"

Remy sighs. "I can't believe you're making me go to that place, it's so depressing and miserable and… ugh."

"Miserable? Sounds like you'll fit right in!" Jessica pulls a shit-eating grin which Remy swiftly dispels by swiping the Pop Tart in her hand and wolfing it down like a Tasmanian devil.

"That was the last one!" Jessica shrieks as the bathroom door slams in her face. She throws her arms up in the air and storms off.

Helen presses herself against the door. "You wouldn't have to go if you hurried up and got a job!"

"I've been unemployed for, like, five minutes!" Remy yells from the other side.

"It's been six months!"

"You're exaggerating."

Eager to confront her daughter with reality, Helen tears the calendar from the kitchen wall and forces the bathroom door open.

"Jesus, Mum, privacy much?!" Remy tries to uphold a modicum of dignity sitting on the toilet.

"It's been six months!" Helen triumphantly points to a date on the calendar, where circled in red are the words 'Remy fired' and then a few weeks later, 'Remy home'.

"You wrote it down?"

"I write everything down." Helen points to a highlighted strip on the calendar with the words 'Remy cycle' written across it.

Remy shakes her head. "Why would you write *that* down?"

"Trust me, the rest of us need warning." She leaves the bathroom and her daughter utterly mortified.

Remy honestly believed the job centre would be the lowest point of her day, but oh how her mother has lowered the bar.

"Could you at least close the door?" Her plea goes unanswered. She sinks her head into her hands and imagines herself anywhere but here.

*

Lauren closely inspects a life-size statue of the Dread Knight Grimoirh. She prods the fibreglass armour then runs her hand along the wide beaten sword, which is almost as tall as she is. A cold shiver runs down her spine and the hairs on the back of her neck spike up. She scans the office, unable to shake the feeling she's being watched. Most of her colleagues are mingling or picking at the considerable spread laid out over several tables by the caterers. No one's looking her way, but still, she feels unnerved. Glancing up, she notices Eric standing in his office, looking down at her through the glass. She quickly looks away, but can't help but look back over her shoulder, only now he's gone. She spots him descending the staircase to the ground floor, then he stops about halfway down and clears his throat. The room falls quiet as everyone gathers towards him like a flock to a sermon. Lauren lets others push in front of her; she's eager to be as far away from him as possible.

He puts on his round specs and a charismatic smile, though having just seen his severe expression she deems it to be utterly false.

He signals at one of the developers, who passes him a glass of champagne then hurries back down the stairs.

Eric takes a breath. "It's been a long road. A lot of overtime. *A lot* of overtime. A lot of pressure, but we're finally here. Over 500,000 pre-orders. Contender for game of the year? Definitely. Tomorrow, the Ultimate Adventure VII remake ships. Tomorrow, people will become totally immersed in what you've all created…" He pauses and savours his employees who hang on his every word. "… A masterpiece."

The staff erupt with applause. Even Lauren can't contain a little smile. The atmosphere in the room is electric.

"Work hard, play hard, right?" Eric raises his glass. "Let's do it." He downs his drink, music turns up, lights go down and people break off into groups to chat as the pre-drinking starts.

Lauren notices him eyeballing her again through the crowd. It's strange but she can almost feel him looking at her, and a dull ache swells from her forehead and shoots through her skull. She clutches her head in her hands and lets down her hair; maybe it was tied too tight? She looks back, but once more Eric is gone. Something about his stare was sort of inhuman, and nothing about Vincent quitting makes sense – why would he miss this? How could the driving creative force behind the remake give up so close to the launch?

Sanctuary, at last. Remy flops onto her bed – well, bed might be stretching it a bit. In reality, she sleeps on a lumpy futon mattress laid on the floor in the corner of her sister's bedroom, surrounded by boxes full of her worldly possessions, erected like a makeshift barricade. The bright, colourful room hidden behind Remy's wall of angst is adorned with all the things a typical teenage girl would own. Plushie emoji pillows litter Jessica's large bed in the opposite corner; the headboard is wrapped with fairy lights, and the walls are plastered with posters of synthwave musical idols. Electric Youth, Lazerhawk, Miami Nights 1984, Dynatron, Kavinsky and Timecop 1983 are but a few that grace Jessica's mural of inspiration. Nothing in the room offers Remy such comfort, quite the opposite. Every chip in the pastel pink paintwork, the view from the window overlooking the street full of identical brick houses; the dreaded familiar only serves as a bitter reminder of how little she's achieved in her twenty-seven years of existence and evokes a nauseating fear that she'll be stuck here forever.

Taking solace behind her wall of stuff, Remy draws her phone from her pocket. Social media isn't something she's particularly adept at, unlike Jessica who has built up a sizeable TikTok following, posting short dance videos and occasional synthesised covers. Remy has always been more of an internet wallflower, utilising it as a window into other people's worlds. Not that it does her any good. Her face becomes a road map of frustration and self-loathing as she scrolls through the stream of wedding photos, carefully curated selfies at trendy bars and epic holiday vistas. All are enough to make her feel physically ill, and that whisper in her head returns. *Wasted your life nothing to show pathetic useless no good to anyone.*

Then comes the finishing blow, a wrap photo from her former employer, of the 'dream team' on location in sun-soaked

Tulum. It was a rat-pile-heap-of-dog-shit situation she'd got herself into – long hours, impossible deadlines, unpaid overtime, stress and misery in spades. She found herself at the bottom of a bottle every weekend just to cope with the pressure, until finally she snapped. April 28th would forever be emblazoned in her mind as 'Black Thursday'. When she had received the schedule for that day's shoot, she had pointed out to her boss – a man named Simon, with a ponytail and the interpersonal skills of a snivelling rat – that he had neglected to allow time between set-ups for location moves. Naturally he ignored her until the shoot began and wouldn't you know it, by midday they were drastically behind schedule. The client wasn't happy, the crew weren't happy and, naturally, Simon pinned the mistake on her. When she overheard him shit-talking her to the client rep something in her snapped. She'd bitten her tongue for so long she drew blood, and the copper tang sent her into a berserk craze. She called him out, in front of everyone, which granted her a moment of euphoric catharsis, but which was sadly obliterated when he responded by terminating her contract immediately. Looking back it wasn't really that one thing that caused her to snap, it was more like an undercurrent of suppressed rage evoked by a litany of injustice that broke her. A week later she was out of her flat, and after couch-surfing burned a few more bridges, she haemorrhaged what pittance she'd saved on a hotel room, which she'd lived out of for almost a week to get her head together. Once the money dried up, Remy was back on her sister's bedroom floor before she knew what had hit her. She hasn't spoken a word to any of her former co-workers since, but seeing them with beaming smiles against a white, sandy beach really twists the knife. *'Dream team'* – *hah!*

It's like she's been erased. As if the last three years of toil had meant nothing, and to salt the wound, they're all in paradise while she's stuck in her dingy childhood bedroom. Tears well up in her eyes as she thumbs through their Insta-story, but she doesn't let them out. Instead she hurls her phone away. It crashes into a box of her belongings, which tumbles over, spilling its contents across the floor.

She stares at the mess a while – a fitting visual metaphor for the state of her life – then reluctantly drags herself out of bed to collect her things. As she lifts the box, out falls a dusty old games console, which she regards fondly. She gathers up the video game cartridges scattered on the floor around it and notices one of them has slid under Jessica's bed. She reaches for it and whacks her head against the bed frame as she comes back up. Gritting her teeth, she breathes through the pain and inspects the cartridge in her hand. It's worn, the label is faded, but she can still make out the title: 'ULTIMATE ADVENTURE VII'. A smile creeps across her face. All the hours she'd clocked traversing the mystical world of Pangea Ultima come flooding back. It was her escape when things got tough. When she got in a row with her parents, if she had a rough day at school, if a boy broke her heart, she'd plug in and play for hours on end and stuff her face with all sorts of crap. God, those were good times. Simple times, where right and wrong, good and evil were clearly divided and justice always won out in the end.

She scrambles through the other boxes for the cords that power her ancient console and doesn't waste a minute hooking it up to a boxy CRT TV buried in Jessica's walk-in cupboard. She powers up the old Game Station and waits expectantly. After all these years it works. Well, why wouldn't it? Everything back then was built to last.

The screen flickers as the pixelated Ultimate Adventure VII logo fades in, underscored by a honky-tonk melody. The picture is slightly warped but she doesn't care. This is bringing back hella nostalgia. She creates her avatar, a crude little sprite that sort of resembles her – were she a two-dimensional pudgy midget with no discernible features but eyes and hair. Ultimate Adventure VII is certainly not a graphically advanced game.

Hours pass as Remy levels up her character, battling monsters, storming castles, looting dungeons and saving townspeople. She can be anything she wants in the game, she can be successful here, it's easy. She meets other 'non-player characters' like the roguish Bengeo the Bandit, daring swordsman Regis the Good, Astrid Amethyst the exiled princess turned assassin, and the crow-headed wizard Ozrune, who join her quest to stop the notorious Dread Knight Grimoirh, from obtaining the legendary magic crystal, a powerful relic capable of destroying the world.

Remy's avatar slays a bunch of monsters and rescues some NPCs, and one of them thanks her for her help.

Thank you, brave stranger! Thanks to you this village will be safe from harm! Here's a reward for your troubles.

For a moment, she enjoys the validation and triumph that is so sadly lacking from her real life right now. The sprite throws a gold blob to Remy's avatar, who picks it up and gains five hundred runa – the game's fictional currency. If only money was as easy to come by in reality.

Alas her enjoyment is cut short as a mess of glitched pixels and streaks of colour flood the screen. Her face turns sour as she remembers how much of a beating the box has taken over the years. The old trick of blowing the cartridge doesn't make a lick of difference. It's bricked beyond all recognition. She snaps back to reality. It's dark now.

Too stubborn to admit defeat, Remy flips open her laptop to scour the internet for a replacement cartridge. Her search immediately leads her to an article on Kotaku, a gaming news site. In big, bold, black letters the words 'Ultimate Adventure VII remake' are written at the top of the page.

An Ultimate Adventure VII remake? Her eyes dart across the screen, devouring all information – the same wonderful story that she loved remade with a new state-of-the-art game engine. She scrolls down to a video beneath the article, which starts with two men on a stage at the annual E3 convention in Los Angeles, where developers showcase their games. A little graphic pops up listing their names and job titles: 'Eric Garland – producer' and 'Vincent Golbez – director'. They introduce the game before screening the trailer, but Remy impatiently skips ahead to the good bits. All the characters she remembers make an appearance – Bengeo the Bandit, the Dread Knight Grimoirh, the crow-headed wizard, the wicked kingdom of Runegard, the monsters, the towns, the airships – all rendered in breathtakingly beautiful high-definition 3D graphics running at a smooth sixty frames per second. It's a sight to behold. Not buying it isn't an option and she doesn't waste any time ordering a copy. She hammers in her details and waits with bated breath until the transaction is rejected due to insufficient funds. Her lips purse in frustration at the realisation she doesn't even have fifty quid to her name.

Jessica bursts into the room in a flurry of drama and collapses face first into her pillow before releasing a muffled scream. Remy, ever the sly fox, pops her head above her box wall and sees a means to an end.

She moves over to the end of Jessica's bed and asks, "What's up?", feigning sincerity.

"Mmmmmmphhhhrughshlob." Jessica's pillow garbles her words.

"Lift! Lift!" Remy prises up her head.

"Barefoot Keith broke his fingers trying to surf down the stairs, so Blue Raid can't open for Neoncop."

"I have no idea what you just said. Who's Barefoot Keith? Why is he called Barefoot Keith?"

"Forget that, what matters is now we're opening for Neoncop!" she exclaims. "Our first paid gig!"

Remy shrugs. "Isn't that a good thing?"

"Yeah but no, it's tomorrow night! I'm so not ready."

"Then bail."

"I can't just bail! It could be a real break for us and didn't you hear me? It's paid! Somebody has to contribute around here, I can't freeload like you."

Jessica notices Remy retreat into herself and her bleeding heart pangs with regret. Her strict conscience gets the better of her, even though she suspects her sister is up to something.

"Sorry, that was harsh. You're not a freeloader."

Remy forces a smile to mask her misery. "I guess I'm just… I don't even know."

"Yeah…" Jessica can relate; playing in her band and pursuing music is her goal, but her parents are pressuring her to walk a more conventional path.

The sisters sit a moment and ponder their futures.

"I've got it! Down some Dutch courage before you go on. It'll take the edge off. Once you get into it, you'll forget why you were even nervous."

"You think so?" Jessica asks.

"It always worked for me," Remy says, and sensing the glimmer of gratitude on her sister's face figures it's a good time to ask, "Uh… hey, can I borrow some money?" She flashes Jessica wide, soppy eyes. Subtlety isn't her strong suit.

Jessica relents with a sigh; good advice doesn't come cheap. She reaches for her purse and pulls a couple of notes from it.

"Actually, your card? It's for online stuff." Remy puts on a smile that says, 'I know I'm asking a lot', but asks anyway.

She hesitantly draws her bank card, which Remy snatches before leaping like lightning to her laptop to purchase the game, leaving Jessica alone and clueless on the bed. Behind her box wall she furiously hammers in her sister's card details. Escape, here she comes.

II

NEW GAME

Remy's eyes flutter open to dapples of light shimmering through the curtains above her. Slowly she comes to her senses and her vision shifts into focus. Then she remembers the game and throws back her covers, leaps out of bed like a kid on Christmas morning and scampers barefoot downstairs to check the post. Her search turns up nothing, so she parks herself on the sofa and waits expectantly, like a passenger for a train that never comes.

She awakens again, hours later, face buried in the sofa. She cracks her neck and winces as she sits up, then glances at the clock on the wall. It's late afternoon now and the sun is beginning to set. She approaches the front door, and a small card on the doormat catches her eye. Staring back at her are the four words nobody wants to read: 'Sorry we missed you'.

Why didn't I hear the doorbell? she wonders, and leans outside to test the button. It's broken, like everything else in her life right now. With a sigh she flips the card over and scans the back. Her game has been left with a neighbour.

She lands three hard knocks upon the door of the house

opposite hers and waits. No answer. Three harder knocks. Still nothing. A patient person would just come back later, but patience isn't her MO, so she hammers the doorbell and pounds the door in a frenzy.

After an age – well, a couple of minutes – it creaks open and Ed peeks outside, clearly wary that there's a maniac at his door. He takes one glance at her and pushes the door shut, leaving her confused and alone on his porch.

She pounds the door again and again, almost in a monotonous rhythm until finally the door creaks open again. Oblivious to the frustration plastered across Remy's face, he leans, like Jimmy Dean, against the doorframe. It's not every day a girl comes knocking, but you bet your ass he's practised for this.

"Sup?" he nods. If you could bottle confidence, he'd be wearing it.

Remy glances up at his hat and then back at him. *Was he wearing that a minute ago?* "You get my mail?" she asks.

"Uh, like email?"

She looks at him incredulously. "No. It says my parcel was delivered here." She shoves the delivery card at him. He hooks his neck back to read what it says, but she lowers it before he can process what he's seen. "So do you have it?"

"I guess," he says with a grin. He thinks this is going well. It's not.

Remy blinks expectantly waiting for him to retrieve her game, but he just stands there like a gormless fool.

"So can I have it, then?" she asks.

"Right, sure." He retreats inside, leaving his confidence on the porch like a flogged corpse laid before Remy, who taps her foot impatiently until he returns carrying a small box branded with the game shop logo.

"Let me guess, the Ultimate Adventure remake?" he asks with a hint of sarcasm while inspecting the box.

"Mmmhmm," Remy nods, and her hands itch to grasp it.

Ed lights up like a Christmas tree. " Really?" He can't believe it – a girl gamer, the stuff of legend. "I never imagined you'd be into RPGs."

Remy shoots him a look that asks, 'What's that supposed to mean?'

"Uh...! I meant... I just didn't take you for someone who plays video games... but I totally get it, you could definitely do that cam stuff."

Her eyebrows shoot up her forehead. *Just what exactly is that supposed to mean?*

"N-no! Oh God, I didn't mean... You know, like on Twitch. People game and they film themselves in the corner and stream it..." He trails off, distracted by her clothes – a pair of short checkered blue shorts and a stained grey vest with two illustrated fried eggs on her chest. "... Sorry, are those pyjamas?"

Shit. She snatches the parcel from him and covers herself with her arms.

"Cheers, perv!" She storms back towards her house but pauses at the end of his drive and glares over her shoulder. His mouth hangs open while he tries to concoct words that won't make everything worse.

"Don't stare." She shakes her head then crosses back to her house, leaving him alone on his porch.

*

Remy admires the game box. Finally escape is at hand. She stands in her living room, before her stepfather's media centre: a 55inch 4K flat screen, surround sound system and a barely used Game Station 5 – the most powerful games console in human history. Wasted on her parents, whose only use for it is watching Blu-rays or streaming Netflix. These are her stepdad's most prized possessions, and she's not supposed to touch any of them, but to hell with that. The console powers up with a beep. She inserts the disc, and it begins installing the game. With a huff, Remy plonks herself on the sofa and endures an agonising wait. After a few minutes of watching the installation bar crawl one pixel a minute to completion, she dons a pair of headphones, jacks them into her phone and boots up a playlist titled 'Depression you can dance to'; she'd always considered herself a New Romantic, despite being born a decade or two too late.

Overjoyed that she's about to escape her sucky reality for the next hundred-plus hours, she shakes, bops and bounces her way into the kitchen and tears off the note taped to the fridge. Her mother's handwriting reads:

'We'll be back tomorrow afternoon, don't make a mess and don't kill each other!'

She faintly recalls hearing something about a wedding, but who cares? She tosses the note aside and promptly raids the kitchen for food, finding only a tray of leftover lasagne. She bungs the whole thing in the microwave and dances with the grace of a three-legged deer whilst, unbeknown to her, Jessica leans in the doorway, watching her prance about to the sound of her bare feet slapping the linoleum.

She smiles for two reasons: firstly, this will make excellent ammunition in their next inevitable argument, but secondly, Remy actually looks sort of happy as she jives left and right while staring at the spinning dish as it's nuked. Maybe she'll just give her five more seconds of bliss before she ruins the moment.

"I'm going out." Jessica's words fall on deaf ears. "I'm going out!" she cries louder as Remy spins around on one heel.

Her heart spikes on seeing Jessica, and she sprays beer everywhere.

"How long have you been there?" She wipes the sticky ale from her chin and slides her headphones back around her neck.

23

"Long enough." Jessica grins like she just checkmated Remy in some messed-up game of one-up chess. "Did you even get dressed today?"

"Don't judge me."

Jess rolls her eyes. "I'm going out."

"Oh yeah, you've got your thingy." Remy looks her sister up and down. She's dolled up to the nines, but no amount of eyeliner or voluminous hair can hide her shaky nerves.

She bids Remy farewell with an anxious smile and throws her red silk bomber jacket over her shoulders on her way out the door.

"Dutch courage, remember?" Remy cries over the beep of the microwave. She opens the door, releasing a burst of piping-hot steam. By the time she looks back, Jessica is gone, and the slam of the door signals her departure.

With a satisfying ping, the game finally finishes installing. Remy eagerly grasps the controller in her hands, watching as the 4D Games logo fades in and out to black, then a gorgeous rendering of a crimson moon hovering over a cloudy sky fades up and the main menu options appear. She takes a moment to bask in the stunning menu screen while the remastered melody plays, then she presses start and the familiar chime gives her goosebumps. Once again she creates her avatar, but instead of a deformed two-dimensional sprite it's a fully rendered 3D character, and the resemblance is pretty damn uncanny. After a few small 'enhancements' to give her avatar a more idyllic physique, the game begins with a title crawl…

**The world of Pangea Ultima is teetering on the edge of oblivion.
A surge of ancient evil has tainted the land, spreading like wildfire across the continent.
The Dread Knight Grimoirh seeks three crystal shards. The remains of a legendary relic that will**

grant him unfathomable power. Few dare to stand
against him and his accursed horde.
You awaken, a prisoner of the Dread Knight, taken
in a raid that destroyed your home. Destiny
has chosen you. Steel yourself, your ULTIMATE
ADVENTURE begins...

Her avatar awakens in an iron cell. The dungeon looks incredible, every brick in the dilapidated wall seeming almost real, and she's mesmerised by the glistening ray-traced light refracting against the damp cave like glittering diamonds. She doesn't dare glance away even as she shovels lasagne into her mouth with a serving spoon. She's regressing to a time before responsibility infected her life like a debilitating disease.

*

Jessica pushes her way to the front of a queue formed outside a narrow building wedged between a chicken shop and an estate agent. The bouncer grants her entry with a nod and she enters through the black doors into the Underbelly, a dive bar, which in this case means a poorly ventilated basement that serves overpriced drinks and is undoubtedly in violation of a dozen health code regulations. Tonight the entertainment is live, and she's it.

Unbeknown to her parents, she's the vocalist in a retro synthwave band called Berserk Statement. This is a secret she's kept for two reasons: firstly, her bandmates, Ziggy, Tyler and Scuzz, are a bit older and way too edgy for her mother to approve of, and secondly, because she's bloody petrified of performing live. Music is something she loves and something she's good at, just not in front of people. A frontgirl with stage fright sounds like an exciting hook, but it doesn't exactly get a crowd going, and tonight the crowd look a little dicey.

Following her sister's advice Jessica leans against the bar standing on tiptoes, and tries to look as adult as possible. The bartender greets her and she naively asks, "Do you have any Dutch courage?"

The bartender looks her up and down.

"You got ID?" he asks.

"Come on, man, I turned eighteen in May." Her petite stature and dimples don't do her any favours.

"ID." He arches one eyebrow. The eyebrow means business.

She hands over her learner's licence, and the bartender inspects it closely, then her even more so.

"Doesn't really look like you," he says.

"It's a bad picture, I was going through a phase." What a phase it was. She wanted an edge, a little more Siouxsie and the Banshees and a little less Sailor Moon. What she got was more akin to Rocky Horror. So many regrets.

He concedes and pours her a drink, which she knocks back, then raises her hand.

"Hit me again."

Another four downed and Scuzz waves her over, but the butterflies in her stomach are rampant. She takes a deep breath to calm her nerves before taking her place on stage. All eyes are on her, and she glances back at her band who nod giving her the go ahead. No time like showtime.

"Uhh… Ahem," she coughs into the mic, which screeches, silencing the audience. "Hi. I'm Jessica, and we are Berserk Statement." She looks stunned amidst the blinding stage lights and the crowd's blank stares.

"Show us your boobs!" a heckler cries.

Jessica looks disturbed by the crass comment but decides to let it slide.

"This song is called 'Strange Girl.'"

On her signal Ziggy drops a beat, Scuzz strums his bass, then Tyler comes in with his homemade synthesiser, releasing a swell reminiscent of John Carpenter. Jessica closes her eyes and counts herself in.

"Walking alone, in the shadows of night
Her eyes dark, but gleaming with light
Her smile, both sweet and wild
Wandering this life in exile
Why can't you just trust
She's not a strange girl
Why can't you?
Oooooah ha ha, ahhhh ahhhhha"

Despite her nerves, the crowd is pretty enthralled by her dulcet tones and peppy moves. It's all going rather well until she opens her eyes and sees dozens staring back at her. The butterflies in her stomach wither and die and fester. She's fighting her way to the chorus when nausea hits her like a truck, and before she can think she blows chunks all over the stage, showering the first two rows in 'Dutch courage'. The crowd howl with horror and raucous laughter as she flees the scene. She doesn't know it yet, but she'll be a fleeting internet sensation for all the worst reasons.

*

Bluish light flickers in the window on the fourth floor of an aged tower block, an eyesore amidst the gentrified Highgate Village with its tall red-bricked Georgian houses and leafy roads. In a room some would consider no larger than a utility cupboard, George sits on the end of his bed, so engrossed in the Ultimate Adventure VII remake that he doesn't hear his mum calling him.

Down the hall of the flat, Lauren is also a world away. Her vacant eyes stare out of the kitchen window at nothing as her mind replays yesterday's conversation with Eric, while she absently soaks the dishes.

Her mother, Lin, the author of Lauren's East Asian heritage – who looks a lot like her daughter plus a few decades of stress and killer hospital shifts – approaches the sink muttering.

"I swear he's going to get square eyes sitting in front of that thing all day." She places the last dirty plate by the sink and leans against the counter.

Lauren, only half listening, lets out an agreeable murmur.

"You alright, love? You've been very quiet. How was work?"

"Meh." She rinses her hands of soapy water and turns away to put the dry dishes in their place.

Lin senses something is off. She watches her daughter and smiles. "I'm proud of you, you know."

Lauren shrugs. "It's not like a real job, they're not exactly paying me."

"It's a start," Lin says, "a foot in the door. It's all who you know these days."

Unconvinced but appreciative, Lauren smiles. "I guess so."

"It's a competitive industry. There were probably a lot of applicants, but they picked you. You're special, you're going to do something great. Your dad always thought so."

Lauren notices the glimmer of pain in her mother's eyes, and with it, the ember of hope that life will ever be normal again fades. Their family was hit hard by her father's sudden passing, and although it's going on two years, they're all still reeling from the loss. Lauren was always shy, but since her dad's death she's really receded, and not just mentally. Her clothes hang off her waifish figure, her hair falls to her waist like a sleek black waterfall; she hasn't cut it since that godforsaken day. Honestly, she looks like a ghost, the sort you'd see in those Ringu movies. Lin can't help but worry that she's losing herself.

She kisses Lauren on the forehead. "I'll finish up. Go tell your brother to get off that bloody game."

Lauren tosses the dish towel on to the counter and heads into her brother's room. She lingers by the door and watches the game a moment. She's proud to have been a part of it, however small. She wonders whether her name might even be in the credits somewhere.

"Mum says bed," she says softly.

"I'm going, I'm going. I just need to find a save point."

"Nice try, but Vincent told me the game auto-saves like every five minutes."

"Who's Vincent?" George asks, clearly padding for time.

Lauren hesitates to answer. She was going to say a friend, but he did just up and leave without a word. She looks at the TV, then at George's Grimoirh figurine displayed on his shelf, and sighs.

"... He directed most of the game."

"Whoa, cool!" George says.

"Yeah..." Lauren puts herself between her brother and the TV. "Come on, enough. You've been playing since you got home. When's my turn, huh?"

"But I wanna stay up, it's the weekend!" He tries to play on looking past his sister.

"If it were up to me... but mum's the law around here." Unswayed by his pleas she holds out her hand until he reluctantly passes her the controller.

Behind her the game glitches and flickers to an image of a strange cavern. A distorted silhouette moves in the darkness, but before the shape comes into the foreground, Lauren absentmindedly switches off the console. The screen goes black, and George throws his hands over his head and hurls himself against his mattress with dramatic flair. Lauren takes his pillow and throws it at him playfully, but the boy just lies there like a slug.

*

Time slips by like rain against glass. Flashes of blue illuminate the night sky and thunder rolls in the distance, but tonight,

29

reality can suck it! Remy is too busy fighting alongside Bengeo the Bandit, looting dungeons and levelling up. Unwilling to miss a second of the captivating cut scene, she brings her drink to her lips without looking and misses her mouth entirely. The cold spillage sends her leaping off the sofa with a gasp. She pauses the game, hightails it upstairs to Jessica's room and ploughs through her boxes in search of clean clothes. She throws off her beer-soaked vest and picks up a scrunched-up T-shirt from the floor then sniffs it – *Not terrible, it'll do*. The room lights up for a split second then goes dark, and Remy presses her face to the glass to look up at the stormy sky. Then something catches her eye in the window parallel to hers. It looks like Ed is pounding against the glass to get her attention. Her first thought is that he's spying on her while she changes, so she swiftly pulls the curtains shut and pulls the T-shirt over her head. Untucking her hair from her collar, she mutters to herself in disbelief.

"What a freak."

*

Downstairs a wet and weary Jessica steps in from the downpour, still reeling from the burning aftertaste of vomit and whisky. She wrings the rainwater out of her hair and moves into the house. The hallway lights strobe before the house goes dark with a deafening boom overhead.

"Hello?" she calls out to the darkened hallway.

The house is eerily quiet save for the patter of rain on the windows. Drawn like a moth to a flame she approaches a soft glow emanating from the living room. She expects to find Remy, but there's naught but burnt-down candles, half-empty beer bottles and the dregs of last Wednesday's lasagne – clear signs she was there at least.

She tries the lights but no luck. Strange then, that the television is still functional. As Jessica moves into the room she notices that the perspective on the screen shifts, as though she were looking through a window and not at an image projected on an LED screen. She inches towards the television, fixated on a shape moving through the long dark tunnel towards her. A stale breeze brushes her face and offends her nostrils with a damp earthy scent. She kneels before the TV and as the figure draws closer, she can make out its form; a cryptid monster emerges, shrouded in black robes, its gangly body draped with a large rusty chain.

Jessica jolts back with a bloodcurdling scream as the creature thrusts its gangly arm through the television and into the room. Three unearthly fingers grasp her face and curl around her head, and her wide eyes tremble while her panicked shrieks are muffled by the creature's coarse, leathery palm.

*

Upstairs, Remy fumbles around the dark bedroom for her phone and after grasping it tightly, activates the torch app. The thunder booms, shaking the house, and she swears that she heard a scream, but it was so faint she could've imagined it.

She stares at the darkened room and frowns. *Ugh, I better not have lost any progress.*

She returns to the living room and peers in from the doorway, but no one's in there. Her eyes race back to the television screen, which is still glowing despite the power being out – weird. Weirder still, she spots Jessica's phone lying on the floor, and knowing that her sister would never willingly abandon it, Remy braces herself and cautiously enters the room.

"Jess?" she whispers, and looks curiously at the strange mist swathing around her feet, and as she bends down to retrieve the phone a shadow creeps across the wall behind her. The clacking rain is interrupted by a strange murmur, an alien croaking that makes the hairs on her neck stand tall. Her eyes widen. She feels a presence behind her, but not someone, something.

If I don't look, maybe it'll go away. Fat chance. This is one problem she can't ignore. Those are the worst kinds of problems.

She turns around slowly so as not to antagonise whatever *it* is. Her lip trembles as the hooded reaper stretches itself out. Remy has always been tall for a girl, yet this being towers over her. The creature races towards her taking long strides. Its hulking foot cracks her mother's beloved coffee table in half, before stopping dead in front of her. She stands paralysed with fear as it appears to examine her from behind its eerie, featureless mask. She glances at its belt and clocks several game controllers crudely tied to it like trophies. This creature is evidently a collector of sorts. Her breathy gasps and pounding heart mute the storm outside. She flinches as the being raises its hand to its face and removes the mask, revealing a hideous fleshy face devoid of features, save for a ringed maw lined with razor teeth, now stretching wide. Flashes of a gory, violent death dash through her head.

Here it comes. She braces herself, shutting her eyes tight. A guttural warble sends a shiver down her spine. She flinches and opens one eye. A blinding light emanates from deep within its throat. Like a living lighthouse it shines at her and Remy loses herself in it. Her muscles seize up, her vision blurs, she feels drugged and utterly docile, like a prisoner in her own body. She can barely muster a scream as the abomination sweeps her up in its arms.

Booming thunder extinguishes her helpless cries. The room illuminates like a supernova. Light pours out of the house, streaking through the torrential rain lashing the driveway. Then, as quickly as it appeared, the light retreats. The house sits empty. Remy watches her living room drift away, and it's as though she's looking at it through the reverse side of the TV screen. It quickly fades out of sight entirely, and like a satellite drifting into the abyss, she is engulfed in black.

III

LET'S PLAY

Drip. Drip. Drip. Cold droplets splatter against Remy's forehead as her eyes flutter open and see a rocky ceiling. She comes to her senses quickly, her chest tightens, she jolts upright with a gasp then a whisper disturbs the silence.

"You alright?" A young man, of similar age to her, leans into her view.

His crystal blue eyes shine like a beacon of hope in their dark surroundings – a crude prison cell. Black iron bars, dug into the rock, surround them on three sides and a rusty iron gate bars any notion of escape. The last time she awoke in a place she didn't recognise she was twelve Cuba Libres down, but her head wasn't throbbing half as much as now.

"Where am I?" she asks.

"Hell if I know, I'm still not convinced I'm actually awake," the young man replies. "Last thing I remember, I was playing—"

"Ultimate Adventure VII?"

"Yeah!" He looks at her as though she had read his mind.

The image of Jessica's discarded phone and her bloodcurdling scream come rushing back to Remy. She notices a girl in the

33

corner of their cell and recognises the red bomber jacket immediately – a staple of her sister's wardrobe.

"Jessica?" She crawls over to her sister and shakes her limp body. She's so flustered that she doesn't even notice the chain fastened around her ankle.

"It's alright, she'll come around soon," the young man assures her. "We rolled her onto her side, that's what you're supposed to do, right?"

Remy checks she's still breathing and sighs with relief. "Yeah, I think so. Thanks."

The young man smiles. "I didn't get your name."

"Remy."

"I'm Matt," he nods to the opposite corner of the cell, where another young man is curled up away from them with his head slumped between his legs, "… and that's Ed. He's not coping so well."

Remy glances at Ed but doesn't recognise him from the back. She's more transfixed by her surroundings. It feels so familiar.

"Are we…? Is this… the game?" A fleeting smile graces her lips. She wanted immersion, and for fifty quid, this is pretty damn immersive. She runs her hand across the floor, and stares at the cave walls through the bars of her cell. Everything looks and feels as real as she is. "… Amazing."

"Amazing? This is a nightmare." Ed turns around and faces Remy mad-eyed, his hair a wild mess. "Those things, you know what they do? They eat people!"

"You!" she gasps.

"Pyjama girl?" His severe expression softens, and he looks vaguely happy to see her.

Realising that she's still in her pyjamas she sighs. Awkward. "Of course it had to be you."

"You know him too?" Matt asks.

Ed nods. "Yeah."

"No," Remy says at the same time.

34

Matt looks a little confused but shrugs it off. "Well, he's got a point, we shouldn't hang around in case those monsters come back."

"Agreed, you with us?" she asks Ed, who mulls it over for a second.

"I guess whatever is out there can't be worse than waiting in here to die," he sighs.

"We're not going to die," Remy laughs. "This is a game."

A chilling scream resounds through the dungeon hallways, and their eyes fixate on the dark tunnel beyond their cage, but thankfully nothing emerges from it.

Then Matt stands up, a bastion of bravery. "If this is a game, then let's play."

The other two rise with him and they all try to take a step towards the cage door but tumble over; each one of them is shackled to the other and to the wall.

"Oh yeah," Matt groans.

*

A tall woman with hourglass hips traverses the ruins atop the tunnels, once human, now something much more twisted. Her slinky figure cloaks a wicked bloodlust. Ice-white hair flows behind her as she stalks through the long passageway beneath the crumbling stone arches. A black-scaled body suit covers her torso and arms, with patches of the fabric removed to expose her ample cleavage and various parts of her toned abdomen – well, it *is* a video game after all.

The end of the corridor widens to the remnants of a coliseum long laid to waste, and standing in the centre of the circular platform is a figure encased in pitch-black plate mail and draped in a ragged cloak, gazing out at the blood-red moon looming in the night sky, bathing the vast wasteland before him in crimson.

"More have arrived." The woman's voice is softer than her striking features would lead one to expect; with cheekbones that sharp she hardly needs the decorated short sword hanging on her hip.

"Are they capable?" The Dread Knight's low voice reverberates from beneath his demonic helmet, framed by two horns like a ram's skull.

"Some of them have potential," she smirks, relishing the grim fate that will likely befall the poor 'players'.

His gaze turns from the moon. He pauses. It's impossible to tell what he's thinking beneath that cold metal, but that doesn't stop her from wondering.

After a moment he looks back at her over his shoulder. "Show me."

*

"This is useless!" Ed moans as he, Matt and Remy pull harshly at the iron chain binding them to their cell.

"Shut up and keep pulling!" Matt replies through gritted teeth.

At his behest, they pull again, but the chain doesn't so much as budge. Remy and Ed collapse huffing and wheezing while Matt wastes little time conjuring a new plan. He frowns at the shackle linking the chain to the wall then focuses on the wall itself. After a moment he lights up.

"Maybe I can punch the brick to loosen the shackles!" He pulls off his T-shirt, revealing a muscular physique.

Ed rolls his eyes. That's got to be the dumbest thing he's ever heard, but Remy finds herself a little impressed by Matt's display of sheer undiluted masculinity. He slams his fists into the wall around the shackles, and after the first few blows, his shrill screams and bloody knuckles quickly banish whatever fleeting attraction she felt. She winces and exchanges a disturbed look with Ed while Matt pummels the brick with desperate, sweaty ferocity.

Unable to endure this horror show any longer, Ed searches for a more practical means of escape and stares at the iron gate.

"A game… If this is a game then there has to be a way out," he whispers to himself.

His eyes widen with the promise of an idea and the bobby pins in Jessica's hair provide a method to his madness. He shakes her gently; first impressions aren't exactly his forte, but he reasons that her coming around while he's stealing her hair pins might set off red flags. Thankfully, however, she's still out cold. He carefully slides one of the pins from her hair and tries to pick the lock on the shackle binding his ankle. Matt's screams and the crunch of his knuckles beating the stone make it difficult to concentrate, but after a bit of finagling, Ed cracks it. He can't believe his eyes. Back home he'd tried this once after he'd locked himself out – failed miserably, busted the lock. Dad was furious – who's laughing now?

He stands, free from his bondage. "Hey!"

Matt pays him no heed. His punches are fewer now, sluggish, but he refuses to give up. Better to break every bone in his hand than look foolish.

"Hey!" Ed shouts again.

"Not now!" Matt snaps. "I need to focus. If I can just channel all my strength—" He clenches his fist. Blood seeps from his raw swollen knuckles.

"Seriously, just gimme one second."

"What?!" Matt turns to him, red-eyed, nostrils flared.

Ed motions to his ankle, and Matt and Remy realise he's no longer chained to them.

"But how did you—?" Remy asks.

"I picked the lock," he says with a shit-eating grin.

"Nice." She punches him affectionately. "Now do us."

Matt quietly concedes defeat and nurses his split knuckles

and his pride while Ed unshackles them, and then Jessica who's still unconscious. After they're all free he turns his attention to the cell door and starts to jimmy the lock while Remy and Matt watch closely over his shoulder.

"Could I get a little room?" He motions for them to back off, and they oblige but lean in again as soon as he turns back to the gate.

He twists and turns the pin slowly until the lock clicks. They watch with wide-eyed trepidation as Ed pushes the creaky gate open.

"What are you, a locksmith?" Remy asks.

Ed shakes his head, still barely believing it himself. "I just thought, what would I do in the game?"

"It doesn't matter how he did it, we need to move, and we need to stay quiet," Matt says, like a general commanding his troops.

Jessica's eyes flutter open, but her head throbs so she doesn't sit up right away. As her vision clears, she stares fearfully at a centipede scuttling from the eye socket of a human skull buried in the dirt beside her and lets out a piping scream as it crawls towards her face. She jolts upright flailing her arms.

"Jess! You need to be quiet! Be quiet!" Remy grabs her from behind, which only worsens her panic. They wrestle while she tries in vain to subdue her sister's hysteria.

"I'm surprised those creatures aren't here already!" Matt frantically scans the tunnels for danger. If they're really in the game, it'll never be far away.

Remy mounts Jessica and pins her arms to her sides. She presses her palm against Jessica's mouth, but Jessica bites down on her hand. Remy sharply retracts it with a yowl, then Matt pushes her aside and strikes Jessica with his hand, silencing her instantly.

She stares at him with wide, fragile eyes as a bright pink handprint materialises across her stinging cheek. Ed and Remy look amazed and appalled that he'd smack a scared teenage girl half his size.

Oblivious to the controversy, Matt looks up to the stretching tunnel and squints his eyes. He feels like a goddamn action hero.

"We need to move," he growls as the tremor of metal footsteps draws near.

*

The Dread Knight Grimoirh and his wicked accomplice approach the cell. Her face turns woeful at the sight of the door ajar and the 'players' gone.

"Domina," the Dread Knight says.

She turns towards him, looking shameful, and can't bring herself to look him in the eye.

"Find them. Quickly!" he commands.

She grits her teeth and storms off, leaving him to inspect the empty cell.

*

The four unlikely adventurers wander the winding dungeon in search of an exit. Matt takes the lead, of course, steeling himself for any danger that may lurk around the corner. The rugged tunnels stretch on for miles, lit by flaming torches mounted at various points along the walls.

Remy treads barefoot over the rough cave floor and stumbles with a sharp cry. Matt rushes to her side like a knight in blue jeans.

"What's wrong?" he asks.

She inspects her blackened sole and carefully prises a jagged fragment from her skin, releasing a trickle of crimson. She can't be sure but it looks like a piece of bone.

"It actually hurts…" she mutters to herself as her mind races with thoughts of what this could mean. Surely no game would let the player feel actual pain, and so far her experience has been way too linear to be a dream. Her tawny eyes meet Matt's over the fragment. "It actually hurts."

Despite not understanding the gravity of her words, he nods empathetically, then he tears off his T-shirt sleeve and tenderly wraps her foot.

"Oh, you don't have to—" Remy insists.

"Don't be silly, don't want it to get infected…" he says with a warm smile that puts her at ease; it's been a long time since anyone looked after her, "… besides if you're hurt you'll just slow us down."

And there it is. Her sense of ease quickly fades as she remembers the reason why no one has looked after her in a while; because despite how they appear, in her experience people only ever have their own interests at heart.

Ever the pragmatist, Ed searches for a more permanent fix and backtracks a short way to loot a pair of boots from a rotting corpse slumped against the cave wall.

"Here, put these on." He offers up the putrid shoes and as Remy reaches for them, a decaying foot slips out of the left boot and lands between them with a thump.

"Oh God!" Jessica retches, covers her mouth and shies away.

"No way am I sticking my foot in there," Remy cries.

"It's either these or bloody feet." Ed tosses the dusty boots to her.

"So poetic."

She holds them up with her forefinger and thumb and peeks inside to ensure there aren't any more surprises. The smell knocks her back; no doubt who ever died in these met their end sometime ago. The boots squelch as she presses her feet in them and she shivers as her toes sink into the mushy insoles, which are damp and slippery but also somehow gritty. It feels like she's wearing a dead fish.

Jessica looks back but catches a whiff and immediately regrets doing so. "I think I'm going to be sick." She backs away from her sister.

Remy stands, and the boots are about ten sizes too big, but in the blink of an eye they shrink to fit her perfectly. She gasps as the cold leather wraps her feet and tightens around her calves.

"Did you see that?" She marvels at the ratty boots as though they were ruby slippers.

"Think about it… In the game you loot enemies for their stuff and it always fits, right?" Ed says.

Matt shakes his head. "You really think we're in Ultimate Adventure VII?"

"Makes sense to me. How else do you explain this?"

Remy scoffs, "It doesn't make any sense at all. This doesn't feel like we're in a simulation, we're all wearing our own clothes and my foot actually hurts, that can't be good, right?"

While the three of them try to rationalise their situation, Jessica stares into the darkness behind them. A faint murmur has caught her ear.

"Do you guys hear that?" Her question lands on deaf ears. The others are too busy bickering to notice.

"… Everything looks so familiar. This place, I'm pretty sure I've been here." Ed presses his palm against the stone wall, recalling the first major dungeon in the game.

Remy lights up. "So you know a way out?"

"Not really, I always just follow the quest marker on the mini-map," he sighs, quashing any glimmer of hope.

Jessica takes a step closer to the others. "Guys, I think we've got company!" Her voice trembles.

The four of them huddle together and fix their eyes on the tunnel behind them, imagining all manner of horror as a rising symphony of hoarse groans echoes towards them. Then comes creaking bone and crunching cartilage. A herd of walking corpses emerge from the dark. As good as the graphics in the remake are, they don't stand up to the realism of the withered flesh hanging from their yellowed bones, bound in remnants of broken armour, the glint of rusted blades clasped in their skeletal hands and the permeating stench of death. Their groans turn to gnashing, snarling cries as their pale, dull eyes lock on the four 'players', and the creatures snap their rotting jaws excited by the prospect of a fresh meal.

"Run?" Ed trembles with the fear of God.

Remy nods. "Running sounds good."

"I like running," Jessica whimpers.

"Go!" Matt takes off like a bat out of hell in the opposite direction, leading the others through the winding cave passages that cross and intersect each other, each as identical as the last, making it impossible to tell whether or not they're retreading the same path.

"Does anyone know where we're going?!" Jessica struggles to keep up. Her short legs aren't doing her any favours. She knows if she looks back, it'll make everything worse, but she does it anyway. The corpses' lack of eyelids make their white, decaying eyes pop at her and their half-rotted lips give way to crooked, bloodstained teeth and demented, bloodcurdling shrieks. Yep, definitely made it worse.

"This way!" Matt darts left through a slim passage in the crumbling wall. They wrestle their way through and stumble into a bricked corridor, and at its end, a worn stone staircase.

Something about the spiral staircase fills Ed with overwhelming dread. He opens his mouth to warn the others but trips over a living corpse crawling out of the wall on its arms. This one looks fresher than the others and is wearing modern clothes – a T-shirt and a pair of bloodstained Levi's. Ed lands on top of it and lets out a yelping scream. The mangled corpse hisses back at him, but before it can taste his milky flesh, Remy pulls him onto his feet and leads him away by the arm up the staircase.

More undead writhe from every nook and crevice, clawing at the 'players' as they tear through the ruins atop the caverns in a breakneck sprint. These creatures aren't the shuffling, empty, dull undead like you see in zombie movies; they move with purpose. Their hunger may be what drives them, but there's more than a remnant of consciousness behind their skeletal faces – almost a flicker of emotion, of hatred.

"Piss off!" Remy scowls as she hurls herself at a rotter blocking her path. She shoves it to the floor and leaps over it, but Ed trips behind her and plants his foot through its rib cage as he passes.

"Sorry!" he cries, wrestling his leg free as he hops away.

The corridor ends at a towering wooden door, which Matt hurls himself against.

"We can lose them in here!" He pushes, but it doesn't budge until the others throw themselves against it too.

Their combined strength forces it open, and the door creaks as it drags across the stone, setting Matt's teeth on edge. He presses his palms through the grime, against the coarse grain of the oak, and pushes with all his might until there's enough room to squeeze through. Once clear, they force it shut quickly behind them and press themselves against it as the dead pile up on the other side.

"Find something to bar it with!" Matt cries.

Jessica scans around for something, anything, but it's too dark to see much. Her eyes lock on a long, thick branch planted in the dirt, which she grabs without a second thought. She shoves it through the iron handles, barring the door shut. Only after she steps back does she realise that it isn't a branch at all but a bone, probably a femur or maybe an arm, hard to tell.

The others collapse huffing and wheezing and look around them. Save for a couple of lit torches mounted on the wall either side of the door, they are faced with seemingly infinite darkness.

It doesn't feel like they're outside, more like a large chamber or hall of some kind.

"Turn back. Nothing but death awaits you." Grimoirh's foreboding warning bounces around the darkened space, disturbing the silence of the void before them. From a balcony above, he watches the poor souls huddle fearfully by the door.

"Who's there?" Remy shouts into the shadows.

"This is so messed up," Jessica frets.

"Show yourself!" Matt takes another bone from the floor, lifts it high and hurls it.

They watch the bone be swallowed by the abyss and listen on tenterhooks, but it makes no sound. Then the deafening silence is broken by a bellowing roar that shakes the room.

Out of the black, hundreds of pale green tentacles slither over one another towards them. They stumble backwards against the door in a heart attack-inducing fright and watch as the mass of slithering appendages part, revealing a ball-like head from which the ungodly creature gazes through a single malevolent eye. It brandishes a wide maw filled with rows of jagged teeth and roars again.

"What the fuck is that?!" Jessica screams. "I've seen Hentai, I don't like where this is going!"

"I knew I recognised that door," Ed cries. "It's the dungeon boss, a giganeye!"

"Why didn't you warn us?" Remy scolds him.

"I... I tried!"

Matt defiantly steps forward as the tentacles swoop overhead. "We can beat this!" He puffs his chest ready for a fight. "We just have to work toge—" BOOM!

A tentacle lands on him with a bone-crunching thud. Remy shields herself with her arms and peeks over them as the dust clears. The appendage retreats, and nothing of Matt remains but a red mist and fragments of bone and sinew stewing in a pair of blood-soaked Yeezys. She wants to scream, but all she can do is stare, mouth agape, thinking she was so very, very wrong. This is anything but a game.

Jessica lets out a shattering scream, while Ed stands frozen in breathless silence. The giganeye roars thunderously and, as if by magic, torches along the walls burst aflame, illuminating the chamber and the mutilated remains of dozens of players who came before them.

IV

OUT OF THE FRYING PAN

Remy and Ed scramble in opposite directions leaving Jessica trembling by the door. Her knees buckle, and she lets out another hair-raising scream as the tentacles writhe towards her.

"Jess, move!" Remy pulls her sister aside before the appendages come crashing down.

"What do we do?!" Ed cries, cowering behind a toppled pillar.

"The hell do I know!" Remy screams back.

She stumbles over a rusty beaten sword discarded on the floor. Picking it up, she shakes off the dismembered hand still clinging to the hilt.

"Find weapons!" she yells.

Ed grips a fist-sized rock, briefly contemplates its uselessness then tosses it aside. "I've got nothing!"

"I can't babysit you right now!" She swings her beaten sword, cleaving a tentacle in half. The monster howls and Remy watches the detached limb squirm at her feet before it melts into a bubbling toxic goop.

"Get out of there!" Ed cries, pulling Remy back to the danger at hand.

She drags Jessica along behind her, and together they trip and dive over and under the surge of tentacles hounding them. As the creature turns, Ed spots a spear pinning a mutilated carcass to the wall and brazenly makes a play for it. He crawls on his belly through the battlefield and frantically tugs the shaft, but before he can prise it loose, the creature swats him away, and the spear goes flying across the hall.

He rolls across the stone floor and picks himself up with a groan, watching the abomination gurgle and retch. It dawns on him that its movements mirror the animations of the boss in-game, and he realises what untold misfortune is to be unleashed.

"Get to cover!" he screams, scrambling onto his feet and sprinting back to the toppled pillar. "Bad breath!"

"What?!" Remy can barely hear him over the beast's thunderous bellow.

"Bad breath!" he cries like a madman. "Bad breath!"

Panic takes her by the throat and hits her in the pit of her stomach. All Remy can think is, *Oh shit.* Then a tentacle sweeps her off her feet in the worst way. Her back hits the ground and she crawls to cover on her elbows as the giganeye parts its humongous jaws. Through its jagged teeth pours a tidal wave of toxic smog, which engulfs the hall. Jessica's muffled screams fall silent amidst the shroud, and once it dissipates, she is revealed, petrified in stone.

"Jessica?!" Remy howls and trips over her own feet as she clambers towards the statue that was her sister. She presses her palm to poor Jess's face, which is frozen in a twisted scream.

Ed watches her desperately try to pull Jessica out of her affliction and his heart sinks.

This is definitely not a game! We're dead. We're gonna die! No, no, think, Ed! What do we know?

He recalls his battle in the game with the giganeye, which didn't end well either. He hadn't levelled up enough before trying his luck, but there are no second lives, revive potions or save scumming now. He ducks back behind cover as the creature's malevolent eye sweeps the room in search of him, then his eyes snap wide as a strategy presents itself.

"The eye!" he cries. "Stab it in the eye!"

The creature fixes its gaze on Remy standing out in the open, and sends its squirmy tentacles to grapple her legs and arms. Tightening her grip on the rusty sword, she erupts in a fit of primal rage. The creature's black blood sprays everywhere as she lops off one appendage after another until her sword arm is constricted. The giganeye pulls her upwards into the air kicking and screaming, and brings her towards its maw. It unfurls a long, slimy tongue, which dances, eager to savour her flesh and spit out her bones.

Ed, recalling the giganeye's toxic blood to be extremely flammable from the info listed in his special edition monster manual – totally worth the extra hundred quid now – hurriedly prises a torch from the wall and hurls it into the mass of tentacles. The blood ignites like gasoline, and the giganeye roars and spits as the flames scorch its putrid flesh, allowing Remy to wrestle her sword arm free. She jabs the blade into the tentacle around her waist, splaying it open like a sausage. With a deafening yowl, the dungeon boss releases her and she tumbles onto its huge face. Balancing on her knees, she plunges her sword as hard as she can into its vile eyeball again and again. The beast lets out an ungodly cry as it dies, and the entire ruin shakes while the monster festers into a rancid tar beneath her feet. Remy slides through the muck and hits the ground on her front, saving herself with her elbows. Then a gleaming flash steals her attention. Above her, a shard of green crystal floats downwards from where the monster stood, glistening with a pale, hypnotic light. Remy is captivated by the jewel's soft whisper. It's not quite a voice, more like a craving, slithering between her ears and into her mind, body and soul. She reaches out and brushes the gem with one finger and its light pulses at her touch. Despite appearing as smooth as water the gem pricks her fingertip, drawing a drop of blood.

*

Seeing the crystal, Grimoirh erupts and leaps over the balcony. His obsidian greaves shatter the stone floor as he lands with a whomp.

"Don't touch that shard!" his voice booms. He strides towards Remy with intent and draws the oversized 'God Cleaver' sword on his back, but a tremendous blast tears down the stone roof above them and hurls everyone across the chamber.

Ed rolls onto his back and cups his ringing ears, while through dust and smoke he spies a great galleon floating above the dungeon. Armed bandits rappel into the hall on long ropes as the walls around them collapse, letting loose the undead horde that had pursued them through the dungeon. Ed stumbles onto his feet, but before he can orient himself a gruff-looking fella takes him by his underarms and carries him up towards the airship while the hall floods with walking corpses.

Remy crawls towards the crystal shard and grasps it tightly in her right hand. The jewel shines between her fingers and sears her flesh like a hot iron. She howls as the shard bores into her palm like a parasite and embeds itself there.

Grimoirh picks himself up, ready to cut the relic out of her. He staggers towards her as she drags herself towards poor petrified Jessica, but she's stopped shy of reaching her sister by another bandit who takes hold of her waist and hoists her out of the mayhem.

Grimoirh's dark eyes watch her from beneath cold metal as she wrestles her captors and cries out to Jessica while she's pulled kicking and screaming on board the vessel. The airship ascends, leaving Jessica amidst the undead.

*

The bandit airship *Skywark* – a floating galleon, kept aloft by huge gas balloons that hover in place of sails – soars through the dawn sky. Remy and Ed sit on the bow, beaten to shit, wrapped in a coarse blanket to shield them from the frigid air. They behold the blinding sun born anew over the brown barren wasteland to the east, and to the west, nothing but dense forest that stretches beyond the horizon.

Ed steals glances at Remy. Her windswept hair flutters across her blackened face, and her eyes, flush with grief, gaze into nothingness as she sits deep in thought, rubbing the palm of her right hand. He searches for words to ease her pain, not that any could, and is certain that reassuring her it was 'just a game' would not be appropriate. Still, he musters something.

"She'll be alright..." his voice cracks as he speaks, "... petrification doesn't mean you're dead, we just need the remedy – a golden needle, I think – then we can go back. How hard can that be to find?"

She pays him no mind and just sits quietly ruminating on how mad this all is. If that crystal is what she thinks it is then she had better get rid of it fast.

Marcus, first mate of the *Skywark*, approaches them.

"Come with me," he growls, strands of long blond hair dancing across his rugged face in the breeze.

Remy doesn't so much as glance in his direction, but Ed quickly conjures all the worst possible scenarios of what's about to play out – visions of torture or being thrown overboard. He gulps, quashing the awful scenarios from his mind's eye.

"Hey, you hear me? I said come along."

"I think we better do what he says." Ed nudges Remy, who

50

shoots the bandit a dirty look as she reluctantly gets on her feet.

He ushers them into a small cabin on the deck and shuts the door behind him, then stands in front of it and folds his arms like a bouncer denying them entry into a nightclub.

"You can't just take us like this. It's super-dysfunctional." Remy squares up to him, but he isn't the least bit intimidated.

"Hey, cool it." Ed's attempt to pacify her proves useless; she's already right in the bandit's face, standing on her tiptoes to meet his gaze.

"Listen, you dick, stop being a dick and tell us who you are!"

The bandit locks eyes with her and frowns, but keeps his lips shut tight.

"What an ass," she spits. Unsurprisingly, interpersonal skills weren't listed on her résumé.

Marcus arches a stoic but disapproving brow. Sticks and stones and all that.

Ed sighs. "You're only making things worse for us."

"Well, at least *I'm* doing something." Remy walks over to the wooden desk in the centre of the room and takes a seat behind it.

Spurred by her stinging remark Ed decides to do something. "Ever heard of killing with kindness?" he whispers with a smug grin before perching on a crate beside the door.

"I'm really digging your whole dieselpunk biker pirate vibe."

Marcus shoots Ed a threatening eye. Nevertheless, he prattles on.

"No, really, wish I could pull off that much leather... Anyway, look, we've had a really, *really* long night, she's cranky, she's rude, she's loud..."

"I can hear you!" Remy scoffs.

Ed leans closer to Marcus, taking on a hushed tone. "See what I mean? So how about you just do us both a favour and tell her something so we can all get a little peace and quiet? What do you say, my man?"

The bandit weighs up Ed's proposition. One glance at Remy's tempestuous face is enough to concede. Threatening she is not, but annoying, well, that's a skill she's more than levelled up over the years. Raising his eyes to the heavens, Marcus complies with a sigh.

"The boss wants to talk to you."

"And who exactly is your boss?" Remy kicks her feet up on the desk in a petty act of rebellion.

Before Marcus can reply, the door behind him opens and light from outside casts a tall silhouette of the man at the door. He steps into the cabin, ducking as he enters. As Remy gets a look at him her eyes widen in awe.

"No way," she gasps.

Bengeo the Bandit stands proudly before her, no longer a tiny pixelated sprite or an animated 3D model but a solid oak tree of a real man, heavy-set and muscular with rich, dark skin and sporting a ragged leather vest, dull green trousers, big dusty boots and a burly battle axe on his back, exactly like his character model from the game. He rubs his hair, which is cut similar to a hi-top fade and runs a hand across his stubbly beard. He's a goddamned specimen of strength, that's for sure.

"Boss," Marcus greets Bengeo.

"Well, well, what do we have here?" he asks, grinning.

"The girl's a real pain in the ass," Marcus warns.

Remy is too star-struck to pay that insult any mind. "You! You're...! You're...?!" she stutters trying to string a sentence together, "... Bengeo?"

Bengeo glances at Ed who is too enraptured to speak. "Looks like my reputation precedes me," he grins.

Remy approaches him like a squeeing fangirl. "I can't believe it's really you!" She slaps a hand on his face, squeezes and pulls at his cheeks to see what he's made of – feels like flesh and bone.

"Girl, get your damn hand off me." He swats her away with fists as big as her head.

"You're my favourite character," she beams, admiring the gnarly scar on his cheek, an X that he got in a duel with the former captain of this very airship, but that's a story for another time.

"Whad'ya mean character?" Bengeo frowns.

Remy looks to Ed for an explanation, but he shrugs. It seems Bengeo is unaware he's a work of fiction.

The bandit eyes up his captives noting their unusual clothes. "So how'd a pair of milk drinkin' weeds like you two end up in that crypt? You don't look like you're from around here."

"Beats me." Ed rests nonchalantly against the wall with his arms behind his head.

Remy rolls her eyes at his try-hard cavalier attitude. "We were kidnapped. Sort of. Taken from our home by some creature," she says.

"And where is *home* exactly?" Bengeo asks.

"I'm not sure…" Again, Remy looks to Ed for an explanation and again he shrugs.

"Uh, a galaxy far, far away…" Ed sighs. He can't believe what he's saying. "… Another world. I guess."

"Maybe the old crow wasn't crazy…" Bengeo mutters.

"Look, my sister is still back there, trapped like a living statue. You need to turn this ship around and go back for her!" Remy says.

He shakes his head. "Sorry, kid, there's no going back now."

"Why not? The Bengeo I know isn't afraid of anything!"

"Not afraid but not stupid or suicidal either. We're lucky we got away at all."

"Well, if you won't go back then let me off, and I'll go get her myself!"

Bengeo sighs. "Can't do that either."

"Why the hell not?!" Remy squares up to him.

"I don't know about all this 'other world' stuff you're spoutin', but I sure as hell know the old man is gonna want to talk to both of you. I got orders and we all gotta do our part, see? That includes you two." He matches her wicked gaze and stares her down.

Remy grits her teeth. "Not interested, let me off."

"You wanna go up against Grimoirh? Save your sister? Well, you can't do it alone. You're just one annoying girl. You're gonna need an army and real power."

She knows he's right, in whatever weird new reality they've found themselves in, but she's too stubborn to admit it. She perches on the desk and folds her arms in a huff.

"What were you guys doing storming that dungeon anyway?" Ed asks.

Bengeo turns to him and ruffles his hair. "We were looking for you, Red."

Ed tries to tidy his mop when a loud bang rings out around them.

"The hell was that?" Bengeo looks worriedly at Marcus and bursts out of the cabin.

Remy and Ed follow the bandits onto the deck and look up as a shadow looms overhead. They gawp at the trail of black smog spewing from a gargantuan metallic airship pursuing them. This other craft dominates the ship they're riding and looks far more advanced, like a flying diesel gunboat blackening the skies.

"No way we can outrun that, boss!" Marcus cries.

"Get those cannons firing and give the engines all we've got. I'm taking them outta here! If shit goes south, rendezvous at the Legless Arms!" Bengeo replies.

"Aye!" Marcus nods, and the two bandits bump their forearms together like a salute before he runs off to command the other bandits rushing about the deck, readying their cannons to return fire.

Bengeo turns to Remy and Ed with a foreboding look. "Stick by me. This is gonna get messy."

Ear-popping gunfire rains from above, and the burning stench of gunpowder permeates the air. Monstrous henchmen rappel from the marauding airship and besiege Bengeo's vessel. The bandit crew hold their own but are vastly outnumbered, and as the bombardment blows the floating galleon to bits around them, they are slaughtered too.

Cleo, one of Bengeo's fiercest, calls out to her captain, "Get 'em outta here, boss! We'll hold 'em off!" She cuts down an ugly goblin charging at the 'players' with her curved sword and downs two more in a flurry of kicks and slashes, while Bengeo drags Remy and Ed down a flight of creaky wooden stairs below deck.

"What are we doing?! The fight's up there!" Remy snatches her arm back.

"Ship's lost, we gotta run."

"Are you kidding me? Grimoirh's up there. We can finish this now!"

"We're outgunned and outnumbered. Now shut yer trap and do what I tell you!" The bandit lifts a wooden hatch and retreats down a ladder to the deepest level of the ship. Ed follows quickly and Remy reluctantly behind him.

The barrage blasts great holes in the galleon's hull, causing splinters and shards to litter the air as the three fight their way to the cargo hold in the ship's belly. In the centre of the room sits a large contraption covered with a grotty tarp, which Bengeo promptly tears off and tosses aside.

"What is that thing?" Ed stares worriedly at the strange machine, a primitive aeroplane of sorts. Its small cockpit sits atop a long oblong metal chassis, which is framed by two wings stacked above one another on each side – four in total. Each has a series of propellers. Another larger propeller sits on the front and two more on the tail.

"Our lifeboat," Bengeo replies with a smug grin. "I call it the *Dragonfly*."

"Oh no, I don't think so. I'm not getting in that thing." Ed looks wanly at the panels and parts crudely welded together.

Bengeo ignores his cowardice and cranks open the cargo hold doors.

"You're going to abandon your crew?" Remy shouts over the blustering wind.

"It's you they're after, and it's you they'll follow!" He climbs into the cockpit and starts the machine's engine. Its propellers roar to life like an angry warthog.

"You're using us as bait?!" she scoffs.

"That's the plan. Grimoirh wants you for some reason, so get your asses up here!"

Remy glances at her right hand, knowing she possesses the exact reason Grimoirh is relentlessly pursuing them, then takes Bengeo's arm, and he pulls her into the cockpit behind him, but Ed hesitates; he really doesn't like flying. Well, actually it's not so much the flying he fears, it's the idea of dying in a steel death trap.

"It's now or never, kid!" Bengeo extends his hand.

Ed glances behind him and sees several bloodthirsty goblins clobbering their way towards him through the bowels of the airship. Looks like it's certain death either way, might as well take his chances in the air. With Bengeo's help he scrambles into the cockpit.

The bandit looks back at the pair and smiles excitedly. "Hold on to your butts."

The goblins force their way into the room and leap onto the hull of the plane as it rolls forward.

"Uh, we've got some stowaways!" Remy cries.

Bengeo punches it, the plane lurches downwards out of the cargo hold and the goblins let out a shrill cry as they're tossed into the air by the sudden drop. Remy hurriedly slides the cockpit shut while Ed screams hysterically and clings to her like his life depends on it.

"Do something before we crash!" she shouts.

"Not yet!" Bengeo replies.

"What do you mean not yet?! We're going to die!"

"Not yet!" he snaps back and counts in his head.

Remy shuts her eyes tight, but Bengeo keeps his cool as the plane hurtles towards the earth, and tightens his grip on the yoke.

"Three... two... now!" He throttles the engine and jolts back the yoke. The plane's four wings extend outwards from the chassis and catch the air, and it suddenly soars upwards.

"Whooooooohooooooo!" the bandit cheers and guides the plane towards the warring airships. "How you two holding up?" He looks back at Remy who, white as a ghost, props up Ed's limp body.

"He fainted," she sighs.

Bengeo lets out a raucous laugh as the *Dragonfly* whizzes through the sky and zips past Grimoirh's ship. "We gotta get their attention somehow. Hey, kid, how's your eyesight?"

"Stop calling me kid, and it's fine!" she snaps while trying to keep Ed from flopping everywhere as the plane zigs and zags through the sky.

"Put this on." Bengeo tosses her a leather body harness and a pair of goggles.

"What the hell is this?" she asks, trying to make sense of the tangled mess of straps and buckles.

"Just put it on, I need you to shoot."

"Shoot? Shoot what?!"

"There's a cannon mounted on the rear, you gotta go out there to reach it."

Remy looks behind her and spots the gun mounted on the tail. "Are you kidding me?! Why did you put it on the outside?!" she shrieks.

"If you get thrown off, just pull the red cord," he laughs.

Remy glances at the harness, which is covered with dangling red cords. "Which one?"

"Bah! You'll figure it out, now go!"

She hastily fastens the harness and pulls the goggles over her eyes. Her hair whips violently in all directions as she slides open the cockpit window and climbs out on to the hull. She clips a chain on the harness to a steel loop on the chassis, tethering herself to the plane, but can't bring herself to climb out.

"C'mon! Before they blast us to scrap!" the bandit yells.

"Jesus Christ, give me a minute!" she roars back, and with a deep breath hoists herself out of the cockpit, then shuffles her way along the tail to the cannon. Despite the brutal wind resistance she miraculously reaches it without falling and clings onto it desperately. On inspection, it looks like a crude proto-machine gun of sorts, like the early Gatling guns she once saw in an American Civil War movie, then she comes to a frightful realisation. *I don't know what I'm doing!*

Turning back to Bengeo she yells over the roaring engines and cannon fire, "I don't know what I'm doing!" but he can't hear her. She's on her own.

The plane passes over Grimoirh's vessel, and varicoloured fireballs hurl past Remy, erupting all around her like a lethal firework show. She chokes on the thick smog as Bengeo manoeuvres between the blasts.

She frantically examines the Gatling gun again and notices that the trigger and handles strongly resemble her game controller.

"It's just a game. It's just a game..." She repeats the phrase like a mantra. "It's just a game. It's just a game!"

Planting a firm hand on the controls, she squeezes the triggers, releasing a spray of red-hot metal from the six spinning barrels.

"Here we go, kid!" Bengeo steers the *Dragonfly* over Grimoirh's ship again and Remy lets rip.

Gunfire showers the deck, shredding cannons and blasting the monstrous goblins to chunks of odorous meat around

Grimoirh, who stands fearless as the shrapnel ricochets like glittering stars against his black armour.

"Blow them out of the sky!" he barks at his monstrous minions who aim their cannons at Bengeo's plane.

BOOM! The blast narrowly misses the *Dragonfly*.

"Hey, watch it!" Remy shrieks. "I nearly lost my eyebrows!"

She rubs soot off her goggles and blasts away at the cannons as Bengeo doubles back for another pass. Wicked vibrations rattle her bones as she hails Grimoirh's ship with piping-hot lead. She can barely see through the smeared lenses as she shreds a few mounted cannons and turrets, but just when she starts to believe she might actually survive this... KABOOM! Another blast clips the *Dragonfly*, blowing two of the wings clean off, sending the ship spinning wildly out of control and hurtling towards the forest below.

The G-force tears off the tail of the plane, sending Remy spiralling earthbound. Her stomach churns like she's strapped into some hell-bound carnival ride, while her heart thuds in her chest, and she clumsily clambers for a red cord. Her hand finds one and tugs it hard. A large pouch on her back blows open, and a bunch of egg-shaped rocks, a frying pan and a small duck shoot up above her. Wrong cord.

"What the hell is that for?!" she screams.

The treetops come spinning towards her. Her hand stumbles on another cord and she yanks it, praying for a parachute – no such luck. Instead, the harness glows bright teal, and in a flash, a sphere of protective energy envelops her. It doesn't slow her descent one bit, but as she tears through the treetops and into the forest, the sphere shields her, incinerating anything it touches.

She hits the ground like a meteor and the magic burns through the earth until she slows to a halt and hovers amidst the shimmering energy, like a hamster in a zero-gravity ball. The sphere sharply and suddenly dissipates, and she drops into the crater head first. She lifts her face, caked in thick clots of mud, and spits out dirt. Adrenaline surges through her. Her arms and legs tremble fiercely while she suppresses the overwhelming urge to vomit. She hugs her bruised knees and brings them to her chin as she comes to terms with what just happened, and slowly her panic turns to rejoicing that she's still alive. But before she can gather her thoughts, Bengeo tears out of the treeline, carrying Ed's limp body over his broad, muscular shoulders.

"Told you you'd figure it out! Now run!" he hollers as he sprints by.

She looks skyward, and to her horror, massive pieces of debris are raining down from the airship battle. Her fingers clasp the dirt as she claws her way out of the crater and immediately breaks into a clumsy sprint. She catches up to Bengeo and follows him, leaping and ducking through the thick forestry as the debris bursts through the trees and into the ground like a flaming hailstorm.

"Keep up, kid!" Bengeo charges through a hollow tree, using Ed as a shield.

Remy hasn't run this much since PE when she was in school. Nowadays her lackadaisical lifestyle consists mostly of sitting before a screen and a diet of carbs on carbs on carbs – hardly fitting preparation for a hardcore survivalist jungle run. Bengeo notices her wheezing, and as she falters, he pulls her sideways over a drop. The three of them tumble violently down a steep gorge, crashing through vines, thorns and thickets which scratch them to ribbons, until they hurtle off the cliffside into the raging river below. Remy fights to stay afloat. The river thrashes the rocks and pummels her while it sweeps them through the forest. Bursts of air are interrupted by swelling currents pulling her under. She's not the best swimmer, but she's too damn stubborn to drown.

*

In the real world, it's mid-morning, and Remy's parents are returning from the wedding they had attended. Helen looks glazed at the passing street and ponders what state the girls have left the house in.

"I bet the place is a tip," she mutters.

"Mmm," Ray mumbles half-heartedly.

"Remy won't have done any washing."

"Mmm."

"Honestly, that girl." Helen shakes her head, and purses her lips.

"Mmm," Ray grumbles again as he turns a corner.

"She's so... I mean, Jesus, was I ever that mopey?" She knows Ray is paying more attention to the radio but vents anyway. "Am I too hard on her? She never listens to me. She just... It's like she knows exactly what buttons to push to drive me mad. Oh, I just don't know..." Helen lets out a long sigh and bites her fingernails.

Ray notices his wife's sombre expression and, unable to endure her sadness, he – in a rare act – emerges from his psychological man cave and gently takes her hand. Bringing it away from her mouth, he rests it in her lap.

"She's just lost her way. She's angry at the world and she has a right to be, it's a hurting place sometimes. Life, it can be hard. There are times when you don't want to get out of bed, all you want to do is tune out the world. She needs to realise that just because she made some mistakes, and things aren't panning out how she expected, that doesn't make her a failure. She tried, she just needs to try again and accept that sometimes bad things will happen to her. But if she's going to make a success of her life, she's got to put the past behind her and move on so she can grow and be open to the opportunities that will come her way, but it's something she needs to realise on her own. She'll be alright. She's tough, like her mother." He smiles at her tenderly, turns onto their road and parks.

Helen's face is shock and wonder. His uncharacteristic bout of wisdom and tenderness is something wholly unexpected, but something she desperately needed to hear. Lost for words, she puts a hand on his knee and squeezes it.

Ray kills the engine and returns to his usual docile self. They exit the car and gather their bags, blissfully unaware that they're about to step into a crime scene. Helen unlocks the front door and it swings open. The daylight casts a harsh spot on the living room. Furniture is toppled over, there's broken glass littered about, the candles have burned to nothing, and the TV is idly displaying a Game Over screen. It's clear there's been a struggle, and brazen as Remy may be, she'd never leave the house in this much of a state.

"Remy?!"

"Jessica?!"

They call out, but no answer. The parents exchange a look of grave concern, both of them fearing the worst.

V

INTO THE WOODS

Where the winding river calms, Remy's hands sink into the cold mud and she drags her drenched, encumbered self further inland. Rolling onto her back, she flicks her sopping hair off her face and breathes a sigh of relief – finally a break in the madness. As she lies there like a beached corpse, she realises that this is the first moment in a long time that she's felt truly alive; a string of near-death experiences will do that to you.

Staring up at the foreign sky, the weight of everything hits her like a train. She grasps deep breaths to quell her shot nerves and clutches her thumping chest. A surge of emotion floods to the surface. She can't stop it. She's been holding it all in, just going through the motions, but now there's nothing to stop the cruel whisper in her head. *You're lost you're dead you left Jessica unforgivable terrible person no one will miss you.*

She wanted to get away from her life, and often fantasised about woodland retreats, spending time with nature, but this is certainly not what she had in mind. The grass, the water, the wind on her skin, the brisk air filling her lungs – it all feels too real, which only terrifies her more. She lets out a hateful scream at the universe for punishing her like this. Everything she's got comes spewing out – bloody fury, a big fuck you to the world. She's still here – wherever that may be. Still alive. Her voice cracks. She screeches until breathless.

*

A little way downstream, Bengeo strides out of the river, winding his shoulder while rubbing it with his other hand. Ed, who's lying face down in the muddy riverbank, abruptly comes to and coughs up murky water as he lifts his completely blackened face out of the muck. His greyish eyes and white teeth shine from beneath the filth and he takes a deep breath then lets out a prolonged scream that slowly winds down.

"Again with the screaming," Bengeo remarks.

"Wha—? Where are we?! We were flying and then—!" He rolls onto his side and tries to piece it all together.

"Calm down, boy, we're alright for the moment," Bengeo replies.

Ed feels something coming up, a wrongness stirring in the pit of his stomach. "I think I'm going to—!" He opens his mouth wide and retches. "Yep, definitely... urrrgghh... feels like I'm... ueeegggggghh!" He brings his knees to his face and pants like a sick dog. "There's nothing, there's nothing there. It's just... uuuuuuugggggggghhhhhhhh!" He rolls back onto his side like a stuffed pig. "I'm good, I'm good," he waves. "False alarm."

Bengeo stares in disbelief. He's never witnessed a more pitiful sight in all his life.

"Just breathe, kid. It'll pass. Got to figure a way out of here, though. This is the last place we want to be when it gets dark..." The bandit looks up at the crooked trees around him and frowns.

"What happens after dark?" a welcome voice asks from

behind him. Remy steps out of the brush, soaking wet and beat to hell.

Bengeo and Ed, who uncurls from the foetal position, both look very happy to see her.

"You good?" the bandit asks.

"Not dead yet." She slings the muck off her face with her forearm.

A smirk creeps across Bengeo's lips, commending her resilience. "We move in five. So get on your feet." He nudges Ed with his foot before splashing himself clean in the river.

"I'll be right with you." Ed rests his face in the soft mud. If he pretends real hard, it sort of feels like a cold, squelchy pillow, and right now, that's enough.

*

A world away, Lauren is on a mission of her own. She's standing on the doorstep of Vincent's flat staring at a string of unanswered texts on her phone. It's been months since she's heard from him, and now he just up and quits without a word. It doesn't make sense, and she's not buying Eric's story. She wants answers, or at the very least to know he's okay. After a mind-numbing internal back and forth, she finally plucks up the courage to ring the doorbell. It was all for nothing, though, no one answers. But then, she didn't really expect him to. Determined not to leave without at least visual confirmation he's okay, she peers through the kitchen window of the flat on tiptoes. It's a struggle to make out much through the crack in the drawn curtains, but looks like no one's home.

With her nose pressed against the glass, she doesn't notice an old man wrapped in a grey dressing gown sneaking up behind her.

"What are you doing?" His gravelly voice startles Lauren, who headbutts the window and screams.

The old man screams too and clutches his chest. "Christ, girl! Are you trying to kill me?" He readies his newspaper to strike her.

"Wha—?! What?"

"Give a man a heart attack screaming in his face like that." He lowers the newspaper, surmising that she's as scared of him as he is of her.

"S-sorry, you… you startled me," she says.

He eyes her up and down. "Too right. What are you prowling round here for anyhow? You one of them peeping toms?"

"What?" Lauren looks mortified. "No! I'm not a… What?"

"Going round peeping through windows. That there is the *modus operandi* of a pervert, that is."

"I'm not! Well, I was but—"

An old, white-haired woman pokes her head out of the neighbouring door. "Roger, who's that there?" she asks.

The old man turns to his wife. "Caught a prowler."

"It's not what you think," Lauren says.

"Then what are you doing?" Roger probes.

"I'm looking for Vincent Golbez. He does live here, doesn't he? He quit his job. I'm just worried, so I thought I'd stop by."

"What did she say?" the old woman asks from behind the door.

"Said she's looking for Vincent," Roger replies.

"Who?"

"Vincent!" The old man rolls his eyes to the heavens.

"Who?"

"Vince…! Oh for God's sake, woman, the weirdo from next door!" He gives a false smile, hoping not to have caused any offence.

"Oh," the old woman says. "Haven't seen him in ages."

The three of them stand in deafening silence while Roger and his wife stare at Lauren expectantly.

"Well… If you see him will you tell him to call Lauren?" she asks.

"Who's Lauren?" Roger replies.

"I'm Lauren." And she's contemplating throwing herself off the balcony to escape this conversation.

"What did she say?" the old lady shouts again.

"She said she's Lauren."

"What?" the old lady cups her ear as Lauren lets out a pained groan under her breath and wonders whether she'll be trapped here for all eternity.

*

"If we stop, we die!" Bengeo's warning lingers in Remy's mind as she struggles to match his gruelling pace through the sprawling forest. She savours every breath, planting one leaden foot after the other over twigs and branches while her sweat-drenched pyjamas cling to her. Her foot catches a rock, and she tumbles over and rolls to a stop. The boots on her feet, however disgusting, at least provide adequate protection from the terrain. She barely felt the rock as her foot slammed into it. Ed hurries back to her and offers a hand, but she shakes her head as she sits up and rests her arms on her clammy thighs.

Bengeo calls to them, "What's the holdup?"

"No more running. We've been running all day," Remy heaves in a raspy voice. "Running from cannon fire or monsters or crap falling from the sky. You know how hard it is to run without a bra? So I'm not taking another step until you tell me what is so bloody dangerous about this forest after dark!"

"Can't you just do what you're told?" Bengeo puffs his chest and flares his nostrils. He's sick of her incessant whining.

Remy gets on her feet, stands as tall as she can and puts on her toughest mean face. "Maybe if I knew why we were in danger I would!" Bengeo dwarfs Remy, but she doesn't relent.

Her attitude is a match for any hulk-sized sky pirate.

They stare each other down until Ed steps between them. "Guys, can we not?" But they only eyeball each other harder, so Ed throws his hands up and leaves them to it. "Look, just tell her and then we can resume running for our lives."

"Fine. It's the trees, they eat people," Bengeo says matter-of-factly.

"Come again?" Remy looks dumbfounded at the bandit.

"The trees eat people. After dark, they come alive, and they'll eat you right up."

Remy opens her mouth then pauses. "… Yeah, alright that's a pretty good reason."

"Man-eating trees, huh?" Ed eyeballs the forest with suspicion.

"Happy now? It's not long before sundown and I ain't being eaten by no tree." The bandit ploughs on ahead like a man on a mission.

"I want out. Take me home, please God. Why is everything here so deadly?" Remy sighs.

"You don't have man-eating trees where you're from?" Bengeo asks.

"No! Of course we don't have man-eating trees! Of course not, because that's not a thing. Trees don't eat people in the real world. They're vegan," Remy exclaims.

"Huh, sounds like a weird place," Bengeo smirks, but his face quickly turns sour as the echo of a war horn tremors through the forest. Casting his eyes behind them he spots plumes of smoke rising in the distance. "They're relentless. Whatever you did it must have really pissed them off."

Ed looks at Remy's hand. "I think they're after—"

"Ed!" Remy quiets him.

"What? We should tell him," Ed replies.

"Tell me what?" Bengeo asks.

Ed looks encouragingly at Remy until she reluctantly

confesses, "I might have picked up a magic crystal shard back in that dungeon you pulled us out of."

Bengeo's face darkens and he takes on a serious tone. "Crystal shard? Show me."

She wiggles her fingers and balls her right hand. "The thing is it's, like, hidden."

He snatches her hand and inspects it closely before she wrestles it back, but he couldn't tell from looking whether or not the crystal was really in there.

"Hey!" she snaps, but Bengeo looks gravely worried, as though the man-eating trees were suddenly of no consequence compared to the shard in her hand.

"So the old crow wasn't lying. You've got no idea what that is, do you?" he asks in a condescending manner.

"Trust me, I have some idea," she replies, knowing all too well, having played the old game, what trouble this little jewel will no doubt bring her.

"Well, we're in the shit now. If that's what I think it is, they'll hunt you across the world." He casts his gaze through the trees as the war drums and bellowing horns resound through the woodland.

*

Smoke and fire engulf all life. Stubby goblin men with sallow, lumpy skin cut their way through the trees atop clunky steam-powered traction machines that look like crude tanks, only with blades, grinders and saws welded to the front and back. Each one is piloted from a seat atop the base, behind a console full of levers and buttons. The creatures cackle in shrill voices as the trunks snap under the unforgiving caterpillar tracks.

Domina rides atop the largest machine ahead of the others. Her cold eyes regard the forest with scorn and contempt. She does her best to conceal a malicious grin while the whirring buzzsaws decimate the sprawling lush greenery before her and all manner of woodland critters flee for their lives.

*

Remy, Bengeo and Ed take off, desperate to put as much distance between them and Grimoirh's search party as possible. They don't stop until they reach a clearing that overlooks the sprawling forest, which stretches for miles and miles.

Bengeo's eyes tighten with worry at the scorched-dusk sky. "We're not gonna make it," he says.

Ed turns back towards the smoke plumes. He can hear the throaty rumble of the engines crawling towards them, and watches trees topple over in the distance, then he frowns at Grimoirh's airship which hovers ominously above, an imposing sight if ever he's seen one.

"What if we weren't on foot?" he grins, alluding to a plan forming in his mind.

Bengeo glances at him and then over to the smoke and cottons on. "You've got balls, kid. I like how you think."

"Are you crazy? There's probably dozens of them," Remy says.

"What if we had help?" Ed grins again.

"You got an army we don't know about?" the bandit asks.

"What if I do?"

Remy snaps, "Stop answering everything with a question, it's really annoying."

"Sorry. I thought it sounded tough."

Bengeo draws the axe on his back. "So what's our play?"

"We wait till dark and lure them into an ambush. Then we let the flesh-eating trees do the fighting for us while we roll out of here on the sly."

Remy's impressed. "Okay, that's not a bad idea. But how do we lure them to us?"

"Leave that to me," the bandit smiles.

*

The grey skies over London shroud the setting sun and rain befalls the city. In the northern borough of Barnet, outside 15 Forest Hill, a dirty white Vauxhall Corsa pulls up. Behind the wheel sits Detective Inspector Scott Valentine – a real man out of time, with no patience for technology and little idea how to use it. He pulls on an old, musky leather jacket before stepping out of the car, using a folded newspaper to shield himself from the downpour. He stares at Remy's house a moment, gathering a sense of the neighbourhood before he darts to the front door. By the time he reaches the porch the rain has soaked him through.

A policewoman greets him by the door – Nitya Alapati, a young and warm-hearted constable, newly promoted, looking to prove herself and friendlier to Valentine than most, maybe because he sort of reminds her of her dear old dad. The sight of him evokes a smile. He looks like he walked straight out of a 90s detective show, probably because he hasn't bought any new clothes since then.

"Scott," she nods.

He nods back. "So what brings us to this charming place?" He brushes back his dripping charcoal hair and follows her into the house.

All is quiet, save for the flash of a camera from a photographer snapping pictures of the living room.

"No signs of forced entry anywhere, the doors and windows were all locked, but obviously looks like there was a struggle." Alapati points at the broken coffee table and strange imprints marking the wall and floor. "The two daughters are missing. Remy, twenty-seven, and Jessica, eighteen."

Valentine picks up a smashed family picture from the floor and stares at the girls. "Maybe they threw a party that got out of control?" He rubs his tired eyes then peers into the kitchen to see a bewildered Ray and Helen sitting at the dinner table, wrought with worry. "I mean, these aren't exactly missing children. Young people do crazy stuff, it's a generational thing," he says in a hushed tone.

"A generational thing?" she asks.

"Yeah. Every generation at that age does wild, reckless stuff. I could tell you some tales. Ha."

"Oh yeah? I'd love to hear what Churchill was really like," she jests.

Valentine frowns and places the picture back on the mantle. "Very funny."

He walks into the living room and takes a minute to absorb the scene before approaching the television, which is idly displaying Ultimate Adventure VII's Game Over screen. He stares a moment, but nothing jumps out at him until he notices what appear to be large, filthy footprints staining the carpet. They're far too big to be human.

He signals the photographer. "Make sure you get a shot of this."

The photographer nods and snaps the picture. "I've taken a 360 recording of the room."

"A what?" asks Valentine.

"You know, those cameras that film in all directions. I took a recording so you can look back over it later. It lets you pan around the room like you're actually here."

"But I am actually here," Valentine replies.

The photographer is taken aback by the look of disdain on the detective's face. "Uh, yeah I suppose so." He laughs nervously and steps away from Valentine.

The grisly old policeman lets out a tired sigh as he steps out onto the porch for a smoke. Before he can light it, Alapati interrupts him.

"So what you thinking?" she asks.

"I'm thinking why am I here? Both girls are adults. You said no signs of a break-in. Could be they had a wild night and are sweating off a hangover at some greasy spoon café, or maybe one of 'em just decided to take her aggression out on the living room set. Maybe they threw a party that got out of hand. Did you ask the neighbours about any noise last night?"

Alapati shakes her head. "Not yet… Something feels off about this one, and Sarge said we've had four other calls like this last night. I'm not buying your 'party got out of hand' theory."

Valentine shrugs. "People do weird shit." He goes to light his cigarette but is interrupted yet again by the cries of a man jogging towards him from across the street. "Case in point," he says.

"Police? You're the police?" the man cries.

"Yeah, we're the police," Valentine replies.

"I called, but they said no one would be over for hours! Inside, it's my son… he's gone and… and the house—?!"

"Whoa, slow down." Alapati steps off the porch and approaches the man. "What's the matter?"

"Just come and see for yourselves!" He takes her by the arm and pulls her across the street.

"Hey, hold on." Valentine shoves his unlit cigarette back in his pocket and jogs after them.

They're led up the stairs. A trail of scratches and scuff marks scar the wall, the banister is partially torn from the staircase, and more weird footprints stain the carpet leading along the upstairs corridor.

"Well, this just got a lot more interesting," Valentine says.

"This can't be a coincidence," Alapati whispers.

"Hard to say…" Valentine trails off as he follows the carnage into the bedroom, which looks like a bomb hit it.

"You just get home?" he asks the father.

The man nods. "I work nights, stopped at Tesco after. I had no idea—" He shakes his head and looks worriedly at the mess.

"This your son's room?" Valentine rubs his chin as he tries to make sense of it all. Feathers and broken figurines are scattered over the floor; shelves have been ripped down. He breathes in every minute detail, and immediately recognises the same Game Over screen sitting idle on the upturned television.

"Hmmm," he mumbles.

"What do you make of it?" Alapati asks.

Valentine inspects the wall next to her – more fingernail scratches, leading into the room. "This looks like someone was dragged upstairs..."

"The door was locked when I got home!" Ed's father says.

The detective runs his hand along the wall, then stepping into the room, he moves over to the window where he notices palm prints smeared on the glass.

"What is it?" Alapati asks.

"Looks like someone was banging on the glass..." Valentine stares at the Winters' house across the road. The rain is heavy now.

*

Bengeo kneels over a bundle of sticks and dead leaves, and strikes a piece of flint against the head of his axe to generate a spark. With every failed attempt he grows more heavy-handed. Patience is a virtue that he does not possess. Likewise Remy, who lurks behind him, hawkishly watching his every move.

"Do you want me to try?" she asks.

"I can do it," the bandit insists.

"I know how to light a fire, okay?"

"I said I can do it!" He grits his teeth and smashes the flint faster.

"Let me try, your hands are too big."

"My hands are not too big!"

"You're doing it too hard," she nags.

With a thwack the flint breaks into smaller pieces.

74

Remy sighs. "Told ya so."

He lets out a seething moan then he tosses the flint to Remy, who kneels by the fire pit and strikes the axe with careful precision. Feeling warm breath on the back of her neck, she turns her head and sees an enraged Bengeo looming over her, judging her every move to see how she likes it.

She shoos him away, so the bandit perches on a log, rests his arms on his knees and watches Remy work. After a couple of strikes, she gets a fire going.

"Ha! Still got it," she grins.

"I'll get firewood," Bengeo growls and approaches a dead tree, which he punches to splinters with his massive fists.

Ed watches him pound the bark and then glances at the bandit's axe resting by the log next to Remy.

"Wouldn't it make more sense if—"

Bengeo glares at him with furious intensity, and Ed shuts up, fearful of incurring the bandit's wrath.

"Forget it, you're doing great. Keep it up!" he laughs nervously and backs away.

Bengeo gathers the bark and watches the last glimmer of sunlight disappear below the treeline. The leaves rustle in the howling wind. The forest is waking up. He pulls his charges behind a hollow log on the far side of the clearing and watches with anticipation as the search party closes in on the smoke from their campfire.

The trees topple with a deafening crash as Domina's traction engine roars to a halt, and several goblin foot soldiers leap off and search the perimeter.

Fifty yards away Ed's eyes lock onto the machine.

"That's our ride," he whispers, watching Domina dismount the engine to search the site herself.

She sniffs around the area before casting her eyes directly towards the hollow trunk that they're hiding behind, almost meeting Remy's eye line.

"No way she can see us," Remy whispers.

"She's something alright," the bandit replies.

Remy rolls her eyes. "Yeah, if you're into that kind of thing."

Bengeo frowns. "What? I meant she ain't as human as she looks."

Domina approaches cautiously, listening intently for their whispers, their breath, their heartbeats.

Bengeo clutches his axe tightly. "Get ready for a fight."

"I'm always ready," says Ed as he peers through a hole in the rotting bark.

Remy frowns sceptically at him. That statement couldn't be farther from the truth, but hey, ignorance is bliss.

Domina unsheathes the short sword hanging on her belt and as she calls to her underlings all hell breaks loose. Contorted branches snap to life and whip the goblins off their feet, hurling them into the air. Great ravenous mouths break open from the thick tree trunks and brutally devour Domina's henchmen. The trees are angry and eager to punish the creatures responsible for burning and trampling their forest.

"Now's our chance!" Bengeo leads Remy and Ed through the mayhem, and they scurry across the clearing on their elbows while the goblins are tossed about like rag dolls and mashed into the ground by the living branches.

Ed grimaces at the stomach-churning sound of snapping bone. A mangled corpse crashes beside him with a whomp. He freezes and stares fearfully at the goblin's mushed head, until Remy grabs his collar and drags him towards the bulky traction engine that has been left unguarded.

Domina spies the three of them climbing aboard and furiously cuts a path to her prey. With a flick of the wrist, her sword falls limp and extends like a bladed whip, which she wields with mighty prowess, lashing the ravenous trees to splinters.

Ed examines the machine's controls and runs his hands over

his face. He hesitates to press any of the buttons, levers and dials for fear of breaking it.

"What are we waiting for?!" Remy kicks a goblin in the face as it clambers aboard to capture her.

"I don't know how it works!" Ed snaps.

"Well, figure it out!"

"Here we go then." Ed mashes the controls at random and the machine roars to life with a puff of black smoke that erupts from the tall copper pipes on the rear. "It's working! It's working!" he cries.

"Make it work faster!" Bengeo bashes a goblin with the hilt of his axe and kicks it off the machine. It's caught mid-air by a branch and dragged into the jaws of a carnivorous tree.

Domina thrusts her snake sword at Remy, who cries when she feels its sharp sting across her back. She tumbles off the engine with a shriek and looks up at her striking assailant.

"Give me that shard, or I'll cut it out of you!" Domina hisses.

Picking herself up, Remy scowls. "Bitch, it's been a really long day. So try me!" she braces herself. This is probably gonna hurt.

Domina grins with malice, revealing her fang-like teeth. She raises her arm, spinning her flail in a figure of eight between them until one of the serrated edges catches Remy's cheek.

"How about death by a thousand cuts?" Domina cackles.

"How about you piss off!" Remy spits and wipes clean the blood trickling down her cheek, then picks up a crooked club dropped by one of the dead goblins.

Domina relishes the girl's fighting spirit and shines with twisted glee as she readies a killing blow. She casts her whip down upon Remy, who raises the club in defence. The whip wraps her weapon and compresses it to dust. Defenceless again, Remy is out of ideas and out of luck. Bengeo is too busy protecting Ed from the marauding goblins and trees to lend any help.

The wicked woman winds her arm back to strike Remy, but

a cursed branch latches onto her wrist and constricts her like a python does its prey, then whisks her into the air in an instant.

Remy drops to her belly and crawls towards the engine, dodging the branches that swoop over her while Ed cranks lever after lever. The machine grinds forward and Bengeo extends his arm to Remy who scrambles onto her feet as the traction engine accelerates. She bounds after it through the trees as blood seeps from her cuts and scrapes. Her vision begins to tunnel as exhaustion and shock take their toll.

"Slow down!" Bengeo cries.

"I can't!" Ed jams the levers back and forth, desperate to make the machine obey him, but its speed is ever increasing. Bengeo leans out as far as he can to Remy, who jumps and catches his hand. He pulls her up in one swift movement as the machine really takes off into the forest like a stampeding rhinoceros, flattening trees beneath its bulky caterpillar tracks.

"Oh God, let me off!" Ed clings tightly to two vertical rods that protrude from the console-like joysticks as he's thrown up and down by the rough terrain. The machine flattens a tree stump and throws him sideways, making him jerk the joysticks left, and the machine judders with him. Finally it dawns on him how to pilot this contraption.

"Motion controls!" he squeals as they hurtle at breakneck speed through the living forest, smashing and sawing everything in their path to oblivion. He grips the joysticks with renewed confidence and does his best to steer them away from the larger obstacles. Leaning left and right, he guides the machine with his movements but struggles to keep his eyes open in the wind.

"Hey, stay with me!" Bengeo shakes Remy as her eyes slowly shut. She goes limp in his arms, and everything falls silent as she blacks out.

*

Sprawling meadows surround the outskirts of the forest. The vast rolling fields bathe in the light of the crimson moon while fireflies flutter around the tall swaying grass to the song of crickets. The roaring steam-powered bulldozer bursts out of the treeline on a gnarly rampage and sweeps through the meadow, obliterating the tranquillity and leaving the most obvious trail possible. Ed tries to slow the machine down by pulling back on the lever that started it, but nothing he presses, pulls or pokes makes a damn bit of difference.

"We gotta jump!" Bengeo shouts over the roar of the engine.

"Are you insane? We're going too fast!" Ed cries.

"Will you just man up and do what I tell you!"

"I will not be pressured by toxic mascu— ugh!" Ed gasps as Bengeo throws him off the machine, like Donkey Kong hurling a barrel.

Then the bandit lifts Remy over his shoulder. "This is gonna hurt," he sighs before plummeting into the long grass.

Wincing as he readjusts his aching back, Ed watches the machine plough over the horizon, and rain starts to fall around him. As he peers up at the sky a drop lands right between his eyes and trickles down his nose.

"Great…" Letting out a deep sigh, he strides through the long grass towards Bengeo who is standing tall with his head tilted to the heavens. "That was a dick move you pulled back there," Ed groans while massaging the back of his aching neck.

A sly grin creeps across Bengeo's lips. Ed glances at Remy who is lying still in the soft grass.

"How's our girl doing?" he asks the bandit.

"I'm not your girl," Remy whispers weakly and rolls onto her side.

"I thought we'd lost you for a second there."

Remy smirks, her eyes still shut. "You worried about me?" she croaks.

Ed runs his fingers through his tangled hair. "Well, yeah..." he mumbles, "... you're all I've got in here."

Remy quietly rests her eyes amongst the damp grass.

"What a day," Ed says.

"You did good, kid. Got us outta there alive." Ed winces as Bengeo pats him heartily on the shoulder. He bruises like a peach.

"Thanks." As crazy as this all is, for a fleeting second he almost feels glad to be here. "We should get out of this rain."

"Just another minute," Bengeo smiles, looking skyward.

*

The rain pitter-patters against the windows of Valentine's office. He's working late, as he often does, mostly because he has nothing but a microwave dinner waiting for him at home. The old man sifts through photos of both crime scenes on his computer, squinting intently, and he leans forward into the screen visibly frustrated by the thing's mere existence. Lord knows his eyesight isn't what it used to be, but he refuses to get glasses.

He clicks 'file' and 'print' and a dialog box offering an array of options pops up, which only fuels his rage against the machine.

"Bloody hell," he mutters to himself. "Nitya!" he calls out to the next room. "Nitya!"

Detective Alapati pokes her head through the door. "Yes?"

"It's doing that thing again," he sighs.

"You're gonna have to be more specific. Words, Scott, use your words," she quips.

"It won't let me print."

"You select the right printer?"

"I don't bloody know." He slams his hand on the mouse and angrily clicks about.

She sighs and leans over him, and in a series of quick and precise clicks gets the printer to spring to life. Photos of a third crime scene come etching out – a man's bedroom, trashed like the others, belonging to twenty-six-year-old Matthew Dermont. Valentine pins them up on a large board hanging on the wall of his office alongside pictures of Remy, Jessica and Ed.

"That's three similar disappearances on the same night," Valentine says.

"Is Matthew as connected, though?" Alapati replies. "Other than his age, I don't see what he has in common with the others. Far as we can tell he doesn't know them."

Valentine inspects his evidence. Rough timelines of Remy, Ed and Jessica's last few days are mapped out beside pictures of each of them. He inspects images of the crime scenes, studying each in meticulous detail.

One thing in particular stands out to him: a television sitting idle, displaying the same Game Over screen. His eyes tighten with intrigue as they dart from one photo of the game in Remy's living room to another photo of Ed's bedroom to the third in Matt's bedroom. It could be just a coincidence that all the missing parties happened to be playing the video game shortly before something tore apart their homes, but Valentine has never been one to put much stock in coincidence.

He swivels back on his wheelie chair towards his computer. His hands clack away at the keyboard, punching Ultimate Adventure VII into his web browser's search engine. Looks like he's got a lead.

VI

SIDE QUEST

Remy looks downcast at her bulky leather boots, which slop in and out of the mud as she trudges through a sprawling, waterlogged meadow. Squelch, squelch, squelch, with every broad step. Her breath fogs in the frigid air. She shivers in the ice-cold drizzle and kicks herself for ever touching that godforsaken crystal shard. It's brought her nothing but misery and strife, and as far as she can tell doesn't do anything useful. The worst of her cuts are crudely bandaged with torn pieces of Ed's T-shirt – which now stops above his midriff. He looks back at her, his warm expression a stark contrast to the sight of her all bundled up in his hoodie, her hands balled inside the frayed cuffs to keep warm, her bare legs red and raw from the cold and clumps of wet hair falling either side of her face. She looks like she's on a serious comedown after the world's worst music festival.

"Ever b-been to G-Glastonbury?" he asks through chattering teeth.

She shakes her head. "Spending a week in a muddy field isn't my idea of a good time."

Ed laughs. "Well, look at you now, having the t-t-time of your life."

Bengeo, tough as nails, takes the weather in his stride. He glances at the sorry pair and smirks. "Not far now."

Ed gazes at the gloomy sky. "I c-can't believe this rain. Non-stop since last night."

"Yep," Bengeo grunts.

"I'm s-s-soaked. Can't wait to get s-somewhere dry."

Bengeo murmurs in agreement.

"So we must be in the 'rainy plains', huh?" Ed sniggers. "It always rains b-back home. We get like t-t-two days of summer and a year of rain."

His babbling preys on Bengeo's last nerve. "You always talk this much about the weather?"

Ed shrugs. "I'm English."

Bengeo frowns, unsure of what exactly that means. He notices Remy shaking like a leaf as she slogs along behind them. "You alright back there?" he asks.

"F-f-f-f-fine." She bites her quivering bottom lip to stop it shaking.

"I know a tavern with warm beds and strong drinks. On the horizon, there!" He points to a plume of smoke rising beyond the ridge and rallies them up the grassy knoll towards the town. "Trout, here we come!"

They approach a crooked wooden gate guarded by a single man in a rusty suit of armour who's sound asleep, slumped against the wall.

Some security, Remy muses. He looks as aged and withered as the wonky perimeter fence. The man does at least put up a formidable attack on one's senses, from his eyesore of a moustache to his repellent body odour. Even his phlegmy snore is an assault on the ears.

Smoke rises from the chimneys of the square stone houses spaced about. Each modest abode is stacked two or three metres high with muddied bricks and a thatched roof. There's a bit of bustle along the craggy streets as people go about their business, mostly flooding towards the town square, which sits in the middle of the village. At its centre is a round fountain adorned with a statue of a creature with a fish head and human legs – kind of like a reverse mermaid.

"Where are we?" Remy asks, staring at the butcher hanging strange beastly carcasses in the filthy window of his shop.

"Just some backwater hole," Bengeo laughs as he leads them through the village.

They pass a rickety wooden wagon, and sitting atop it a small furry creature about the size of a fox, with beady eyes that look in different directions, presides over a display of random odds and ends.

"Greetings, travellers!" it says in a yappy voice.

Ed, having still maintained a little of his childlike wonder at the strange game world they are in, immediately perks up at the sight of the little critter. "Is that what I think it is?" he smiles, pointing at the small furry salesman.

"Pay him no mind," Bengeo barks, but Ed has already dashed back to the merchant's wagon.

"Good morn to you, handsome traveller! What brings you to the quaint little village of Trout?" The critter addresses him with the enthusiasm of a used car salesman who hasn't seen a customer in some time, and Ed examines the items displayed before the wagon with great interest. Before he can respond the creature continues his spiel. "Fascinating! Buckle has wares if you have coin? I've quite a selection of healing and fortitude potions."

"Is that supposed to be a midgey merchant? Those roaming trading creatures you see in towns?" Remy frowns at the little fella as she approaches his stall.

"Yeah," Ed replies, grinning like a kid on his birthday.

"I thought they were supposed to be bigger."

"Well, this is a remake. Maybe they redesigned them."

Upon seeing Remy and Bengeo, the midgey merchant brandishes a devilish grin. "Ah! There is a party of you! You are adventurers, questing from afar?" He takes on a hushed tone of voice as he leans towards the group. "Your coming is a blessing, for I fear foul woodland spirits—"

"Oh no you don't!" Bengeo hurries Remy and Ed along. "We're going to sit and do nothing until my crew show up, so keep your heads down, and stay out of trouble."

"We don't exactly blend in." Pulling at what's left of her tattered pyjamas, Remy wipes her filthy face with the sleeve of Ed's ragged hoodie and sighs.

Bengeo looks her over, and then at Ed, who's standing slouched, bare-bellied in his torn T-shirt and mud-caked skinny jeans, his sopping wet hair clinging to his sickly pale forehead.

"Ugh," Bengeo winces.

Remy folds her arms and frowns at the bandit. "I refuse to spend another second in this world wearing my pyjamas. I want clean clothes and a hot bath."

Exhausted from their arduous journey, Ed sits down in the street while the two of them bicker again.

"You got any gold stashed somewhere? Cos I forgot to grab my coin purse when we were being blasted outta the sky," the bandit snaps.

"Come on. You must have something?" Remy insists.

Bengeo pats his pockets. "All tapped out, princess."

"What about that axe you carry?" She eyes the gleaming weapon on his back.

Bengeo frowns. "The only way Annabella here is getting sold is if you loot my cold dead corpse."

"Well, what else are we supposed to do for money?" She sticks out her bottom lip and looks pleadingly at Bengeo who shakes his head. "Fine!" She storms over to the midgey merchant. "Hey, you, I need money. Got any work?"

Bengeo slaps his hand on his forehead as she accosts the little critter. "Oh boy," he sighs.

"Ho ho ho, how fortuitous!" the merchant chirps. "I fear my business partner, Barnabas, has fallen prey to foul forest spirits. He was due three days ago with a shipment of pelts and supplies from Parousia, but I've not seen or heard from him."

"Yeah, yeah, whatever. Just tell me where to look and I'll bring him back for a fee," Remy says.

"Of course, stranger, I suspect he'll be north of town on the outskirts of the Witched Wood."

Bengeo and Ed approach the market stall. A disapproving look is plastered across the bandit's face.

"What are you getting yourself into?" he asks.

"I'm being proactive, seeing as you refuse to help," Remy replies. "Hell, if only it were this easy getting a paying job in real life. That idiot didn't even ask for references."

"So what's the job, then?" Ed asks.

"Nothing crazy, we just need to find this guy's business partner in the woods and bring him back with the merch," Remy grins. "Easy money."

"A fetch quest?" Ed groans. "Fetch quests are the literal worst. Come on, don't make me do one for real."

"You want clean clothes, right? Food? Maybe a weapon seeing as how everything is trying to murder us."

Ed thinks a moment. She's talking sense, his stomach is rumbling something awful, and there's nothing worse than wet jeans. "... Fine," he sighs.

"Great! Let's hurry up and get it over with! Which way is north?"

Bengeo laughs. "You really think you two numbskulls can handle this?"

"You heard Ed, it's a fetch quest. How hard can it be? Besides, we've got you to protect us," she grins wickedly.

"You know, this isn't going to go how you think. Nothing ever does when some dopey peasant is asking you to deliver some tea to his granny or find his father's missing do-dah," Bengeo replies, "and have you forgotten Grimoirh is still hot on our heels?"

"The way I see it you've gone to a lot of trouble to keep the two of us alive. I'd bet we're pretty important to you, and I think you're gonna help us no matter what. So are you gonna whine like a little bitch or point me north?"

Bengeo lets out a long groan. Of all the other-worlders – assuming there are *other* other-worlders – why'd he have to get stuck with this tempestuous brat?

"Fine," he grunts and raises his hand to the north. "Just don't come crying to me when this all goes belly up and bites you in the ass."

With a bitter glare, Remy storms out of the village.

*

In the hold of his airship, Grimoirh stares at petrified Jessica, frozen in a scream, and wonders about her connection to the girl who possesses the shard. He reaches out, pressing his black iron gauntlet against the cold stone, then draws a long golden needle from a satchel on his belt. Bringing it to the statue he pushes the needle through as if piercing butter. It shines before disappearing with a glint. Slowly Jessica thaws. Her dull, greyed eyes return to moist glacier blue and dart fearfully about as her form returns to flesh and blood. Her legs give way. She falls onto her knees with a gasp and hunches over on all fours to catch her breath. Her throat, dry and raw, begs for water. She glances up to see the Dread Knight looming over her and opens her mouth but can only conjure a rasp.

"Thirsty!"

Grimoirh offers her a clay flask, which she eagerly reaches for, but he pulls back at the last second and her eyes shimmer with desperation.

"The girl you were with, tell me about her."

Before Jessica can answer, a lumpy-headed goblin bursts into the room and interrupts them with a hiss. "She's back."

Grimoirh nods at his minion then hands Jessica the clay flask, which she swiftly knocks back, spilling water down her cleft chin while the goblin takes her by the arm and drags her away.

Visceral cries echo throughout the tight iron corridors of the ship. In a small bedchamber, a group of goblins hold Domina down as she writhes and shrieks in pain. Grimoirh enters the room, and the goblins scamper away as she sits up on the bedside. Her hair falls over her face, masking her feral expression. He notices her right arm is mangled and bloody from her skirmish with the carnivorous forest, and she's spitting and hissing like a rabid animal. He places a hand on her cheek and holds her face. From beneath the black iron mask, his dark eyes bore into her.

"Sleep." He utters the word like a spell and just like that her eyes roll back into her head as she drifts away. He catches her as she slumps over and lays her gently on the bed.

"Make it known to every cutthroat, goblin, troll, ogre and harpy in the realm, that the girl must be brought to me alive. Coin, weapons, power – whatever they want in return."

The goblin men bow to his command and swiftly take their leave before he kneels at Domina's bedside and sweeps her hair from her face.

Bowing his head, he whispers to her, "Is any part of you still in there? Can you hear me?" After a moment, he sighs mournfully and leaves her to rest.

*

Remy, Ed and Bengeo come upon a smashed wagon strewn across the dirt path leading into the woods. Now that the rain has cleared, the forest that recently tried to kill them looks serene and peaceful as the high sun shimmers through the leaves, bathing everything in dappled light.

"Looks like we're close," Ed says.

"I hope he's not dead." Remy looks worriedly at the ransacked cart. "I mean, we probably won't get paid if he's dead, right?"

Ed cups his mouth with his hands and shouts into the forest, "Hey, Barnabas!"

Bengeo swats the back of his head. "You want to draw whatever smashed ol' Barnabas' cart right to us?"

Ed rubs his head and frowns at the bandit. Remy steps into the brush and follows the debris like a trail of breadcrumbs through the thicket. She stalks through the trees and comes upon a campsite in a clearing. A small campfire crackles and spits, surrounded by a few large tents, crudely patched from the hides of various beasts. The site appears deserted, and Remy's eyes light up when she notices a pile of fur skins atop a rock and more strung up around the tents.

She ducks down in the bushes and points. "Those have got to be the pelts that the merchant mentioned."

"Alright, let's go get 'em." As soon as Ed stands up from their position in the trees, Bengeo yanks him back down before he can take a step.

"Wait!" the bandit exclaims. "Look!" He points at a huge wooden club resting by a tree. "Looks like trolls, ogres maybe."

"Trolls?" Ed looks aghast, recalling their description in his Ultimate Adventure VII monster manual. "Trolls are bad, Remy. Let's bail. I don't want to end up as lunch." He stands to walk back the way they came, but Remy pulls him down before he can take a step.

"Shhh! I didn't hike back into these cursed woods to leave empty-handed. We're getting those pelts!"

"What about Barnabas?" Ed asks.

"Oh yeah, him too." Remy squints to get a better look at the camp. "I'll sneak in and swipe the fur. You guys wait here. Back me up if anything goes wrong."

"Back you up how?" Ed whispers as she creeps towards the camp. "Back you up how? Remy?!" But she's not listening. He turns to Bengeo with a foreboding look. "I've got a bad feeling about this."

"You and me both," the bandit sighs.

Remy creeps into the campground and notices the spit above the campfire. Her eyes widen in fear as she inspects the blackened overcooked meat hanging off it. Looks like they roasted Barnabas, and what's more, he smells pretty tasty.

The sound of rustling fabric catches her ear and causes panic as one of the tents jostles. Remy pulls the fur skins off the rock and over her, and watches as a large grey-skinned troll emerges from its tent. The creature stretches its long, clumsy limbs and lets out a wide yawn, bearing crooked, yellow teeth. Around its neck hangs a tribal necklace of strung-together bones, likely trophies from past hunts. It rubs its oddly sized eyes as they blink open and stumbles about, picking its stubby nose with a fat finger. If there is such a thing as an ugly tree, this creature is certainly the fruit it bears.

The troll staggers over to the far side of the camp and rests its forehead against a tree, then moves its loincloth aside and lets loose a stream of steaming hot piss. The rancid, pungent scent carries to the other side of the campsite where Remy is hidden. She pinches her nose and retches as it hits her in the throat.

Unable to endure another second, she gathers as many pelts as she can carry and tiptoes towards the treeline, but the troll finishes up with a shake and spots her as he turns around. Remy stops dead in her tracks and the troll stares at her, unsure of what's going on.

"Uhh, you're dreaming," Remy says, waving one hand wistfully. "This is all a dream."

Over in the trees, Bengeo throws his head in his hands. "What the hell is she doing?"

"Beats me," Ed shrugs.

"Dream?" asks the troll. "I never had dream before," it grunts in broken English.

"Well, you're having one now. I'm not really here, and neither are you."

"Then where am I?" The troll examines its clumpy hands closely, searching for proof that he's real.

"You're asleep." Remy points to his tent. "If you go in and lie down, you'll wake up, and I'll be gone."

"Lie down sounds nice," the troll says with a toothy grin. "But who are you?"

"I'm... uh, your subconscious. A figment of your imagination." *Oh God, please don't eat me.* She feigns cool composure, but her eyes are screaming.

"Sub-con-kers?" The troll burps, sits down in the grass and rubs its bald head. "I feel bad," it groans.

"Just lie down and close your eyes, you'll feel better. I promise," she says.

The troll sluggishly reaches for her and drags her over to its side. "No feel good! Rub belly, make feel better."

"Oh God," Remy gulps, regretting every decision in her life that led her here. She drops the pelts and resigns herself to the unthinkable.

Ed and Bengeo watch in horror from the bushes.

"Now what the hell is she doing?" Bengeo grimaces with disgust.

"I'm not sure..." Ed can't believe his eyes, "... but it looks like she's buffing that troll's banana." He tries to rationalise what he's seeing, but nothing can make it look any less than what it looks like from where he's sitting.

Remy fans her hands around the troll's belly in small circles. The creature's skin is surprisingly rubbery and tough –

an evolutionary trait handy for deflecting arrows. She can feel pockets of gas moving through its body. After a few minutes, the troll dozes off and snores like a warthog with a deviated septum.

"Oh thank God," she whispers to the heavens and tiptoes back to the pelts, then gathers them in her arms before striding back to Bengeo with a shit-eating grin plastered on her face.

"Got 'em."

"I've seen a fair few people deal with trolls in my time, but none of 'em like that," the bandit laughs. "Guess you really want out of those clothes."

"Whatever, you're just mad because I managed without your help."

Bengeo shakes his head and turns back towards the dirt road.

"Hey, aren't you going to carry some?" she asks.

"Nope," the bandit grins. "Didn't I tell you not to come crying to me when this bites you in the ass?"

Remy mutters crude obscenities under her breath as she shifts the pelts from one shoulder to the other.

Upon arrival, the party are greeted in the square by the midgey merchant and a crowd of townsfolk. Remy and Ed exhaustedly drop the pelts in front of the little critter, who inspects them with glee while Bengeo looks on, unimpressed.

"Thank you, brave strangers. Now the town will have furs to warm them in the coming winter months and best of all my pockets will be weighty with gold," he cheers.

"It was no big deal," Remy smiles. "Now, about our reward?"

"But what of dear Barnabas?" the midgey merchant asks.

"Uh…" Remy hesitates. "He—"

"He didn't make it." Ed bows apologetically. "So sorry."

The midgey merchant hangs his head. "Poor Barnabas. Oh well. Ho ho ho. Here's your reward. You can have his pay too seeing as you delivered the pelts." The critter tosses Remy a modest bag of coin in exchange for her hard work and then addresses the townsfolk. "Behold the furs have been recovered."

The crowd cheers and shuffles towards the merchant's stall to purchase the furs before stock runs dry. Although not everyone is pleased. A crooked-nosed man, cloaked in a dark robe, eyes the would-be adventurers with suspicion before he slinks off into a back alley.

Bengeo approaches Remy and Ed, clapping slowly. "So much for keeping your heads down."

"How much did we make?" Ed asks.

As Remy peers into the bag, her eyes gleam with the glow of gold. "Enough for a shopping trip!" she grins.

She scampers across the square and into the town's general store. Its walls are adorned with all sorts of fantastical items – breastplates, helmets, spears, swords, clubs, axes. It's a one-stop shop for all your bludgeoning needs – though most of them aren't in the best condition. Ed examines the displays with awe, drooling like a dog who's just got his paws on a rib eye steak. Years spent collecting action figures, tinkering with avatars, crafting cosplays and that one LARP experience he'd rather forget all pale in comparison to this one glorious moment. Finally he can actually purchase real fantastical wares.

"I'm getting everything! One of everything!" He spins, taking it all in.

"Cool it. Let's not blow all our cash in one go." Remy speaks from experience.

"Well, we should get weapons though, right? *'Seeing as how everything always wants to kill us'.*"

"We shouldn't spend it all, we should be responsible…" She trails off, her attention stolen by a glittering elfin battle suit. Its aquamarine scales shimmer in the light, and what's more it looks stylish, practical and comfortable – an impossible combination for a woman to find in the real world.

Ed pulls on a chain-mail shirt which is far too big for him.

"Hey, it's not shrinking?"

"Well, of course not," Bengeo says. "That only works if it's enchanted."

"Enchanted?" Ed looks disappointed as he pulls off the chain mail, then glances at Remy who is standing in the corner. His eyes wander across the small of her back and up to her shoulders as she pulls the tunic over her head. Her skin is marked by a dozen cuts and scrapes, shades of pink and purple. Worst of all is the great welt inflicted by Domina's flail.

"Fits nice," she says, moving her arms up and down. The outfit glistens and twinkles, like a battle-hardened disco ball.

"Wow... uh, not bad," Ed mumbles. "This looks good too." He quickly lifts a sword from one of the weapon racks and its weight immediately sends him crashing to the floor.

Remy shakes her head and looks apologetically at Bengeo while Ed tries to put the sword back. Why she feels responsible for his buffoonery she cannot say.

He quickly becomes engrossed by an unusual mirror whose moonstone frame is decorated with carvings of different faces. He wipes the dust from the glass and as he peers into it, his hair changes in the reflection. He gazes at himself, sporting long, flowing, red locks, and can't believe his eyes. He's found the one thing he could never get in the real world: a perfect haircut.

"Hey, how does this work?" Ed asks.

His interruption visibly irritates the shopkeeper who is leaning on the counter with his nose buried in a book entitled 'CHARMANCER: Casting Spells on the Opposite Sex'.

"You keep away from that, it's broken." He half-heartedly shoos Ed away before returning to his literature.

"Seems fine to me..." Ed peers into the mirror and imagines a different hairstyle, and like magic, it materialises on his reflection.

Bengeo sighs. "This is taking too long. I'll meet you in the tavern across the square – the Legless Arms. Can I trust you two to be left alone for five minutes?"

"We'll be fine," Remy assures him, "we're not children."

He raises an eyebrow and gestures at Ed, who claps and giggles with glee as he cycles through an array of ridiculous hairstyles. "Don't dally. Finish up and come straight over."

"Sure thing, Dad," quips Remy, much to his disdain.

*

Outside, the crooked-nosed man watches Bengeo exit the general shop and make for the tavern. He slinks behind a house and rolls up his sleeve, revealing a tattoo on his forearm of a black winged lizard. He clenches his fist and whispers strange words under his breath, bringing it to life. It slinks along his arm and prises itself out of his skin, then with a hiss, takes off into the sky.

Inside the shop, Ed is still playing around with different hairstyles – a feathered bob cut, a medieval monk do, an afro, crazy anime spikes, long, pushed-back hair, a fringe that covers one eye – until finally, he settles on something resembling a coiffed pompadour.

"Perfect!"

Before he can run his fingers through his new do his hair suddenly leaps off his head leaving him utterly, cartoonishly bald.

"Shit!" Remy stares wide-eyed at Ed's immaculately smooth and shiny head.

Their cries alert the shopkeeper, who is not pleased. "I told you it was broken and still you tamper?!"

"You didn't tell me my hair would leave me!" Ed whines.

"It was implied!" screams the shopkeeper. "Subtext! Subtext!" He smacks the cover of his book.

"Oh God, catch it! Catch it, Remy! Please catch it!" Ed chases his enchanted fro as it runs riot about the shop and leaps at it with full force, but it evades him, and he crashes into a pile of shields.

"Whatever you break, you buy! I told you not to go near it, but do you listen? No, of course, the customer is always right!" the shopkeeper cries while cowering behind the counter.

Remy manages to corner the hair, mirroring its movements as it darts left, then right. Seemingly out of options, Ed's mop then leaps directly at her and clings to her face like something from an *Alien* film, muffling her screams. She struggles to prise it off, toppling into a cabinet of glass bottles, which shatter on the floor.

"Those are expensive rarities!" The shopkeeper cradles his head in his hands.

"Don't hurt it!" Ed grabs his hair and tries to yank it off Remy, but his fingers slip through and he trips over backwards.

Her muted cries grow angrier as some of the hair gets into her mouth. With all her might she wrestles it off and hurls it at Ed who catches it with both hands before firmly thrusting it onto his head. As it touches his scalp a shockwave of blue light pulses out as the magic dissipates, returning the hair to its normal, untameable state. Remy and the shopkeeper take cover as the dispersing energy sends everything hung on the walls crashing down.

The shopkeeper slowly rises from behind the counter and trembles looking at his beautiful wares scattered all over the place. His enraged eyes dart to Remy, who emerges from behind a large iron shield.

"Uhh, we'll just finish up and get out of your... hair." She looks downcast, realising her poor choice of words. "... Sorry."

In his unbridled fury the shopkeeper is unable to conjure a sentence. His left eye twitches with rage at Ed, who sits up amidst the carnage, his hair a wild mess. He caresses it gently and sighs with relief.

*

Bengeo ducks as he enters the crooked tavern. It's the only building in the village made of wood, and not particularly well made at that – but it's just how he remembers it. A wonky bar takes up one side of the room, while mismatched chairs and tables crowd the other. There is a small staircase at the back of the tavern, which leads up to the second floor, where the guest rooms are located.

The place is packed with villagers drinking from tin tankards and revelling in each other's company. Bengeo approaches a slender old woman with greying hair, who zips about the place, picking up empty tankards and wiping down tables.

"Bar wench," he cries.

The barmaid smirks. "Call me that again and I'll string you up myself, bandit."

Bengeo lets out a raucous laugh as he approaches the barmaid and embraces her. "Esmerelda, long time no see."

"Get off me, boy," Esmerelda insists. "Honestly, you're more muscle than man these days!"

"What can I say, a bandit's life ain't an idle one." He smiles, but Esmerelda catches a glint of pain in his eyes. She always could tell when he was hurting – women's intuition and all that.

"You look like you've been through hell, Ben. Where's that ship and crew o' yours?"

The bandit looks ashen as he swallows his pride and tells her of his troubles.

*

Having earned themselves a lifetime ban from the store, Remy and Ed make their way towards the inn as instructed. Ed adjusts his tatty green tunic and ties a rusted, beaten dagger to his belt. He had chosen the garment, not just because it was all he could afford after they covered the damages, but also because it reminded him of the tunic the hero Link wore in the Legend of Zelda games.

"I can't believe we had to give him almost all of our gold because you couldn't keep your hair on," Remy sighs.

"At least we had enough left to get you out of your pyjamas," he replies.

Remy inspects her new outfit of simple, grey peasant clothes. It's not the glistening elfin battle suit, but it'll do. Why, oh why can't she have nice things?

Ed draws and sheathes his knife like a kid playing with a toy. "I think I'm more of a sword guy, y'know? I always used swords in the game."

Remy looks disappointed at the dinky little blade in his hand. "Whatever..." she groans. "We can't fight Grimoirh with that. We need real weapons." She eyes a longsword hanging from the belt of the town guardsman, who is now napping beside the fountain. Her eyes light up with a wicked thought. "You distract everyone, and I'll swipe it!"

Ed looks horrified at her. "We can't steal from people, we're not renegades."

Tired and irate, Remy snaps, "They're not real, Ed! They can't really exist! None of this does!" She stomps over to the midgey merchant's stall and thrusts her finger at the little critter behind it. "And that's not what a midgey merchant is supposed to look like!" She storms off towards the inn, leaving Ed and the merchant dumbfounded.

The tavern door creaks open and Remy steps inside. She lingers in the doorway a moment and gauges her surroundings. It's a den of debauchery. Everyone inside looks like they have a story to tell. Busty tavern girls wearing low-cut bunchy white blouses serve huge tankards of mead and ale to muscular louts who knock them back by the dozen; the surly barkeeper with the gnarly scar across one eye wipes down the bar top with a filthy rag; and huddled around a table, a warrior in a blue cape plays cards with a bard in a flouncy red outfit and mage in a purple hood. There's even a cat-person smoking a long pipe as he's served raw fish and a glass of milk.

Ed catches up to her and together they make for the bar, avoiding the drunken louts and menacing glares. He tries not to antagonise anyone but accidentally locks eyes with a shirtless brute, who cracks his knuckles and grimaces until Ed swiftly averts his gaze. Another surly sell-sword slaps Remy's arse as she passes his table, which breaks out in raucous laughter after the fact. She turns sharply towards the perpetrator with eyes full of wrath, but Ed hurries her along, not wanting to cause any more trouble than they already have.

They approach the bar like two underage kids trying to buy beer, and the barmaid leans over the counter to greet them.

"What'll it be, handsome?" she asks in a sultry voice. Her bosom is anything but subtle.

Ed strives to maintain eye contact but can't help steal a glance. His eyes glaze over, fixated on a shiny silver ring worn on a chain as it bounces between her ample breasts.

Remy swats the back of his head, breaking the sway her hypnotic chest holds over him. "I could use a rum and Coke," she says.

"Never heard of that. We got Bandit's Brew and Runegard Rye, or if you're feeling brave we just got some Ether, but it's got a helluva kick to it," the barmaid replies.

"Uh, we'll take two brews." Remy places their last few coins on the counter.

"Two brews, coming up." She winks at Ed before she pours their drinks. He blushes lobster red much to Remy's infuriation. The barmaid returns and plonks two heavy tin tankards on the bar, each about the size of a kettle and full to the brim with a bubbling liquor.

Remy scrunches her nose. It smells like kerosine. "What's in this?"

Before the barmaid can respond, Ed takes a sip and spits it out. Just a taste and he can feel all five senses dulled. They pick up their tankards and mosey over to Bengeo, who is quietly sipping his at a table in a dark corner.

"What took so long?" he asks, eyeballing their new threads.

"It's a long story," Remy sighs and glares at Ed who takes another sip and struggles not to spit it out again.

"How do you drink this?" Ed coughs.

"It gets easier. After the first one you can't feel anything," Bengeo laughs and takes a hearty swig, savouring the bitter aftertaste.

Remy scans the room. "This is where you told your crew to come meet you, isn't it? Any sign of them?"

"They'll be here," Bengeo replies.

"What if they don't show?"

"They'll be here."

"I'm just saying, it's been a while. We barely made it out of that forest, maybe they—"

Bengeo slams his fist on the table to silence Remy. The whole tavern falls quiet as everyone cranes their necks to see what the ruckus is. After a moment the chatter resumes.

"Whatever, just don't forget you promised to help me save Jess." Remy folds her arms and slumps in her chair like a child refusing to eat their greens.

"Like I said, the wise man'll help you," Bengeo replies.

"Who is this wise man?"

"Can't talk about it and can't talk about why."

"Well, how long are we gonna wait? How far away is he?"

Bengeo's eye twitches. "No more talking," he grunts.

"So what, we're just gonna sit here in silence?" Remy lets out a condescending cackle, which Bengeo ignores. He quietly sips his tankard and stares dead ahead at the door. "Oh that's really mature."

"Remy." Ed shakes his head to discourage her from pestering him any further.

She rolls her eyes and then notices the look plastered across the bandit's face. Those men were his brothers, and he was in charge of keeping them safe. Guilt swells in her throat and she regrets pressuring him to leave. If it were Jessica, she'd wait – well, probably. She sighs and takes a sip of her brew, wincing as it goes down.

They drink silently, and Remy overhears the conversations of the people around her – rumours about a talking sword, a haunted forest, growing civil unrest in the kingdom. The tavern is a hub of worldly information. Faint cries from outside catch her ear, making her listen intently as the chatter in the bar dies down. It sounds like screaming.

Bengeo hears it too. He downs the rest of his drink and slams the tankard on the table. "Stay close."

He bursts out of the tavern ready for a fight, while Ed and Remy stay safely behind his tank of a body.

Across the square from the tavern, six nasty-looking trolls ride atop gnarly boar beasts with stubby snouts and great tusks that curl from their snarling jaws. The riders dismount, and each troll towers at least eight feet tall. Some have short, rounded horns protruding from their foreheads. All of them are adorned with welts and scars worn proudly like medals on their thick grey hides, which are cloaked in patchy armour, crudely stitched from animal skins and odd pieces looted from travellers.

Their leader, a troll named Terak, is a head taller than the tallest of his men – an imposing giant with only one good eye, his other lost in some skirmish long past.

He speaks with a gruff roar. "Hear me well! You have stolen from us, so we come for what we are owed. Your gold and silver!"

Oh shit. Remy kicks herself as Bengeo's earlier warnings about how even the most straightforward quest will snowball into a colossal mess come flooding back to her. Oh, how she wishes she heeded those words now. Honestly, what is this compulsion to resist authority that has confounded her entire life?

Bengeo draws his axe and steps forward to face the trolls. One of them takes aim with his bow and lets loose a hand-carved arrow which pierces the bandit's side. He falls to one knee with a roar.

Remy and Ed run to his defence, and he lets out a breathy groan as she examines the arrow sticking out of his ribs.

"Who stands with these three?" Terak cries.

Every villager in proximity to Ed, Remy and Bengeo takes a large step backward, leaving the three of them alone in a patch of empty space.

Terak eyes them and is not impressed.

"Bwahaha!" he chortles as he approaches the would-be adventurers. "You have until noon tomorrow to present your coin or we will burn this feeble village to the ground." He addresses the terrified villagers. "Let this be a lesson to all who incur the wrath of the Boulder Clan!"

With that, Terak and his men ride away from the village in tight formation as the whole town stares.

"Ugh…" Remy groans, "… side quests."

VII

Disappearing

Lauren taps her finger on the space bar of her keyboard, not hard enough to press it but enough to make a repetitive clacking noise that reassures her time is actually passing. She slumps in her pleather office chair and frowns at the sign hung on a string above her desk – a red-eyed, sad-looking cartoon chimpanzee operating a laptop. The caption below reads, 'Social Media Monkey'. Poor Lauren has been given the unfortunate job of trawling through forums and responding to all the inane queries, maddening qualms and facepalm-inducing questions posed by the oh-so-vocal gaming community. It's a thankless, mind-numbing task, which is undoubtedly why it's fallen to the intern.

She skims over various threads. People are bickering about graphical capabilities, whether or not Ultimate Adventure VII will be released on PC. After rolling her eyes at a complaint about the lack of skimpy armour options for female characters, she notices the blinking notifications at the top of her web page – '1,462 unread messages and 1 call pending'. Her curiosity is piqued – who calls anyone anymore?

She opens the call log, clicks the recording and dons her earphones. It sounds like heavy breathing and then a young man speaks in an almost unintelligible whisper. Before Ed's message can play out entirely Lauren slides her headphones back, becoming distracted by an elderly man standing in the office looking wary – for this is a place of computers, and Detective Valentine prefers not to be surrounded by them.

"Excuse me." He approaches Lauren at her desk.

She looks up at him as though he has caught her doing something she shouldn't.

"You're the only one who looks like they want to be here less than me," he smirks, stealing a glance at the open web page on her monitor – a gaming news website, the headline reading, 'DEVELOPER DEFENDS CONTROVERSIAL CHANGES TO REMAKE'. There is a black and white picture of Vincent beside the article. He looks to be in his early-to-mid-thirties with dark, tangled hair swept off his face.

"Can I help you?" she asks.

The old man flashes his police credentials causing Lauren to sit upright in her chair and straighten her posture. She's never been in the remotest bit of trouble in her life, but goddamn does she feel guilty for no reason at all.

"Scott Valentine, DI. Who's that?" He points to the screen.

"Oh, nobody." She quickly minimises the window.

"I'm looking for Eric Garland. Is he here?"

She stares blankly for a moment, then stutters, "D-do you have an appointment or something?"

"I find the badge usually works all the same."

"Well, everyone is out prepping for the Comic Con presentation. A new game just launched and it's kind of a big deal so there's a huge promo thing next week, and, well, some of the guys needed to blow off steam, so—"

Valentine looks around at the mostly empty office. "So you got left behind, huh?"

"Just unlucky I guess," she shrugs.

He reaches into his pocket and hands Lauren a crumpled post-it note with his email and phone number scrawled across it. "Here's my card. Ask Mr Garland to call me."

"*This* is your business card?"

"Have a nice day, miss," Valentine nods then heads back towards the door.

Lauren plucks up the courage to speak before he leaves. "What did you want to talk to him about?"

The detective turns back on his way to the door. "Eh?"

"Is Eric in some kind of trouble?"

Valentine has good intuition about people, and it's roused by this girl. He senses she knows more than she's letting on, so he opens up a little, hoping she'll do the same.

"There have been some recent disappearances and they all owned copies of your game. I wanted to ask some questions about the player community."

"Disappearances?" Lauren's eyes widen. *Could this be connected to Vincent? Or that weird message?* she wonders.

"What's he like? Mr Garland. If you don't mind me asking?"

"He's very... professional. Kind of coldly, scarily professional, to be honest. Um. I probably shouldn't have said that. Maybe you'd better come back when he's here, I'm just an intern."

Valentine surveys the office again. "That card goes for you as well, miss. Don't hesitate to get in touch, if you think of anything we should know."

His smile bears more resemblance to a grimace than anything else, but still Lauren senses a sincerity to it. She turns the post-it note over in her hand thoughtfully as she watches him leave. Letting out a hopeless sigh, she glances longingly at Vincent's empty desk. He would always make sure that she never got lumbered with the menial jobs just because she was an intern, but it seems those glory days are over.

She recalls one summer evening they had spent together, one of her fondest in recent memory. After all, there haven't been that many lately...

*

The hot, sticky air had made the office unbearable. The building wasn't air-conditioned, so Vincent and Eric had wheeled in big fans, which did nothing but blow heat in circles. Everyone had escaped to enjoy the sunshine while it lasted, but not Vincent. Like always he had stayed later than the others to work on one thing or another. He'd lock himself away in the office upstairs for hours on end, and Lauren too would often find some excuse to linger behind. Anything to avoid going home, where the sadness in her mother's eyes reminded her of all she had lost. Most nights she'd watch video tutorials on YouTube, teaching herself to get to grips with Unreal Engine 4. The only chance she had to play around with the software was when no one was around. Her ancient computer at home couldn't dream of running the program, and she'd seldom do any actual designing during work hours unless she was shadowing someone. So she seized every opportunity to broaden her skills, hoping to one day wow everyone and maybe land herself a paying gig doing something she could be proud of. She'd usually duck out around nine-ish before the cleaners came in, but the light would always be on in the upstairs room when she left. Except this time, when Vincent caught her practising on one of the computers.

"Didn't expect to see you here." His voice startled her, and she leapt out of her seat and spun around to see him descending the stairs.

"S-sorry!" She thought she was done for.

"What're you apologising for?" he asked.

"I don't know... Sorry."

"There you go again," Vincent laughed, then caught a glimpse of the monitor behind her. "What's that you're working on?"

"Oh, it's nothing."

"Doesn't look like nothing." He leant over the desk, took hold of her mouse and clicked his way around the lush forest she had created in the program. His eyes glistened with wonder as he gazed at the tall green trees swaying in the wind, and scattered in the tall grass were strange creatures that prowled nearby ruins as the volumetric god rays shimmered through the dancing leaves.

"You made this?" he asked with a hint of disbelief.

Lauren looked guilty. "I know I shouldn't be using the computers for personal stuff—"

"But *you* made this?"

"I swear I saved everything to an external drive so it wouldn't interfere with—"

"Relax, you're not in trouble. You shouldn't be so modest, Lauren, this looks way better than my first game."

Lauren shuffled uncomfortably as she often did when receiving a compliment and asked, "What was it, your first game?"

Vincent smiled, recalling it fondly. "It was this little space-shooter RPG called Runners. It's how I got started here actually. Feels like a lifetime ago now, though."

"Is it on Steam?"

"Nah, might be able to find an emulation online, but I think I have one of the old cartridges lying around at home. I'll bring it in for you."

"Yeah, I'd love to play it."

Vincent turned his attention to her creation. "This is good work. How long did it take?"

She hesitated at first, but ultimately figured it better to be truthful. "About three weeks."

"Three weeks? You've been staying late for three weeks?"

Lauren nodded shyly, noticing a flicker of panic wash over Vincent's face as he ran his hands through his dark hair.

"I never noticed. How did I not see you?"

"You're a world away, working up there. I always left before you came out so—"

"Smart. You didn't peek inside, did you? While I was up there, I mean."

Lauren shook her head. "I promise I won't do it again," she said.

"No, it's fine, just as long as you stay down here. It's just super-confidential stuff. You'd have to sign a bunch of NDAs and I could get in a lot of trouble if you leaked anything."

Whatever he was doing up there, he clearly didn't want her to see it. Usually, her curiosity would have got the better of her, but she felt like she was already treading thin ice.

"So what inspired this?" Eager to change the subject, he clocked another look at her creation.

She shrugged. "I was just thinking of a place."

It was obvious to him the reason was more than she was letting on. "Come on, we're friends, right?"

She could see he wasn't going to accept anything less than the truth and so relented. She pulled her phone from her pocket and untethered her earphones as she explained.

"The summer after I finished school, my family went to Donegal for my uncle's wedding."

Vincent looked perplexed. "Donegal?"

"Believe it or not I'm half Irish," she smirked. "While we were out there, we spent a day in these beautiful woods. My parents taught my brother to swim in the lake – well, they tried. I spent most of the day under this tree listening to *Lost in the Dream* over and over until I fell asleep. You know it?"

Vincent shook his head.

"It was probably the most relaxing moment of my entire life. All my worries about the future and moving away to uni just melted away. It was like nothing mattered."

"Sounds peaceful."

"I think about that trip a lot. It was the last one before… well, yeah." She passed him an earphone. "Ready?" Her thumb hovered over track five, 'Disappearing'.

Vincent placed the bud in his ear. Lord knows the pressures of game design often left him with yearning visions of relaxing breaks far, far away from everything and everyone he knows.

As soon as she hit play his head was flooded with a swell. The calming bassline vibrated in his chest. The music washed over their souls like waves against the rocks. Chills ran through him and then it came all at once – warmth, peace, escape. The song was the most bittersweet sound, evoking longing wanderlust as it carried him away. He closed his eyes, felt the warm air on his skin and sighed.

"Whoa."

"I know," Lauren replied. "This song makes you feel like you can just—"

"Disappear?" he grinned.

"Yeah," she smiled, but her eyes radiated sorrow as she gazed longingly at the forest on the screen and lost herself amongst the trees, imagining the wind on her face and the grass between her fingers.

They stayed a while, listening to the song on repeat for almost an hour as they talked about all kinds of things, then he took her out to this little burger bar on James Street. He spoke little of himself, but she got a sense that he felt as burdened as she did. Little did she know by summer's end he'd be the one to disappear.

*

The rest of the afternoon moves by painfully slowly, and being late autumn the darkness creeps in early. She can't take it any longer. There's no one else here, and nothing to do – might as well duck out a little early.

She throws on her coat and buzzes herself out. Rain hammers the street outside so she stops under cover by the entrance and waits for the shower to die down so she can dash to the bus stop.

Across the street, Eric watches her from inside his car. He pulls up alongside her then lowers the passenger-side window.

Lauren's heart skips a beat at the sight of him. *Shit, why did I leave early?! He's probably going to fire me. Can he fire me if I'm not getting paid?*

He leans over the empty seat to better see her. "Need a lift?"

His smile makes her feel uneasy. Although much more aesthetically pleasing than the old detective's, there's something false about it. After a second she realises why. His eyes aren't smiling, they look cold, almost dead. She hadn't noticed they were green until now, but they seem oddly vivid, like he was wearing coloured contact lenses or something.

"I'm okay, but thank you." She clings to the hood of her baggy raincoat and pulls it tightly over her head.

"Come on, it's pissing down."

"No, really, it's okay."

"As your boss, I'm ordering you to get in the car." His jest comes off more like a threat.

Looking out across the street she can see that the rain shows no sign of letting up, so reluctantly complies.

She pulls her hood back down as she gets into the passenger seat and shuts the door. The car is quiet save for the patter of rain against the roof and the wipers zipping back and forth.

"I was hoping I'd catch you before you left." Eric sweeps his hair behind his ear and looks at her. "About the other day, if I seemed off—"

Lauren, all too painfully polite, tries to put him at ease. "Oh no, you didn't, it's fine." He did, and it wasn't.

"With the launch… it's just stress. You know how it is. I was anticipating a world of bug fixes, but thankfully QA didn't shit the bed. In retrospect, I might've come over a bit curt. I know Vincent leaving was probably a shock for you."

"Yeah, maybe a little," she says.

"It hit me hard too. Truth be told, I think the pressure was too much for him. He just couldn't deal with it anymore. I mean, those last few months the crunch was pretty bad, but he never left. One Saturday I found him working and he just broke down, let it all out. I thought it was best he took some time. Got his head straight. I think it just burnt him out."

Lauren smiles agreeably, but she's not buying it. He's not as good a liar as he thinks he is.

"Anyway, look, I just want you to know that your work hasn't gone unappreciated, and I wanted to reassure you that just because Vincent's departed, doesn't mean you're job is in jeopardy."

"Thanks, um, I appreciate that."

"What are we paying you anyway?" Eric asks.

"… Nothing," she laughs half-heartedly.

"Oh." His smile drops.

"It's fine, I knew when I applied—"

"That's not cool. Let's do something about that. Come talk to me tomorrow, and we'll work something out."

"Really?" She tries to downplay her elation. Getting paid would mean she could actually contribute at home and ease the pressure on her mum, not to mention update her dinosaur of a computer.

"So where to?" Eric hands his phone to Lauren as he gets ready to drive. "Punch in your postcode."

"It's okay. The station is just down the road."

"Nonsense, it's bloody torrential out there."

She hesitantly takes the phone from him and thumbs her address into his map app. The journey is mostly filled with uncomfortable silence while Lauren steals glances at him when he's not looking, in a bid to suss him out. She appreciates the gesture, but her intuition is telling her he's got an agenda, and she wonders whether or not he was waiting for her to leave. His appearance just seems too convenient.

"Left up here," she says, reading the directions from his phone. *His phone.*

She wonders what trove of information might be stored on the device – texts, DMs, emails. If Vincent did up and quit or have a breakdown or something, there would have to be some kind of correspondence to back it up. She spies Eric from the corner of her eye. His attention is on the road as he drives, so she quickly swipes through his messages. There's nothing from Vincent for a while. The last text reads like he had something important to show Eric, but it's months old. She minimises the chat and slyly opens his email, but it's password protected.

"Keep going straight for a while," she says, hurriedly returning to the map before Eric glances at her. "Uhh, it's just up ahead here," she mumbles.

Eric pulls over to the roadside and peers out of the window at the tall red-bricked Georgian house to his right. "Nice place."

"Actually it's that one." She points at the grotty tower block on her side of the road.

"Oh." Eric stares up at the building with a glint of pity.

"Thanks." She passes his phone back and pulls up her hood as she climbs out, then waits until Eric pulls away. Her eyes tighten with distrust, watching his tail lights drift down the road. Once the car turns a corner, she glances up at the rain and sighs, letting the downpour wash over her for a fleeting minute before she goes in.

She pulls her hood back as she steps inside and shoves her keys back in her bag. She finds her brother at the edge of his bed, utterly immersed in Ultimate Adventure VII. Having played virtually nonstop since he got it, his character is now a level thirty-three assassin – a limber beanpole of a man dual-wielding a pair of enchanted daggers while sneaking through the shadows and silently picking off goblins. She flops onto the end of his bed, but he's far too engrossed in the game to pay her any attention.

"Mum's on lates?" she asks, staring at the ceiling.

"Uh-huh," he nods.

"So she probably won't leave the hospital until two-ish."

"Uh-huh."

"But she texted me, don't wait up. Because she's never coming home…"

"Uh-huh."

"… Because after her shift she's moving back to Hong Kong to find herself."

"Okay."

Lauren rolls her eyes, not that George notices, then sits up and watches him play over his shoulder. His avatar creeps through the shadows of some ruin, avoiding detection from enemies until he reaches a locked door, and rather than find a way around, George decides to pick the lock. She straightens herself as an idea forms in her mind. If she wants answers about Vincent she's going to have to find them herself. Even if that means overcoming a few locked doors.

"I've got to go out for a bit," she says. "You okay to fix yourself food?"

"Mmm hmm." His glazed eyes remain fixed on the screen.

"I think there's sticky rice casserole left over."

She hurries to her bedroom, which is cluttered with back issues of gaming magazines, sketchbooks and university documents she never threw away. The walls are covered with drawings and pixel art of quirky characters, all her own work. Most prominent is an old self-portrait drawn in charcoal that she had hung as a sort of grim reminder of how she used to feel before everything went to hell.

She pulls open the small chest of drawers beside the single bed in the corner of the room and takes out dry clothes. Everything she owns looks two or three sizes too big. They used to fit a bit better, but the grief and the stress of everything surrounding her father's death saw her appetite diminish with her confidence. After throwing on her raincoat, she gathers some tools – hair pins, a screwdriver and her phone.

"Don't answer the door to anyone." She pops her head into George's room on her way out. "And don't forget to eat!"

He mumbles a reply that she doesn't hear, but she's certain that he won't even notice her absence, and ventures back out into the rain.

It isn't long before she's sitting in the shadows outside Vincent's building, waiting patiently for someone to buzz in or out so she can sneak in. Eventually, a drunk couple let themselves into the gate and she dashes through unnoticed before it closes. She climbs the stairs to Vincent's floor and kneels in front of the door. Channelling her inner sneak thief, she pulls the screwdriver and bobby pin from her pocket and tries to pick the lock for a good few minutes.

What am I doing?

She sits back against the door and sighs. In hindsight this was a dumb idea, but she's come all this way, and determined not to give up at the first hurdle, she conjures another plan.

After rehearsing for a good twenty minutes she knocks at the apartment next door.

Roger, the old man who interrogated her the other day, answers the door. "You again?"

"Sorry to bother you so late but, could I please use your bathroom? It's an emergency." She pleads with doe eyes and scrunches her nose, feigning agony while she clutches her stomach.

The old man's wife calls out in a shrill voice from inside the flat, "What did she say?"

"She wants to use the bog," Roger says.

"We don't have a dog," his wife replies.

Roger hangs his head in despair and steps aside to let Lauren in. "Just be quick and don't steal anything!"

Lauren skirts by him and hurries into his apartment.

"It's down the hall, first door on the—"

She finds it and shuts the door behind her before he can finish. She moves over to the window, taking care to open it quietly, then assesses the drop. She looks her reflection in the eye in the mirror above the sink. *This is insane, are you crazy?* she asks herself, then splashes her face with cold water and looks determinedly at the window. *No, Eric's lying for sure. I need to find Vincent. What if he's in trouble? What if he needs my help?*

She takes three slow breaths and counts to five, then climbs out onto the balcony and carefully edges her way across to Vincent's apartment and proceeds to prise open a window with her screwdriver. Her waifish figure allows her to slip inside with ease, but she trips on the other side and tumbles to the floor, landing head first. She slicks her damp hair back and scans her surroundings as she ties it back in a messy bun. The room is dark save for the glow of streetlights piercing the blinds and curtains. The whole place is a state. Stacks of paper, clothes and books are strewn about, all blanketed in dust. It makes her room look tidy. She activates the torch on her phone and searches the apartment for a shred of info that could point to Vincent's whereabouts.

Peering into the kitchen, she sees a single plate and cup in the sink. She opens the fridge, and a fetid aroma hits her in the back of the throat. The food is all mouldy and looks like it's been there a while. She starts to fear the worst as she moves towards his office.

Sure, Vincent was stressed, and I guess I don't really know him that well, but he wouldn't... No way! She scolds herself for entertaining the notion.

The door creaks open as she presses a finger on it, revealing a large desk in the centre of the back wall. Resting atop it are stacks and stacks of external hard drives. Computer monitors are placed all about, some of them modern, others retro CRT types. It looks like the lair of some super-hacker, but really he's just a pack rat that can't bring himself to throw things away. She approaches the desk and spots a retro action figure of Grimoirh on a shelf above, and next to it an old photo – Vincent and Eric posing with their first game, Runners, the retro space shooter that he had mentioned. They're both smiling from ear to ear and look quite a bit younger. She examines the picture carefully. Eric looks relaxed, and happy – not at all like the man she knows. She gently prods the mouse which rouses the screens to life. The room lights up from the glow of the monitors which all display the same login page.

Of course, it's password protected. She eyes the figurine on the shelf above the desk. *Grimoirh? Runners?* No luck. She slumps back in the desk chair and asks herself, *What am I doing here?*

The reality that she might not get the answers she hoped for starts to sink in when a ruckus from the front door startles her. Hoping it's Vincent, she peeks through the office doorway at a mirror in the hall, which faces the front door, and wonders how the hell she's going to explain what she's doing in his apartment. The door creaks open and a figure steps inside. She eyes the silhouette closely and determines it too slim and short to be Vincent. She hesitates to reveal herself and creeps back into the office, quietly pushing the door shut. Her heart races while she frantically searches for a place to hide, and she darts beneath the desk as the footsteps grow louder. She tucks herself as far back as possible just as the intruder approaches the room she's hiding in. The mysterious stranger lingers outside before the knob turns and the door creaks open. A masked man enters the room and moves towards the desk, stopping right in front of her. Her heart practically beats out of her chest while she clasps her hands tightly over her mouth to muffle her anxious shallow breaths. The silence is broken by the clacking of a keyboard and the Windows login chime. Lauren listens intently while the intruder uses Vincent's computer, and her eyes dart wildly as her mind races. *Could it be him? Who else would know his password?*

After a few minutes, the intruder stops fiddling with the computer and exits the room. Lauren listens as he speaks in a hushed whisper.

"Why her?"

His voice is familiar, but she can barely make it out, and who is he talking to?

"If victory proves elusive seek new allies... or foes," a chilling disembodied voice replies.

She clutches her forehead as a splitting pain crackles through her head, fading as quickly as it arrived. Strange, it felt like that voice was inside her head, but at the same time it was something she wasn't supposed to hear. Her eyes snap wide as she notices a discarded post-it note on the floor, triggering her to remember that she still has that detective's number. Her intuition is telling her she's in danger, so she rifles through her raincoat pocket and quietly uncrumples the post-it note. Sliding her phone out of her jeans she taps in the number, taking care not to make a sound.

*

Valentine slurps the last of his ramen soup from the bowl. It trickles down his stubbly chin and wets the edges of his thick moustache. The dim restaurant is lit only by a couple of neon signs and backlit posters of Japanese flicks like *Battle Royale*, *Hidden Fortress* and *Spirited Away*. The room is empty save for a young couple in the front, a bartender, a waiter and the tired old detective.

His phone buzzes on the table, but his tired eyes linger on a blank birthday card lying in front of him. It's his daughter's birthday, but they don't talk. Haven't for years. He doesn't even know where to send it, but every year he buys one anyway. The bartender sets a drink down in front of him. Scotch, neat.

"Thanks," he mutters, knocking back the half-finished drink he had already.

"You got a text." The young woman motions towards his phone.

Valentine nods appreciatively as he rubs his hands clean on a napkin before picking it up. His brow furrows with all seriousness as he scans the message.

Please help me, trapped inside flat 211 Caledonian Square, not alone.

It's Lauren from 4D Games.

He shoves his phone in his pocket, pulls some bank notes from his wallet and drops them on the counter as he gets up.

"Call me a cab, will you?" he asks the bartender.

"You don't have Uber?" she replies.

Valentine squints with displeasure, downs his drink and heads outside to flag down a taxi. He holds out his arm and the black cab approaching him screeches to a halt and mounts the curb.

"Where to, boss?" asks the driver who's barely tall enough to see over the steering wheel.

Valentine shows him the text. "Can you get me there fast?"

"Fast?"

Valentine flashes the driver his badge, and the little old man brandishes a devious smile, like he's been waiting his entire life for this moment.

"Strap in, boss," he chuckles and guns it down the road.

Valentine doesn't get a chance to blink before he's tossed back into the seat as the car speeds off.

"Mother of God." He tries to settle his stomach as the cab speeds around a corner, blows through a red light and narrowly avoids a collision with a car crossing by. Then his phone buzzes again.

Are you here? Please, please, please. Can't call for help, you're my only hope.

Valentine tries to send a coherent response, but between the five Scotches he drank and being tossed around the back of the cab as it zips and winds through traffic, he can't quite type actual words.

Lauren's phone buzzes. Her heart spikes with dread as the footsteps suddenly come running down the hall. The intruder stops outside the door and peers into the office and then into the living room opposite.

Lauren presses her phone to her chest to cover the light emanating from the screen. Her eyes are popping out of her head for fear of being discovered, but thankfully after a few seconds the intruder strides back down the hall. She lets out a slow, calming breath and hurriedly checks the message she received.

Oh me way, star hiddeb and be quite.

She scrunches her nose, trying to decipher the text, then catches a whiff of something burning and notices slender traces of smoke coming in through the crack below the door. She scrambles out from under the desk and tears into the corridor to find the living room ablaze. She bolts for the door but stops dead on seeing the masked man blocking the way at the far end of the hall.

Lauren gazes at him like a deer in headlights. "V-Vincent?" She tries to stop her legs from buckling with fright.

"Vincent is gone..." the man replies in a raspy voice as fire blazes from the kitchen between them, "... and now, so are you." He traces his finger across the wall and Lauren can barely believe her eyes as, like some sort of spell, a line of fire ignites.

She stands frozen as he turns away, leaving her to burn with the apartment he's just torched. The flames spread quickly across the hall and block the door, and with the living room burning she can't escape via the balcony where she came in. Her whole body seizes up, the voice in her head is screaming at her to get out, but fear paralyses her like a deadly toxin.

Outside, Valentine's cab pulls up, and he flings a wad of cash into the front seat, then scrambles out of the car.

"Keep her running," he orders the driver, then sprints into the building and up the stairs, clinging cautiously to the railing to maintain his balance. As he rounds the third floor the intruder dashes past, knocking him down as he flees the crime scene.

"Hey, stop!" Valentine cries, but of course the man doesn't heed his command. "Bah, damnit."

He picks himself up, stumbles up the steps and notices smoke pouring from the ajar door of Vincent's apartment. He barges it open, only to be confronted by roaring flames and the ear-piercing ring of the fire alarm. He chokes down the smoke and waves it out of his face, spotting Lauren frozen at the far end of the hall.

"Hey! Can you get out?" he yells over the chaos.

Her eyes are fixed on the flames, but she's too panic-stricken to even notice he's at the door.

"Hey!" he cries again, this time grabbing her attention.

"I... I can't move!" she yelps.

Panic sends her senses haywire, her vision tunnels, her head spins, her muscles seize up as the stench of smoke burns her eyes, evoking fractured glimpses of the worst day of her life.

"Shit," he mutters. "Okay, I'm coming to get you!"

The flames crawl up the walls, charring them black as the wallpaper melts away.

Valentine backs up for a running start. "Shouldn't have drunk so much. I'm probably flammable." He pulls his coat over his head and charges through the fire. Incredibly he makes it to Lauren unscathed and pats his smouldering coat down before turning back towards the door. The flames are too high now, and walls are starting to give way. There's no going back.

"We're gonna die," Lauren whimpers.

"Enough of that now." Valentine pushes her into the office and slams the door behind them.

Lauren covers her ears and tries to get a handle on her shot nerves while Valentine calls the fire brigade and shouts for help over the blaring smoke alarm, then he hurls the computer monitors off the desk to reach the window behind it, and wipes the sweat from his brow as he assesses the drop. Looks survivable. Probably. Maybe. He pushes and pushes the window, but it won't budge, so he draws a retractable baton from his jacket and smashes out the glass, which rains onto the street below. Only after does he notice the window was on the latch. He lifts the handle up and the frame swings open into the room.

"Shit," he grumbles then looks back at Lauren, taking her by the arms. "Look at me! I promise I'm not going to let anything happen to you. Alright?"

She nods affirmatively through teary eyes as he ushers her towards the window. "Just listen for sirens, they'll have us out of here before you know it."

Neither of them notice the computer screens blink on and off. Lauren takes a step back from the window and feels cold water fill her shoe. She covers her mouth with her sleeve and chokes on the smoke while she tries to ascertain the source of the water rising above her ankles. "S-something's happening!"

"What is it?" Valentine coughs, and looks baffled as the room floods. It isn't but a few minutes before they're both waist deep. Then things get weirder. They look in fright at a bright, shivering light pulsing from beneath them.

In the Bakers' flat, George's television flickers, then the lights in the whole flat blink on and off. He looks curiously at the LCD screen on his TV, which ripples like water and jolts back as the collector's gangly arm shoots out from the screen to grasp him. He hurls his controller at the creature before bolting out of his bedroom, screaming like a banshee. The collector tumbles out of the television and in a fluid swoop scurries into the hall and snatches the boy up with its long arms. It cradles him and covers his mouth muting his pleas for help, then it pulls him back through the screen before he can even process what's happening. In a flash of blinding white, his home is gone, and he's drifting through a dark empty void.

*

While Lauren tries in her head to make sense of the water's origin, Valentine is busy trying to force the office door open, hoping the rush of water, which is now up to their chests and climbing, will have doused the flames.

Then her eyes light up as she pinpoints the source. The water is surging out of the screens! "This doesn't make any sen—!"

The floor beneath her gives way, and they both plummet into what seems to be a deep ocean. The apartment disappears and the blaring smoke alarm is drowned out until all falls silent. Lauren holds her breath as she tries to keep her eyes open long enough to see what's happening. She kicks about in the murky water and desperately propels herself upwards towards the surface. She's not in Camden anymore.

VIII

TROLLS AND TRIBULATIONS

Bengeo roars in agony as Remy and Ed struggle to lug him up the stairs of the crooked tavern.

"You're so bloody heavy," Ed groans.

"Muscle weighs more than fat," Bengeo replies through gritted teeth.

"Well, I wish you were fat, then."

They stagger through the narrow corridor, carry him to one of the guest beds and drop him on his back. The bed frame almost cracks in two as he lands on the straw mattress, and the bed itself is far too small to accommodate him. His legs hang off the end as he lies groaning while Esmerelda the innkeeper tends to him.

Remy looks around the small crooked room – wooden walls and boarded floors; the two small beds are separated by a beaten treasure chest. Daylight enters through a single window, and a small wooden door leads onto a balcony outside. It's woefully bleak, and for a moment she finds herself lost in a flashback to a depressing family holiday in some dreary seaside town she can't remember the name of. A smile creeps across her face as she fondly recalls playing cards with six-year-old Jessica, who seemed so happy that her big sister was paying attention to her. Bengeo howls as Esmerelda yanks the arrow from his side pulling Remy back to the crisis at hand.

"Poison tip, just as I thought," the innkeeper scowls as she tosses the arrow aside.

"Is it bad?" Ed asks.

"Nothing too serious, but he'll be sore for a few days."

She scurries out of the room. Remy and Ed look worriedly at each other and listen while she clatters about and mumbles to herself in the hall. She returns with a bowl of juniper, hornwort and white hellebore petals, which she mixes into a salve and rubs over the wound.

"Never did like your medicine," Bengeo grunts.

"It's put you back together all these years, ain't it?" Esmerelda places a hand over Bengeo's side. The air under her palm fizzles green, and soon enough, his grimacing subsides and his head lolls on the pillow. She stands and wipes her hands against her linen frock. "That boy's tougher than a Chromatoise shell. He'll live."

"How did you do that?" Ed asks.

"It's good business for an inn to offer healing," she replies.

"Could you teach me?"

Esmerelda looks him up and down and notices his dirty Converse sneakers. She frowns. "I don't know who you two are, but you look like trouble to me. You can have the room until he's better, but then you're out, you hear?"

They nod like children scolded by a teacher and sit quietly until Esmerelda leaves the room. Ed kneels before the treasure chest. The lid has rusted shut, but he attempts to force it open while Remy plonks herself on the empty bed and stares at Bengeo, wrought with worry.

Noticing her grave expression, Ed looks surprised. "I thought none of these people were real?"

Remy looks away and bites her lip guiltily. "Nothing about this place makes sense," she sighs, and flops onto her back and stares at the ceiling just like she'd do back home when throwing herself a pity party.

"Sure it does," Ed replies. "It's kind of like Tron, and I guess you're Tron."

After a moment of trying to figure out what he means by that, Remy sits up and shakes her head at him. "What?"

"You've got that magic thingy in your hand, so you're the one who has to save the world."

"Ha!" Remy gives a pained laugh. "I'm on the dole. I'm not saving anyone's world." She flops on her back again and stares at her hand.

"Well, do you feel any different?" he asks.

"Not really." She wiggles her fingers and balls a fist. "Aches a bit, I guess, but so does the rest of me..."

"Well, if that really is one of *the* three magic crystal shards then it's all powerful, right? Maybe it could be our ticket home. Try and use it."

"Use it how?"

"I don't know, maybe we should ask Esmerelda? She can do magic stuff."

Remy turns her hand and frowns. "I don't think we should tell anyone about it."

"Why not?"

"Because, Ed, if this really is what we think it is then the worst kind of people will do anything to get it."

"Worse than Grimoirh?" Ed replies.

A scream from outside steals their attention. They exchange a worried glance before Esmerelda bursts back into the room with a severe look on her face.

"Both of you, come with me quickly!" she barks.

Outside the tavern, a mob of angry townsfolk surround another troll, shorter and more slender than the others that came before her, with wild dark hair plaited behind her head. Two villagers jab their pitchforks in her direction, and another tries to grab hold of her from behind while the rest jeer and spit.

Esmerelda bursts out of the inn, flanked by Ed and Remy as a man takes hold of the troll girl, locking her arms behind her.

"Away from her!" Esmerelda barks.

"But she's one of them!" a villager cries.

The troll girl wrestles herself free from the man holding her and whirls around, drawing two knives from her belt. She snarls at the villagers who raise their pitchforks, rakes, hatchets – and in one old woman's case, a limp fish – ready to run her through.

Remy places herself between the mob and the troll. "Everyone, just chill out!"

The troll speaks. "I said I came in peace!"

"And you'll leave in pieces!" cries the old crone with the fish.

"She's an animal, string her up!" shouts another villager.

"Filthy troll sympathiser!" The haggard old woman hurls the fish at Remy. "Shaaaaaame!" she howls, pointing her decrepit bony finger.

"Enough!" cries Esmerelda, with sparks and flames erupting from her hands. Bringing them together she unleashes the energy, hurling a fireball at the crowd's feet and with that, they reluctantly retreat.

"It's alright, you can put those away now," Remy says.

The troll stares her down, and after declaring that Remy is no threat to her, sheathes her knives.

"Are you alright?" Remy asks.

"Avarice," the troll grunts.

"Sorry?"

"My name. Avarice."

"Oh, err, Remy."

Avarice nods.

"Get her inside," Esmerelda says as she shoos the last of the villagers away.

126

Avarice perches like a cat on the empty bed and watches Bengeo cautiously while the room quakes with his snoring.

"What are you doing here? Are you with the others?" asks Remy.

"Trolls never break camp before a raid. Out with it, child." Esmerelda folds her arms and tightens her eyes with suspicion.

"Terak has changed his plans. He has heard that you two…" Avarice points to Ed and Remy, "… are wanted by the Dread Knight. He will come at first light, to take you and burn this village to ash."

"What makes you so sure?" Remy asks.

"Because," Avarice mutters, "Terak is my father."

"He's the leader, right?" asks Ed, covering one eye impersonating the troll chieftain's eye patch. "Scary guy."

"Ignore him," Remy says. "So why are you helping us?"

"Grimoirh is a monster and cannot be trusted. Trolls are a proud people, not monsters. We should not align with him. No matter the reward."

Esmerelda gestures for Remy to follow her and steps outside onto the rickety wooden balcony overlooking the square.

"What do you think?" Remy asks.

"Run," the innkeeper replies. "Take your friend and make your way west through the forest."

"Please God, no more running," Remy jests. "I've had enough of forests too."

Esmerelda looks irritated. "Last we met, Bengeo had a ship and crew, now he's got you two and a hole in his gut. If you're just another couple of would-be heroes flouncing through the realm then go on off to the next village and leave this one behind."

Remy leans over the balcony and hangs her head. She knows she's a burden to Bengeo and without him would likely be dead.

Seeing the dour look on her face, Esmerelda takes pity on the girl and softens her tone. "I'm sorry, but I've seen far better adventurers die for less."

Remy gazes out at the village as life unfolds before her. An old man hobbles across the market square, a young woman cradles her baby in her arms, a group of children laugh and chase chickens as the evening light paints everything gold. She sighs, tired of treading circles. Her head tells her this is just a game, that they're all works of fiction, but her senses deem them real enough, which only weighs heavier on her conscience, because she can hardly abandon them to a mess she created.

"We're not going to run," she says.

"I figured as much," Esmerelda sighs.

"Bengeo needs time to rest, but the rest of you could run?"

Esmerelda scoffs. "What kingdom do you hail from, girl?"

"Uh, Greater London I guess."

"Well, Remy of Greater London, if someone threatened your home would you abandon it so easily?"

Remy thinks for a second. "Well, yeah. Probably."

That wasn't the answer Esmerelda was hoping for. This girl is trying her last nerve. "Well, there is nowhere for us to go. This is where we have built our lives. This is where we belong."

"You've got magic, can't you fight?"

The innkeeper laughs. "My fighting days are long behind me, child. Trolls come raiding sometimes. If we hide and let them have our things, maybe they'll let us live in peace."

"Sounds like an awful plan."

Esmerelda looks downcast and descends the creaky wooden stairs leading to the street.

"Wait," Remy calls to her. "About Bengeo. Me and Ed, we'd be dead without him. He's the hero."

Esmerelda smiles with pride. "Don't let him hear you say that." She winks and leaves Remy to watch the villagers as they close up their shops for the day.

With a deep breath she sweeps her matted hair off her face and thinks. She longed for Ultimate Adventure VII to get away from her stress and problems, but here she is, neck deep in both without a hope in hell.

Inside, Ed manages to prise open the chest between the beds with his dagger. Beaming with triumph, he draws out its contents – a very, very rusty sword.

"I knew it!" he cheers. "Rooms at inns always have good loot."

Bengeo watches Ed examine the sword thoughtfully and laughs. "That old thing ain't gonna do squat against a troll. Besides, you even know how to use it?"

"Oh, I know how to use it," Ed grins with unfathomable confidence, spinning the sword elegantly with a flick of his wrist and, immediately, it slips from his grasp and crashes against the wall. "… Guess I'm a little rusty too."

"Just take Remy and journey west. Along the coast, there's a village—"

"Not a chance. You wouldn't abandon us."

The bandit's expression indicates otherwise, but Ed isn't buying it.

"You grew up here, right? You'd really just run away?"

Bengeo laughs. "I ran away soon as I was able. My ma feared that the outside world was full of strange and horrible things that would corrupt me. Course she was absolutely right, but that's mothers for you." He tries to stand, but the pain proves too much and he slumps back onto the bed with a groan. "Aghhh, you and Remy are scrappy. You might make half-decent bandits, but heroes? It doesn't pay well, and it always ends badly." He rests his head on the straw pillow and with a sigh, shuts his weary eyes.

The boisterous tavern below is now empty except for Avarice, who's tearing a roasted chicken to bits as she glugs down tankards of brew. Plainly, the townsfolk have boycotted the place in protest of the dirty troll sympathisers.

"Bah, this is weak!" She hurls her tankard, which clangs off the wall.

The commotion causes Remy to investigate, and she enters the room cautiously, then pulls up a seat beside Avarice who watches her like a cat stalks a mouse.

"Can we talk?"

"I am not interested in talking anymore," Avarice grunts.

Avarice is obviously glum and resentful of the world around her. Maybe it's because she's a troll – a social outcast hated and ostracised wherever she goes – or maybe it's because that's how the game developers wrote her. Either way she's a bit of a teenager, and Remy can't help but be reminded of herself at that age, not least because of the permanent scowl plastered across her face.

"I know coming to warn us can't have been easy with your father—"

Avarice snaps, "Careful when you speak of my father."

Clearly some unresolved daddy issues there. Remy changes her approach. "Look, our friend is hurt, and no one else is strong enough or willing to stand up to the trolls."

"I have given you fair warning," Avarice says. "If you do not leave this place, it is on your heads."

"I get it. You don't want to stand against your dad. Families are complicated, believe me I can relate, but—"

In one swift, abrupt motion Avarice whips a knife from her belt, slams it into the table and speaks with a calm, dangerous rage.

"Long ago, before my father was chief, soldiers from Runegard raided the forest, attacked my clan and stole me away. They caged me like an animal, beat me with sticks and called me cruel things. I was a child, weak and afraid, but all they saw was a monster. They held this very knife to my throat and threatened to cut me open. Back then, it was forbidden for any troll of the Boulder Clan to venture beyond the forest, but my father left

130

anyway. He tracked me for days, far beyond the Witched Wood and into the realm of men. He did not sleep, did not rest until he had found me, and when he did, he crushed my captors' bones to dust and carried me home on his back. He risked everything, even lost his eye to save me from people who look like you, and you would have me betray him? You would have me fight my father? My family? Would you do the same for me, human?"

It occurs to Remy that her own family drama pales in comparison – first world problems and all that.

She looks Avarice earnestly in the eyes. "I'm sorry that happened to you. Really I am, but not all humans are alike. I don't think trolls are monsters, but if your father does what he's threatening to do then that will show all these people that he is exactly that. I don't think you want that any more than I do."

Avarice glares at Remy, who sighs and stands to leave. As she turns her back the troll mutters, "Five hundred runa."

"Huh?"

"There is a mercenary company camped at the river east of here. For five hundred runa, they will fight. My father is bold, but he will not fight if he is outmatched."

Atop the stairs, Ed eavesdrops on their conversation, and realises his gaffe with the mirror may have cost them dearly. There's no way Remy could pay for that company of mercenaries now. He shamefully hangs his head and sneaks out the back door of the tavern for some air.

He walks the streets with his hands buried in his pockets. It's dark now, and the red moon looms over the village. All but a handful of people are huddled in their houses, savouring what could be their last night. The midgey merchant still sits at his little caravan, and Ed, in desperate need of a shoulder to cry on, perches next to the little creature.

"Hey, it's Buckle, right?" he asks.

"Greetings, traveller. Come to browse my wares?" the merchant says in a chipper tone.

"… I screwed up," Ed sighs. "I'm an idiot." He notices Avarice leaving the tavern from across the square, and watches as she rides off into the night. Holding his head in his hands, he pours his heart out to the merchant who struggles to keep his bulgy eyes open while Ed prattles on.

"… I'll admit at first I freaked out, I mean who wouldn't, right? But then I thought I'd be in my element here. I mean, it's a role-playing game so why shouldn't I get to be whomever I want? At least I think it's a game, I don't know anymore…" He picks up little trinkets on the merchant's stall and examines them curiously before placing them back. "I can't believe I got us killed for cosmetic customisation. Now we'll never get home…"

The midgey merchant slumps over his stall and begins to snore.

"… Yeah, I guess you're right," Ed replies as though Buckle has said something to him. "Why worry when we're all gonna die in the morning."

He rests his chin philosophically on his hands and sighs at his reflection in a small, decorated mirror sitting on the stall. After a second he turns his attention to the mirror itself and then his eyes light up with the spark of an idea.

*

Lamp light flickers in the downstairs window of the Legless Arms. A gaunt elderly man, with uneven patches of white hair scattered around his otherwise bald head, sweeps the floor with a single-minded intensity, repairing some of the damage caused by Avarice.

Remy sits at the bar, staring at her right hand in deep thought. She clenches and releases her fist, trying to figure out a way to invoke the crystal's power. With a deep breath, she stretches her arm in front of her, tenses every muscle in her body, and focuses her mind on the very rusty sword which is now resting on the counter top. Her hand trembles. She looks constipated. With all her might she tries to summon the sword as if the crystal would give her Jedi powers or something.

Come on, come on! Work! She strains so hard she turns purple and the veins in her forehead bulge, but it's no use. That voice she despises clouds her mind with doubt. *This is so stupid worthless useless can't help anybody all your fault run away now now now.*

Defeated, Remy plants her head on the bar. "Guess it chose wrong."

The old man passes by her, swishing the mop over her boots. "Beware the forest. Dark and meddlesome spirits dwell there," he mumbles.

Remy regards the old coot quizzically. "Sorry?"

"Beware the forest. Dark and meddlesome spirits dwell there." The old man repeats himself in the exact same flat, lifeless manner as before.

"Thanks for the advice, but you're a little late." Remy takes another swig of her drink as she swivels back towards the bar.

The mad old man drifts away to sweep the other side of the room as Bengeo staggers down the stairs and sees Remy feeling sorry for herself.

He walks awkwardly towards her and gestures at her drink. "May I?"

She passes him the bottle. "Feeling better?"

"Getting there." He takes a swig and savours the taste. "Still have time to run."

"And leave all these people?"

The bandit shrugs. "They're simple folk. Live or die, they'll never make much difference in the world."

"Yeah, been there." Remy frowns. Taking the mead from Bengeo, she downs what's left then glances at the old man sweeping in the corner. "I get it. He's an NPC, I shouldn't care. But how do you not care about someone when they're standing right in front of you?"

"He's a what?" Bengeo looks at the old man, puzzled. "Old Baul got lost in the Witched Wood when he was a kid. Scrambled his mind something awful. Ain't that right, Baul?"

"Beware the forest. Dark and meddlesome spirits dwell there," Baul mumbles again.

"Poor old bastard," Bengeo sighs.

Remy shakes her head, and picking up the sword she examines the pointy end. "I guess real enough to kill me is as real as anything gets."

Bengeo goes behind the counter, rummages through the bottles and takes an ale that looks to his taste.

"You're a weird girl, you know." He pops the cork and swigs.

"Well, it's a weird world you got here."

"Drinking helps." They share a smile as he hands Remy the bottle.

Whoosh! The tavern door suddenly bursts open and Ed looks elated at them both.

"I've got a plan!" he gasps.

Bengeo and Remy look sceptical, but his face beams like a ray of sunshine on a stormy day.

*

The sun creeps over the thatched roof of the inn and a chilling wind blows through Trout's empty streets. The market is unmanned, the square, desolate. Ed and Remy stand alone in the centre of the village like gunfighters in a spaghetti western.

"This is an awful plan," Ed whispers.

"What?! It's *your* plan!" Remy gasps, anxiously tapping her fingers against the handle of the rusty sword.

"Yeah. But I'm starting to have doubts."

Remy winces slightly and massages her head.

Ed looks appalled. "Are you hungover?"

"Shut up," she mutters. "… A little." She glances at Bengeo

134

who's standing before the inn. He gives her a little nod, signalling he's ready.

Before long, a thunderous stampede tremors through the village, heralding the notorious Boulder Clan. They approach the main square and Terak raises a hand, halting his men. The troll chief dismounts and as he approaches, weapon in hand, Ed pushes Remy forward to greet him.

"We... we don't want to fight," she croaks.

The trolls erupt in raucous laughter.

"We do, Meat!" Terak raises his great club, fashioned of rock and bone, to smash Remy into pulp, but Ed pulls her back in the nick of time and the club strikes the pavement.

"That's it! Let 'em have it!" Remy cries.

Bengeo boots open the tavern door to unleash hell, and the trolls peer at the doorway in anticipation, but nothing comes.

"Bah!" laughs Terak. "You think you—"

"Look!" cries one of the trolls.

Terak's jaw hangs wide as a wave of living hair scurries out of the tavern towards him and his men. Interwoven locks of all colours separate into smaller bundles, which scatter like a swarm of spiders and wrestle the trolls from their mounts while the bald villagers watch the mayhem unfold from the safety of their homes. Honestly, Remy can't recall a stranger morning.

Terak claws a bundle from around his throat and clobbers it into the ground. He looks at the 'players' with flared nostrils and charges toward the source of his ruin.

"Oh crap!" Ed squeals at the mad-eyed chieftain, who swings his club with such brutish barbarity that he tears the fish-headed statue asunder in a single strike. Remy pulls Ed away as the rubble crashes down around them and raises the rusty sword to the troll chieftain, but he disarms her effortlessly, sending the sword flying across the square.

"Whoa! Whoa! Whoa!" Remy implores Terak to show mercy, but he doesn't know the meaning of the word. She shuffles away on all fours as the troll's clunking huge feet shake the ground around her.

Ed, with all his might, lifts a chunk of the broken statue and drops it onto Terak's foot, making the troll let out a mighty yowl. He thumps Ed in retribution then sets his sights on Remy. He raises his club to squash her again, when a knife plants itself in the haft of his weapon. He examines the blade and seems to recognise it.

"Stop this madness!" a voice from above cries out. Avarice leaps from the roof of the general store into the square and approaches her father.

"Insolent daughter, you shame me!" Terak cries.

"Enough, Father," Avarice pleads, "these people did you no wrong. They merely took back what we took from them. Spare them and leave this village."

"Why do you ask this of me?" the chieftain grunts.

"Because, Father, you taught me our clan is proud, we have honour, we answer to no one. How am I to believe that if we are pawns of the Dread Knight?"

Terak is inspired by his daughter's pride for her people, but he is old, and male, and a troll, so of course his stubbornness gets the better of him.

"The Dread Knight offers power. He is turning the tide for our kind. Too long have we been shunned by the world, a world that we too are part of. Mankind has no greater claim to it than us, but still, they push us to the brink, force us into the wilds, hunt us like animals. You are but a child, you know nothing of what it means to provide for your clan. This Dread Knight can change things. Any blight to them can only be a beacon to us."

Avarice, unwavering, stands tall and proud. "Grimoirh cannot be trusted! He knows only malice and death. We are trolls, Father. We take what we need. We do not beg for scraps! We must be better, better than the Dread Knight, better than humans."

"You should listen to your daughter," Remy whimpers from where she's cowering in as dignified a way as one can cower.

Terak hesitates to strike her, thinking on his daughter's words. "You warned the humans of our coming?"

"Yes..." Avarice bows her head shamefully, "... I have seen you kill for less."

"Yes, you have..." Terak lowers his club, "... but they were not my daughter."

He opens his arms wide. Avarice hesitates for a moment, but unable to resist the lure of her father's love, runs to his embrace.

Remy sighs with sweet relief that their plan actually worked... well, sort of. A bit. Her moment of repose, however, is tragically short-lived. Any hope of respite fades as Grimoirh's airship casts a foreboding shadow over the town. The wind dies down, and the birds and critters of nature go deathly quiet. The villagers and the trolls all stare in fear at the ship, then a moment later dozens of goblins rappel from it and start burning the houses with torches and flaming arrows.

Terak holds Avarice tightly. "Run, Daughter!"

"No, Father, I will not leave you!"

"Stubborn, like your mother was," he grins.

"Remy, we gotta go!" Ed's cries fall on deaf ears.

Remy looks stunned as Grimoirh's forces tear the village apart. The bundles of hair scatter about the square in a blind panic. Even the magic enchanting them fears the darkness Grimoirh brings.

"Remy! Let's go!" Ed tugs at her arm, but the familiar thud of footsteps – cold, hard metal greaves grating against stone – steals her attention.

Then she spots Grimoirh himself across the square, while screams of terror echo around her. The Dread Knight raises a hand, conjures a fireball and hurls it into the tavern, setting it ablaze.

"What's the matter with you?! Come on!" Ed continues to pull at her desperately.

"No, I'm sick of running." She tears her arm away from him and charges without a second thought, taking up the rusty sword as she crosses the square.

"She is crazy!" Avarice gasps.

"Bah, forget her, come." Terak raises his club to the goblin soldiers, and with his daughter's help, he cuts Ed a path to the burning tavern where Esmerelda and Bengeo, axe in hand, smite any goblins that rush them.

Remy lunges at Grimoirh who lifts his God Cleaver to block her attack. Her blade prangs off his and in a flash he strikes back, knocking her clean off her feet. A second strike breaks her rusty sword in two.

"You have the shard?" he asks.

"Take your shard and shove it! Because of you my sister's a statue!" She clambers on her feet, swipes a shield from the midgey merchant's market stall and readies herself for another hit.

"What is that idiot girl doing?" Bengeo looks on in disbelief as Remy tries to hold her own against Grimoirh. "Everyone with me!" Like a raging bull, he charges through a group of goblins, toppling them like bowling pins.

Amidst the chaos, the cowering midgey merchant throws a sword to Ed. "Take this, stranger! May it aid you on your quest!" the little critter cries before he tucks himself underneath his wagon.

Much to his surprise, Ed catches the thing and with a renewed sense of bravery backs Bengeo in his charge while Avarice and Terak cover their rear.

He unsheathes the sword ready to fight the three armoured adversaries blocking their way, but the blade goes limp and droops to one side. Bengeo looks at Ed to demand an explanation, but he shrugs at the bandit. Determined to make the best of it, he flails it wildly and bashes his foe until Avarice hurls a knife into the monster's face. Terak brings his club down upon another, smashing it to mush, and Bengeo finishes off the last one, severing its head with his axe.

The head rolls at Avarice's feet, and she removes the helmet to gaze upon her foe. The creature is no goblin. In fact it looks as though it were once human. Now its pale, sickly flesh is rotten, with eyes sunken and faded.

"Accursed! Corrupted!" she exclaims, holding the head up to the others. Ed heaves at the sight, while Terak looks on in horror.

"You were right, Daughter." The troll chief bows his head shamefully.

Determined to save Remy from her own recklessness, Bengeo hurls his beloved axe at Grimoirh. The weapon soars across the battlefield and lands true, pranging off the Dread Knight's plate mail, bringing him to his knees. Remy leaps onto his back while he's down and furiously tries to prise off his helmet. In defence, Grimoirh conjures a burst of fire that hurls her across the square and into the fountain with a whopping splash.

Bengeo lunges at the Dread Knight, picking up his axe again and swinging it in a violent rage, but a few ferocious blows against Grimoirh's seemingly impenetrable armour break the head to pieces. Countering the bandit, Grimoirh plunges his great sword forward, stabbing visciously. Bengeo stumbles backwards but turns the tide and, like a brawling sailor, hits back with his hulking fists. For a brief moment, it looks like he has the upper hand until a hard strike to his arrow wound sends him tumbling down with a cry.

Desperate to help somehow, Ed brazenly rushes the Dread Knight too and leaps onto his back, yanking his head backwards and clinging onto the horns of his helmet while Grimoirh tries to swing him off.

Avarice rushes to help, but her father takes her arm and pulls her back.

"No, Daughter. You are no match for that demon! We must flee."

Avarice looks back at him and reluctantly complies. The two trolls slip away as mayhem tears apart the town. Around them, the village burns to ash and goblins cut down many of the townsfolk as they scatter.

Esmerelda leads a group safely into the meadows surrounding the town and towards the forest. She pauses at the treeline and looks back at her home with a heavy heart before fleeing into the woods.

Grimoirh hurls Ed over him, and his back slams against the craggy street. He fights to breathe as Grimoirh presses a foot on his chest and grips the God Cleaver with both hands, raising it to guillotine Ed in two. For a split second Ed wonders whether dying here would truly end his life or would he awaken back in his room, sweating over the whole thing like it was some vivid fever dream, but after seeing Matt reduced to a bloody soup he's more than certain it's the former.

"Wait!" He gasps what could be his last word as Grimoirh shunts the sword inches from his head. Braced to meet his maker, Ed squints one eye open and breathes a sigh of relief before Grimoirh thumps him in the face.

Remy picks up her dazed self and staggers out of the fountain. She looks up as the Dread Knight strides towards her. Lunging forward, she hurls her fist at him but almost breaks her hand as it collides with his plate mail – rookie move. He takes her by the throat and throws her to the ground, kneels over her and presses a thumb on her forehead.

"Sleep." Once more, he utters the word like a spell, and in an instant her eyes roll back in her head, and she drifts away. Sheathing his sword on his back, he takes her in his arms.

Ed takes up a spear from one of the fallen goblins and charges to Remy's aid, screaming bloody fury.

"You bastard!" he roars at Grimoirh, who turns to him just as the blow lands. The spear tip shunts the faceplate of his helmet, but he doesn't flinch.

He glares at Ed, who for the first time gets a proper glimpse at the man beneath. Dark eyes burn with a cold rage, but hours spent people-watching while working in retail has gifted Ed with an ability to see between the lines, read a person for what they really are, and there is something distinctly human about Grimoirh's gaze, something hidden beneath the malevolent intent.

In a flash he headbutts Ed, who collapses with a groan. All he can do is helplessly and hopelessly watch as Grimoirh steals Remy and the crystal shard away. Defeated and deserted, he mops the blood from his brow and stares up at the looming airship through the plumes of smoke, then Ed's eyes grow wide as a second much larger airship unexpectedly eclipses the sky.

The few remaining townsfolk cheer as the *Thanatos* – the flag gunship of the Runegard Army – fires upon Grimoirh's vessel as it retreats. At its helm stands a tall man clad in gleaming golden armour. General Gilbertus Gigas, famed leader of Runegard's military, a renowned tactician, warrior and not to mention a notoriously difficult to beat in-game boss, grins, eager to decimate Grimoirh's airship and bring an end to the scourge desecrating the realm.

"Blast them to oblivion," the general orders his second in command, Captain Diamond, named for the unbreakable ornate rapier hanging on her belt.

"Yes, General," the captain salutes. Turning to the crew she relays his order. "Give them hell!"

Cannon fire roars across the sky, and smoke and fire engulf Grimoirh's ship as it is bombarded.

"Looks like the cavalry showed up," Bengeo growls, clasping a firm hand on his side.

"They're gonna blow them right out of the sky!" Ed cries.

"That's the idea, I expect." The bandit grimaces as he tries to get on his feet, but the shooting pain in his abdomen keeps him down.

"But Remy's on board that thing!"

Leaning on Ed for support, Bengeo looks up at the warring ships. "Worry about us right now."

IX

DUNGEON CRAWL

*Y*ou're dead no escape nowhere to go. The whisper in her head becomes a desperate scream, which she silences by pulling against the iron binding her wrists until they're red raw. Remy glances at the pointy implements laid on a table in the corner of the dark metal room and cycles through a variety of grim scenarios in which they might be used to extract the crystal from her hand. But hell, she'll tear her arm off first if she has to, whatever it takes to escape.

At once, nerve-shredding pain lances through her right hand and down her arm. She curls her toes in her soles and howls wildly, stretching her fingers to try and keep her muscles from going haywire. Glancing up through tears, she watches as pale eldritch light pulses from within her hand, and it feels like her arm is splitting in two. Then as quickly and suddenly as it appeared, the agony subsides and fades to a dull ache. *What the shit was that?!* she wonders. Undoubtedly this was something to do with the crystal shard, but what caused it? And what did it mean?

She hangs in the dark by her wrists and catches her breath as her hair falls over her face. The iron door opposite her swings open, and the light behind Grimoirh casts an intimidating silhouette as he looms in the doorway. Remy watches him with eyes ablaze as he approaches her.

"Let me go!" She lunges towards him, stopping inches short as her chains pull taut. "Well? Say something!" she hisses.

"Who are you?"

His cold voice reverberates from behind the iron mask, which unnerves her, but damned if she'll show it.

"Piss off," she spits.

Then, unexpectedly, he lifts the horned helmet from his head to assure her that he's no monster, but a man. Her curious eyes study his gaunt face, scrutinising every detail – the deep scar across his nose and the dark bags under his eyes. Strangely he looks familiar to her, but she can't place why.

"You played the game?" he asks.

Game? How does he know it's a game? None of the other characters have. Her eyes dart back and forth as she tries to fathom what this could mean. "You know about—?"

"Of course. I created it."

For one of the few occasions in her life, Remy Winters finds herself lost for words. She wasn't expecting Grimoirh to be entirely human, let alone the creator of Ultimate Adventure VII.

"*Created it?* You mean—?"

"I'm as real as you." He glances up at her hand. "The crystal, you have it?"

She keeps her gaze locked on him and clenches her fist. He looks deep into her eyes and notices glimmers of teal. Strange, he's sure they were brown before.

"I wonder… can you help me?"

"Help you? Help *you*?" she scoffs.

"Help me save the world, Remy."

Her eyes snap wide on hearing her name from his lips. *How the hell does he know my name? Doesn't matter, don't let on that you're bricking it. You're tough. Be tough.*

"Isn't Grimoirh supposed to end the world?"

"The irony isn't lost on me," he replies. "You've played the game, then you know the power those crystal shards hold. To retrieve it that monster had to be destroyed. I was right to think it was only a matter of time until one of us would do it."

"One of *us*?" Remy pulls defiantly on her chains. "I'm nothing like you!"

"We're both stuck here and if we want to change that we'll need to work together. I'm sure by now you know, this world is very, very dangerous."

Her eyes narrow to a bitter glare.

"Those shards contain unfathomable power, and if I can gather them all then maybe I can fix this mess."

"Why would I trust you? You tried to kill us! Hunted us through the woods! Chained me up like an animal! You almost got my sister killed!"

"No, that was you. I warned you to stay away from the giganeye. I locked you all up to protect you. If you had stayed put things might have gone differently." He turns towards the doorway. "Bring her in!"

At his command, one of his odorous underlings shoves Jessica into the room and onto her knees.

"Rude!" She pokes her tongue out at the goblin, then her eyes sparkle as she sets them on her sister. "Remy?!" She throws her arms around her and squeezes tight.

"Jess?! You're... you?! Are you okay? Did he hurt you?"

"I'm fine," Jessica replies. "They just locked me up, alone. It wouldn't kill you to find a magazine or something!" she hisses at Grimoirh, who signals to the goblin to remove her.

Its clumpy hands grab her arm and drag her away. "Get off me, you ugly son of a—!"

The door slams behind them, but Jessica's muffled insults echo as she's dragged kicking and screaming back to her cell.

Remy eyes him with murderous intent. "I swear to God if you hurt her—"

"Hurt her? I saved her. I could've left her in that pit like you did, but I didn't. This isn't a game anymore. I'm not some evil villain, and you're not some plucky heroine. I'm trying to put an end to all of this before it gets any worse." His tone darkens. "There's more at stake here than you think. Sinister forces are at work. Your sister has got fire in her, just like you, but do you think you can keep her safe for long in a world like this? You've already lost her once..." He leans closer. "... Not all of us are capable of surviving this unforgiving place. So help me, help yourself, help your sister, and you might both survive what's ahead."

"And what's that?" she asks.

"Tell me, are you afraid?"

She looks scornful, and tries as hard as she can not to show even a flicker of fear.

A smirk plays on his lips. "Good, that fear will keep you alive."

With a frustrated sigh, she relents, knowing this is a decision she'll surely regret. "Do I have a choice?" she asks, feeling as helpless and out of control of her life as ever.

"There's only one choice." Grimoirh unshackles her wrists, and lets them down, "Adapt or die."

*

Lauren bursts to the surface with a gasp. Her heart races at the ocean surrounding her, frigid waves pummelling her as she fights to keep her head above the water.

"This way!" Valentine cries.

She spins around, and her chest flutters at the sight of land and Valentine swimming towards it. She focuses all her attention on the beach ahead as she battles her way ashore. It takes all she's got not to get swept out further.

The detective gasps for breath as he drags himself onto the bleak sand, while Lauren wades out of the water behind him and falls on her knees. She looks to the dawn sky and savours sweet air, her aching arms and legs shivering in the sea breeze. She scans this alien place and wonders how the bloody hell she got here.

The sun isn't the only thing crawling over the horizon. An airship sails overhead, and the morning light gleams off the slender metal hull, blinding her as it passes. The hairs on her neck prickle like a hedgehog's spines. She recognises that ship – but that can't be possible.

Hunched on all fours, the detective has his head literally buried in the sand and misses the floating ship entirely. "What… Where are we?" he asks, spitting seawater and sand out of his mouth. "Hey, you alright? Shit, what was her name again?" he mutters. "What's the last thing you remember? The fire and then… Hey, you with me?" He waves a hand in front of her face, snapping her out of her trance.

"Ye-yes," she shivers.

He shoots her a crooked smile before pulling his mobile phone from his pocket. "You'd think these things would be waterproof by now," he curses, tapping the screen aggressively. "Can't call for help… Keep it together, Scott, get a lay of the land…" His incoherent mumbling is mired by the squelching of his shoes with each step further inland.

They cross the beach and stagger over the ridge into a sprawling meadow of swaying grass. All the while the detective impatiently taps his phone screen. Lauren checks hers too, praising herself for buying the waterproof case, but it makes little difference, no signal – not that she expected any.

"I don't think that's going to work here," she says.

He tuts and stuffs his phone back into his pocket. "Where is *here* exactly? Don't see any roads. Penzance? Dungeness maybe?

But how did we get to the coast? How the hell could we be in a burning apartment one minute, then in the ocean? Where did all that water come from? What's going on?!" The detective rubs his head as he tries to make sense of what doesn't. "Maybe we're dead."

He laughs while Lauren quietly tries to subdue her swelling anxiety with steady breaths.

"Maybe this is just a dream?" He examines his hands and wiggles his fingers. "Doesn't feel like a dream, though." He slaps himself across the face. "Definitely not a dream."

Lauren shudders as something whips past her leg and the grass rustles around her, as though a shark were circling its prey.

"Uh... he-hey! De-Detective!"

"What's wrong?"

"I think there's something in here with us." She looks white as a ghost.

"Like a dog?" he asks.

Lauren catches a glimpse of whatever is lurking in the grass – a leathery tail with a barbed stinger.

"Not a dog!" she whimpers.

A blur leaps at her, and she ducks in the nick of time before the creature flies overhead and tumbles onto the ground, sharply rolling onto its paws. She gets a good look at it now – a sizeable, blueish, panther-looking thing. Two long tendrils writhe from its shoulders while its menacing tail sways behind.

"Christ, what the hell is that?!" Valentine's shaking hand reaches for his telescopic baton, which he draws on the creature as it takes a run at him, and whomps it in the face as it leaps. The beast tumbles over in the grass.

He prods the limp carcass. "What the ever loving...?! You ever seen anything like this?"

"Random encounter... random encounter!" Lauren cries as the reality – for lack of a better word – of her situation dawns on her.

"Random what?" he asks, unnerved by the look of dread plastered across her face.

"We have to get out of this field, right now!"

"You think there's more?"

Lauren gulps. "A lot more."

The rustling grass indicates packs of creatures stalking towards them.

Valentine looks warily about the field. "On three, we'll run together. One. Two. Thr—!"

A gelatinous blob with two black button eyes rises from the grass behind him, and Lauren recognises the creature immediately – a blobkin, a common monster that has appeared in all the Ultimate Adventure games, often found dripping from dungeon walls or lurking in damp areas. It's comprised of a bright-coloured ooze which swallows Valentine's baton as he strikes it. The detective stumbles backwards, watching his baton dissolve inside the creature's acidic body, then it bounces towards him like a malevolent space hopper.

"Run!" He takes off through the meadow like a shot.

Lauren bolts too and quickly catches up to the aged detective who wheezes like a sick dog as he clumsily hurls himself through the long grass which bleeds into a marsh scattered with crooked black trees.

More blobkins give chase and cut them off, their black button eyes staring with a cold unwavering hunger to kill. Valentine stumbles through the bog and picks up a rock then hurls it, striking one of the oozes, which retreats with a wobble.

"Watch out!" Lauren shrieks as a walking corpse rises from the water. Valentine turns as the creature lunges and clocks it hard, knocking its head clean off.

"What is going on? What *are* these things, and why are they after us?!" He looks aghast at the decapitated body thrashing in the water.

"Random encounters," Lauren replies.

"Why do you keep saying that?"

"It's part of the game. Monsters show up to battle when you're in the wilderness."

"*Part of the game?*" He looks at her like she's crazy or high or both.

She points up at the airship hovering in the distance, far above the rising fog that swathes over the murky water. "There, we need to get to it and out of the wild!"

Valentine's jaw drops at the stark sight of the floating ship. "Maybe we are dead..." he gulps.

*

Remy trudges behind Grimoirh through the veiled bog. With every step the airship fades further into the mist, which washes everything in pale grey. She watches him cautiously, and the thought of trying to escape crosses her mind, but there's nowhere to go, and he still has Jessica prisoner. She examines her right hand and rubs her palm softly. The faint glow of the jewel resonates from under her skin. If only she knew how to wield its power, if only she knew how to get herself home.

Her mind swells with questions. *Who is he? A player like me? He said he created the game. He does look a little familiar. How is that possible? What if he wants to be here? What if he's living out some sad fantasy? What if this is a trap? If he wants the crystal why didn't he just take it?* She winces as the icy water swilling around her legs trickles into her boots, then asks for the umpteenth time, "What are we doing here and where are we going?" She thinks back to the original game, but the boxy 16-bit graphics hardly translate to the realism of her experience now, and there are dozens of swamps in the game that all reused similar tilesets. She jolts at the caw of a crow perched atop the husk of a dead tree, and its beady eyes follow her as she passes it by.

"I feel like that bird is watch—"

"Shh!" Grimoirh snaps and grabs the hilt of his sword. "We're not alone."

Remy can't make out much through the fog, but a foreboding groan unsettles her. She tightens her eyes and peers through the mist at a humanoid silhouette shambling closer. She edges backwards, keeping her attention fixated on who or what is before her. A decrepit wet hand suddenly clasps her shoulder from behind. She shrieks and wrestles with a walking corpse until Grimoirh buries a dagger in its head and it topples back into the marsh.

"Undead!" He draws the God Cleaver from his back, which erupts with an enchanted yellow flame, and the fire spits and crackles across the black iron blade as dozens more silhouettes sprint out of the mist. Snarling, hissing, shrieking wights – bald, festering and sunken-eyed – charge the Dread Knight who swings his sword with great gusto, cutting them into pieces that plop into the water. Remy's heart races as one corpse after another hurls itself at her, but she manages to evade their advances and spots a worn longsword impaling one of the dead. Determined to reach it, she ducks and dives her way through clambering hands and clasps its hilt. She pulls at the sword, but it's lodged too deep in the wight's breastbone to budge. Thinking fast, Remy shoves the sword further through its guts and runs another through as it comes towards her. Wielding the sword like a giant shish kebab, she swings the skewered creatures into their kin while desperately trying to break it free.

"Oh for God's sake!" She lifts her foot against the corpse and kicks. One big tug and the sword finally breaks loose from its chest cavity, spraying her head to toe with rotting bodily fluids as she trips backwards into the bog. She wipes her eyes clean and swings the blade around as she stands, beheading the monster in front of her. Its gnashing head splashes at Grimoirh's feet, and he crushes it with his boot then brings his flaming sword down on another, splitting it like a log. Remy covers her mouth and retches at the rotting guts spilling into the marsh.

"There's no end to them!" Grimoirh cries. "Stick close to me." He cuts a path through the biting abominations, and together they wade through the mist and shallow water while the horde relentlessly pursues them. More and more dead rise feverishly from their watery graves, each as starved of flesh as the last.

The shape of a towering ruin appears through the fog as they advance, but hundreds more undead surround them from every direction. Grimoirh cleaves ten corpses in half with one broad slash. He stands firm, back to back with Remy, and in a flurry of fire and steel, they slice and dice the wights to ribbons. Body parts and putrid guts litter the murky water, tainting it brownish red, but the endless rush overwhelms them.

"Brace yourself!" the Dread Knight warns.

"For what?!" yelps Remy.

Gripping his sword in both hands, Grimoirh raises it high, then shunts the blade into the earth and drops to one knee. With all his might, he twists the sword in the ground, unleashing a burst of enchanted fire, which forms a wheel of flame around them.

Remy looks amazed as the fervent dead hurl themselves into the fire and explode into clouds of ash. As he tears the sword out of the earth, a gaping sinkhole crumbles beneath their feet and they slip through muck and bones into a long-forgotten ruin buried beneath the marshland.

Dust litters the air. Rancid water pours in from above and splashes against the cold stone floor. Remy picks herself up after a rough landing and leans against an old sarcophagus to catch her breath. She watches Grimoirh while he busies himself with prising open an ancient chest in the corner of the room.

"That was mental!" she gasps. He ignores her yet again. At least he doesn't see her rolling her eyes. "Anything in there?"

He lifts a small black stone out of the chest and holds it up to her. "Something that might prove useful."

"More magic rocks, great."

"It's a ferry stone." He almost smiles as he admires its perfectly smooth edge. It looks more like glass than stone, and its core glows amber.

"Ferry stone?"

"I thought you played the game? They're used to fast travel across the map to locations you've already visited. It only works once, but it'll help if we can't find a way out."

"Well, I didn't get very far before being dragged through my parents' flat screen and I don't remember any ferry stones in the original game."

"We needed a way to encourage players to avoid shortcuts. We wanted you to experience the world as if you were there. Ferry stones are rare, and we can't exactly purchase more on the Game Station network."

"I think I've 'experienced' enough." Remy massages her sore ribs.

"You're hurt?" It almost sounds like he's genuinely concerned for her wellbeing.

"What do you care?"

"Let me see." Grimoirh moves his hand towards her, but she swats it away.

"Back off, don't touch me," she hisses.

"You're no good to me dead," he says coldly then turns his attention to the large stone door on the far side of the chamber. "We should keep moving."

Judging by the stone sarcophagi spaced evenly throughout the room, Remy surmises they're in a crypt of some kind. Its tall bricked walls are obviously ancient and were swallowed by the marshland and lost to unforgiving time. The musty, damp scent is a little reminiscent of her grandfather's house, which provides her with the tiniest comfort.

"Another dungeon…" she mutters under her breath.

"Give me a hand with this." Grimoirh presses against the door, and together they push with everything they've got, but it's sealed shut.

"There's got to be a switch or something. Isn't there always a switch? Or a puzzle?" she says.

"Stand back." Grimoirh picks up his sword and Remy ducks for cover and cups her hands over her ears while he hacks and smashes the ancient door to rubble.

"It's open now," he says.

"You want to let the whole dungeon know we're here?"

"Let's push on then." Resting his blade on his shoulder he ducks through the hole in the door.

Remy shakes her head and warily follows him into the deep, still none the wiser about where they're going or why.

*

Above ground, Lauren and Valentine sprint through the mire. The fog grows thicker as they draw closer to Grimoirh's airship, and the roaming corpses rise in greater numbers.

"It's okay, I don't think they've spotted us," Lauren reassures the detective, who gasps for air as he struggles to keep up. He spies a structure through the fog – the very same dilapidated ruin, half sunken into the marsh.

"Quickly!" He takes Lauren's arm and leads her to its crumbling walls, then points at the ship floating above them. "How the hell are we supposed to get up there? What is that thing?"

Lauren points to a tall crooked spire atop the ruin. "Maybe we can signal for help from there?"

"Not a bad idea." Valentine composes himself and points to the crumbly entrance of the ruin. "Let's go."

Lauren glances back at the ship, which glimmers in the

morning light breaking through the fog. It's too high to make out the insignia on the hull, so she prays that whatever is on board isn't worse than out here.

*

Jessica clasps the iron bars of her cell and stares at the sliver of light illuminating a patch of the dark empty room around her.

"Let me out of here!" She rattles against the cage hoping to loosen the bars, but she's far too puny ever to accomplish such a feat.

"You can't treat me like this. It's, like, inhumane!" she sobs.

The iron door on the far side of the room blasts open and a husky figure approaches her cage. She backs away as the wretched goblin hisses at her to shut up and takes a bite out of something in its hand.

"I'm hungry!" Jessica assertively stomps her foot.

The goblin grins with spite and tosses the rancid slab of meat into her cage.

Her teary eyes regard it with disgust. "You don't expect me to eat that?"

The henchman lets out a belly laugh and slams the door behind it, leaving her alone in the dark once more. She hugs her knees and stares at the strange meat.

"This is a nightmare. It has to be. Wake up! Come on, Jess, wake up!" She slaps herself across the face. "Wake up! Wake up! Wake up!" again and again, harder each time, until her cheeks turn pink.

"What are you doing?" a little voice squeaks from the darkness.

She jumps out of her skin and retreats to the far corner of her cage. "Who's there?"

Bracing herself for the worst, her wide eyes fixate on a small shadow emerging from a grate in the wall. Nothing she has seen in this world has been anything but horrifying beyond all recognition. As the little creature steps into the light, she realises it's not a creature at all, but a young boy wearing grubby denim dungarees and a yellow T-shirt. Inadvertently he's dressed like a DreamWorks minion, which Jessica has never been fond of, nevertheless his appearance is a welcome sight. She was beginning to wonder if she'd ever see anyone nice again.

"Why are you slapping yourself?" the boy asks.

She looks him up and down a second time to make certain she's not imagining him. "Who...?! What are you doing here?"

"Escaping," he says rather nonchalantly and squeezes through the bars of her cell. "I've been crawling through the vents trying to find a way out without those goblins seeing me."

"You're all by yourself? How long have you been here?" she asks.

The boy shrugs. "Dunno. A few days, maybe." It's been a few hours tops.

"You poor thing." Jessica's maternal instincts kick in. The boy reminds her of Newt from *Aliens* – a film that traumatised her after Remy made her watch it at far too young an age – but that makes her Ripley, which if she remembers correctly is somewhat of a silver lining because she survives until the end.

She throws her arms around the boy, constricting him. The kid stands limp and confused. Honestly, she's scaring him more than the monsters.

"Please stop." He wriggles free of her death grip.

"What's your name?" she asks.

"George. George Baker."

"George. I'm Jess," she smiles. "Can you help me get out of here?"

He slips back through the bars of her cage with ease. "Can't you squeeze through?"

Jessica tries to slide her arm out, but her head and hips get stuck.

"Your butt's too big," George says. Savage.

"Watch it! I'm a size six, you know!" She wriggles and squirms, but it's no use. "We need the key."

"But that monster has it…" He shakes his head fearfully.

"I know. They scare me too, but you know what? I bet you're really brave! You must be to have survived on your own in here. Once I'm out, we can find my sister, she'll know how to get us home."

"Home?" George's eyes twinkle. Jessica's warmth reminds him of his own sister.

"Yeah, I bet your mum and dad are worried. Mine are gonna flip out when I get back." She looks doleful and wonders how her parents are coping with her disappearance.

"It's just my mum," he says.

"Your dad's not around?" she asks.

George shakes his head and looks downcast.

"Well, then we've got to get you back to her, haven't we?" Determined to rescue this boy, with a devious grin she hatches a plan. "So you're good at hiding, huh?"

Down the corridor the goblin jailer is busy picking muck from between his crooked toes. He gets a good chunk loose and sniffs it when a scream startles him.

Jessica lets out a howling cry, a tantrum worthy of legend. "I demand to speak to whoever is in charge! If you think I'll get bored and stop you're wrong! I'm told I can be very, very annoying!" She kicks the bars and shrieks at the top of her lungs. "I know you're out there, you meatball-headed arsehole!"

Outside the door the goblin carefully feels the shape of its head, looking insecure.

"Meatball head! Meaaaaatbaaaaall head!" she shouts until the door slams against the wall, startling her.

The guard storms over and reaches through the bars to grab her, while George creeps out of the duct and pinches the key hanging from its belt. He's almost home free when the goblin

157

spots him out of the corner of its lazy eye. It hisses with spite and lunges for the boy, but Jessica wraps her arms around its head and with all her might pulls backwards, pressing against the bars with her feet for extra support. She slowly chokes the goblin until it passes out and collapses in a heap. She and George look at each other, both amazed that they actually pulled it off.

The kid tosses her the keys, and she unlocks the cell door. Together they drag the unconscious monster inside and lock him in.

"Let's go." She beams like sunshine.

Years of sneaking out of the house to attend band practice have unwittingly granted Jessica the stealth of a seasoned sneak-thief. She takes George by the hand and silently sprints through the winding corridors of the airship. A gleam of light at the end of the long hallway calls to her, and she bolts towards it. Halfway there, another goblin bursts out of a room to their left. Jessica and George dart behind the door as it swings open and the goblin wanders down the dark end of the corridor seemingly clueless to their presence. They tiptoe quietly to the end of the corridor and force open the metal bulk hatch, flooding the dark corridor with white-hot daylight. It feels like forever since Jessica has seen the sun. Desperate to breathe fresh air, she practically leaps outside. After her eyes adjust to the brightness she takes in her surroundings, and her jaw drops. Leaning over the railing of the airship's deck she sees nothing but clouds and swathing mist below. All this time, she had assumed she was underground.

"What the actual fuck?!" she cries, spiralling with despair. Her knees tremble like jelly. She's trapped on a flying ship full of monsters, stranded hundreds of feet in the air.

*

Deep underground Remy and Grimoirh traverse the crypt in silence, which she of course finds tortuously boring. But she's also burning to question him and doesn't know where to start, so she enacts a plan to gauge more information about her captor, under the guise of honest conversation. '*Killing with kindness*' as Ed put it.

"So how did you end up in the game?" she asks.

Grimoirh glances back at her, over the gigantic blade rested on his shoulder. "It doesn't matter."

"Well, if you really did create the remake then shouldn't you have some idea about how this is possible? Were you the first of us to get stuck here? What's your plan to get us back? And you still haven't told me what we're doing here."

His patience wears thin, and her voice grates on his ear, but he remains quiet.

"If you're not going to contribute I'll keep talking, and we both know you don't want that." A sly grin creeps across her face. If there's one thing she and Jessica share, it's their ability to gnaw away at someone's patience. "So how'd you end up stuck in your own creation?"

"I found myself in a small mountain village. Monsters came in the night and killed everyone. I froze up and I got cornered."

"So how did you get away?"

"I didn't. I thought I was done for, then it came to me. This cursed plate mail and the magic sword."

"It came to you?" she asks as a dismembered carcass springs to life and seizes her ankle. She gasps and Grimoirh swiftly crushes its head with a firm stomp.

"Th-thanks." She nods appreciatively, and kicks the husk to make sure it's dead. "What's with all the corpses anyway? You couldn't have filled the dungeon with chickens or something?"

"It's the shard. Its power perverts death."

"You don't have to explain it, I played the classic. I just meant you changed a bunch of other stuff, so—"

"Like what?"

"Well, the midgey merchants should be taller, and a man-eating forest? That wasn't in the old game and—"

The sound of stone grinding churns her stomach, and she feels the slab beneath her foot click into place. Grimoirh turns back to her with a look that says, 'you can't be serious'.

"Please don't say we're gonna die, because if I die due to my own reckless abandon, then my last thought will be that my mother was right, and I don't think I can rest in peace if that's the case."

"Just don't move!" Grimoirh snaps.

"Why would you say that? Now I can't not move!"

He shoots her a look of absolute disdain.

"Shouldn't something have happened by now? Maybe it's broken?" She gingerly shifts her weight onto her other leg.

"No! Don't mo—!"

Her foot is barely an inch off the plate when the ground crumbles, sending them both cascading through a hidden tunnel, deeper into the crypt. Remy covers her face as she glides through thick cobwebs until she's thrown out of the loathsome slide onto a huge pile of bones. Grimoirh crashes down shortly after her.

"My bad." She brushes cakes of dust off herself as she sits up.

"I'm starting to think I was wrong about you," the Dread Knight growls.

They find themselves in a buried ritual hall littered with empty sarcophagi, and towering stone pillars prop up the high ceiling. The slabbed floor is cracked at the centre, where a large pit is filled with piles of rotted corpses – possibly the former residents of the ruin or maybe ill-fated adventurers that fell prey to whatever abominable creature resides here.

A single undesecrated coffin stands out, much bigger than the others. Remy's chest spikes, and she remembers, just as a deep bellowing roar emanates from within the coffin, what foe she is about to face.

The stone lid cracks open, and a hulking suit of armour rises from the sarcophagus. The screech of metal against stone sets her teeth on edge as the dungeon boss drags its clunky body from its resting place. The armour looms above them appearing to move by itself, possessed by some transcendental force. From beneath its battle-scarred helmet two points of crimson light burn, like flaming ghostly eyes. The entity throws back its tattered brown cape and drags a colossal greatsword from the coffin. Its gargantuan bloodstained blade dwarfs them both.

Remy turns pale as it finally dawns on her what they're doing in this hell hole. "Nope! Hell nope! I'm out." She scrambles onto her feet to turn tail and leg it, but Grimoirh pulls her back.

"There." He points to the glowing green shard embedded in the armour's breastplate. "We have to hit the—"

"The shard. Yeah, I know." The Spectre Knight was a soul-crushing boss battle that took Remy weeks to best in the summer of 2002. She spent days grinding in the underground ruins to level her party up enough to withstand the monster's devastating attacks.

Grimoirh charges in while she scrambles amongst the bones in search of her sword. Taking it up in both hands, she whispers words of encouragement to herself.

"Don't die. Just don't die."

She approaches while Grimoirh has the spectre's attention and strikes the monster's leg, her blow recoiling off its armour, and she trips backwards.

Grimoirh lands a heavy blow but barely blemishes the spectre's armour. The Spectre Knight, in turn, launches a brutal assault. Again and again its tremendous blade comes crashing down on him. He parries a downward strike and counters. The creature howls as the jewel reverberates in its chest, and by no coincidence, a searing, nerve-shredding pain courses through Remy's hand. Her muscles writhe in a silent scream, and she tightens her fist and clenches her jaw until it subsides.

"Two more should do it!" Grimoirh cries. The rule of three always applies in a video game after all.

Shaking the pain off her hand, she nods determinedly and waits for an opening as the wraith obliterates a stone pillar, bringing down part of the ceiling with it.

Whoosh! Grimoirh narrowly avoids the blade soaring by him. He strikes the wraith's sword-wielding arm, knocking it off balance, then spins and sweeps its leg with his sword causing the spectral armour to come crashing down.

"Now!" he cries.

Remy seizes the opportunity and hammers her sword against the shard in its chest. A wave of pale green energy knocks her off her feet and the shard in her hand glows like a red-hot coal. She screams as the unbearable pain returns, only far greater this time, and grapples her arm as it contorts beyond her control. She could swear her flesh is moving in ways it couldn't possibly be.

"What is this?!" she howls as tears roll down her reddening face.

"The shards are connected, fractured pieces of a single living entity. You hurt one, they all feel it." Grimoirh stares at her hand with great interest. "You'll have to push through it."

"Easy for you to say." She grimaces as the pain subsides, and switches her sword to her left hand as she stands.

The dungeon boss too regains its footing and erupts in a frenzy, swinging blindly in all directions.

"How are we supposed to get near it now?" Remy asks.

"I'll distract it. If you see an opening, take it!"

Remy nods affirmatively and Grimoirh charges at the spectre again. His first strike prangs off the armour, then he unleashes a flurry of slashes and swipes, beating the dungeon boss back towards the pit filled with corpses. The God Cleaver bursts ablaze and he thrusts it forward to guard against the wraith's mighty blow. His blade's enchanted hellfire sears through the dungeon boss's weapon like a blowtorch, rending it in two. The top end hits the stone floor with a resounding clang, and as the spectre examines its broken weapon, Grimoirh plunges his sword through its right leg guard and with a twist, brings the dungeon boss to its knees.

"Hurry!" he shouts, before the wraith tosses aside its broken sword and grabs hold of his arms. He releases a roaring scream as it tries to tear his limbs from their sockets.

A profound breath summons courage, and Remy charges. Springing off the wraith's knee, she leaps and thrusts her sword into the shard with every ounce of might. Pure fiery energy bursts from the armoured shell, and the creature releases Grimoirh as it haemorrhages in pain. Remy reaches out with her right hand and grips the shard tightly. At her touch it resonates with the piece inside her, and the jewel glows bright as she prises it from the spectre's chest plate. The spirit beneath the plate mail vanishes with a bang that hurls Grimoirh across the room. Piece by piece the armour crashes to the floor, along with Remy, who clutches her right hand tightly while her muscles slither like serpents around her bones. She clenches her jaw and shuts her eyes until her suffering lessens. Her arm jolts forward as though possessed and reaches for the crystal shard lying amongst the heap of armour. She seizes her right hand in her left and squeezes it until she regains control over its movements. Letting out a thankful breath, she stares worriedly at her hand, and her pinky finger twitches, then her hand jerks again and snatches up the shard they've won.

She stares into its shimmering core, which throbs in her palm like a gentle heartbeat and resonates with her own pulse. She winces as the jewel bores into her flesh and her fingers seize up as the shards fuse beneath her skin. She shakes her hand, and balls and opens her fist to ensure that it still works like it should.

What was that? she wonders. *My arm moved like it had a mind of its own...*

163

She wiggles her fingers as the thought of going home and putting an end to this nightmare fills her with hope. "So how does this whole crystal thing work?" she asks. "If we have two now, can we use them to get home yet? Or do we need all three?"

"Where is home?" he asks.

"London, at least for now," she sighs.

"You don't like it?"

Remy shrugs. "Sometimes. It's crowded and expensive. Everyone that lives there acts like it's this amazing place to be, but it's not. It's suffocating and lonely all at the same time. If you don't have money then you're always fighting to stay above water. I hated living my life that way, but what else can you do? All the work is there. I guess I'm just sick of feeling like I don't matter."

"You matter now," he says.

"I don't know about that. Whatever these shards actually do, they don't seem to work for me."

"Maybe you lack conviction," he replies. "Only an unyielding will can command its power. You're too unsure of yourself. We survived that by the skin of our teeth. You need to be better if you're going to endure what's ahead."

She looks at his worn, scarred face and wonders, what did he have to become to survive, and was it worth it?

"What happened to you?" she asks.

He looks doleful as he recalls something he'd rather forget.

"Why are you pretending to be Grimoirh? You said you locked us up to protect us. If that's true then why not come with us? Together we'd all have a better shot at finding a way back. Don't you want to go home too?"

"What if..." he pauses, thinking on how to soften the blow of cold, hard truth, "... what if we couldn't go back?"

"But we can't stay here, this place isn't real, I mean, is it? I don't know anymore."

"It's all too real, and that's why this world has to end. What happened to me, to you and the others, can never happen again."

"But if this place is real then what happens to all the people that live here if you end it?"

"It doesn't matter. Ending the game world is the only way to stop all of this. If we don't act fast, more players will keep coming. We're only the beginning."

"The beginning?"

"Your sister told me a lot about you. You seem frustrated and lost. Your life lacks purpose and direction. Well, I'm offering you one. Help me. Help me destroy this abominable world."

"But if we can't go back... what happens to us?"

Grimoirh smiles sadly and reaches out, offering his hand to her. "Help me."

She takes a step back. "I don't understand."

Sensing her growing hesitance, he reaches out further. "This world is anything but a fantasy, Remy, it's a nightmare. It's cruel and rotten and very, very dangerous. It was never supposed to exist. So I'm asking you, forget the past. There's no going back for any of us, but together we can stop this from happening to anyone else. I'm offering you a choice. Isn't it better to die with purpose than live a meaningless life?"

"Die? You'd throw your life away? Just like that?" Noticing his eyes are locked on her right hand, she balls her fist.

"Do you really believe the crystal will help you? That thing is evil, it brings only death and ruin."

"From what I've seen, the only thing that brings death and ruin is you."

A moment's silence feels like an eternity. The cold look in his eyes makes plain there's no getting through to him, and her heart races as his intent dawns on her.

"You were never going to help us get home, were you?"

"No."

The word hits her with precision and sends a shiver down her spine. Her eyes dart to her sword discarded on the floor. She knows she'll never reach it before he reaches her, but maybe, just maybe, she could call on the crystal's power. Like he said, all it would take is a little conviction, and nothing breeds conviction like staring death in the face.

She thrusts her hand at the sword, and her palm shimmers with pale eldritch light, and, like magic, her sword flies towards her. Before she can catch it, Grimoirh's blade ignites with a roaring flame, and he strikes in a flash. Her right hand hits the floor with a thud. Spitting, hoarse screams swell from Remy's throat. She clutches her burning forearm, her bulging eyes fixed on the smoke rising from where her hand should be. She stumbles backwards in a desperate attempt to flee and tumbles into the pit of withered corpses.

Grimoirh takes her severed hand in his and looks regretfully at her stumbling around over the dead, which begin to wake up. He abandons her to her grim fate. The haunting scent of burnt flesh stings his nostrils, and her inhuman wails echo through the dungeon as he turns his back.

Hundreds of wights awaken around her. Clambering from every direction, they drag her into a lake of undead. Her jagged cries fall quiet as she's submerged, like a baptism of death.

X

RESCUE MISSION

E d sits outside the smouldering husk that was until recently the Legless Arms and gazes at the grand airship *Thanatos* hovering above. Following the battle in Trout, the Kingdom of Runegard has seized the village. Few townspeople remain. Most fled during the conflict and the others – well, they lay scattered about. Men, women, even children, struck down by the marauding goblin men, whose corpses are now piled up in the main square ready to be buried. All that survived of the midgey merchant's wagon are the blackened iron wheels. The little critter salvages what wares he can from the charred remains of the wagon box before the soldiers move him along.

A striking dark-skinned woman in shining silver armour points at Ed and Bengeo. "Bring them here," she commands.

Two soldiers drag them before her and throw them to the ground.

The woman grins spitefully. "Bengeo."

"Lieutenant Diamond." Bengeo grimaces as he sits up.

"It's captain now." She glares at him with piercing eyes.

"You know this lady?" Ed asks.

He grins. "Intimately."

"Where is the crystal shard?" Diamond asks.

"The shard? Remy has it, and Grimoirh has her," replies Ed.

The captain frowns. "You were supposed to deliver that shard to me, Bengeo. Take them to the ship."

At her word the soldiers pull Ed and Bengeo onto their feet.

"But what about Remy?" Ed asks.

"If Grimoirh has her, then she's as good as dead."

Her words hit him like a gut punch, and he hangs his head as the soldiers shove them aboard an air balloon.

"What are they going to do with us?" Ed whispers.

"Just let me do the talking," Bengeo replies.

The balloon ascends and Ed gazes at the floating warship with wonder as they approach. The moonlight glints against the decorated hull, which widens towards the bow. Deep crimson sails flap in the wind, and the gargantuan engines hum and whirr, rattling Ed's bones as they pass. Countless cannons and rail guns line the starboard side, and the weather-worn deck is awash with soldiers and ship hands readying the airship for departure. Ed and Bengeo are promptly escorted through corridors of iron and rosewood to the airship's bridge – a large oval room, from where the ship is piloted. Ed's wandering eyes drink everything in. The control consoles scattered around are all attended by crewmen all dressed in naval-looking uniform, and dozens of armoured soldiers stand alert along the edge of the room. The whole place has the feel of a military command centre about it.

General Gigas stands before a huge circular window, overlooking the prow of his ship. He notices Bengeo and Ed from the corner of his eye as they are brought to him.

"This war is going very badly, Bengeo." The general's voice is gruff and commanding.

"And just how many are you fighting these days?" Bengeo quips.

"How many are *we* fighting? You are, after all, a citizen of the Empire."

"Us bandits aren't real big on citizenship."

"Honestly, Bengeo, all the errands you run for me, how long until you realise you're as much of a soldier as I?"

"Forever, if I have anything to say about it."

Ed clears his throat and hesitantly asks, "General Gigas, right? We're after Grimoirh too, so why don't we work together?"

"What is this little man prattling on about?" Gigas arches his brow, perplexed by Ed's odd appearance and mannerisms. "I heard about your ship, Bengeo. We picked up a few survivors but not many."

"They knew the risks," the bandit laments.

"Indeed," Gigas nods, and eyes Ed one more time, intrigued in particular by the raggedy Converse trainers on his feet. "Are you one of them? An other-worlder?" he asks.

"Me?"

Ed glances at Bengeo, who shakes his head as if to say, '*tell him nothing*'.

"Uhh, I'm just a poor village boy—" Ed pretends to cough. "I hear the forest is haunted, you shouldn't go there," he says in a monotonous tone and utterly blank-faced, poorly imitating a non-player character.

Gigas isn't buying it and stares hawkishly while Ed sweats under the pressure. He's never been one to tangle with authority.

"He's just some kid that joined my crew. Whelp of a boy, survived the crash by some miracle," Bengeo laughs nervously.

The general sees right through their facade and glares with vitriol at Ed. "You people are a blight on this world as well. I don't know for what purpose Grimoirh is summoning your kind, but be certain I will hunt and destroy every last one of you. The shard, do you have it?"

"Our friend has it, and Grimoirh has her, but if we hurry—"

The general interrupts Ed's outburst. "If your little crystal-harbouring friend isn't dead already, rest assured I'll kill her myself."

"But you can't kill Tron!" Ed cries. "Wait, Tron was actually part of the game so that would make Bengeo Tron, and Remy Jeff Brid— Ugh!" Bengeo jams his elbow in Ed's stomach, silencing him.

Gigas sighs. "You've always been a remarkably loyal scoundrel, Bengeo, so long as the coin was good, but to think you've thrown your lot in with these foreigners? Heresy!" he hisses. "For your treason, you shall hang with them." The general signals to his men to take them away.

"Wow, he's got some real prejudices, huh?" Ed whispers as the guards drag them into the bowels of the airship and toss them into one of the prison cells divided like the spokes of a wheel about the circular holding room. All of them are empty save for one, which is occupied by two badly beaten men who are sound asleep in only their briefs. Ed dreads to think what was done to them. He slumps against the bars and releases a doleful sigh.

"I'm right back where I started."

"Swings and roundabouts, kid," Bengeo says, hoping, but failing, to lift Ed's spirits.

"Whatever…" he sulks as the severity of the situation sinks in.

Bengeo places a hand on his wound, which is aching somewhat after his brawl with the Dread Knight.

"You okay?" Ed asks, to which Bengeo shrugs. "Come on, let me see."

"It's fine. If I'm lucky I'll die before Gigas hangs me. Heh heh, that'll really piss him off."

Ed plants himself opposite Bengeo. "I did not see my life going this way," he says.

"This is exactly how I pictured mine," Bengeo smirks, but Ed doesn't share his cavalier attitude.

Instead he twiddles his shoelaces while his mind is flooded with what-ifs. What if he had been able to stop Grimoirh from taking Remy? Or prevent Jessica from being petrified? Or spoken up about the dungeon boss sooner and saved Matt from being squished? What if he hadn't befriended Barney in secondary school? He would never have got into role-playing games and so never would've played Ultimate Adventure. What if he hadn't spent so much of his time in fictional worlds, pretending he was someone stronger, or smarter? Someone people could rely on, someone that could protect his friends. Toxic thoughts poison his mind and tears well in his eyes. He blinks them away and wipes his face with his sleeve.

"Phwoar, the dust in here is making my allergies flare up." He pretends to cough and tries not to let on how emotionally fragile he feels to the hulking specimen of manliness sharing his cell.

But Bengeo takes pity on the poor boy. "You... You want a hug or something?"

"What?"

"I dunno, isn't that what... Forget it."

Ed grins ear to ear.

"I was just trying to... Shut up."

"Look at us. What a pair we are," he says.

"We're not a pair. We're nothing alike."

"Sure." He places his hand on Bengeo's shoulder, which the bandit swats away.

"I tried to be nice, but my head said don't do it, you give this boy an inch, he'll take a mile. But I looked at you, your soft girlish frame, tears in your eyes and I felt such pity. I just couldn't stand by and watch, but you proved me right."

"Usually you just punch me in the arm and tell me to sack up."

The bandit lies down and faces away from Ed. "Wake me before our execution. Wouldn't wanna miss that."

"Come on, don't be like that."

"Like what?"

"All closed off. We've been travelling together for a few days, and I don't know much about you. I got kidnapped before I could play your backstory quest."

"My what?" Bengeo looks back at Ed, more confused than ever.

"Uh, never mind," Ed mumbles.

They sit for an awkward minute until Bengeo reluctantly decides to participate. "Well, what do you do? Where you come from?"

Ed looks pleasantly surprised that he's taken an interest. "I work in a comic shop, the hours aren't bad."

"What's a comic?"

"It's like a book, but the story is told with pictures."

"People don't read words in your world?" the bandit probes.

"Not as much as they should," Ed laughs.

"So do you like it?"

"My job? I dunno... I guess it's nice to be surrounded by what you love." Bengeo nods as Ed continues, "It's not what I want to do forever, but for now it's okay. The whole country's in the shitter at the moment so—"

"So what do you want to do?" the bandit asks.

"What do I want to do?" Ed rubs his hand through his hair and twiddles it between his fingers. "I guess, I mean, I've always wanted to create my own graphic novel." He braces himself, expecting ridicule, but Bengeo seems nonplussed. "You don't think that's dumb?" he asks, with wide, vulnerable eyes.

The bandit shakes his head. "I can definitely see you creating a graphic novel. Follow the road your heart takes you down, I say."

Ed beams with renewed affirmation. "Thanks, man. I think I needed to hear that."

Bengeo smiles. "Don't mention it. Now, sleep."

The two lie top-to-toe on the floor of the cramped cell. After a moment, Bengeo sits up. "Hey, Ed?"

"Yeah, buddy?"

"What's a graphic novel?"

Ed's chipper disposition fades, along with his confidence.

"Forget it." He rolls on his side, away from Bengeo, and stares out through the bars at a little spider crossing the rough wooden floor. His eyes begin to feel heavy. After a few minutes he's out like a light.

*

The last of the soldiers return to the *Thanatos* in their air balloons, and Captain Diamond takes one final look at the ruined town before boarding hers. Black scorches marr the few houses left standing. Piles of black ash and charred wood are all that remain of the general store. A faint wind scatters the ash across the bloodstained cobblestone, over to where some villagers muck together to clear some of the rubble. She notices a young girl, covered in soot, sitting atop the smouldering ruins of her house. Her life has been destroyed by the conflict. Her parents likely didn't survive the battle, or fled without her. The orphan watches the captain from across the courtyard, admiring her shiny armour and gleaming rapier.

"Are you coming, Captain?" a soldier calls to her from the last balloon on the ground.

"What kind of empire abandons its people?" She looks shamed and leaves the villagers to pick up the pieces of their tattered lives.

Her balloon docks on the portside of the warship where she is greeted on the deck by General Gigas, whose crimson mantle dances in the wind as the rising sun glints off his armour.

"At ease, Diamond," he nods.

"Aye, sir." She relaxes, and follows him towards the nose of

173

the ship. "Our scouts say Grimoirh fled south-west towards the wetlands."

"Well, I'll be glad to see the back of this hole," he says.

"Aye, sir," she nods. "... Sir, can we not spare a few men to help the townsfolk rebuild?"

"Absolutely not," he scolds her. "We need every man available for the war effort. Grimoirh, his accursed army, attacks ever more prevalent on the roads and now these invaders from this other world. I would conscript every able man and woman from that village were there any left."

Diamond winces at his disposition. "But sir, surely—"

"Enough of your bleeding heart ideology, Captain. Fret not, there will always be more poor people. They're like rodents. They breed quickly and spread like a disease," he scoffs at her sentiment. "The *Thanatos* is yours. Find the Dread Knight, I'm going to have a talk with our other-worlder captive."

Diamond breathes a sigh of relief at his departure, and steels her heart before returning to the bridge.

*

Ed awakens from his nap in a completely different room. It's dark, save for the flicker of the oil lamp placed on a table in front of him. He motions to sit up, but his arms and legs are bound to an iron chair bolted to the floor. Gigas looms opposite him, wearing a stern expression on his old, weathered face, illuminated from beneath like the villain in an old horror flick.

Ed looks worriedly at his restraints. "How did I get here?"

The general nods to the guard by the door. "She carried you. You wouldn't wake up. One would think you were dead."

"I'm a heavy sleeper, my dad says it's because—"

Gigas jabs a dagger into the table, which springs back and forth as he releases it.

"Some do not take the threat of your kind seriously. I, however, am under no illusion that your coming is a declaration of war."

"Whoa, wait a minute! We're not trying to start a war with anybody. Swear!" Ed laughs nervously as the general tightens his eyes. "Look, I'll tell you whatever you want, just please don't hurt me. I mean… I don't know anything, I don't think, but I'll tell you what I do know, whatever that is."

Convinced Ed's blathering is part of a ploy to confuse him, Gigas grows angry. "Silence, you impotent worm! How did you come here? What is your goal?"

"Hell if I know, all we're trying to do is get home and rescue Jessica and now Remy, I guess and, well… now me?"

"What are you babbling about?" The general curls his lips back across his gritted teeth.

"One minute I'm eating Pot Noodles and playing video games and the next I'm facing off with a giant tentacle monster in a real-life dungeon."

"What monster?"

"It had this glowing gem inside, that's what Grimoirh wanted!"

"Yes, the shard." Gigas' interest is piqued. "Tell me everything you know about it." He grips Ed by the throat.

"I don't know much, I avoided spoilers!" he replies in a raspy voice as the general tightens his grip. "Ugh! Too tight! Too tight!" He squirms but Gigas' hold is relentless. "Wait, wait, the game! The game!" he gasps as Gigas releases him.

"What game?"

"In the game, Grimoirh's goal is to reforge the crystal and use it to destroy the living world."

Gigas turns wan. "Until now the crystals were mere myth, some even doubted their existence, their location was lost to time. How does he know where they are?"

Ed shrugs. "Beats me."

"You know things you shouldn't, other-worlder, perhaps too much to be allowed to live." The general draws the dagger from the table and wonders whether or not he should end Ed, who sweats under the general's spiteful eye.

The interrogation room door bursts open and a soldier enters the room.

"Sir, Grimoirh's ship is on the horizon. You're needed aboard the bridge!"

Gigas places the dagger down. "Watch him!" he barks at the female guard by the door and storms out of the room with the other soldier.

Ed slumps back in the chair and tries to soothe his shot nerves. "I can't take much more of this," he groans. "A guy shouldn't have to face his own mortality more than once a day."

The female guard slinks towards him and picks up the dagger from the table. "Well, I'm sorry to say it's about to get worse." She cuts Ed's arms loose.

"Is this some sort of trick?" He clings on to the chair.

"No trick. Follow me if you want to live." After freeing his legs she pulls him onto his feet. "Stay quiet and keep your head down."

"Who are you?" he asks.

"A friend," she whispers.

*

Bengeo examines the wound on his side, which, thanks in no small part to Esmerelda's magic, is healing nicely, but the bandit is weary from his travels. He rubs his tired eyes, which are framed by dark circles, and sighs.

"You don't look so hot," a guard jests as he enters the holding room.

"Yeah well, at least I don't have to hide my ugly mug under a tin can," Bengeo quips.

"Something tells me this ugly mug is gonna put a smile on your face." The guard throws off his helmet, letting his long blonde hair loose around his rugged face. "Been a while, boss!"

Bengeo grins widely. "Marcus?! Ha ha! I knew you wouldn't get eaten by a tree!"

"Looks like you've been through some hell." Marcus motions to Bengeo's wound.

"Ah, ain't no thing." Bengeo covers the wound with his jacket. "Who else made it after the crash?"

"Just Cleo. She's gettin' your boy outta interrogation." Marcus unlocks Bengeo's cell and pats his old friend on the shoulder.

"How'd you two get out?" Bengeo asks.

Marcus points at the pair of naked, beaten men lying unconscious in the adjacent cell. "You know Cleo," he smiles, "she knows how to work her assets."

As the bandits turn the corner out of the holding room they come upon Ed and Cleo skulking down the corridor.

"How's your boo boo?" Ed asks Bengeo.

"Sore, but it ain't gonna stop me from bashing a few skulls should the need arise." Bengeo cracks his knuckles. "It's time to blow this scene."

*

The *Thanatos* finally comes upon Grimoirh's ship, hovering above the misty mire.

"Tear that thing out of the sky!" Gigas commands his crew. "Launch the tethers! He won't outrun us again."

The soldiers stand to attention. "Aye, sir!" they salute in unison, then mobilise.

Gigas turns to Diamond with a malicious grin. "He'll rue the day he stole that ship from us."

Diamond nods and glares out at the ship across the sky, a bitter reminder of Grimoirh's one-up over Gigas and the mighty

Kingdom of Runegard. Her eyes tighten. Today they take back what's theirs.

*

Jessica scurries on all fours through a maze of sweltering ducts that wind through the bowels of Grimoirh's ship. She mops the sweat running from her forehead to her eyes and looks irritably ahead at George who scuttles in front of her.

"Are you sure you know where you're going?" she asks.

"I've been in plenty of ships like this, trust me," he replies, with more certainty than a lost child should possess.

"I can't believe I'm taking orders from a nine-year-old," she mutters.

"I'm eleven! And *I can't believe* I'm stuck on an escort mission."

"Hey, I'm the one escorting you!"

The grate beneath her gives way and she plummets with a squeal and dangles above a giant chasm overlooking the colossal cylindrical engine chamber. George grabs hold of her arm, but neither of them possess the strength to pull her back up.

"Don't look down!" he warns.

Jessica immediately looks down and gasps at the enormous roaring machines powering the ship.

"Can you swing over to that platform?" George points to a metal walkway suspended below that runs throughout the centre of the engine chamber.

Jessica assesses the distance and nods.

"I'll find a way down. Be careful." He races through the rest of the vent, to greet her before she lands.

Jessica brings her other arm up and grips the edge of the vent with both hands, then she swings her legs forward and back to gain momentum.

She begs the universe, *Please don't let me die,* and with one great swing lets go of the vent, free-falls through the air and crashes into the side of the walkway. She clings for dear life to the railing and hears George's trainers squeak against the metal as he sprints towards her. He grabs her jacket tightly, and with his help, she pulls herself over the railing and collapses on the bridge.

As her pounding heart slows and her legs stop shaking, she asks, "So what now?"

George looks panicked. "What? I thought you had the plan?"

"I do. I do," Jessica assures him. "Just let me think."

She runs her eyes over the massive gears and giant pistons that whirr and grind, and notes the numerous consoles suspended throughout the chamber on platforms that branch off the long walkway, which she assumes must control the engines somehow.

"Hurry it up before those goblins catch us," George says.

"You know, you're a pretty demanding kid!" Her mind races for a solution to ground the airship. She approaches the nearest console and stares at the metal block covered with dials, gauges, levers and buttons – not exactly the smartphone technology she's used to. An idea forms in her mind. She reasons that if she can damage the engines, then whoever is flying this thing will have no choice but to land it.

She pokes a long brass pipe protruding from the console and tries with all her might to prise it loose, so she can use it to jam one of the gears, but alas, the pipe's welded on. Like her sister and mother, patience doesn't top her list of redeeming qualities, so it isn't but a minute before she's kicking the pipe as hard as she can. The clank of her boots striking metal resounds through the chamber, alerting a goblin engineer to their presence. The crooked creature lifts its welding goggles and spots them both. With a grunt it strides across the walkway towards George who has his back turned and is too engrossed by Jessica to notice.

The umpteenth kick dislodges the pipe just as the goblin reaches George and inadvertently blasts it with scalding hot engine oil. The creature shrieks, trips backwards over the railing and lands between two massive cogs which crush and mangle its body to mush, swiftly grinding the starboard engines to a halt.

"Wow, that worked!" George cheers.

"Oh God! S-sorry!" Jessica covers her mouth, and the sight of the goblin's innards dripping out of the machinery burns itself into her mind. She'll never sleep soundly again.

A deafening bang reverberates through the chamber. She and George look worried at each other as the centre of gravity shifts and the airship tilts to one side. The explosion draws a pack of monstrous henchmen onto the walkway, and as soon as Jessica spots them, she pulls George in the opposite direction.

"Don't look back!" she cries, sprinting across the skewed catwalk.

George, being an eleven-year-old boy, absolutely has to look back now that she's told him not to and glances over his shoulder at the bloodthirsty monsters chasing him.

"I looked back!" he whimpers.

"How bad is it?" Jessica asks.

"It's bad!"

They skid to a halt as more goblins cut them off on the far side of the catwalk blocking their escape. It gets worse.

*

From behind a stack of supply crates aboard the deck, Ed and the others watch the captain mobilise her men. Soldiers rush about, readying cannons and manoeuvring large turrets to draw on the Dread Knight's ship as they approach.

Bengeo tightens his eyes, across the sky, as Grimoirh's vessel leans to one side. "Something's wrong."

"It's gotta be Remy," Ed grins with renewed hope. "She's giving them hell over there."

"Prepare to fire on my signal!" Diamond raises her rapier. "Now!" she cries.

BOOM! A volley of massive harpoons hurtle through the clouds and tear through the hull of the Dread Knight's airship. The crew wind massive wheels, which in turn retract the chains, reeling in their target like a captured whale.

Bengeo creeps up on two soldiers operating one of the huge harpoon cannons and grabs the men by their helmets, then he slams them into each other with enough force to knock them out cold. Cleo and Ed arm themselves with the guards' weapons while Bengeo and Marcus finish aiming the turret.

"Boss, you sure this is a good idea?" Cleo asks.

"Ask him," Bengeo nods to Ed, "I'm just along for the ride." He releases the lever and a harpoon soars across the sky and pierces the starboard side of Grimoirh's ship.

"Go on ahead, I'll stay back to cover your escape," Marcus says, tying his long hair back.

"You sure?" Bengeo asks.

"That thing is going down, you better make sure you ain't on it when it does. I'll buy you some time on this side." The two bandits bump forearms in a sort of brotherly salute before Marcus takes off across the deck screaming at the top of his lungs.

Captain Diamond spots him fleeing from the guards, and her first instinct is to give chase, but she senses something is afoot and surveys the area for more trouble. Her predatory eye spots her prisoners, attempting the unfathomable. The three of them are skirting along one of the chromium chains tethering the two airships.

*

The goblin men surrounding George and Jessica move in for the kill. She pulls the boy close to her as the nasty creatures charge

181

with ill intent. As all hope seems lost, one of the harpoons blasts through the side of the ship and tears the edge of the catwalk to shreds. She shields George as another harpoon rips a gaping hole in the hull behind them, and she clings to the boy with one hand, while lunging for the railing with the other as the blustering wind sucks the goblins out into the sky.

"Hold on to me!" she shrieks.

George wraps his arms around her waist, locking his hands tightly as they're both lifted off their feet.

*

"You still sure this is a good idea?" Cleo yells to Ed who looks sickly as he shimmies along the chain. The mist and cloud shroud the earth below, making it difficult to tell exactly how high they are, but the fall is undoubtedly fatal.

The chain wobbles abruptly, up and down. Looking back towards the *Thanatos*, Ed spots Diamond sprinting towards them, like some nimble cheetah stalking its prey along a tree branch.

"Hey, Bengeo! Your girlfriend is coming right at us!"

The bandit looks back at her and growls, "Keep going, I'll deal with it." He climbs around Ed and Cleo to cut her off.

In one swift leap, the captain unleashes a flurry of swipes, which the bandit barely evades.

"Damnit, woman, give it up, will you?!" Bengeo barks.

"You know I hate when you call me that!" she hisses, thrusting her blade again. He parries and catches her arms, and the two of them wrestle with one another thousands of feet in the air until she slithers from his iron grip and strikes him in his arrow wound.

"Bah, cheap shot!" Bengeo loses his footing but catches the chain in his hands and dangles below her.

The captain raises her rapier and grins victoriously. "You never should've forsaken the kingdom, Bandit!"

"You should've come with me," he smirks, hoping to charm his way out of the precarious situation he's found himself in – fat chance.

She jabs her sword as he swings perilously between chain links, dodging her attacks, until finally, that smug look on his face gets the better of her and she loses her ice-cold composure. With a broad slash, her diamond blade severs the chain between them.

"Ha ha! Got you," Bengeo laughs raucously as the chain breaks into two halves and he swings away.

She curses his name as she clings to her end of the chain and hurtles through the air back towards the *Thanatos*.

Ed and Cleo, having made it across, wait at the gaping hole in the hull caused by their harpoon, watching as the bandit climbs towards them.

*

With all her might, Jessica drags herself and George off the collapsing walkway and scrambles through the ship's labyrinthine passages. Her wide eyes dart left and right as she desperately tries to find a way outside. A sharp turn finds them at a criss-cross of corridors and faced by a pack of bloodthirsty goblins, clasping knives, rusty cleavers and beaten old shields, but before the monsters rush them, three more figures emerge from the corridor to her left.

"Hey!" she recognises Ed as he sprints past.

He skids to a halt and looks at her with a wide grin. "You're not a rock?!"

The goblins shriek, immediately dispelling his joy. He hooks his neck the other way at the angry mob.

"Uh, run!" He pulls Jessica by the arm and chases after Bengeo and Cleo who ran ahead.

"Where's Remy?" Jessica asks.

"I don't exactly know, she should be on board somewhere," he replies.

"You lost my sister?!" she barks as he pushes her up a set of coiling iron stairs.

The goblins pile on behind them. Their snarls and shrieks resound up the staircase, sending Jessica's heart racing. Cleo reaches the top first, but the exit is barred by a door she can't open. Bengeo rams it with his shoulder again and again while the goblins' harrowing chants grow louder with every second.

"I always imagined I'd die like this," Ed whimpers.

"Why would you ever imagine dying like this?!" Jessica shouts.

Ed shrugs. He's always been blessed with an overactive imagination.

"Well, I'm not going out easy!" Cleo twirls her sword, and braces herself for their last stand while Bengeo attacks the door with increasing ferocity.

"Won't budge!" Bengeo throws his arms up, then steps in front of his companions, ready to defend them to the death.

As the goblins round the final flight of steps, the mangled corpse jammed between the huge cogs in the engine chamber breaks loose and the overheated engines surge and combust in a violent explosion.

The stairway rattles and a surge of blazing fire rips through the bottom half of the ship, which crumbles towards the mire below, tearing all but the top few steps of the staircase with it. The party cling to the railings and each other for dear life while the monsters pursuing them are sucked into the chaotic hellfire below.

"Holy shit!" Ed screams over the roaring gale force winds.

"What now?!" Jessica asks.

"Let's get this door open!" Bengeo insists.

"Uh, sorry but who are you?" She looks warily at the hulking bandit.

"It's cool, he's on our side," Ed reassures her. "He saved Remy and me."

Bengeo nods proudly and shakes her hand, squeezing with hearty enthusiasm.

"Whoa, you're strong," Jess laughs nervously and rubs her hand as the blood flows back to it.

*

A deafening crackle from above halts Lauren and Valentine's ascent of the ruin. They stare wildly at the *Thanatos* bombarding the airship, which is now breaking in two. The bottom half plunges into the swamp in a spectacular blaze.

"Christ almighty!" Valentine says. "Can you believe what we're seeing?" He perches against the crumbling bricks and holds his head in his hands while his mind tries to comprehend the unreal events of the past few hours. He stares at the flaming shipwreck, which incinerates the roaming undead as they blindly wander towards it, and frowns. "Well, whoever's up there isn't going to help us now."

Lauren looks guilty as she contemplates whether or not to share her theory that they're somehow inside Ultimate Adventure VII. Ultimately she decides against it, reasoning that it probably wouldn't make him feel better anyway, and she's not sure if she believes it herself. She looks downcast and spots a figure striding out of the ruin across a crumbling stone bridge beneath them. She instantly recognises the black armour and hulking greatsword on his back. It's Grimoirh. The sight of him fills her with dread. The last thing she wants is to cross paths with the game's big bad, so she ducks behind some rubble and signals for Valentine to do the same.

He shakes his head, unable to interpret her frantic gestures, so she pulls him down beside her and points to the man in black from cover.

"Who's that?" he asks.

Lauren's eyes tighten on Grimoirh as he stops and gazes up at the warring airships. Immediately she realises something isn't right. In the game, Grimoirh is a suit of living armour possessed by the malevolent will of the crystal, but there's a man under that black plate mail. She watches him curiously as he beholds the catastrophe unfolding above. They're a distance apart, but Lauren can just make out his face as he turns their way. It's Vincent! There's no mistaking him. Her dread is instantly dispelled and without a second thought, she leaps over the rocks and stumbles down the ruins after him.

"What the hell are you doing, girl?!" Valentine hisses at her, but she pays him no mind.

She trips onto the crumbling stone bridge with a thud but wastes no time picking herself up and jogs towards Vincent.

"Hey!" she waves her arms to get his attention. Her voice gives her away before he sees her.

His face turns wanly in surprise and then sadness. He had hoped she wouldn't be drawn into any of this. Turning away in shame, he foolishly prays that she'll leave him be.

"Vincent?!" Lauren gasps. He turns back slightly, hesitant to show his face.

The wind howls across the bridge as booming cannon fire echoes from on high. Vincent stands tall, clad in his black plate mail, the God Cleaver resting on his back, but Lauren is looking only at the man beneath it all.

"It *is* you!" she smiles. "What's going on?! Are we... Are we in the game? Is this why you disappeared? How is this possible?" She blurts question after question. "I was worried something awful had happened to you, but... are we really in the game?! I can't believe it!"

She's as naive and goofy as he remembers. The sight of her beaming at him while her long bedraggled hair dances in the wind brings a flicker of a smile that he quickly banishes.

"You're okay, right?" she asks.

"You shouldn't be here."

His words stagger her. She'd played this moment over in her head the last few days but had never considered he'd greet her so coldly. She also never considered their reunion would take place inside a video game, but right now she'd rather sweat the stuff that can be explained.

"I don't understand, Vincent, what's going on?"

"I'm sorry this happened to you," he croaks.

She notices the dismembered hand he's clutching and asks in horror, "What is that? And why are you dressed like Grimoirh?"

He glances at Remy's hand and then back at Lauren. "This world is too dangerous for you. Where I'm going you can't follow. Find Bengeo the Bandit, he's sheltering other players, you'll be safe with him."

"Bengeo? So we really are in the game? How is that possible?" she asks, but he seems reluctant to share the answers she craves.

"Hey!" Valentine cries out as he jogs over. "Don't go running off like that!" He hunches over once he reaches her and rests his hands against his knees.

Startled by the detective, Vincent draws his weapon.

"Easy there, fella." Valentine holds his hands up, clearly intimidated by the ridiculously oversized sword pointed at him and wonders, *How could a man lift that thing?*

"It's okay, he's with me." Lauren urges Vincent to lower his weapon.

"Who's this guy?" Valentine asks.

"Uh, he's my boss," she replies.

"Eric Garland?"

Vincent looks thunderstruck on hearing Eric's name. "Eric? Eric's alive?!"

Lauren nods, confused, and Vincent's searching eyes dart wildly while he contemplates what this could mean. Before she can ask why he would think Eric was dead, Valentine yelps and points at a hunk of debris hurtling towards them from the warring airships above. The three of them don't make it two metres before the flaming scrap decimates the bridge beneath their feet and they crash into the crypt below.

Smoke and dust scatter the air, bathing the room in streaks of sickly light. Valentine groans before he picks himself up.

"Christ, that hurt…" he winces as he cracks his neck.

Vincent is already on his feet and shifting the rubble. "Help me find her!" he barks.

Valentine springs to action and they claw through the soot and rocks until they come upon her.

"Come on, you're alright!" Valentine brushes Lauren down as she coughs the dust from her lungs. He examines the nasty gash on her head. It's bleeding pretty badly but thankfully appears superficial.

A hiss from above heralds danger amidst the dust cloud. The crash has attracted a horde of undead, which stagger over the collapsed bridge and flop into the room. Landing with a wallop, their bodies crash and writhe towards their prey.

Vincent picks up his sword. "Take her and go." He pushes Lauren towards the detective.

"Wait!" she protests. "Come with us! We can find Bengeo together!"

Vincent looks distressed, and she senses there's a lot he's not telling her.

"There's too many of them!" he cries as his enchanted sword ignites with unholy fire. "Go, I'll hold them back." He cleaves a walking corpse in half as it rushes him.

Lauren gasps as the dismembered pieces slide across the stone floor.

"Come on, girl. We best listen to the man." Valentine pulls her away as dozens more undead rain down around them and ushers her through a narrow passageway leading into the crypt.

She looks back over her shoulder as she runs, stealing glances at Vincent, who contends with the frightening wights and living skeletons, until he's out of sight. Faint echoes of his battle swell before the passage collapses behind them.

Little does she know, Vincent had collapsed it purposefully to protect them from any stragglers and to stop her coming after him. He cuts the monsters down then takes a moment's rest. Leaning against his sword he watches as his ship is decimated by General Gigas and the *Thanatos*. The top half of it is barely kept afloat by the massive helium-filled balloons supporting it. He picks up Remy's severed hand and examines it. Gripping it tightly he pictures in his mind the most powerful creature in the game. The hand pulses with shimmering light and the fingers twitch as he raises it to the heavens and calls upon the crystal's power. Magical glyphs emanate from the blackened palm and call forth a monstrous dragon that materialises from an otherworldly void. Pitch black and crystalline, it spreads its wings with a shattering chime. Vincent mounts the great beast and takes off, roaring into the sky.

XI

A Light in the Darkness

In the deepest, darkest depths of the crypt, Remy wrestles against the dead, who clumsily fumble over one another and drag her deeper into the pit of corpses. Reeling from the loss of her right hand, she struggles to push them off her and chokes, between raw unanswered screams, on the permeating stench of their necrotic flesh. Any splinters of hope diminish as the surface slips out of sight.

I'm dead. Fuck. I'm dead. Dead, dead, dead! Her mind races and her bounding heart thuds in her chest. Exhausted, hurt and alone in the dark – she's found herself here before but never quite so literally. With nothing to look forward to but a grim and painful demise she thinks back to the dark void when she crossed worlds and tries to imagine the freeing weightlessness it brought, but coarse leathery hands pull her in all directions like warring forces of gravity. Certain her thread is about to be cut, she closes her teary eyes and drowns out the haunting chorus of a thousand shrieking corpses. Flashes of her life come to her like a cresting wave. She remembers vividly the first time she laid eyes on little Jessica, this bright-eyed little thing looking up at her with promise. She remembers when her mother told her their two families would become one, that this was to be her little sister, and it was her job to look out for her – a task her young self spurned. She wonders why, as one of the corpses sinks its rotten teeth into her shoulder. The pain jolts through her body. Snapping her eyes wide open, she lets out a blubbering cry as transient glimpses of light catch her eye. She's sure that this is the light everyone talks about, the one at the end of the proverbial tunnel. It takes every ounce of strength she's got to climb and claw her way through the ravenous tide. She bursts to the surface with a heart-rending cry and is met by shimmering, radiant warmth. Glowing like life itself, the light takes the form of a bird as it hovers over the pit and scorches the undead with its divine rays. The creatures cower and scramble into the recesses of darkness as the glowing apparition signals Remy to follow it. She drags herself over the rotting horrors until her left hand clasps the pit's edge. Her fingernails scrape against the stone as she throws her weight forward, pressing her feet against a wailing corpse's head to push herself up, then she drags herself to safety using her burned stump. Her knees quiver like a newborn deer. She can barely stay on her feet long enough to take a step, but she presses on after the ghostly apparition which flutters through the winding tunnels. Tripping and staggering on the uneven floor, she skins her knees and drags herself up against the walls for support, glancing fearfully behind her all the way.

The insatiable hunger of the undead proves greater than their fear of the divine light, and they crawl after her. They've tasted her sweet flesh, and they want the rest.

The spectre leads her to a dead end. With a twirl it zips around her then passes through the solid wall.

"No! No! Come back!" She beats the stone with her balled fist and skims the wall in search of a secret switch or something, anything, to get her out of this mess.

Snarling, gnashing and shrieking resounds through the tunnel, hitting her like waves of terror. She spins around, presses her back to the wall and sweeps her matted hair out of her eyes.

Weapon, need a weapon! She snatches the burning torch mounted on the wall to her left, and the stone behind her grinds open, revealing a secret passage. She slips through and tumbles down wide steps, while the torch rolls ahead of her, throwing strange shadows across the dome-shaped hall.

Picking herself up, she gazes frantically at the intricate murals painted and carved onto the spherical walls around her. A twinkle catches her eye. In the weathered hand of a crumbling monument to some long-forgotten warrior sits an unusual sword. The undead tumble out of the passage entrance and hurl themselves down the stairs after her.

"Fucking hell." She rushes towards the statue, leaping onto it with arms flung wide. It's a struggle without the use of both hands, but she manages to scale it, wrapping her thighs around its shoulders, and she reaches for the blade held over where its head used to be, then pulls it free. At her touch the sword jitters and the sleeping eyeball carved onto the ornate hilt blinks open.

"Hello there." The sword speaks in a chipper voice, startling Remy, who loses her footing and slips off the monument. Her back strikes the floor with a thud, winding her. Still, she crawls towards the sword lying in the dirt. Her hand grasps the handle and again the weapon springs to life, bobbing up and down, slashing and swishing in all directions. She can barely hold on to it as it pulls her onto her feet and charges the monsters.

"Fight me! Fight me! Fight me!" the sword cries, and in one broad swipe, it splits a walking corpse from hip to shoulder, spraying Remy with blood and guts.

"Ugh!" She spits the rancid fluids from her mouth as she's thrown about like a rag doll.

"Pathetic, bring me a worthy opponent!" the sword cackles before making short work of the remaining monsters. As the last decapitated head rolls onto the floor, the blade instantly returns to its inanimate state, and the eye blinks shut as all life seemingly fades from it.

Remy collapses on her knees, resting her head between her legs, breathing slow and deep to ease her nerves. Once she's got a grip, she inspects her strange sword. Its peculiar handle appears to be carved from some kind of bone, bound in strange leather, and the hilt is sculpted to resemble a demonic face. The blade itself is dark, like black iron or obsidian, and is edged on both sides. She grips it tightly in her quaking hand and looks about the darkened hall, at the decaying statues and murals, which appear to tell a story of how the great crystal came to be and was subsequently shattered and scattered across the world. She can only make out fragments as most of the mural has crumbled and rotted, but thanks to the plot points she already knows from playing the old game she can piece it together. Some malevolent force came to Pangea Ultima long ago and spread a foul sickness that rose an army of the dead – could they be the undead remnants that wander this dungeon?

The adrenaline drains from her body and the searing pain in her right arm returns. She examines her swollen burned stump, buries her hand in her tangled hair and clutches her head as the pain sends her spirit howling. She curls on her side in the darkness and thinks of her parents, her sister, of Ed and Bengeo. The thought of never seeing any of them again breaks her heart. She's sure that she'll meet her end here, a forgotten nobody, who died alone and afraid, and shuts her eyes as tears spill down her face, resigning herself to fate.

A gravelly voice disturbs her isolation. It echoes from the blackness, reverberating through a passage high above her, that leads out of the chamber she's trapped in.

"Hello?!" she calls out but gets no answer. "Is anyone there?"

After a moment the voice calls back. "Who's that?"

Remy's eyes widen and twinkle with hope. She's not alone. "H-help me! Please!" she begs. "I'm hurt!"

"Ah, this better not be a trick! Who are you?" the ill-tempered voice asks.

"Remy! My name's Remy!" Her eyes dart wildly about the dark hall as she waits on tenterhooks for a reply. "Hello?!" she croaks.

No reply, but the sound of footsteps fast approaching renews her hope, then a silhouette of a man appears above her, obscured by a lit torch he's holding in front of his face – but not the flaming kind, the light is white and focused like a flashlight.

"Remy Winters?!" the voice asks.

"Y-yeah?" She shields her eyes from the light as he points it at her face.

"Well, shit," the man mutters, "I've been looking for you."

His gravelly voice certainly isn't the stuff of angels, but it sounds like rescue. He crouches down and raises the torch to light his face. It's Detective Valentine, and Lauren stands warily behind him. They both climb down from the ledge to meet Remy. He gets a better look at her up close and she's a sorry state, that's for sure, caked head to toe in filth and muck, tired bloodshot eyes and cracked lips, and of course one hand short of what she had in the picture her mother had shown him.

"Bloody hell, girl, what happened to you?" he asks.

She doesn't know where to begin. No words come, only breathy gasps as she struggles to endure the pain.

"What about your sister?" he asks. "And your neighbour?"

Remy looks quizzical. "How do you—?"

Valentine reaches into his coat for his badge. "Your parents reported you missing…" He rummages through his pockets before patting himself down. "Ah, I must've dropped it." He sighs and looks at poor confused Remy. "I'm the police. We're looking for all of you. Can you tell me where the hell we are? And how it is you came to be here?"

Remy frowns at Lauren and looks back at Valentine. "You mean you don't know? Didn't you come here on purpose?"

Valentine shakes his head. "Not exactly."

"So you're stuck here just like us, then." She slumps onto her knees.

Lauren nudges Valentine and points at Remy's missing hand.

"... Right," he whispers, "let's get you out of this hole." Offering Remy his hand, he asks, "Can you walk?"

She nods and pulls herself up then picks up the enchanted sword and hands it to Lauren. "We're probably going to need this."

Lauren looks out of her depth as she takes the weapon. The closest thing to a sword she's ever held is a steak knife. "I... I don't know how—"

"Don't worry," Remy assures her, "it does all the work for you."

*

The Runegard soldiers mobilise a deadly magi-cannon – a cutting-edge killing machine, melding science and magic that fires with precise and devastating force – and take aim at the smouldering remains of Grimoirh's airship. As the cannon charges, the Dread Knight swoops down on the back of his crystal dragon, which lands on the deck with a cacophonous roar and crushes the soldiers beneath its razor talons. Reinforcements charge to aid their comrades but are blasted to ash as the creature spits hellfire at them. Gigas himself steps onto the deck wielding his great enchanted lance, Blazerush. His weapon ignites with a roaring blue flame as he rushes the dragon and pierces its crystal hide. The beast lashes its tail, but the general evades its fatal sweep then strikes the creature again. Vincent leaps off the dragon's back and, drawing his God Cleaver, he attacks Gigas from above. Their weapons clash in a ferocious blaze.

"The Dread Knight himself," the old war hawk smirks. "At last."

Vincent strikes at Gigas again and again with furious overhead cleaves, but the general is an experienced warrior and is more than a match for him. He blocks each attack with relative ease, spinning and swinging his lance with grace.

"Your strength is fuelled by rage." Gigas strikes Vincent in the chest plate, stunning him. "You lack discipline."

With a spiteful grin he sweeps Vincent's legs from under him. Brute, barbaric strength might not cut it this time.

"I expected more," Gigas goads him further.

Vincent falls for the general's ploy and lunges clumsily at Gigas, who parries then counters, cracking his lance against Vincent's back.

"Weak."

The war hawk's laugh provokes Vincent, who erupts in a fit of rage, unleashing a mighty spin, and he cleaves off the tip of Gigas' lance. The general's face sours. He's done playing. In a flash he pummels Vincent with a series of devastating blows, flooring him, then brings his lance down on Vincent's arm, breaking it.

"That sword will make a fine trophy. As will your head," he spits, and beats Vincent relentlessly.

The Dread Knight roars in agony and tries to crawl away as his body is broken by the general's blows. Gigas stays his attack and grins victoriously over the mighty Grimoirh, beaten to a pulp before him.

"Seems the stories were just that. You're no demon, only a man," the general laughs, his mind flush with visions of adoration and fanfare from his kingdom. This victory will cement him in history as a legendary hero of Runegard. People will sing songs and tell tales of this battle long after he makes his way to the great spirit in the sky.

Vincent, spitting blood, releases a haunting cry as his armour takes life. Contorting and constricting his body, it pushes his ribs back into place and bolsters his broken bones. Gigas looks aghast as the Dreadmail forces Vincent on his feet, and he laughs madly, his crazed eyes burning through the straggled hair in his face.

The crystal dragon roars with his master and releases a stream of white-hot fire across the deck, then leaps into the air before nose-diving through the ship, wreaking havoc in its wake.

As the *Thanatos* falls apart around them, Vincent strikes with such unfathomable force that every blow cracks Gigas' lance until it breaks. The general trembles at his opponent's unbelievable recovery.

"You're right, I'm no demon..." Vincent grits his bloody teeth, "... I created this world and nothing will stop me from ending it!" He brings the God Cleaver down on Gigas one more time and with a mighty shunt, impales him.

The general's last look is one of pain, confusion and disbelief. He collapses with a breathless groan as Vincent draws the sword from his chest and glares at the soldiers who surround him, watching rife with fear and awe as he mounts the crystal dragon once more and tears into the sky, leaving the *Thanatos* in ruin.

*

Plumes of black smoke billow from the crumbling wreckage of Grimoirh's ship, eclipsing the sky. Ed and the others sprint across what's left of the deck as it breaks apart around them. Having found no sign of Remy and no way off, hope is faltering.

Jessica trips and hits the deck with her palms. "I'm too young to die!" she sobs. "I have so much I want to do! My band, travelling. Oh God, I'm going to die a virgin!"

George, seeing the frightened look on her face, starts to panic too. "I want to go home," he says as tears well in his eyes.

"Me too!" Jessica throws her arms around him.

"Quit your whining, we're getting off this heap!" Bengeo scans around, but there are no lifeboats or any way to land or steer the wreck. The only thing keeping it afloat are the tethered air balloons.

"What about Remy?!" Ed says. "We can't leave without her!"

"For all we know she was on the half that broke off already," Bengeo replies.

Jessica looks horrified, but Ed rebukes the bandit.

"I don't believe it!"

Bengeo can see deep down that Ed knows that she could be gone, but can't or won't bring himself to admit it. The bandit sighs and rests a hand on his shoulder. "It's not gonna hold much longer. We gotta go."

"Go without me!" Ed pulls away. "I'm not leaving until I find her."

Bengeo nods. "Might make a hero outta you yet." He throws his arms wide and walks towards Ed.

Ed smiles. "That means a lot coming fro—" WHAM!

Bengeo knocks him out cold with one punch, and his body topples like a plank of wood.

"Sorry, kid. But I'm not leaving anyone behind this time." He hoists Ed over his shoulder. "We're getting off this tin can," he cries, instilling embers of hope in his comrades.

He glances up at the enormous balloons keeping the wreck in the air. "Climb on and cut the ties behind us. Without this weight dragging it down we can float a while until it runs outta gas."

"Sounds like a plan, boss." Cleo quickly scales the ropes ahead of the others.

"You really think Remy made it out okay?" Jessica asks, trying so hard to hold it together.

"No doubt in my mind. Your sister is like a force of nature." His words instil comfort and pride.

"What is that?" George points towards the *Thanatos* and gasps at the glimmering crystal dragon soaring towards them.

With a deafening roar the dragon crashes onto the remnants

of the deck and Grimoirh dismounts the beast, paying the 'players' no mind as he rushes into the ship. He stumbles through the wonky corridors until he reaches Domina's bed chamber, where she's still lying unconscious from her ordeal in the forest. He shakes her, but she doesn't wake, so he takes her in his arms. On his way back to the deck, an explosion blows a gaping hole in the wall, tilting the remnants of the ship even more on its side. Vincent fights his way across the upturned room as the furniture tumbles towards him. The bed clips his shoulder, throwing him off his feet and out into the sky. Hurtling at incredible speed, he clings to Domina and wonders if his magic armour could withstand the impact of a thousand-foot drop. Unlikely.

A thunderous roar tears through the sky. Vincent's summoned dragon glides towards him and catches the pair in its enormous claws. Its broad wings spring wide, and it pushes its way above the carnage and soars past the floating wreck and rips through one of the balloons, igniting a firestorm.

"Hold on!" Cleo slides down the ropes and hits the deck as flames rain overhead and the balloons deflate, along with any chance of escape.

"What now?!" Jessica's hair thrashes in the wind, and she looks to Bengeo for answers, but the look on his face makes it clear he's plain out of ideas. Her heart sinks. She knows she's done for. They all are. She comforts George who looks frightened at the smoke-stained sky. Cleo and Bengeo exchange a respectful nod as he lays Ed down beside him.

The bandit kneels and hangs his head. Guess his luck had to run out sometime. A foreboding creak and the ship begins to descend, but the full-throated growl of an engine catches his ear. Bengeo looks up as a round balloon bearing the Runegard sigil – a rising sun – arises before him.

"I don't think now is the time to be sitting on your ass!" Marcus cries, piloting a stolen air balloon from the boat-shaped carriage hanging beneath it.

Bengeo grins with unwavering determination as raw survival instinct floods his veins.

"Asses and elbows, people! We got ourselves a shot off this wreck!"

*

Miles below, Lauren and Valentine drag Remy up the spiral steps of the spire atop the ruins. The raspy hisses and inhuman groans of the undead swarm echo closely behind. Lauren glances back, and the sight of withered skeletons scrambling up the coiled stone steps shakes her to her core.

"Don't stop for anything!" Valentine cries.

Remy's feet drag along the stone rooftop as they pull her towards the edge and lay her by a crumbled wall.

Lauren looks worriedly ahead and turns to Valentine, with wide, fearful eyes. "They're coming!"

The detective kneels before Remy, who's slumped half conscious against the stone. "Don't worry, we'll get you home," he assures her, "somehow."

Remy weakly lifts her good arm and points at the sky behind him.

He looks over his shoulder and, hovering above, a dinky little air balloon sails over them.

"Well, I'll be a lucky son of a bitch." He runs to the edge, waving and leaping frantically. "Down here! Heeeeeey! Heeeeeellllp!"

On board the balloon, George tugs at Jessica's jacket.

"That's my sister!" He points over the side of the carriage at the two leaping lunatics screaming at them from atop the dilapidated ruin.

She notices Remy slumped against the wall beside them and looks elated. "That's *my* sister!" she screams and pulls on Bengeo's arm. "Remy's down there!"

"Take us down! Quickly!" He orders Marcus to bring the air balloon in close.

Valentine lifts Remy over his shoulders and carries her towards the lifeboat where Bengeo pulls her aboard. Cleo helps Valentine on, and Jessica leans out and extends her hand to Lauren, but the remnants of Grimoirh's ship break apart with a bang, raining debris over them like a meteor shower. Hunks of scrap crash into the ruins, caving whole sections inwards, and a flaming chunk of metal soars past them causing Lauren to trip back onto the rooftop, while Marcus tries to regain control of the air balloon as it sways violently.

"We gotta go! That whole thing is coming down on us!" he cries.

"We're not leaving her!" George barks.

"I can't get it any closer, we'll be torn apart!" Marcus points furiously at the flaming hail above.

Jessica's heart breaks at the sight of George's teary, panicked face. Her eyes dart wildly around for anything that can help. She takes up one of the coiled ropes hanging on the side of the carriage and fastens it around her thighs and waist like a harness then throws the other end to Cleo. "Throw me!"

"What?" Cleo looks at her like she's mad.

"Just do it! I'll catch her." Cleo nods and secures the end of the rope to the lifeboat while Jessica climbs onto the edge of the safety rail surrounding the carriage. She keeps her eyes dead ahead. It's taking everything in her not to look down at the fatal drop.

Valentine leans over the carriage and shouts to Lauren, "Get ready to take a run and jump!"

She peers over the edge of the tower and turns sickly green at the drop. "You have got to be kidding!" she cries.

"It's now or never!" the detective calls back. "Take a leap of faith!"

"You can do it!" George's head bobs up over the side.

"George?!" she gasps. "What are you doing here?!"

"What are *you* doing here?!" he replies.

She shakes her head. Now she has no choice, not that she ever really did. She looks back sharply as the dead spill onto the rooftop. One glance at their vacant eyes and rotting flesh and she takes off running as fast as her beanpole legs will carry her.

"Live to fly, fly to live." Jessica recites the lyrics like a mantra psyching herself up, but her curiosity gets the better of her and she glances down for just a second then recoils from the edge. "I won't make it, I won't make it," she panics, slapping herself in the side of the head. She glances at George who looks at her with wide, worried eyes and steels herself.

"Shit," she whispers. "Hey, muscles, give me a boost."

Bengeo nods and readies himself. She takes a quick step towards him, and he javelins her into the sky.

Lauren sprints into a leap off the tower, and both girls soar towards one another. Jessica throws her hands forward and they catch each other before they drop.

Marcus manoeuvres the balloon sharply as more debris shoots past. Lauren's grasp falters, but Jessica catches her raincoat and clings to her with all she's got while they hang precariously amidst the shower of flaming wreckage and watch the undead hurl themselves off the edge of the ruin after them with ravenous desperation.

"Pull us up! Pull us up!" Jessica shrieks as Bengeo, Valentine and Cleo hoist the rope.

The girls collapse in a heap on the deck, and Lauren throws her arms around Jessica. "Thank you!" she cries. All at once the adrenaline hits her, and she jerks back as a force rises from the pit of her stomach and throws her head over the side before she vomits.

"Don't sweat it." Jessica holds back Lauren's hair and rubs her back tenderly.

The others watch, transfixed, as the last vestige of the wreckage crashes into the mire in a grand spectacle, dispersing the mist as bursts of flame erupt like primordial geysers. Bengeo glances at Ed and Remy, who both lie unconscious beside one another in the carriage, and smirks. He chalks this up to a win. Looking back across the sky, he sees the *Thanatos* descending in the distance in a trail of black smoke. Double win.

"What now?" Jessica slumps against the side of the carriage and lets out a big sigh.

"We're going somewhere safe," he replies.

"*Safe*?" She arches her brow.

"Well, safe enough." Bengeo leans back and throws his arms behind his head, and onwards they sail through the ash and war-torn sky.

XII

Harbour

Seeing her big sister broken like this evokes more despair than anything Jessica's faced in this world thus far. Growing up, Remy was always a hurricane that went her own way and spoke her mind no matter the consequences. She knew exactly how to push Jessica's buttons, as though she were solving an intricate puzzle and the prize was Jessica's emotional distress, but truthfully she has always looked up to Remy, though she'd never admit it. She casts her forlorn eyes over the rusty canyons passing below, the view reminding her of the default desktop background on her laptop. It occurs to her that she's never been anywhere exotic before. Her parents couldn't afford holidays abroad when she was young, and these days most of her earnings go towards sound equipment or rent, which helps her parents cover their mortgage payments. One of the reasons she wanted to be a singer in the first place was because they get to tour. She figured she'd see the world once she caught a break. This isn't her world, sure, but she can still appreciate the view.

She glances over her shoulder at George who rolls his eyes while Lauren rubs the dirt off his face with her thumb. A sad smile graces her lips. She never had that kind of relationship with Remy either. Tough love was more her thing.

Maybe that's not so bad, she thinks. *I guess I need to be the tough one now.*

"Stop it." George swats Lauren's hand away. "What are *you* doing here?" he asks.

Lauren exchanges a guilty look with Valentine – probably best not to mention the fire or the fact she broke into Vincent's flat. George can't keep a secret after all.

"Are you okay? Are you hurt?" she asks, checking him for cuts and scrapes.

"Me? What about you?" His eyes widen at the gash on her forehead. "Is that blood?!"

In all the chaos she had forgotten all about it, but a splitting headache comes rushing back. She touches the wound with the back of her palm. It's sticky and warm; probably needs a good clean.

"It looks bad," George says.

"I'm okay," she smiles, trying not to worry him.

Thankfully her brother's attention shifts to Ed, who releases a long groan as he sits up. Before he can make sense of anything, pain comes rushing to his face.

"How's the head?" Bengeo looks remorseful.

"Feel like I got hit by a train." He rubs his blackening eye.

"What's a train?" the bandit asks.

Ed shakes his head and looks confused at his surroundings. "We made it off the airship?" He points quizzically at the newcomers. "Who…? What did I miss?"

Bengeo motions to Remy, sleeping soundly in the corner of the carriage. "We picked up a few strays."

Ed grins ear to ear. "You found her!"

"Actually she found us, thanks to them," Jessica replies.

"It was nothing," Lauren says.

"Nothing? Ha!" Valentine coughs. "Nothing but trouble."

205

Lauren nudges him with her elbow, so he softens his tone. "Uh...
but, of course, we're glad she's safe." He fumbles a cigarette from
his pocket, only to realise he has nothing to light it with and
stares longingly at the smoke before shoving it back in his coat.
"Your parents are worried about you. I can see now that they're
right to be."

"Our parents?" Ed asks.

Jessica looks elated. Since the moment she stepped foot in
this godforsaken world she's wanted to leave. The cranky old
detective is hardly a knight in shining armour, but at this point
she'll take whatever she can get. "You were looking for us?"

Valentine nods. "Detective Inspector Scott Valentine,
whatever that's worth, wherever we are."

They look at Lauren, expecting an introduction.

"Oh, I'm not with... I'm just, um, Lauren." She tucks her hair
behind one ear and looks down at her shoes. First impressions
aren't her strong suit.

"Yo, boss. We're almost there," Marcus says from behind the
steering wheel at the back of the carriage.

"Almost where?" Jessica asks.

Bengeo points overboard. "Take a look."

A small cove tucked behind the sprawling canyons rears on
the horizon. Dull waves spill onto a beach of blackish sand, and
built into the cliffside overlooking the ocean, a small village.
Crude wooden shacks are propped up by rickety scaffolding
spread across the cliffside like a web.

The balloon eventually kisses the sand a little way from the
village, and as the party disembark they're met by a group of
small children running along the beach.

"Bengeo's back! He's back!" cries one child.

"Woohoo!" cheers another.

They maul the bandit and pull him towards the village.

"Easy now," Bengeo says, "we've got some newcomers, gotta
see to 'em first."

"Are they yours?" Ed asks.

Bengeo shakes his head and laughs. "They're refugees, from villages burned by the Dread Knight or Runegard. The wise man looks over 'em. My crew ferry supplies to the camp, least we did before my ship got blown to dust."

A little girl with rosy cheeks and braided hair approaches George. "Did your home get burned down too?"

"Uh, no." He looks coy as the girl takes his hand and drags him along towards the village. He looks back at his sister, who nods encouragingly for him to go.

Ed takes in his surroundings. The houses and huts appear to be fashioned from driftwood and scrap; the wooden beams bolting them to the cliffside creak loudly in the wind as though the village itself were groaning. Most of the villagers are huddled around a large pyre at the base of the settlement, gaunt and weary, dour-faced and baggy-eyed, warming themselves by the flame roaring defiantly against the sea breeze like a beacon of hope in this forlorn land. This sad little place is certainly an eyesore juxtaposed against the towering canyons that cradle it above the endless ocean – although he supposes the view offers some comfort to the people sheltered here.

"Doesn't look like much," he mumbles to himself.

"Wasn't 'til we fixed it up," Cleo replies. "People took to calling it Harbour. Name stuck."

"The wise man founded it, said the land here is special," Marcus says.

"Special how?" Lauren asks.

"Something about a well of spirit energy deep beneath the ground."

"Is that, like, something superstitious?" Jessica asks.

Marcus shakes his head. "Nothing superstitious about it, seen for myself, magic is stronger here. Especially the healin' kind. So don't fret, your sister is in good hands."

He lifts Remy under her arms and Cleo grabs her boots.

Together they cart her off the air balloon and towards the village.

Jessica shoots Lauren a sceptical look. "Did he say magic?"

Lauren nods earnestly.

"So are there more missing people here? Like us?" Ed asks.

"All sorts of displaced folk, but afraid you're the only other-worlders we could save," Cleo replies.

"Which is why we had to get you here!" Bengeo says. "We hoped you'd be able to shed some light on what's going on."

"I think we're as clueless as you are," Ed replies.

"Just talk to the wise man. Maybe you know something you don't know you know. Y'know?"

"Whatever you say, man." Ed rubs his swollen eye and follows the bandits into the village. They carry Remy to a small cave at the foot of the cliff shielding the settlement. Ed and Jessica follow but are stopped from entering by a bald man clad in layered robes, who looks kind of reminiscent of the Hare Krishna that parade through London.

"Let the healer do her work, and you can come see your friend in a while," the monk says.

"Please be careful with her, she's the only sister I've got." Jessica watches them carry Remy deeper into the cave.

"You have my word." The monk smiles kindly then pulls shut a round wooden door.

"Well, might as well look around." Ed feigns an upbeat can-do attitude despite the others being too tired or too fed up to appreciate it.

"I need a drink," Valentine grumbles, and wanders off alone in search of somewhere to wet his whistle.

One of the refugees points him to a creaky hut on the east side of the village. There's no door, only a faded curtain hung in place of one. He pulls it back and enters the rickety tavern – well, tavern might be stretching it. It's a modest shack, filled with a few chairs and tables and a small counter. A barrel of something stands on wooden supports behind the barman who has his back turned as he polishes the rusty brass tap.

Valentine approaches the bar and perches on one of the wooden stools.

"Hey, can I get a—?!" He looks dumbfounded at the bartender, who looks identical to the monk that barred them from following Remy into the cave. "Didn't you just—?" Valentine motions to the doorway.

"Oh. You new here? You're probably confusing me with one of my brothers," the barman chuckles. "I'm Tiwo. See, I wear this sash." He smoothes the yellow silk belt around his waist.

"You got any other brothers I should know about?" Valentine asks.

"Most of them are over there." Tiwo points to a group of bald men sitting around a table at the back of the room, each one as identical as the last save for some small accessory.

*

On the edge of the village, George watches the children play-fight with sticks and chase each other about the beach.

"I'm Regis the Good!" yells a kid with fluffy black hair.

"It's my turn to be Regis," cries another with a bowl cut and a bandage over his forehead.

"Yeah, you're always Regis," says the rosy-cheeked girl with braided hair. "Let the new guy be Regis."

"Uhh, that's okay." George looks warily at the girl. He's never met an NPC before. He didn't expect them to be so lifelike. "How long have you been here?" he asks her.

"More than twenty-four days. After that, I stopped counting," the girl replies.

"That's 'cus you can't count any higher," the fluffy-haired kid snorts and laughs until his friend swats him with a stick while he's not looking.

A bell rings out and the refugee children drop their sticks

and run off into the village, where some of the more able-looking men and women are handing out food to the townsfolk.

Each of the 'players' is handed a clay bowl by one of the villagers as they join the long queue of hungry people. One by one their bowls are filled with a hearty stew and a small portion of rice.

Ed and the girls eat quietly together on the beach, their tin spoons scraping every morsel of food from their bowl as they wolf it down. It's been a while since any of them ate a hot meal.

*

Glimpses of pale green light and murmuring familiar voices are all Remy can cling to as she dips in and out of consciousness. She feels warm and weightless, and grits her teeth as the severe pain comes rushing back and pushes her beyond her threshold, then everything goes dark again.

Next her eyes open to warm candlelight and the view of a quaint little room from a small bed in the corner. Her pain is less now, how or why she does not know, but she's thankful it's bearable. Her right arm feels numb, as if she'd been lying on it. She catches sight of it thoroughly bandaged up to her shoulder, and the memory of that moment comes flooding back with a swell of rage and regret. Quiet tears roll down her cheeks as she mourns the loss of her right hand. She can hardly believe she'll never be whole again.

Bengeo looms behind the door in the next room, and her quiet sobs rack him with guilt. He was hired to protect her, and he failed. He takes a seat at a small table and hangs his head.

"Now let's get a look at you," a welcome voice says. Esmerelda, the innkeeper from Trout, enters the hut carrying a tray of herbs and poultices.

At her word Bengeo lifts his shirt so she can inspect his arrow wound.

"Looks almost right as rain, no doubt thanks to my magic," she smirks, hoping to rouse the bandit's usual cocksure demeanour, but he just sits, like a stoic giant.

*

Ed squints his eyes like commas at the calm ocean as the last vestiges of light wane beyond the horizon.

"What do you think happened to her?" he asks.

Jessica frowns. "I'm betting that Grimvar had something to do with it."

"Do you mean Grimoirh?" Lauren asks.

She shrugs. "Who cares what his name is. The guy's a psycho."

"What's he look like?"

"Dark hair, serial killer eyes. Oh and he's got this big scar right across his nose. He took off on a black dragon, which I still can't believe, but whatever..." she sighs. "I hope that's the last we ever see of that dick."

Jessica's description matches Vincent. That scar was a new addition that was hard to miss when Lauren saw him at the crypt, and she'd been horrified to notice he was carrying a severed hand, which at the time she assumed belonged to one of the walking corpses.

Lauren hugs her knees and looks guilty as she wonders what could possibly justify wounding Remy like that and leaving her to die. The sight of her battered, alone and on the edge of death in that crypt is one she'll not soon forget.

*

The muffled voices in the next room fall quiet. Remy listens to a door clatter shut and waits a minute or two before throwing off her blanket. Her legs tremble as she presses her weight on them, then she leans against the wall to help her reach the next room.

211

She frowns at the bloody bandages and empty potion bottles discarded on a small table and presses against the wooden door until it creaks open. Her bare feet touch the earth outside sending shivers up her legs, and she finds herself on the peak of a clifftop overlooking the dour village. Rusty canyons stretch for miles in one direction and in the other, infinite ocean, but it isn't the vistas that have her attention. Instead, her eyes linger on a figure facing out towards the watery expanse, cloaked in billowing rattan robes.

"On your feet already?" The stranger's orotund voice rings familiar to her. "Good."

She looks cautiously at the stranger. "Where am I? Who are you?"

"Yes, yes. Many questions. All will be answered in time." The old man turns to her and pulls back his hood with his wrinkled hands, but it's not a man staring back at her. Instead it's a human-sized crow's head, feathers, beak and all.

Remy recognises him immediately. After all, his appearance is hardly commonplace. "Ozrune?"

"It seems no introductions are necessary," he chirps.

"I see you've met the man." Bengeo's brash voice brings a smile to Remy's face. She turns to him as Esmerelda butts past with eyes full of wrath.

"What are you doing out of bed? I barely put you back together and you decide to go strolling outside barefoot! Silly girl."

Is this a dream? Remy tries to piece together how it is she arrived here.

"Good to see you in one piece." Bengeo's smile wanes on realising his poor choice of words. "Uh, well, you know what I mean..." He rubs the back of his head and sighs, while Remy looks mournfully at her arm and swallows her grief like a lump of cold porridge.

"Remy!" Jessica shrieks at the top of her lungs as she appears over the ridge and throws herself at her sister, who grimaces as she squeezes.

Remy groans, "Go easy! Everything hurts!"

She shrinks, like a child refused affection, and looks worriedly at Remy's arm. "Mum is so going to kill you when she sees that." She gently takes hold of it and a little smile creeps across her lips. "Remember when I got my tattoo?" It was a small, tasteful picture of a sound equaliser on the back of her left shoulder. To say Helen had reacted negatively when she saw it would be a gross understatement. Words were exchanged. Threats were made. Dinner plates were harmed. "This is way, way worse."

"So much worse." With a smirk Remy pulls Jessica in and buries her face in her ragged bomber jacket. "I'm happy you're okay," she whispers.

Jessica shines with surprise. Remy never expressed much concern for her wellbeing before now. She embraces her sister. Somehow this small gesture makes her feel warmer and their situation a little less bleak.

Jessica whispers, "Remy..."

"Yeah?"

"What's up with that guy's head?"

Remy chuckles and looks back at the wizard by the cliff's edge. "So you're the wise man Bengeo mentioned?" she asks.

Ozrune nods. "It pleases me greatly that you made it out of that ruin alive."

"Was it you who saved me? In the crypt, that light?"

"You saved yourself, I merely illuminated the way," he replies.

"But why?"

"More questions," he smiles, if a beak could smile. "Come, you must be weary." The old crow leads them into his hut, and they take a seat around the small table.

Remy looks worriedly at Bengeo. "Is Ed here? And the ones who found me, the detective and that girl?"

213

"Don't worry, should be here any minute," the bandit says, and sure enough the door creaks open.

George and Lauren step into the hut, and Ed follows behind them. He tries to downplay how happy he is to see Remy, and likewise, she him, but the growing smile on both their faces gives them away.

"You're alright?" he asks.

She nods, then notices the whopping great shiner around his eye. "What happened to your face?"

He frowns at Bengeo and pulls up a seat at the table. "More like who happened."

Again the bandit swallows his guilt, and Ed notices Esmerelda at the back of the room fixing a pot of tea and looks happy to see her.

"What, you didn't think these old bones could outrun some goblins?" she laughs, then softens her tone. "Glad to see you're still kicking, boy. That stunt you pulled in Trout made me think the two of you might make half-decent adventurers after all."

"Thanks. I think," he replies.

"Although I'd figured it'd be you losing a limb or two, the way you carried that rusty sword," Esmerelda laughs again.

"Who's the kid?" Remy asks.

"George Baker." George extends his hand to her over the table, and for a moment she forgets she's missing hers. He looks awkwardly at her stump. His father had taught him to always shake hands and introduce himself courteously, but he never explained what to do if someone didn't have a hand to shake. Thankfully Lauren quickly lowers his arm and pulls him onto his seat.

"Where's the troll?" Esmerelda quietly asks Bengeo. "Not getting into trouble, I hope."

The bandit shakes his head. "The swordsman took her scouting. She was scaring the villagers." Bengeo leans against the wall behind them and clears his throat. "Well then, everyone, meet the wise man."

They look to Ozrune who stands at the table's end.

"Hey," George squints at the bird-headed man, "aren't you the tutorial guy?"

"Indeed. I am Ozrune. Master of tutorage, teller of truths and seer of sights." The crow-headed wizard bows.

"Man, I always skip the tutorials," Ed whispers to Remy, who nods agreeably. Nobody's got time for that.

Jessica points at him and gasps. "But your... your head?" She looks dumbfounded at her friends and can't believe she's the only one weirded out by a talking crow with the body of a bony old man.

George nudges her and whispers, "Don't be rude."

Ozrune waves his hand and conjures a spark, which bursts like a small firework with the flick of his wrist and ignites the candles placed about the room. He looks empathetically at the 'players' sitting around him and speaks softly. "This conversation is long overdue. As I am sure you are aware, bringing you to Harbour was more complicated than anticipated."

"So you sent Bengeo to find us, why?" Remy asks.

"I'm hoping you can enlighten me as to why you are all here."

"Actually we were hoping you could tell us," Ed replies. "One minute we're playing a video game, the next we're in it."

Ozrune tilts his head. "A game? Most curious. The first other-worlder I spoke with never mentioned any game."

"*The first other-worlder?*" Ed asks.

"A stranger who had found himself lost in a strange land, just like yourselves." The wizard sighs. "He called himself Wanderer and he spoke of another world that existed beyond this one, a world that he had left behind. He possessed knowledge no ordinary man should, of legends I had only read fragments of in ancient tomes. He spoke of the legendary crystal, how it came to be and how it was shattered and hidden across the world. Perhaps most curious of all, he knew the location of each and every shard."

215

Lauren's mouth runs dry. Her mind hisses like static and fires a million thoughts as she cottons on to just whom Ozrune is referring to.

"He warned me that there had been an awakening, a great power slumbered no longer." Ozrune tightens his beady bird eyes. "He claimed he had created our world and that by some cosmic error he was now trapped in it. He implored me to aid him on his quest to seek out the three crystal shards. Only when I asked him what he sought to do with such powerful relics, did the gravity of his malevolent intent become apparent. I didn't know it then, but the Dread Knight himself had crawled out of hell and sought me out."

Remy's chest tightens at the mere mention of him.

"I was sure this man was a threat to all of Pangea Ultima. Our exchange grew heated, we fought and he was no match for me, but that curious armour of his shielded him from every spell I could conjure. I scorched him with fire, crushed him with rock, struck him with lightning, but he endured until I brought a mountain down around him. Even still, he survived."

Remy croaks with trepidation, "He told me that he intends to destroy this world. Is that possible?"

"Tales of the crystals' power are varied and farfetched so it is hard to say," the wizard replies.

"I didn't believe any of it, 'til others started showing up all over the place," Bengeo says.

"Others?" asks Jessica.

"I think he means us." Lauren sits forward in her chair and asks Ozrune, "Did Vincent say anything that stood out to you about the crystal?"

"Vincent?" Remy looks at her sharply. "Do you know who Grimoirh is?!"

Lauren nods tentatively. "He's actually sort of the reason I'm here."

Sombre silence befalls the table, and she glances at the

faces staring back at her, brimming with shock and suspicion, tightening her chest.

"Is it true that he created the game?" Remy asks.

"He is… *was* the director," Lauren replies.

"What are you getting at, Remy?" Jessica folds her arms and frowns. She's sick and tired of being totally out of the loop.

Remy sighs. "Don't you get it? Grimoirh isn't some video game villain, he's a player just like us."

Ed recalls that the glimpse he had of the man under the horned helmet didn't sit right with him. "So then he's stuck here too?"

"Only I think he wants to be." Remy dwells on Vincent's words in the crypt. "*There's no going back for any of us…*"

"But you know him, from back home?" Ed asks Lauren.

"I thought I did, until he just up and disappeared," she replies.

"Disappeared?"

Lauren nods. "It's not uncommon for devs to take stress leave during crunch time, but he totally vanished. I never in a million years imagined he was here." She hopes to appease their suspicion, but Remy is having none of it.

"How can we be sure you're not working with him?" she asks.

"What?" Lauren looks shocked. "But I helped you."

"It's pretty convenient that you just showed up when you did. What were you doing there?" replies Remy.

"We… we were lost. Okay, I saw Vincent at the crypt, we spoke for a minute and sure, he told me to find Bengeo, but he said I'd be safe here. I think he was trying to protect me. I swear I'm just as confused by it as you."

"Don't take it personally, she's like this with everyone," Jessica whispers.

"Jess!" Remy snaps.

"Well, it's true, you're kind of rude."

Ed and Bengeo exchange a quiet look of agreement, much to Remy's infuriation.

"Does any of this matter now that Mr Valentine is here to take us home?" Jessica looks for the detective, but he's not among them. "Where is he?"

"Uh, drinking I think," Ed replies.

Her optimism fades and she shrinks in her chair.

"I can tell you Vincent spent years working on the game, it was his dream. I can't believe he'd really want to destroy it all," Lauren sighs.

Jessica lets out a crass laugh. "I can. This game sucks. Pretty much everything I've seen since I got here has tried to eat me or kill me or both!" She looks sternly at the others. "Why couldn't we have been sucked into The Sims or something?"

"The Sims?" Ed chuckles. "Now that'd be a real nightmare."

"Oh yeah? Well, evil knights, magic gems – isn't this all a little convoluted?" Jessica smirks, savouring the appalled look on Ed's face.

"It's a classic! Ultimate Adventure is a timeless tale of good triumphing over evil!" he replies.

"Sounds pretty contrived to me." Jessica rolls her eyes. "Nothing is totally evil."

"Well, this is literally evil incarnate!" Ed says.

"But why?" Jessica asks.

"Because it's a game, and we need something big and powerful to fight at the end."

Clearly she doesn't share his enthusiasm for fantasy RPG tropes.

"Enough!" Remy snaps. "We need to think about what he might do with the shards now that he has at least two of them, and if they're the reason we're here, can we use them to get home?"

"It stands to reason that their awakening is connected to your arrival in our world. I suspect they will indeed hold the key to returning you to yours," Ozrune says, "but without the gems in our possession, how exactly I cannot say."

"The lore says the crystal was created to imprison an evil entity that manipulated the kingdoms to go to war," Lauren replies.

"Why?" asks Jessica.

"Because where there's war, there's death, and the crystal can raise the dead for its army," says Ed.

Remy frowns, reliving her bitter experience in that dark pit. "That's why there's always undead roaming around near the shards."

George's interest is suddenly piqued, and he sits upright in his chair. "That's right, we need to find Grimoirh and take the crystal back!" he shouts.

"Yeah, but we've got no idea where he went," Bengeo sighs.

"Wait, you've all played the game, right? So don't you know what he's going to do?" Jessica asks.

"It doesn't matter if we've played or not because Vincent isn't the Grimoirh from the game, so he's not going to follow the script." Ed's logic only seems to frustrate Jessica more.

"You said he's got two shards, right? That means there's one more," George says.

"Oh, so now you're an expert?" Jessica quips.

"I'm a level thirty-three assassin," he smiles.

Jessica looks at him blankly. She has no idea what that means.

"The last one is in the north," Remy says. She remembers it well, buried deep beneath the icy mountains in the northern part of the world map.

"Thinking about it, that bastard fled north on his dragon," Bengeo says. "Someone somewhere must have seen something, it's not every day a dragon flies overhead."

"How far north?" asks Esmerelda.

"Don't ask me," George replies, "I'm only, like, forty-five hours in."

"Forty-five hours?!" Jessica gasps. "How long *is* this game?"

George shrugs, so Jessica looks to Lauren for answers, but her expression doesn't bring any assurances.

"I have an idea..." Lauren meekly suggests. "... There's a map. A magic map. When you hold it, it can show you the way to whatever you want."

"How do you know about it?" Remy asks trying, but failing, to mask her suspicion.

"It's downloadable content – actually it's on the disc, but it's locked behind a paywall," she replies. "If we find that map, then maybe we can find him."

"A paywall?! That is so typical. God forbid somebody puts out a full game anymore," Ed groans.

"What's a paywall?" Jessica asks.

"That doesn't matter," Lauren replies. "What's important is, in the game, it's displayed in the Royal Palace in Parousia. You spend ten pounds, and the quest to break it open appears in your journal. There's a whole bunch of other loot in there too."

"Parousia? Not a good idea," Bengeo warns.

"Why? A royal palace sounds better than this smelly hut... Uh, no offence." Jessica smiles politely at Ozrune then buries her hands in her lap and looks downcast.

"The Kingdom of Runegard annexed the city. It's crawling with soldiers."

"And that general guy really doesn't like foreigners very much," Ed says.

"Couldn't we just steal it?" Remy looks at the bandit in the room.

"Bah, not saying it's impossible." Bengeo scratches the back of his head as he mulls it over. "There was a lot you just said that I didn't understand, but none of you seem sure that this map is even there. Besides you lot don't exactly look ready to take on the mighty Kingdom of Runegard."

"Bengeo's right," Ozrune says, "all of you should get

some rest, we all need some time to ruminate on what we've discussed."

The wizard casts his eyes up, specifically at the flickers of moonlight streaking through the holes in the tarp crudely patching a portion of the roof. Everyone leaves the hut and makes their way down to the village via the carved paths and rickety walkways erected on the cliffside, except Bengeo who lingers outside Ozrune's hut with Esmerelda.

"You really think we've got a shot at stopping Grimoirh?" he asks.

"If not, our future is nought but a stillborn dream," Esmerelda replies.

They stare at the sky a while, anticipating the trials that await them.

*

As the crimson moon shimmers above the sparse ocean, the monks show each of the 'players' to a tent for them to sleep in. Remy lets out an exhausted breath as she lies down on the straw bedroll and looks up at the burlap material jostling in the wind. She shuffles to avoid a stone trapped beneath her bedroll and muses that, compared to this, her futon back home felt like a king-size memory-foam cloud. But she's so worn out she could sleep standing up if she had to. Only a few seconds and she's out cold.

XIII

Nabbed

F ar to the north, beneath a primordial sky, an eternal blizzard ravages over the frigid wasteland. Grimoirh's crystal dragon fights its way through razor winds, venturing towards an ancient crater, a place called the Scar, where the world was torn open a millennium ago to forge the magic crystal.

Its power waning, the beast plants itself in the snow. Vincent dismounts and lifts Domina in his arms as she starts to come around. The bitter air chills him to the bone as he stares at nothing but endless white in all directions. The dragon roars, bidding its master farewell before it dissipates into the otherworldly void from whence it came. With that, Vincent takes a deep breath, steeling himself to endure the brutal journey ahead, and sets out with long strides through the deep snow. Every step is a battle as the blizzard rages, and the weight of his sword and Domina in his arms burden him while the echoes of creatures both grand and terrible roll in the distance. No living thing can survive in this land, but that doesn't mean there aren't still things.

Unable to bear the cold much longer he takes refuge in a small cavern – a nook carved into a great glacier that barely shelters them from the deathly conditions. He lays Domina down, dusts the ice off his armour and thrusts the God Cleaver into the ground between them to warm himself by its enchanted flame. He watches her a moment and fleetingly finds himself envious of her supernatural ability to withstand the bitter cold. The fire flickers in his eyes, and the numbness in his face subsides, like pins pricking his skin. He loses himself in thought. Six months ago was the first time he'd physically set foot in the game's world, but maybe events were set in motion long before he could ever have fathomed...

*

Eric and Vincent have known each other forever. In the mid-2000s, at university, they shared a small bedsit. He fondly recalls his old computer, on which he would spend every waking hour programming their first original video game using Visual Studio 6.0. Their living room walls were plastered with posters of late 80s and 90s releases like EverQuest, Chronotrigger, Duke Nukem 3D, Metal Gear Solid, Ocarina of Time, and of course the original Ultimate Adventure VII, serving as both a beacon of inspiration to persevere when times got tough and a wistful token of their adolescence.

One particular night lingers in Vincent's mind – a night, like most back then, spent toiling on their first indie game: a crude third-person space adventure.

"What about—" Eric spoke from his desk on the far side of the room.

"No," Vincent replied without so much as glancing away from his screen.

"I didn't even say—"

"Whatever it is, forget it."

Eric swivelled on his chair towards Vincent's desk and adjusted his round specs, which he wore as a tribute to his idol, the late, great John Lennon. "I just think a few branching conversations—"

Vincent interrupted him again. "It's too late to go changing the whole game."

Eric threw up his hands. "But it would be huge! Imagine, every single decision could totally rewrite the experience."

Vincent finally shifted his attention from the screen. "Eric, my computer is held together with duct tape. We can't make an interactive *Star Wars*."

"Come on, how hard could it be?" he grinned.

"You're right, it's barely an inconvenience." Vincent rolled his eyes and returned to his work while Eric pushed himself across the room to his desk.

"I'm just saying we should be a little ambitious… I mean, we could at least do something about the name."

"What's wrong with the name?"

"What kind of title is Runners? It's a space game, we should come up with something more interstellar."

Vincent scrunched his face. "But they're on the run."

"Yeah, in space!"

Their standoff lasted a full silent minute before Vincent caved and said, "Why don't we actually finish it before we start arguing over a title?"

"If we want games to be viewed as art, then we should start treating it like it is. Don't forget what's at stake!" Eric pointed to an ad torn from a magazine crudely enshrined on the wall. In big letters it read:

4D GAMES ARE LOOKING FOR NEW TALENT.
Show us your game, and you could be working alongside the creative team behind Dead Horizon, Mech-tropolis and the Ultimate Adventure series.

"Don't you want to work on the next Ultimate Adventure game?" Eric grinned.

"You're always harking on about the bigger picture, while I'm left working out the nitty gritty details," replied Vincent.

"That's why we work so well together! I'm the guy with the plan in the ivory tower, and you're on the streets making it happen," Eric laughed.

... That feels like a lifetime ago. They had finished their game in the following months, and in winning the contest had thoroughly impressed the developers at 4D Games. Their efforts had granted them roles on the development team of Ultimate Adventure X. A fleeting smile graces Vincent's worn face as he remembers how out of place they had looked on their first day. Both of them had shown up in suits and ties, which was met by harmless ridicule and garnered them the nickname '*the Men in Black*'.

They spent their first few months debugging with testers. It wasn't until the next iteration of Ultimate Adventure that either of them had actually got to do any work as a designer. Back then the basic framework of the game was set up by the chief developer, and everyone would bring in their own proposals as per his brief. Most would fill theirs with walls of text, but Vincent and Eric wrote theirs by hand and etched doodles and cartoons to convey their ideas. It wasn't long until the chief staff were asking for their ideas at meetings and they had established themselves as a creative force to be reckoned with.

But as the market changed, competitors became more prevalent and players more demanding. Subsequent Ultimate Adventure games garnered less praise. The series fell from grace. After the mess that was Ultimate Adventure XV, the franchise was almost iced, until Vincent approached Eric with the idea to remake the most popular game the company had ever created and the very game that had inspired them both to become developers in the first place. Vincent had always preferred working on the frontlines of development over handling an entire project, but the sacrifice was necessary to ensure that the remake would come out the way he had envisioned, although never in a million years did he envision it would end with him as a popsicle in a frozen wasteland.

*

Lauren stares vacantly at the crackling pyre. She curls up and rests her chin on her knees while her anxious mind drowns the music from her earphones, treading and retreading a maze of thoughts. Vincent, the game, Eric – what does it all mean? The way he was carrying Remy's severed hand around like some accessory seriously disturbed her. What could possess him to do something like that to her? *His eyes were vacant, it was like looking into a void, like a part of him was missing. And why would he think Eric was dead?*

"Can't sleep either?"

A shape pauses in Lauren's field of vision. Jessica approaches the pyre and her eyes light up at Lauren's earphones.

"Oh my God, is that music?" She plants herself next to Lauren, like a dog begging for scraps. "What're *we* listening to?"

Lauren hesitantly passes Jess one of her earbuds as she scoots closer to revel in the music. The tune washes over her like water, cleansing the stress and worry of the last few days from her pores. She was beginning to wonder if she'd ever hear music again.

Jessica smiles like a weight has been lifted. "Ah, The War On Drugs," she says.

Lauren nods. "You like them too?"

"That band is a direct line to all that's true in this life. *Lost in the Dream* is such a perfect album, like, every song is amazing. 'Red Eyes'! No, 'Suffering'! Oh my God, 'Disappearing'!"

"That's my favourite song ever," Lauren says.

Jessica takes the phone from her hand and queues 'Disappearing'. She closes her eyes and lets the song flow through her veins and carry her away. To her, life is music and music is life. All she hears, all she breathes, it pulses through every cell of her body. Her soft silvery voice harmonises with the melody, and she's so swept away that she doesn't notice Lauren admiring her from the corner of her eye. They sit by the crackling fire utterly spellbound until the song's end.

Jessica stares longingly at the phone. She misses hers like an old friend. "What I wouldn't give to go online for, like, five minutes… We could make some incredible TikToks."

"I didn't really look at it that way," Lauren chuckles.

"You use socials much?"

"Don't really have anyone to socialise with," Lauren laughs, trying to sound less pathetic than she feels.

Growing up British-born Asian was at times an isolating experience. The first time she was aware that she was different was in primary school, where other kids would pull their eyes into slits and make vaguely Chinese-sounding noises at her. Technically she's English, born and raised, but whether intentional or not, people's stares made it clear she wasn't one of them – but she wasn't Chinese either. Her Cantonese was nowhere near fluent, her facial features weren't considered traditionally Chinese – something many of her aunts, uncles and cousins on her mother's side of the family had made abundantly clear – and she sure as hell didn't look like her relatives on her father's side either, who were all fair with red and blonde hair. She spent most of her childhood feeling split in two, wishing she looked one way or the other. She even had two names, one English and the other, Yun – Chinese. Eventually she made a sort of peace with it and kept to herself, reasoning that if her people weren't out there, she'd be her own people. The few friends she made during her first year of university didn't bother to keep in touch after she dropped out, and neither did she. Perhaps she's as much an outcast of her own making. Of course she doesn't see it that way, but maybe that's just part of what makes her Lauren.

"So what else you got on this thing?" Jessica thumbs through Lauren's playlists.

"You're really into music, then?" she asks.

"I write my own songs. I figure the more I listen to, the better I'll be. Mostly synth pop stuff. I dunno, haven't really had that much life experience so I don't have a lot to write about... yet!"

"Reckon you'll write a song about all of this?"

Jessica laughs. "I think there's enough material for a whole album, not to mention a lifetime of therapy."

*

Ed pulls back the faded curtain and enters the rickety tavern, where Valentine and six identical brothers are playing cards around a table in the corner. He sits alone at the bar and sighs.

After a moment Valentine leans on the counter next to him. "Good timing, I had a bad hand." He points at the brothers. "Can you believe it? They all look the same!"

"Well, yeah, they're NPCs. To save money sometimes devs reuse character models..." The smell of hard liquor hits Ed like a truck. "Are you...? Are you drunk?"

Valentine shakes his head. "No. Absolutely not. No way." Despite his best efforts to compose himself, his hiccups, bleary eyes and inability to stand still are a dead giveaway.

"You've been here all day?"

Valentine nods. "I was on a hot streak."

"You missed all the important stuff."

"Important stuff?"

"Like what we're going to do next."

"Well, what're we going to do?" Valentine asks.

"Uh, actually we're not sure yet, but we talked about why we're all here."

"Well, let's hear it."

"Uh, I guess we're not sure about that either."

"Sounds like I didn't miss much," Valentine laughs. "Come on, I need some air."

"You sure you can walk straight?" Ed smirks.

"That's why you're coming with me." Valentine plants a hand on his shoulder and staggers out of the bar.

Near the beach they come across the girls listening to Lauren's phone by the firelight.

"Nice night." Valentine yawns and stretches his old stiff body.

Lauren greets him with a polite smile. "Where'd you get to?" she asks.

"Took a mental health day." He laughs a little too hard, then checks his watch, which is totally busted.

"Do you think we'll actually be able to get home?" Jessica asks.

"Honestly, I'm still trying to comprehend how the hell we got here, and where the hell here is." Valentine sits himself down and rests his back against a large rock buried in the sand.

"Mum will be worried," a little voice squeaks, and George pops up from behind the rock.

"Hey, what're you doing up so late?" Lauren asks.

"Couldn't sleep." He totters over and sits next to her.

"How's your eye?" Jessica asks Ed.

"Sore, but I'll live."

"I've been wanting to ask, after that big squid monster everything gets hazy until I was on that floating ship. So what happened to you and Remy?"

"By some miracle, Remy killed the giganeye after it petrified you, and before we knew it we were pulled out of there by Bengeo and his crew. We got shot down by Grimoirh and his goblins and barely escaped, but I can't really remember how..." Ed trails off.

"Can't remember?" Remy laughs as she approaches them, wrapped snug in a blanket. "You fainted. You were out the entire time we got shot down, crash landed and had to outrun the falling wreckage. Bengeo carried you like a helpless damsel."

The others share a laugh at Ed's expense.

"Not my finest moment." He rubs the back of his head and half-heartedly laughs at himself too.

"You seriously fainted?" Jessica giggles.

"After he screamed himself sick," Remy adds.

"C'mon, cut me a little slack," Ed pleads.

"Then what?" Jessica asks.

Ed and Remy exchange a fond glance as he continues to recite their adventure. "Well, we made it through the man-eating forest—"

"Hold up!" Jessica gasps. "*Man-eating forest?*"

"Yeah, it's a thing here," Remy replies, completely blasé.

"Anyway," Ed continues, "we got to this little town where the innkeeper lady sheltered us until a bunch of trolls threatened to rob and kill everyone. Bengeo got shot, so Remy and I used a magic mirror to bring the villagers' hair to life and—"

"Okay, this is getting too weird, forget I asked." Jessica wraps her arms around her legs and curls up to keep warm.

As laughter dies down, Remy looks to Lauren.

"So you really knew Grimoirh before all this? What was he like?" she asks.

The others look at Lauren too, all of them eager to know more about the black swordsman that has made their lives a living hell.

"Well, he was creative, driven. I don't think he had much of a life outside of work, but he seemed to love what he did. Honestly, I thought he might be kind of lonely, but he was the only one who treated me like a person instead of a servant or a child." She sighs. "But now… I don't know… maybe you know him better than me."

Pangs of guilt ripple through Remy. Seeing the downhearted look on Lauren's face makes her regret her earlier accusations.

She bites her lip and rehearses her words before she speaks. "I never thanked you properly for pulling me out of that hole. What I said before, I didn't... well, forget it."

"You'll have to excuse my sister, she's not used to expressing gratitude or remorse," Jessica says. "Let me translate: thank you for saving my life and welcome to the group." Jessica nudges Lauren playfully while Remy looks mortified – but she doesn't refute the claim, so maybe she is growing. Baby steps and all that.

Lauren smiles. It's been a while since anyone made an effort to connect with her – or maybe it's been a while since she made an effort to connect with anyone, the jury's still out – but either way, it's nice to know she and George aren't on their own in this weird world.

"Well, I'm gonna turn in." Jessica yawns as she stands.

"C'mon, George." Lauren holds her hand out to her brother, but he's already asleep in her lap. She wakes him gently and walks him to their tent.

Valentine lets out a throaty snore as he slumps on his side. Remy and Ed smile fleetingly at each other before fixing their eyes on the far reaches of nowhere.

"Not tired?" he asks, glancing back at her.

"Exhausted, but I can't sleep." She sighs. "I keep seeing those dead things all over me. I dreamt that they were... well... whatever."

"You wanna talk about it?"

"Not really."

"How about a walk then?"

She mulls it over, and glances at Valentine who's out cold with his face half buried in the sand.

"He'll be fine," Ed assures her.

They amble down to the shore where the ocean breeze stirs, scattering the sand across their shoes. Remy gazes at the horizon where the calm sea blends into the night sky and the song of crashing waves soothes her tormented soul.

"I can't imagine going home after all of this." She brings her right arm towards her and looks woefully at her injury. "Especially now."

"I don't think I can even process 'normal' after what we've been through," Ed replies.

He looks back at her and she's kneeling in the sand, her head tucked in and her arms wrapped around herself. He can just barely make out her quiet sobs over the tide.

"Remy?" He approaches her slowly.

"Don't. Don't look at me." She sniffs, and with a deep breath pulls herself together and stares ahead at the dark ocean.

"It's okay." He sits cross-legged beside her and rests his elbows on his knees. "You alright?" He sneaks a look at her bandaged stump. "Sorry, that's a stupid question."

"Can we just talk about something normal for a bit? Just pretend we're on a regular beach somewhere and none of this is happening."

"Uh, like what?"

Remy thinks for a second. "I don't know, what's your middle name?"

"Oh… it's… Edward," he answers hesitantly.

"Edward? Wait, so what's your first name?"

He sighs. "… Edward."

"You have the same name twice?"

"Both my grandpas were called Edward and my parents couldn't agree on which one to name me after so… here we are."

"Right. They disagree a lot, then?"

"Not since my mum moved to Spain without us."

"No drama like family drama," she says, recalling a lifetime of chaos.

"Honestly, life is better without her around all the time, she's kind of a crazy mess. I mean, I love her but… yeah. What about your family? Are you and Jessica close?"

"Not really," she replies. "Technically we're not actually

232

sisters, we're not blood-related. My dad buggered off when I was four and never looked back, and eventually my mum started seeing Jessica's dad. Her mother passed away when she was a baby, I think. It's not something anyone talks openly about, obviously. When I was eleven we all moved in together, and we've been your textbook dysfunctional family since. My mum raised Jess like her own."

"Wow, I had no idea. Did it feel weird, getting a sister all of a sudden?"

"I guess… Growing up I felt like Jess was the daughter my mum always wanted and I was just this remnant of my dad breaking her heart and fucking up her life. I was angry and stupid and I said and did things I wish I could take back. I left as soon as I could, went to uni halfway across the country and then I moved into the city."

"So how'd you land back home?" Ed asks.

She looks downcast and ashamed. "I got fired."

"Fired?"

"I called my boss a raging arsehole in front of the entire team."

"Yeah, that'll do it," Ed laughs. "Did he deserve it at least?"

"Yeah. He did." Something of a smile flashes across Remy's face, and as far as Ed can recall it's the first time he's seen her look any sort of happy. "But sleeping on Jessica's bedroom floor was not exactly how I saw my twenties going."

"Bet you didn't see yourself winding up in an RPG either."

"That definitely blindsided me. Although if you'd given me the option a week ago I probably would've taken it. Be careful what you wish for, right? I must have played Ultimate Adventure VII a hundred times when I was a kid. This game taught me so much about life and what kind of person I wanted to be…"
She gazes up at the crimson moon, shimmering against the dark ocean amongst a sky of foreign stars and realises she lost sight of who that person was a long time ago.

Ed watches her hair flutter in the gentle sea breeze as she drapes her arms across herself, and he longs for a window into her thoughts. Something tells him that asking her would be the wrong thing to do, so he waits, admiring the lost expression on her tired face.

She smiles. "… The funny thing is I never even finished it."

"What?"

"I could never defeat the undead griffin in the frozen mountains. I must have tried a thousand times, but I could never do it, so I'd just restart the game after I got to that point."

Ed laughs. "Well, your secret is safe with me."

Remy shakes her head. "Back then I'd have given anything to be here. Now I'm fighting to get home. Funny."

"Is home really that bad?" Ed asks.

"Compared to this? I mean, first-world problems sure, but ever since I was little, I've felt like I don't belong where I am, like I'm supposed to be somewhere else, but I don't know where that is."

She pauses and treads carefully over her thoughts, for her mind is not a place she can safely dwell for long. The whisper is never far away and is always eager to remind her of her faults. *Selfish worthless jealous failure. You could have been so much more, done so much more.*

"When I think about my future it feels like I'm in a room that's spinning but I'm the only one who can see it. I hated my old job, but I stayed because it made me feel like I had worth even if I was miserable. Now I have nothing. And Jessica, she scares the shit out of me. She's always been so sure of what she wants to do, but not me, I'm always drifting. Maybe I take that out on her. I know I shouldn't… I don't think I'm a good person… Sorry I'm just rambling now… Pretty stupid, right?" She sniffs and forces a smile to distract from the tears welling in her eyes.

Ed shakes his head and gives her a look she mistakes for pity, but truthfully he wishes he had the words to remedy her suffering. Not that any could. If only there were spells for mental anguish as there are for physical.

"I know it's none of my business, but if you ask me, maybe you should stop treating Jessica like an NPC and start treating her like a party member."

"What does that mean?" she asks.

"What I meant is, like it or not Jessica will always be a part of your life no matter how much you try to keep your distance."

Somehow his stupid analogy actually sparks a little revelation and Remy wonders, whether intentional or not, if she's caused too much damage to ever repair their relationship.

"Why don't you talk to her about how you feel? Might do you both good to get it all out," Ed says.

"I don't know, we're not really the talk-about-your-feelings type of sisters. We're more like the stuff-it-deep-down-until-one-kills-the-other type."

"That sounds volatile."

She smirks. "You have no idea."

*

A shadow whips past Jessica's tent, and she sits up, rubs her heavy eyes and peeks outside. A primordial fear claws its way up from her stomach. A battalion of Runegard soldiers are sneaking through the village, silently pulling people from their rest and rounding them up. She spots more soldiers descending the cliffside and quickly pulls her head back inside. Before she can formulate a way to warn everyone, two soldiers burst into her tent and wrestle her to the ground. They gag her, bind her hands behind her back and drag her away. She kicks and writhes against her captors, and as soon as she slips her gag loose, shrieks as loud as she can.

Jessica's scream tears through the village, jolting Valentine awake. He staggers to his feet and clutches his splitting skull until the beach stops spinning, then notices two armed soldiers staring him down. The detective's fist flies forward, but he misses and tumbles over in the sand. They draw their swords at his throat, and he holds his hands in the air and sighs. Better sober up quick.

*

Inside the tavern, Marcus and Bengeo snuff out the candles while Cleo peeks out of the tavern window from behind the raggedy curtain.

"They nabbed the blonde one, the quiet girl and the kid. Esmerelda too," she says.

"What's our play, boss?" Marcus asks.

Bengeo rubs his beard and frowns, thinking hard. "Get as many as you can into the caves."

"What about you?"

"Don't worry about me," he says.

At a second glance, Cleo spots several guards approach the rickety stairs leading to the tavern. "They're here," she warns.

Bengeo cracks his knuckles and whispers, "Stay out of sight. Whatever happens, don't help me."

Before the soldiers can position themselves at the doorway, Bengeo bursts out of the tavern fists flying. Wham! The first man drops, then he downs two more in a single punch. The others rush him all at once and drag him to the floor. They bundle on top of the bandit who manages to take out a few more before he's violently subdued, dragged down the stairs and kicked over in the sand. He lands at a pair of shiny metal greaves, and who is staring down at him? None other than Captain Diamond.

"Bandit," she growls. Her face is full of wrath.

"We really should stop meeting like this," he says, wearing a shit-eating grin.

"I ought to cut that smile off your face. For all you've done you'll hang tomorrow, and I'll be the one to kick the stool from under your feet, Bengeo." She scowls at her men. "Take him away!"

At her word the soldiers club him over the head and drag his unconscious heap of a body away.

*

Down at the beach, the wind picks up sharply. Remy and Ed share a foreboding look. The breeze isn't coming from the sea, but behind them. Strange. They turn back towards the village and immediately spot a Runegard gunship descending near the town. Its shiny metallic hull is shrouded by clouds of sand, kicked up by two massive propeller blades beating the air on either side.

He takes Remy's arm and they dart behind a ridge on the beach. "It's an ambush! What do we do?" Ed whispers.

Remy peeks over the ridge and sees the soldiers carry Jessica kicking and screaming up the boarding ramp. "What *can* we do? I can't help anyone like this." She looks defeated as she bites the fingernails of her left hand.

A tinge of hopelessness washes over Ed, but he strengthens his resolve. "I know you're hurting right now but they need us, so spare us the pity party." He takes her by the arms to shake some sense into her. "You killed the giganeye, you faced Grimoirh when everybody else wanted to run, you clawed your way out of a pit of zombies because you were too stubborn to die! So if you think just because your hand got cut off that you're no good to anyone, then I got news for you. There are dozens of heroes who lost limbs and still kicked plenty of ass – Luke Skywalker, Ash Williams, Rick Grimes, Finn the Human, Robocop even. So you're just another amputee that has to conquer evil. Forget what your head tells you and follow the road your heart takes you down!"

Ed's impassioned pep talk quells her doubt. Her eyes dart left to right as she racks her brain, then she lights up with the embers of an idea.

"If I can get to the sword in my tent, we might stand a chance."

"Alright, I'll distract them."

"Okay, solid plan. Well, it'll do." She looks anxious, and with a worried smile he bids her farewell. They split up and sprint across the dark beach towards opposite ends of the village.

*

Valentine is led at sword point up the ramp leading aboard the gunship when he's struck in the arm by a rock.

"Agh!" He looks around to determine where it came from and sees Ed standing in plain sight clutching another rock in his hand.

"Sorry!" Ed cries, then hurls the second stone with more precision. This time he clocks one of Valentine's captors in the head and sends the man tumbling off the ramp and crashing into the sand.

"Hey!" Another soldier raises his sword at Ed, who bolts through the village as more men chase him. Valentine seizes the opportunity to escape and barges the guard in front of him into the sand, then jumps off the ramp and body-slams the poor sod. He rolls on his feet and takes off running towards the tents as more men descend the ramp in pursuit. In his haste, he bumps into Remy who draws her magic sword, which comes alive as the guards rush her.

"Battle, battle, battle!" It jolts at the guards, yanking Remy along behind it.

"Whoa! Wait a minute!" she yelps as the sword swishes about and clashes with a soldier's before swiftly disarming him. Two come at her together, blades swinging. The enchanted sword

238

pulls her out of harm's way and blocks high as one of the men swings for her head.

"Kill, kill, kill!" the sword shrieks.

"No killing!" Remy yells.

Valentine slips the rope binding his wrists and tackles one of the guards into the ground, saving Remy from a nasty back attack. He pins the soldier to the floor and chokes him out until he loses consciousness.

Remy's sword prangs against the guardsman, and she falls back on her arse and tries to pick herself up by shifting her weight onto her right hand, forgetting it was lopped off. Her wound sears with pain as she leans on it and she tumbles back into the sand.

"Well, don't let me die!" she yelps at her sword.

Its morbid eye squints, and the weapon thrusts itself forward, pulling Remy onto her feet. With a flick it smashes against the last soldier's helmet, spinning it backwards on his head. Another strike bashes the top, forcing the man onto his knees, and a third dents the helmet inwards, making it impossible to remove. Remy kicks the guard over and he rolls about, trying in vain to prise his misshapen helmet from his head.

"Where the hell did you learn to do that?" Valentine asks over the soldier's muffled curses.

Remy shakes her head. "This thing has a mind of its own." She shows him the now dormant blade.

"Well, wake it up." He points at ten armed guards charging towards them.

*

Ed sprints into the cave beneath the cliff. His palms beat the cavern walls as he feels his way along the narrow passageways and crashes into Cleo and Marcus, who pick him up. In a panic he warns them of the coming soldiers, but Cleo pulls him around a corner and holds her hand over his mouth. Heavy footsteps grow louder. The soldiers rush in and are met by a surge of roaring flame that erupts from the dark end of the tunnel and incinerates them in the blink of an eye.

Ozrune emerges from the shadows, and behind the wizard, some of the monks protect a herd of villagers and refugees.

"Come with me," the wizard says to Ed, then he addresses the pair of bandits. "See that these people come to no harm." With a graceful flick of his hand he conjures a sphere of light. "This will lead you through the caverns safely."

Marcus nods gratefully and then pats Ed on the shoulder. "Good luck, kid."

"You too," Ed smiles. "Thanks for everything. I hope we meet again."

"No offence, but I don't," Cleo laughs. "Get back to your own world and stay there." She winks, then takes off into the tunnels with Marcus and the refugees.

Ozrune leads Ed back to the village, and as they emerge from the cave they see Remy and Valentine surrounded by a battalion of soldiers by the tents.

"Cast a spell or something!" Ed whispers.

"Wait a moment." The wizard points to a shadow moving across the beach.

*

"Put down your weapon!" a soldier barks at Remy, who grips her sword and stands back to back with Valentine.

"Bite me," she scowls and swipes at him.

The men raise their blades and move to apprehend them, when out of the night sky, like a rain of death, a flurry of arrows fells all of them at once.

"What the—?!" Remy scans the village for the source, clutching her sword tighter still.

"Get them!" another soldier barks from the gunship, and another dozen men descend the boarding ramp, weapons drawn.

From the dark beach leaps a tall figure, which cuts down the first of the men to reach the sand in a spin of swipes and slashes. Remy gasps as she gets a good look at the assailant. It's Avarice, the troll girl she had met in Trout.

Another figure leaps from atop one of the huts, a bow on his back and a gleaming golden longsword in his hand. He runs four men through quicker than Remy can blink. Blood splatters across the sand as the guards topple.

"Come. We must get aboard," the swordsman says.

Remy's jaw drops. Before her stands Regis the Good, every bit as brave and heroic as the game portrayed him. The humble farm boy turned adventurer sheathes his golden blade with a twinkle in his eye and swishes his hair styled in anime spikes.

"Ha, you're still alive!" Avarice laughs.

"Just about," Remy replies.

Their reunion is cut short by the thunderous boom of the Runegard Gunship ascending into the sky.

"We're too late!" Ed cries as he runs out of hiding.

"No, we're not," Ozrune says. "Everyone, come."

Remy, Ed, Valentine, Regis and Avarice hurry to the wizard's side. As he moves his arms with fluid motion, his palms glow amber and the sand around them scatters and spirals around their feet.

"Whoa!" Ed cries in amazement as the wind picks up and lifts them all off the ground.

"Hold on to your butts," the wizard caws before he launches them all into the sky.

Together they glide towards the airship as it sails away, and land on a small observation deck below the hull.

"Shit, here we go again." Valentine looks down at the hazy village as it shrinks into the distance.

XIV

No Time for Mini-games

Remy rests her sleepy head on Ed's shoulder as they huddle together for warmth. There wasn't a chance to pack for the high altitude winds after all. His sight is set on the blinding sun rising over the eastern horizon, flecking pink and red across the boundless sky. He hopes the vista will ease his worries. They barely escaped Runegard last time, and now they're flying right into a city full of soldiers.

"So what's the story with those two?" Regis the Good asks Valentine, who leans against the rails on the other side of the deck.

The detective shrugs. "I just got here."

Regis nods as Valentine rifles through his pockets and pulls out his last cigarette.

"Say, you wouldn't have a light, would you?" he asks.

The swordsman shakes his head and Valentine shoves the cigarette back in his coat with a sigh.

Remy awakens slowly. Prising her heavy eyelids open she sits up and cracks her neck as she stands. "So what's our game plan?"

"First things first, we get off this ship before it docks," Regis insists.

"Can't we just break everyone out now?" Remy asks.

"Not a chance. Even with my blade, Ozrune's magic and her..." Regis looks to Avarice who is attentively picking her teeth with a dagger, "... well, whatever she brings, we're still outnumbered by a few hundred men. Better to play this quiet and enter the city on the sly. They went to a lot of trouble to capture everyone alive, I think it's safe to say they don't plan on executing them, at least not right away. We'll have time to do this smart. It might be a trap after all to nab the rest of you. We've an acquaintance in the city who harbours a grudge against Runegard."

"You think she can be trusted?" Ozrune asks him.

"Maybe, provided our goals align," Regis says.

"Who is it?" Ed asks.

"Better you just meet her. She's a cutthroat who values discretion, if you get my meaning," the swordsman replies.

Remy leans over the railing and sizes up the drop as the gunship soars over rolling emerald hills. "So how do we get off this thing?"

"We'll jump as soon as we descend over the Great Lake," Regis grins.

"Wish I hadn't asked," she sighs and looks out at the glimmering city of Parousia as it rears on the horizon.

It's a beautiful ornate metropolis built over an enormous lake. In its centre, atop a great plateau stands the grand Royal Palace. A breathtaking sight, its spires of ivory and white stone tower hundreds of feet above the crowded city, with limestone streets that wind and weave into a dense nest of houses, arches, shops and taverns stacked in claustrophobic clusters.

"Wow," Ed gasps. "Looks even better in real life."

Remy smiles at the irony of Ed's comment. Her eyes glisten with the shimmering sun which beams off the crystal clear lake below. Parousia was a location in the original game that had always stuck with her, probably because it was packed with side quests and mini-games.

"It used to be something special, now it's pretty much your standard imperial city," Regis sighs. "Obscene wealth surrounded by poverty."

"Sounds like London," Remy quips.

*

"This is total bullshit!" Jessica slams her dainty fists into the cold iron door of her small cell, which echoes down the corridor of the ship's brig, while Lauren sits against the wall and watches her dissolve into a little ball of rage.

"Careful, you're going to hurt yourself."

"Agh! I refuse to be a bloody damsel in distress!" Her balled fist crashes against the iron, and she groans then shakes it vigorously to cope with the rush of pain that follows. "Ow, ow, ow!"

"Lemme see." Lauren takes her hand and inspects it. "Does this hurt?" she asks, bending Jessica's finger gently.

"A little," Jess winces.

"Maybe stop attacking the door. What's your plan if somebody comes and opens it? Please don't take this the wrong way, but you're, like, five feet tall."

"Five foot two!" Jess takes a seat on the rusty cot in the corner of the room. She clenches her fist and a splinter of pain crackles through her finger again. She sighs and reluctantly accepts Lauren might be right, brute force isn't in her skillset. She notices Lauren's severe expression while she stares into nothing and asks, "What're you thinking?"

"Huh?" Lauren snaps out of her trance. "Oh, nothing..." she says, but Jessica's dubious look coerces Lauren to open up. "Well, I was just thinking about George."

"Don't worry, that kid is wicked," Jessica assures her. "If it wasn't for him I'd be monster food."

Lauren smiles, but her worries aren't quelled.

"So it's just you guys and your mum? He said your dad... isn't around?" Jessica asks.

"He did?" Her smile quickly fades. "What else did he say?"

"Nothing, it was more the way he said it that made me wonder."

Lauren sighs. "Almost two years back we lost our dad, but he doesn't talk about it, ever."

"I'm sorry, I shouldn't have—"

"No, it's okay," Lauren insists, but Jessica can tell she's upset and feels guilty for even bringing it up.

"... I lost my mother," she says hoping to put Lauren at ease. Instead she looks shocked. "No, don't worry, it was a really long time ago and it's kinda hard to get upset about someone you can't remember, right? I know it's not the same, but what I'm trying to say is, I kind of get a little bit of what you're going through. Like a piece of you is missing." Jessica's bright eyes shine through smudged black eyeliner, offering more consolation to the wounded girl than she knows.

"Yeah," Lauren nods, "I think the hardest part is that he was just gone. That's what gets me. How could he be there one minute and then in an instant, everything he was, everything he wanted for himself and for us just disappeared and nothing will ever take its place."

Jessica puts an arm around her and squeezes. "I know I don't know you that well, but I bet he'd be proud of the way you're looking out for your brother, and he's a tough kid, I don't think he was half as fazed as I was about being stuck in a video game."

Lauren sniffs and dries her eyes. "Thank you." She smiles again, and this time it's genuine.

"So you worked on this game, right? What do you think they're gonna do with us?"

"You want the truth?" Lauren asks.

Jessica nods. "Hit me."

"They're probably going to hang us. Or torture us and then hang us. Or, if we're lucky, torture us then lock us up in some dark hole forever."

Jessica stares blankly while she plays out the dire scenarios in her mind. Then she erupts like a fireball and charges at the door again screaming.

In the next cell, Bengeo watches George play with a loose thread on his dungarees while Jessica's fury reverberates through the iron wall.

"Chin up, kid, I've been captured by Runegard more times than I can count. We'll be out before you can say dinner."

George mumbles, "My dad used to say it's gonna get bad before it gets good."

"Smart guy."

"Yeah, he was."

"He ain't around no more?" Bengeo asks.

George shakes his head. "Are we gonna die?" he asks. "I heard the lady say they were gonna execute us."

Bengeo smirks. "I wouldn't pay her no mind. Why? You scared?"

"N-no," George insists, but he can tell Bengeo isn't fooled, so he drops the tough guy act. "Okay, maybe a little."

"There's nothing wrong with being a little scared," Bengeo assures him. "You wanna know a secret?"

George nods and scoots closer.

"Being brave don't mean you're not afraid, it means you don't let your fear control you, and you don't need to fret. I bet your dad is up there in the lofty realm right now, watching over you."

"I don't believe in that stuff," George replies.

"Doesn't matter if you believe it or not, he's still watching out for you and your sister. You found each other, didn't you? That was him, he's guiding you both home." Bengeo smiles.

246

"But isn't the lofty realm just a game thing?" he asks.

"Ain't no game, the lofty realm is real alright. It's an astral plane of existence far beyond this one, where all the souls of the dead return to the great powerful spirit after they shed their mortal bodies."

George frowns. "But when you're dead, you're dead."

"Who told you that? Death isn't the end, kid, it's more like a transcendence of form."

"Huh?" George looks utterly befuddled.

"The soul exists partly in time and partly in eternity, so even though the body dies, part of you lives on forever, in the beyond and bound to the ones you love. So as long as your heart's connected, you can find your father anytime."

George looks up at the iron ceiling as if to peer into the lofty realm itself, but it's just a ceiling. Still, it's refreshing to talk about death in such a positive way. Back home his teachers, his friends, even his family tread so softly around the subject, as if they're all afraid to say the wrong thing. Hearing Bengeo unabashedly tell him like it is provides reassurance he didn't know he needed.

*

The gunship descends over the great lake and prepares to dock in the city. At Regis' behest, Remy and the others leap overboard. She plunges into the water, opens her eyes and looks up at streaking light dancing through the blue – must be those volumetric god rays she read about. She allows herself a moment to enjoy the feeling of weightlessness before she surfaces.

"This way!" Regis waves her over to the embankment then submerges and leads them through a large pipe in the city walls. They surface in the sewers beneath the city.

"Holy shit, nearly drowned!" Ed wheezes as Regis lifts him out of the water and onto the stone bank.

"Smells like shit down here." Valentine finishes wringing out his coat and pinches his nose to stop the fetid aroma.

Avarice shakes herself like a wet dog, spraying water everywhere. The others look at her displeased, not that she notices.

"Can't you just magic us dry?" Remy asks Ozrune, who laughs, much to her chagrin.

"Magic isn't a shortcut to all life's inconveniences, I'm afraid. It takes rather a lot of effort to cast," the wizard replies.

Remy rolls her eyes. Magical folk are the most unreliable sort. Perhaps if they spent less time conjuring fireballs and spirits, and more time using their collective abilities for the benefit of the world then Pangea Ultima wouldn't be rife with poverty, strife and war. But that kind of radical change would require mages, wizards and sorceresses to agree on something, which is a task more difficult than mastering even the most complex spell. Why, they can't even agree on what to call themselves. What is the difference between a mage, wizard, witch or sorceress? Nobody is sure, but nobody wants to actually ask a mage, wizard, witch or sorceress lest they're met with a belittling condescending response, which is another trait most magically gifted individuals share, much like people who post their opinions on the internet.

"I don't wanna be that guy, but don't you think it's gonna look a bit suspicious if a troll and an anthropomorphic bird-wizard stroll into town?" asks Ed.

"Those rotten Runegards," Avarice spits, "always treating trolls like we are animals. I will relish burning their city to the ground."

"Nobody said anything about burning the city down," he frowns.

"We will see."

"He's right, it's better if you and Ozrune stay out of sight," Regis says. "We'll rendezvous at the weapon shop in the merchant quarter. Big sign on the outside, you can't miss it."

"Remain wary. The city may seem safe with its high walls, but it's full of cutthroats, sell-swords, thieves and criminals, and that's just the city guard," Ozrune warns. "Don't wait for us, we'll work out an exit strategy and send word. I expect escape will be no small feat after you spring Bengeo and the others."

With that, Remy slings her magic sword onto her back and she, Ed and Valentine follow Regis through the sewers.

"Jesus Christ, look at the size of that!" Valentine gasps as a rat as big as a bulldog scurries across the stone bank opposite.

"I've seen bigger," Regis laughs.

He stops at a ladder that leads to the street just inside the city's West Gate – a huge iron portcullis framed by a white stone arch that serves as one of three entrances into Parousia. The swordsman climbs first, then offers a helping hand to the others as they reach the limestone street, surrounded by tall gothic houses. The people here look mostly wealthier than the peasants of Trout. Women wear bustiers with long gowns and men adorned in quilted doublets and dress coats saunter about, while strumpets and harlots linger outside taverns and brothels down winding alleys. Valentine blushes at one such raven-haired maiden, wearing a skimpy corset, who beckons him for a good time. He rubs the back of his neck and nods to the girl, politely declining her services.

"What kind of game is this?" he asks Ed.

"What do you mean?"

Valentine motions at the harlots.

"Oh. Yeah, there's some pretty racy mini-games. So I've read... Ahem."

"The youth of today," he grumbles as they enter the merchant quarter, the beating heart of the city.

Hundreds of stalls and shops line the streets like a labyrinth of commerce. People flow in every direction. A band of merry minstrels play ballads while peasants dance gleefully around them, maidens stroll the courtyard looking to chat up wealthy noblemen, and vagrants skulk along walls begging for spare coin. Weapons, food, medicine, sex – you name it, you can buy it. In Parousia, everything is for sale. People venture from all across Pangea Ultima to trade at the world-famous bazaar.

Ed is swept up in the river of fair folk. He pushes his way through the maze-like alleys of carts, stalls and stores where dozens of midgey merchants peddle wares gathered from across the realm.

"The hell are those things?" Valentine points at one of the little critters.

"That's a midgey merchant, they're like roaming traders," Remy sighs and shakes her head. "But they're supposed to be bigger."

"They're hideous," the detective says bluntly and the midgey merchant slumps its head and looks upset. "Oh! Uh… S-sorry!" Valentine stutters as the critter sobs. His ex-wife always said he had a habit of putting his foot in his mouth, or did she say that he ought to? The old man never could remember which it was.

He looks over a stall full of livestock. Grotesque bug monsters sit in little crates like kittens at a pet store. The disgruntled beast-master helming the stall curses at him to buy something or move along, so Valentine backs away and accidentally knocks over a ruby vase. He turns sharply, but fails to catch it before it shatters on the ground. An ethereal shape evaporates into the air with a haunting wail, prompting the stall vendor to jeer angrily in his direction. Horrified and confused, he stumbles further into the crowd where a waif of a girl dressed in rags shoves her grubby hands into his coat and pinches his wallet, then a dirty-looking boy swipes the watch right off his wrist.

"Little runts! Get back here!" He shakes his fist at them but is swept away amidst the flow of townsfolk, hopping up and down, keeping a keen eye on them as they pilfer some tarts from a baker's stall then slip through a hole in the wall of a tall building with a bright red door.

"Little shits!" he shouts, much to the shock of the folk around him.

He catches up to the others as Remy spots the weapon shop and points at the big sword and shield hanging above the door with the letters WPN painted across it.

The door creaks open, casting light into the murky store, which is stocked with every melee weapon under the sun. It's more of an emporium than a shop and puts the Trout general store to shame. Ed stares in awe at the rows and rows of blades – iron, steel, ebony, obsidian, mithril silver, even dragon bone, all of them polished to perfection.

Regis approaches the counter, where a burly man clad in tatty leather overalls rests his feet as he sleeps. Behind him, a scalding hot forge crackles while steam rises from the molten metal.

"Hey, wake up." Regis taps the man's boots, and his eyes snap open.

"I didn't touch yer dog!" he snaps, then looks relieved that the furious countess accusing him of dognapping was merely a figment of his imagination. "Well, if it ain't Regis the Good. What d'ya want?"

"Good to see you, Gren," Regis smiles. "I'm looking for our mutual friend."

Gren rolls his eyes. "Oh gods, what has that girl got herself into now?"

"Nothing, yet. We need her help, yours too for that matter."

"Is that so?" He rubs his crooked chin and stands to greet his guests. "Who's this, then?"

"Gren Blacklung, meet Remy of Greater London, the detective Scott Valentine and... Oh sorry," he turns to Ed, "I forgot your name."

"It's Ed," he replies with a deflated sigh.

"Ah, that's right." Regis pats Ed on the shoulder and ruffles his hair. They say never meet your heroes.

Gren runs his filthy calloused hands through his bushy black beard and hawkishly eyes them up, then he looks to Regis. "Well, she ain't here, but I might'a heard a rumour as to her whereabouts. Tavern in the market. The one with the red door."

"Red door?" Valentine perks up.

"Aye. The Lame Adventurer Inn, I think it's called," Gren replies.

"I'll go," Valentine insists.

Remy frowns. "You can't seriously want a drink right now?"

"Of course not. I just want to make myself useful."

"Very well, Ned, go with him, will you?" Regis plants a weighty coin purse in Ed's hands and passes him a small parchment. "Get everything on this list, then stock up on anything that might be useful to us."

"You're giving me all of this?" His eyes twinkle as he peeks into the bag of shiny runa.

"Keep a low profile, and after you've got the gear, retrieve our friend. Pink hair, she'll make an impression."

Ed nods enthusiastically as he jiggles the coin purse in his palm. Along with Valentine, he makes his way outside as Regis lifts Remy's wounded arm and shows it to Gren.

"Now then, what can we do about this?" Ed overhears Regis ask as they step onto the bustling street, shutting the shop door behind them.

He eyeballs the list and then asks Valentine, "What shall we get first?"

The detective reaches into the coin purse, grabs a fistful of runa and shoves them into his pocket. "Get what you want, I'll meet you in the pub."

By the time Ed looks up, Valentine has already wandered into the crowd.

The gunship docks in the air-harbour, high above the merchant quarter where dozens of airships of all shapes and sizes hover by the long embankments that stretch out from the stone plateau and people are busy loading and unloading cargo while others barter for passage to distant lands.

Jessica, Lauren, Bengeo, George and Esmerelda are led onto the bank in chains and are greeted by a regiment of city guards, led by their commander – a hook-nosed man clad in red velvet and half-plate armour.

"You are the other-worlders?" he asks looking past his upturned nose at Jessica's strange clothes.

"They're just kids," Bengeo says, "so let 'em walk and take me instead."

The commander glares at the bandit. "Orders are you all hang. After what you did to the general you should think yourself lucky it'll be quick."

Captain Diamond disembarks the airship and passes Bengeo with her head held high.

"So Runegard's killing children now?" the bandit barks at her.

She gives him a sharp glare, but deep down she knows he's right and it's a bitter pill to swallow.

"Get them off the dock," she orders the commander before striding away.

"You heard her, move!" A guard shoves Lauren to the floor.

"Leave her alone!" Jessica squares up to the guard.

"Or what?" he snarls.

"Or you're gonna have him to deal with." She motions behind her.

The guard looks over her shoulder at Bengeo who glares back, nostrils flared like a bull about to charge.

"No, not him," Jessica says, "him." She points at George, who is also staring furiously at the guard who put hands on his sister.

The guard laughs. "That scrawny kid?"

"That scrawny kid is a level thirty-three assassin!" Jessica yells. "So you better pray that we don't get out of these..." she holds her shackled wrists high and pulls them taut, "... because when we're around, stuff gets wrecked."

The guard takes Jessica by the throat and pulls her close to him. "Let's see you run your mouth without any teeth." He pushes her back and barks at her to get moving.

The townsfolk gawp and whisper as they're marched through the sky harbour gates and into the magnificent palace grounds. Lauren marvels at the elegant white spires atop the palace. The city is clearly not a product of Runegard, whose architecture is far more brutalist and oppressive. She can't but admire its grandeur, and recalls seeing full-motion video sequences being rendered at work, but now, actually standing before the towering ivory palace feels genuinely out of this world. Sadly the feeling is swiftly dispelled as the guards manhandle her into a grotty dungeon beneath the courtyard.

*

Ed enters the bustling city tavern. He barely makes it past the door before a guardsman plants a hand on his chest and barks, "Other-worlders!", at the top of his lungs.

Ed freezes, his heart skips a beat, his knees quiver and he looks worriedly at the guardsman who hands him a leaflet and leans close. It's a wanted poster of sorts, offering a modest reward for any information pertaining to 'other-worlders' and their whereabouts. Below the text is a bizarre illustration of a humanoid lizard creature.

"If you see one then keep your distance, boy, they've red-hot eyes, long snouts full o' razor teeth, and a bewitching gaze that'll corrupt your soul."

"Uh, I'll be careful." Ed swallows his panic and exhales as his bounding heart slows. It's reassuring to him that the locals don't appear to know what an 'other-worlder' actually looks like.

He politely hands the leaflet back to the guard then nudges his way past the drunk nobles and sell-swords clasping a huge leather backpack, stuffed to the brim with provisions he purchased at the market. He sets down the bag to enquire about Valentine's whereabouts and a busty barmaid greets him. She's the spitting image of the serving girl from the Trout inn, save for her dark raven bob-cut.

"What'll it be, handsome?" she asks in a sultry voice.

Ed's eyes are immediately drawn to her exposed bust and the shiny ring bouncing between her ample bosom. *Yep, that's definitely her.*

"Didn't we meet before?" he asks.

She squints her eyes then snaps them wide. "Oh! You're the brave adventurer who stood up to those trolls!"

"Uh, yeah, sort of," he replies.

"Shame the town got burned to a crisp anyway," she sighs and leans over the bar, then subtly pulls on her wig. "And my hair sure isn't growing back anytime soon."

He laughs nervously, remembering how the villagers nobly sacrificed their hair to the magic mirror to ward off the trolls.

"It's not your fault, darlin', I'd always fancied a new look, not that anyone would ever notice."

Ed swiftly averts his eyes from her chest and meets her gaze.

"Warms my heart to see you're still kicking," she smiles. "I ought to thank you for keepin' those nasties at bay so we could escape. I reckon a lot of us woulda bit the dust were it not for you and your friends."

"Oh, don't worry about it," he blushes. "It was nothing. Really, all I did was get hit in the face."

"Nonsense! I saw you charge the Dread Knight himself, so here, it's the least you deserve." The barmaid unclasps the silver chain around her neck and passes it to Ed who examines the small silver ring dangling on it. It's plain except for a fish signet and +3 carved into the band.

"Uh, thanks," he says with the enthusiasm of someone who just unwrapped socks on his birthday.

"I know it don't look much, but my grandfather was quite the rogue in his day. Swore blind that he got that ring from a beautiful mermaiden after he freed her from a wicked lord. Ma said it were only a tale to wind up Grammy, but he told me the ring would let him hold 'is breath for days so he could go back and visit her in the deep sea. Maybe t'were just tall tales, but I figure something like that might be useful to a traveller like you."

"I can't take this." Ed offers the ring back to her, but she closes his hand.

"I insist, hon, you'll get more use out of it than I will. An adventurer's life sure ain't for me. Now, what can I get ya?"

"Actually I'm just looking for someone," he says, fastening the chain around his neck.

"Weren't you lookin' for someone before? You gotta keep better track of your friends, honey. Afraid I ain't seen that big fella nor that crabby girl since I left Trout."

Ed sniggers at her description of Remy. "Actually this time I'm looking for a surly old guy in a long coat and a girl with pink hair."

"Hmm, don't know about the girl, but there's an old guy who looks out of place downstairs."

"Thanks." He lifts his overstuffed bag on his shoulder.

"Be careful down there, people take their card games real seriously in this town."

"Card games?" Ed mutters as he descends the wooden stairs into the basement.

It's a dark bricked room, lit by candles placed atop small square tables spaced apart. Sitting at each one are a bunch of shady-looking customers, all playing a card game in pairs. Against one wall, a feeble old man sits on a throne carved of wood, like some sort of card adjudicator, watching over the other patrons' games.

"Oh no..." Ed groans. There's only one card game in Pangea Ultima: Hexa-clash. A mini-game that appeared in every Ultimate Adventure game since III. Players draw illustrated monster cards from their decks and lay them on a six-by-six grid. If a card is laid, then its attack stats are weighed against the defence stats of the opponent's card. Whichever number is highest wins the clash. There are a bunch of other rules that Ed never bothered to learn, but some players spend hours completing side quests for the best cards to compete in mini-game tournaments. There's even a real-life version of the game; you can buy booster packs and everything. Some of the rarer cards now fetch small fortunes on auction sites. Ed, however, never had the patience to master the game's intricacies.

He spots Valentine at a table on the far side of the room, playing with a deck of his own against a rat-faced man – literally rat-faced. On the table is the detective's wallet. Looks like he tracked it down.

Ed approaches their table. "Hey."

"Not now, lad, I'm winning." He shoos Ed away and contemplates his next move.

Several cards are laid on the grid already, each one displaying a creature or character encountered in the game, and underneath the picture, the card's stats are displayed. The rarest cards are the most powerful and some would even kill for them. Strangely, no one in Pangea Ultima knows precisely where the cards come from or how the game originated, but there's always a bunch of cards in circulation and occasionally new ones pop up in strange places.

"We really don't have time for mini-games," Ed sighs as he pulls up a chair next to their table. He notices a hulking stone wall of a man, clad in a grey suit of armour watching Valentine play from the corner of the room. The man looks familiar.

Ed recognises him from the game's promo material but can't remember who he is.

The knight talks in hushed tones with a short, slight woman whose face is obscured by a black hood, and as soon as he crosses Ed's gaze he hastily ends his conversation, then pulls up a chair beside Valentine's table.

"Your friend is good," he says in a gravelly voice.

"Really?" Ed suspects the knight has an agenda of some kind.

"Five-to-one odds he'll win the tournament."

"Tournament?" Ed plants his face in his palm. "We don't have time for a tournament."

"Relax, get yourself a drink, take the edge off." The knight grins with all the earnestness of a guy selling off brand pharmaceuticals from the boot of his car.

Valentine draws a card that catches Ed's eye. The Brawlin' Bandit displays an illustration of Bengeo, and his stats are formidable.

"Whoa, how'd you get that card?" he asks.

"I won it," Valentine says and lays the card on the table.

His opponent scowls and mutters profanities under his breath as he fans through his hand. The rat-faced man draws a new card, which dispels any hope of winning. He throws the card down on the table – The Scrawny Swordsman, and the illustration looks a lot like Ed. Its stats are dismal.

"Is that supposed to be me?" Ed gasps.

"Don't be ridiculous," Valentine smirks, laying another card – The One-Armed Adventurer, which depicts a chestnut-haired battle maiden wielding a longsword. Her expression is severe and her right hand has been severed and her arm bandaged above the wrist.

"Oh, come on, that's clearly Remy," Ed cries. "Who makes these?" Rumours are the midgey merchants make the cards and distribute them throughout Pangea Ultima to ensure a steady flow of coin to their pockets. Few believe such conspiracies, but then again, how else could the cards stay up to date with current affairs? The network of midgey merchants runs far deeper and is more influential than anyone would dare to admit.

The rat-faced man lays his final card, The Gambling Guardsman, and the picture looks exactly like Valentine does – his grouchy expression, the way he sits with cards fanned in one hand and a tankard by his side. The only discernible difference is the man in the picture is sporting a Runegard guard's uniform.

Ed folds his arms and taps his foot impatiently while Valentine deliberates on his next move, and draws one final card – The Meek Mage – and with it, he wins the game.

His opponent slams his fist on the table. "Blast and damnation!" he spits. "You hustled me! You're a cheater!"

The scoundrel reaches for a club on his belt, but before he can draw it, the knight stands, one hand clasping the hilt of a greatsword on his back.

"I… I didn't mean to offend!" The rat-faced man bows apologetically.

"Pay my friend what he's owed," the grey knight growls.

"Of course." He places a hefty sack of gold on the table then picks up his deck of cards.

The knight growls again and signals to the man's deck. "You know the rules. Winner gets your best card."

"Keep it. I'm only interested in what's mine." Valentine swipes his wallet and watch off the table.

"You're not walking out of here until the tourney is over, old man!" the rat-faced man hisses.

"Like the boy said, we don't have time for your tournament," Valentine replies.

By the time he's finished fastening his busted watch, a dozen rough-looking brutes surround them, armed with clubs, broken bottles and mean faces.

"Anyone ever tell you you've a knack for pissing people off?" Ed whispers to the detective who's busy counting the men.

While all eyes are on them, the hooded woman slinks to the back of the room unnoticed and unsheathes a curved dagger from her belt. The blade glimmers as she positions it at the adjudicator's throat. Ed spots her just as she plunges the dagger into the old man, who dies with a shrill cry and a gurgle as blood sprays from his neck. Pink curls fall in front of the killer's face as she turns to run.

"Oh God!" Ed yelps as the knight hurls Valentine's deck of cards at the rat-faced man then breaks a stool over his head.

"Get 'em!" cries one of the thugs, and on his orders, two more block the door.

The knight rushes the men at full speed grinning like the Devil. He draws the broad sword on his back and cracks one thug with the pommel. Ed and Valentine follow him up the stairs and they tear out of the back alley where they're cut off by a dozen more thugs. The knight grins and raises his sword high.

"Stand back." With a mighty swing he sweeps every scoundrel off their feet and laughs as they roar in agony.

"Appreciate the assist, fellas." He sheathes his sword and escapes through the narrow alley, tipping a cart over behind him to block the road, leaving Ed and Valentine totally abandoned as the ruffians clumsily pile out of the tavern behind them.

"He left us," Ed gulps.

"This way!" Valentine pulls Ed through a narrow gap between two houses and into the heaving market square.

Ed glances over his shoulder at the posse of thugs tailing them and then ahead at the seemingly impassable crowd, and he looks at Valentine, as if to say, 'We're screwed.'

Valentine gestures at the top of the stalls. "Go over!"

He boosts Ed atop a wooden food cart and scrambles up behind him. They hop across the market, leapfrogging from stall to stall with the thugs in hot pursuit. Three brutes come up on their rear. Valentine rummages through Ed's oversized backpack and grabs a potion bottle, which he hurls behind him without a second thought.

"That wasn't cheap!" Ed yells.

Valentine pays him no mind and throws another flask. The bottle breaks against a thug's face, letting loose a swarm of angry bees, which sting the living hell out of the man until he crashes head first into the market with a thud.

"What the hell is in these things?!" the detective asks.

"I got a bunch of different stuff!" Ed replies, trying not to let the weight of his backpack tip him sideways as he leaps across another stall. Angry shoppers and merchants hurl insults at them as they tear past, leaving mayhem in their wake. "Sorry!" Ed shrieks as he steps into a scalding hot wok.

One of the thugs takes a shot at a running tackle, but Valentine pulls Ed down into the market just in time, and the thug flies over them, slamming headfirst into a stall of steaming hot dumplings. They push their way out of the square and bolt down a long crooked alley. Ed clasps his bag in his arms to keep his items from spilling out, but a potion bottle slips from his grasp and smashes on the floor, transmuting several of the townsfolk into chickens.

"He... Bwwaaaarrrk!" A woman's shrill voice morphs into a series of clucks that echo behind them as they tear through another intersecting back alley.

"Sorry!" Ed cries as Valentine drags him around a corner.

"Just when I think shit can't get any weirder!" The wheezing detective wipes his brow and leans against the wall to catch his breath while Ed runs towards the wooden building at the end of the alley.

"Maybe we can hide in here?" He opens the door and a cloud of steam hits him in the face.

Inside, the building is packed with a dozen strumpets fawning over pudgy old nobles sweating in hot tubs.

"Close the door!" a nobleman shrieks while a young woman rubs his hairy chest with honey. "You're letting out the steam!"

Ed shuts the door quickly. Of all the horrors he's witnessed in this world, that woman's slender fingers tangled in the man's gloopy plume of chest hair will haunt him to the end of his days.

Valentine peeks out of the alley and glimpses two musclebound brutes heading straight for them. Just as the thugs turn into the alley, he cracks one in the face, knocking him out cold. He strikes the second much larger man in the chest, but it does little more than infuriate him.

"Christ! What the hell are you made of?" The detective shakes his throbbing hand and throws up his fists, ready to lay down some hurt while Ed rummages through his pack for something that might save them.

The thug slugs Valentine in the nose, and he trips backwards into a heap of trash piled in the alley. Ever the stubborn fool, he gets up and raises his fists. Crack! Another bone-crunching thud and Valentine goes down again.

"Aghh, c'mon, you call that a punch?" He staggers to his feet a third time, rubs his jaw and spits blood.

"For God's sake, Valentine, just stay down!" Ed cries.

The thug looks Ed's way with psychotic eyes. "As soon as I'm done with Grandpa, I'm coming for you."

"For God's sake, Valentine, get up!" Ed prays the detective will save him from a pummelling, or at the very least tire the guy out first.

Valentine rallies, launching a succession of hits on the musclebound bully, who barely flinches. Accepting the futility of his attacks, he drops his fists exhaustedly.

"Okay, maybe we can just hash this out with words? C'mon, what d'ya say?"

BLAM! He slumps backwards and leans against the alley wall, pinching his nose to stay the bleeding.

Ed draws a small bottle filled with a glowing yellow liquid from his bag. "Drink this!" He tosses the bottle to Valentine who catches it in his left hand.

Before he can ask what's in it another blow sends him to the floor. He scrambles away from his opponent and downs the potion like a shot of whisky. His chest burns, his throat stings, he gasps for breath, savouring the fresh air with each inhale, then with a cough, a fireball erupts from his mouth.

"Ugh! What the hell are you trying to do to me, boy?! I'm losing just fine on my own. What the hell was that?!" he gasps.

"Dragon's breath!" Ed cheers.

Another cough and Valentine spits an enormous fireball, which scorches the wall. The thug looks ashen and slings his unconscious comrade over his shoulders, then flees for fear of being roasted while the detective vomits like a flame-thrower, showering the street with fire which sets the bathhouse alight. Black smoke billows from the building's wooden walls as the flames quickly spread.

"We are in so much trouble," Ed whimpers and stands slack-jawed at the mayhem he's wrought.

Naked men and women flee the sauna in terror and scatter into the city while Valentine fights to get a grip on his lethal coughing fit. Ed takes him by the back of his coat and rushes him inside the bathhouse. They crash into the water fully clothed, and Ed attempts to douse Valentine's fire breath by holding his head under the bathwater for extended intervals.

"Enough!" Valentine cries, gasping for air. "It's stopped!" He throws his hands up high as he stands up in the bath, dripping wet.

Ed nods and rests against the side of the pool. "Cool. Cool," he wheezes.

Valentine flicks his sopping hair out of his face and notices thick black smoke pouring into the room from outside. "The building's on fire," he gasps.

"Yeah," Ed nods, still panting.

"We're in the building!"

The imminent danger dawns on Ed and he pulls himself out of the pool, swinging his head in the direction of the door.

"Oh." He gazes at the roaring fire blocking their only exit.

Valentine climbs out of the bath, soaked to the bone, and waves Ed over. They climb the stairs and make their way through the rooms and out onto a balcony.

"You first," he says.

Ed shakes his head and looks at the street below. It looks far and he bruises like a peach.

"You're young, your body is still rubbery, you'll bounce," the detective insists.

"You expect me to believe that?"

"Look, I've got a tricky knee, I can't land hard on it. I need you to help me down."

Ed's conscience gets the better of him, and he steels himself, then climbs over the railing. The flames crawl to the second floor and rip through the wooden building. Planks tumble off the walls and parts of the floor give way.

"We haven't got all day!" Valentine pushes Ed off the balcony. "Remember to bend your knees as you land!" he shouts.

Ed slams onto the limestone street below with all the grace of a suitcase dropped from an aeroplane. Valentine is unsure as to whether or not the fall might have killed him, and he stares at Ed's motionless body and panics – how will he explain this to the others? And the paperwork, oh God, the paperwork. Thankfully his fears are dispelled with Ed's nasally whine.

"That was a dick move!" Ed groans as the detective climbs over the rail and lowers himself down.

"Get ready to catch me," Valentine cries.

"Catch… Ugh?" Before Ed knows it, he's crushed by the 200-pound police officer. With a wheeze, he pushes the detective off him and fights to catch his breath.

The odd couple lie face up in the alley and stare at the burning bathhouse for a minute. The smoke from the fire floats high and in no time at all attracts the attention of the city guard who come rushing, only to find the alley empty save for the charred remains of the bathhouse and a few scattered items trailing into the warren backstreets of the city.

XV

WELCOME TO THE REVOLUTION

G ren fastens several leather straps around Remy's shoulder and bust, connected to a metal pauldron on her right shoulder, which in turn is attached to an elbow guard and an iron bracer buckled around her forearm, on which Gren has rigged an interlocking attachment for a small but sturdy buckler shield. She winces as he tightens the straps on her forearm, then winds her shoulder and bends her elbow testing the prosthetic's manoeuvrability.

"How is it?" Regis asks.

"Feels pretty solid. It's not a robot hand, but I think I can make this work," she replies, trying hard to be optimistic.

"And the wound?"

"It aches pretty bad, but it's bearable. Guess it would hurt a lot more if it weren't for Esmerelda."

She glances down at the shield where her hand should be and burns with rage at what Grimoirh did to her. She draws the magic sword on her back with her left hand and raises her shield arm defensively. If she's gonna make him pay she'll take all the help she can get.

Gren inspects her blade with great intrigue. "Where'd you find a sword like that?" he asks. "Never seen anything like it."

"Got it in some hell hole." She turns the sword in her hand. "Sometimes it talks."

Gren lets out a disapproving sneer. "Talking swords? Bah! Maybe if you'd had one of my blades you'd still have both arms." He lets out a brash laugh that quickly breaks into a violent cough. They don't call him Blacklung for nothing, and it's not like smithing comes with a great healthcare package.

The weapon shop door creaks open and two figures linger in the doorway, one little and one large – clearly not Ed or Valentine.

"Regis the Good? Is that you?" The tall knight throws his head back in laughter. "Well, I'll be a rotting bastard, how long's it been?" He vigorously shakes Regis' hand.

The short one lowers her hood, revealing pale pink shoulder-length hair that falls in curls either side of her delicate face. Remy isn't fooled by her baby-faced looks. She knows this is Astrid Amethyst, the rogue princess of Parousia, who, in exile, spent her formative years venturing from town to town under the guise of a travelling bard, punishing and murdering corrupt nobles in her quest to avenge her stolen crown and slaughtered family.

She twirls an ornate baroque dagger between her fingers as her piercing eyes size up Remy. Accompanying her, as always, is her loyal bodyguard, Tank, the last surviving member of the Knights of Parousia, who was but a lowly squire when he snuck her out of the city during Runegard's violent annex all those years ago.

Remy looks them up and down in awe. Meeting her in-game companions never seems to get old.

Astrid glances at Regis and asks, "Who's this?"

"Remy Winters. I'm a big fan," she says.

"You've heard me sing?" Astrid asks.

"Not exactly, I meant I'm a fan of the way you give those corrupt nobles what they deserve." Remy fangirls hard. "I'm a liberal too – living wage, eat the rich, all that jazz."

Astrid looks wary, as only a chosen few know her true profession deals in death. "You seem to know me, but I don't know you," she says with a scowl.

"It's complicated," Remy replies. "Wait, aren't Ed and Valentine with you?"

"Who?" Astrid looks to Tank who shrugs.

"Never heard of 'em," the grey knight replies.

Remy squints dubiously at the pair. Working for that production company sharpened her bullshit meter to a finite edge.

"Don't fret, they'll be back sooner or later," Regis assures her. "How much trouble could they get into?"

Remy frowns. Regis clearly doesn't know Ed very well.

*

"I can't believe we burned down a sauna." Ed looks over his shoulder to check they're not being followed. His shoes squelch against the cobbled road as they climb a long hill that circles back to the merchant quarter.

"Don't tell the others," Valentine says.

"I don't know, I'm not good with secrets. Speaking of which, are you gonna tell me what all that was about?"

"No." Valentine tosses out the cards, receipts and wet bank notes from his wallet. His face looks flush with panic.

"All that trouble for your wallet?" Ed asks.

"Couldn't care less about the wallet." The old man looks relieved as he pulls out a worn picture of his daughter and stares at it tenderly for a moment.

Ed notices how gently he handles it. "Who is she? A niece or something?"

268

Valentine's silence speaks volumes.

"Your daughter? But you're so old."

The detective frowns, perches on the garden wall of someone's house and stares longingly at the photo. "It's an old picture… I tried the family thing for a while, but all I did was make everyone miserable."

"When was the last time you spoke to her?" Ed asks.

The detective stays quiet. A look of profound guilt and remorse ages him horribly.

Pity stirs in Ed's heart and despite all that Valentine has put him through, he feels like he should say something to ease his pain. "Well, it's never too late, right? You know, Remy told me her dad split when she was a kid and I think that she wonders whether he left because she wasn't good enough for him to stick around. She's spent her whole life walking around with that lie eating away at her. My dad is all I've got. If it weren't for him, I don't know what I'd do."

Valentine looks downcast and sighs.

"I'm not trying to make you feel worse, I'm just saying, so what if you weren't the best dad? You're grumpy, short-tempered, you drink a lot, you're a bit of a dick sometimes, but beneath that dick, there's a good man in there." Ed pokes him in the chest. "You've stuck by us, that means something. So quit wallowing, help us get home, go see her and get a new picture."

The detective hardens his expression, eager not to let on that Ed pierced his shell. He opens his mouth, but no words come, so he carefully tucks the picture in his coat pocket.

"C'mon, we better hurry back," Ed says. "I don't think it's a good idea to leave Remy alone with those guys."

"Who? Regis? Seems okay to me."

"Regis is actually kind of an ass, but no, I meant Astrid and Tank."

"You've lost me, is that the bird-headed one?"

"No, that knight who started the bar fight and the girl who

killed that card shark guy. I'm certain they're who we were looking for. They're probably at the weapon shop already."

"But aren't those the good guys?" Valentine asks.

"More like chaotic neutral," Ed replies. "Astrid's only goal is revenge on the kingdom that murdered her family, and she'll do anything to get it."

"Sounds like a delightful young lady."

"If they're getting involved with us then they're bound to have some kind of agenda."

"Alright. I'll keep an eye on 'em," Valentine assures him as they return to the merchant quarter.

The weapon shop door creaks open and patches of wet trail behind them on the hardwood floor. Remy, Regis and the others greet the pair with blank stares.

"What the hell happened to you?" Remy gasps.

"It's a long story." Ed slings his overstuffed rucksack onto the countertop. "I got everything on your list… well, most of it. I'm not sure what fell out."

Regis takes the rucksack with one hand, and effortlessly lifts it over his shoulder, then he gestures to the newcomers. "By the way, this is—"

"Yeah, we've already met," Ed says.

"Glad to see you boys got away." Tank lets out a brash laugh.

Ed gives the knight a cold stare. "Yeah, thanks for the assist. Fella."

Gren locks the shop door and ushers everyone into the musty basement. He strikes a match and lights the candles surrounding a map of the city laid on a table in the centre of the room.

"Alright, this is what we know. Bengeo and the other-worlders are most likely being held in the dungeon beneath the grand palace." Regis taps the palace's location on the map with the tip of his dagger.

"So we break them out?" Remy asks.

"Not a chance. The dungeon is heavily fortified, and the only way in or out is a bottleneck. You'd never make it out alive," Tank replies.

"Word amongst the guard is, there's to be a public execution tonight," Astrid says.

"Execution?!" Remy looks disgusted.

Astrid scoffs. "No better way to assure the great unwashed that their precious kingdom is winning the war against Grimoirh and these other-worlders everyone's talking about. If you want to rescue your people, the execution is your best window."

Valentine asks, "Won't there be guards everywhere?"

Astrid nods. "Of course, but your friends will be out in the open. The executions are always held in High Cloud Square. There are far too many ways in and out for the city watch to block, and it'll be packed full of gawping peasants."

"So what's in it for you?" Ed asks.

The princess smirks. "Straight to it. I like you, Red."

"The Runegard-appointed regent, that snake General Gigas and his lackey bitch Diamond will all be attending," Tank grins. "We'll have no better chance to snuff them all out at once."

"Your little rescue mission will serve as the perfect distraction. Finally, we can free this city from Runegard's oppression," Astrid says.

"I don't know if I like this," Remy says. "I don't want to put them in any more danger."

"They're dead anyway. At least this way you have a shot," Tank replies.

Remy and Ed share a disapproving look at the knight's callous tone.

"We'll cause a distraction that'll draw most of the guards away from the square. That's what the supplies were for." Regis pats Ed's backpack. "Dragon's breath, blast-powder and hot-rocks."

Ed looks horrified. "You had me buy supplies for a bomb?!"

"Aye," Regis nods. "Though it looks like we're a little light on dragon's breath." Ed and Valentine share a guilty look as Regis continues, "We'll split into two groups. Group one will set off the explosives inside the palace. Should be relatively easy, most of the guards will be at the execution after all. After the palace is blown, group two will rescue the captives amidst the chaos, then we all rendezvous at the sky docks where Ozrune and Avarice will have secured us passage out of the city."

"I don't know, setting off a bomb? What if people get hurt?" Ed asks.

"You joking?" Tank shoots Ed a dirty look. "The more Runegard scum we take out, the better."

"But don't they have, like, families? I know they're the bad guys, but some of them are just doing their jobs, right?" Ed replies.

Astrid and Tank look disgusted at the idea that Runegard soldiers are anything but vermin to be culled.

"Like it or not, this is war. Runegard will kill you just because of where you're from. If you want your friends to survive, you'll have to fight for it," Astrid says.

"I know, I know... I just don't like it, is all," Ed sighs.

Regis nods. "Noted. Tank, you take Valentine and Ed and set the explosives."

"Fine, but you better not get soft on me." He glares at Ed who glares right back.

"Remy and I are on rescue duty," Regis says.

"What about Astrid?" Remy asks.

"I'll cover you from a vantage point. I'll get a better shot at the bastard regent from up high." The rogue princess is a picture of malicious glee. She's long dreamed of this day.

"Well, you're gonna need disguises." Gren drags a chest into the middle of the room and kicks it open. "I've got some old guard uniforms stashed away."

"Alright, let's suit up." Astrid plants her dagger in the map, which prangs back and forth. "Welcome to the revolution," she grins.

Remy pulls Ed back while the others don their disguises. She takes the sword off her back and offers it to him.

"Here."

He grasps it with both hands. "You're giving me your magic sword?"

She smiles. "I'll worry less knowing you have it."

"But won't you need it?"

"Regis showed me a few moves while you guys were out. Besides, he'll watch my back, I don't trust Tank to do the same for you."

"He showed you some moves, huh?" Ed looks over at Regis, whose chiselled muscles glisten in the ray of light catching him through the small basement window as he pulls off his gambeson.

"That's just ridiculous," Ed sniggers under his breath.

"What's so funny?" Remy asks.

"No, nothing. Thanks. I'll look after it." He slings the sword over his shoulder and picks up the guard uniform from the chest.

Remy watches as he pulls off his ratty tunic, revealing his pasty chest and weedy arms. He tries to expand his muscles or at least mask the fact that he doesn't have any while he stands between Tank and Regis – two poster boys for the herculean physiques often seen in comics and video games. Try as he might Ed could never seem to put on any muscle. Well, to be honest he didn't try very hard. Exercise and a healthy diet are adverse concepts to him.

"Oh boy," Remy laughs while he puts on his armour. He looks like a kid on the first day of school, shrinking in a uniform that's far too big for him. He brandishes a goofy smile and strikes a muscle pose at her. A warm tingle flutters in her chest, and before she knows it, a lasting smile has crept across her face. So someone is after her heart again.

*

Lauren stares at an odd brown stain on the floor of her cell, dreading to think what caused it. One thing's for sure, this is exactly how she remembers it from the game, except for the smell. The stench of mildew and rotten eggs permeates the air.

"Ugh, smells like—"

"Shit," George says.

"George!"

"What?" He shrugs at his sister. "You were gonna say it."

"Well, yeah, but..." Lauren lets out a doleful sigh. "Hey, you got a lock pick or anything?" she calls to Bengeo in the cell opposite.

Bengeo shakes his head. "Even if I did, there's a dozen more locked doors and a hundred soldiers between us and freedom. Archers and gunners on the ramparts, bloodthirsty hounds and a portcullis, not to mention the city is surrounded by a lake."

"So you're just giving up?"

"No, just biding my time. Remy and Ed are still out there, and so is Ozrune. They'll come for us, I'm sure of it."

"That's your plan? Just wait and see?"

"Well, seeing is believing."

"Anyone ever tell you that you're insufferable?"

"Every damn day, Freckles," he smirks.

"But what if... what if they didn't make it?" She glances over her shoulder to make sure Jessica didn't hear her. Thankfully she's busy boosting George on her shoulders so he can peer out of the tiny window high up against the stone wall.

"They made it," Bengeo says, reassuring himself as much as he is Lauren.

The dungeon door opens with a thunderous clank. The captain's footsteps echo down the hall and she approaches Bengeo's cell, her crimson cape flowing gracefully behind her.

"To what do I owe this visit?" the bandit asks.

274

"Save it," Diamond scolds him, "this is your last chance to tell us what you know about the Dread Knight and the crystal."

"Why would I tell you anything? You'll kill us anyway."

"The Dread Knight is a threat to the entire world, and I know you, Ben, you act tough, but you're the bleeding-heart type. Tell us what you know so we can stop Grimoirh and save a lot of innocent lives."

"Last I checked Runegard was taking innocent lives," Bengeo sneers. "Do you honestly believe that the crystal would be any better off if Runegard got their grubby hands on it?"

Diamond frowns, with her own doubts about the kingdom beginning to weigh heavy. "Something strange is happening. The undead are marching," she whispers.

"Marching? Since when do the undead march?" the bandit scoffs.

"Until now they've never done anything but roam aimlessly, but after that black dragon took off into the sky, they've all started marching after it. I saw it with my own eyes! When we were pulling survivors out of the *Thanatos* in that marsh, the undead were everywhere. I thought we were done for, but they walked right past us, as though something was calling them! They were like soldiers – when have you ever seen them behave like that?"

Bengeo's interest is piqued. "Where are they marching to?"

"North. All reports say north."

"Nothing in the north. Whole region ain't but ice and snow. I say let 'em have it."

"Legends say the crystal was forged there. In the lost kingdom. The Scar, Ben. It can't be a coincidence. Whatever Grimoirh is doing will spell ruin for us all. So just tell me what you know."

"I'll tell you," Lauren says through the bars of her cell.

"What did you say, girl?" The captain turns sharply to her.

"I said I'll tell you everything you want to know. About Grimoirh, about the crystal, everything."

"Lauren, don't!" Bengeo warns.

"Quiet!" Diamond snaps. She looks closely at Lauren, scrutinising every micro-expression on her face.

"I know who he is, I know what he wants, and I know all about the crystal." Lauren stares the captain down. "Let us all go, and I'll tell you whatever you want."

"How do I know you're not lying?" Diamond scowls.

Confidence in her abilities is something Lauren has always struggled with, but miscellaneous video game trivia is her area of expertise and she knows it. She tightens her eyes and smiles. "Your real name is Annabella La Loire, but everyone calls you Diamond for the rapier you carry. Your mother and father were merchants who died on the night Runegard annexed the city. You were taken in by the army after they found you wandering the streets, soaked in your parents' blood. You were holed up for days in their burnt shop, starving, thirsty. You joined the guard because it was either that or steal, which is where you met Bengeo. You guys had a thing when you were both in the infantry, but you called it off after he deserted the kingdom and pursued the life of an outlaw. You still carry the enchanted ribbon he gave you, though. The one that wards off curses. And you have doubts about whether or not you're on the right side. Sometimes you wonder whether Gigas is just as ruthless as the Dread Knight, and you're right to."

Diamond looks dumbfounded. "How could you possibly—?"

"I read your Wiki page," she replies.

The captain barks to the guard at the door, "Take this one."

"Aye, ma'am." The guard salutes and unlocks Lauren's cell. The iron gate creaks open and the guard clasps Lauren's arm.

"I won't talk unless you let everyone else go." Lauren puts on her best mean face, hoping to mask her crumbling nerves. Unfortunately for her, Diamond can smell her fear.

"Take the little blonde one too." The captain points at Jessica. "If you care so much about your friends, then I suggest you loosen your tongue, lest she lose hers."

276

The guard takes Jessica by the arm and drags her out of the cell before locking it behind him.

"Leave 'em alone, you crone!" Esmerelda shouts as the guards force the girls out of the dungeon.

"You better hope she talks, because after we're done with blondie, I'm coming for you, old woman." Diamond glares with spite, then takes her leave.

Esmerelda looks sternly at Bengeo. "We've gotta do something."

"Not a damn thing we can do," he sighs and looks at poor George, who's wracked with worry for his sister's wellbeing.

*

As Diamond exits the dungeon, three mismatched guards approach the palace from the far side of the courtyard. Tank – tall, broad and strong; everything a soldier should be – effortlessly carries a barrel full of explosives over each shoulder while Ed and Valentine struggle to haul one barrel between them as they bicker with each other. The captain eyes them suspiciously as they cross the courtyard, but Jessica steals her attention.

"Where are you taking us?" she asks.

"If I were you, I'd speak only when spoken to," Diamond barks.

The guards shove Jessica and march the girls into the palace. Diamond pauses before entering and looks back at the three suspicious guards, only now they're gone. She scans the courtyard for them, but they're nowhere she can see.

"That was close." Ed watches the captain enter the palace from behind a tall statue.

"Why are you wearing those?" Valentine points to his Converse sneakers.

Ed lifts the visor on his clunky helmet, revealing just his eyes. "They're my lucky shoes."

Valentine lifts his too. "Lucky how?"

"Well, I've been wearing them this whole time, and I haven't died."

Tank pulls his visor up. "Will you two shut up. You're gonna blow our cover."

"Sorry," Ed bows his head, "but did you see? She was taking Jessica and Lauren somewhere."

"It's almost sundown, we don't have time for distractions. We need to set these kegs in the armoury now," Tank says.

"Saving them isn't a side quest, it's the whole reason we're doing this!" Ed argues. "If they're being taken away, it means they won't be at the execution for Remy and Regis to rescue."

"I'm here to free my country and see Astrid claim her birthright, that's my reason for doing this. If you go after them, you're on your own," Tank warns.

"Fine," Ed replies. "Valentine, you're with me, right?"

The detective nods. "Of course."

Tank scoffs and prods Ed in the breastplate. "Whatever you do you better do it quick, this is the last place you want to be when I blow these kegs." He pulls his visor down and lifts two of the barrels over his broad shoulders. "If you get caught, you better not blab a word about our plan, else I'll kill you myself." With that, he strides across the courtyard like a man on a mission.

"I thought knights were supposed to be chivalrous," Valentine sneers.

"Forget him, let's get the girls." Ed pulls down his visor and the two of them abandon the last barrel in the courtyard and cautiously follow Diamond into the palace.

The captain marches the girls through a long decorated corridor and pauses before a tall white door. The guards open them in unison, revealing an impressive banquet hall. The towering stone walls are adorned with grandiose oil paintings of long-dead Runegard royals. Each looks more pompous than the last. A grand hearth sits against the north wall with two shining halberds mounted above it, and in the centre of the room, at the end of the long dining table, sits a cloaked figure, bathed in the coloured haze pouring in from the oval stained glass window behind him.

"Here and here." Diamond points to two chairs opposite one another at the nearest end of the table. The guards force Jessica and Lauren to sit then exit the room.

The figure sitting at the far end of the table stands slowly and staggers towards them with a limp. It's Gigas, and he looks significantly worse for wear. His skin bears a sickly yellow hue and his crooked, hunched body is draped in a dark velvet cape that trails behind him.

"Who do we have?" he asks in a breathy voice.

"Two other-worlders, sir. This one knows things." Diamond presses her hand on Lauren's shoulder. "Things she shouldn't."

"Is that so?" A droll smile stretches across his mouth.

"Y-you look sick, we can always do this later," Jessica says, drawing Gigas' enraged eyes to her.

He pulls a dagger from his belt and takes a place behind her, pressing the blade under her chin.

"Whoa. Wait a minute!" Jessica gasps.

"So supple, so full of life…" Gigas mutters to himself while he drags the dagger over her soft skin and devours her with his pale sunken eyes.

"Lay one finger on her and I won't tell you anything!" Lauren cries.

Gigas nicks Jessica's collarbone with the blade and grins. "Foolish girl, you think you're in a position to make demands?"

"Oh God," Jessica frets, "I'm too sober for this."

"Maybe we should start with her tongue." Gigas violently grabs her jaw and forces her mouth open. Jessica winces. His foul breath reeks of death.

"Now talk!" the general yells.

"You're gonna let him torture us? Is this the kind of kingdom you fought for?" Seeing the troubled look on her face, Lauren tries to appeal to Diamond's conscience.

"Leave us!" Gigas orders.

"But, sir—" Diamond protests.

"Now! Oversee the execution while I interrogate these two."

Diamond meets his gaze for a moment before stepping outside of the room. She pauses after closing the door behind her. Something about the general's miraculous survival after the *Thanatos* crash doesn't sit right with her. Since then he seems unhinged. Nevertheless, like a good soldier, she departs to carry out his orders.

"I thought she'd spot your shoes for sure. Maybe they *are* lucky," Valentine whispers. He and Ed have taken the places of the guards outside the banquet hall. "So you got a plan to get them out?"

Ed lifts his visor, revealing a twinkle in his eye as Gigas' voice booms through the decorated wooden door.

"The crystal!" Gigas cries. "Tell me of its power, of how it reanimates the dead." He presses the dagger to Jessica's eye.

Inky tears stream down her face as she tries to hide that she's bricking it. He'd only enjoy her sobs and pleas for mercy, so she won't give him the satisfaction. '*Never let them see you cry*' – a piece of sisterly advice Remy had imparted many years ago that always stuck with her.

Lauren trips over her words as she tries her best to explain all she knows. "The crystal was used to seal away a powerful entity that perverted the cycle of life by binding souls to their bodies, so they couldn't return to the lofty realm and be reborn. I guess the undead are just a by-product of when a tainted soul festers in a body that's died."

"You speak as if the crystal is alive?" Gigas croaks and violently coughs.

"I don't know, it might be. The lore is kind of deliberately vague in that area," she explains.

Jessica shuts her eyes tight and grits her teeth as the tip of Gigas' dagger presses on her throat.

"Stop it! I'm telling you everything!" Lauren looks horrified at a droplet of crimson trickling down Jessica's neck.

"Why are the undead marching? What devilry calls them north?" the mad general asks.

"Marching north?" Lauren shakes her head. She doesn't know what he's talking about.

Gigas takes hold of Jessica's wrist and wrestles it against the table. Pinning his weight on the back of her hand, he drives the dagger under the fingernail of an index finger. She lets out a bloodcurdling scream as the blade's tip bores into the soft flesh beneath her nail.

"Stop! An awakening! Ozrune said Vincent... Grimoirh mentioned an awakening!"

Gigas retracts the dagger and poor Jessica cradles her hand while the general hangs on Lauren's every word.

"... Maybe the crystal, or whatever is trapped inside, is waking up?" she says.

"This must be Grimoirh's doing." Gigas grabs a fistful of Jessica's hair, pulls her head back and presses the dagger to the artery in her neck.

"Stop!" Before she realises it, Lauren is on her feet and locking eyes with the general.

"Sit down!" Gigas' voice booms at her, and she collapses back in the seat like a meek little mouse.

He pulls Jessica to the floor by her hair and clears the table with one broad sweep. Plates and silverware clatter to the floor in a thunderous cacophony.

"Stay still!" he screams at Jessica, who struggles against him.

"Piss off!" she spits at him, and he strikes her with the back of his hand.

"Leave her alone!" Lauren cries, her heart stampeding in

her chest and her breath growing shallow – symptoms she's all too familiar with. *No, no, no. Not now!* she berates herself, and tries to subdue her mounting anxiety as it spreads like a toxin through her veins. The cutlery and plates begin to rattle, as do the paintings on the walls. Gigas looks around the room in trepidation and then at Lauren.

"So that's how you know so much. An oracle, are you? Or just a particularly knowledgeable spell-beggar?"

Lauren closes her eyes and, taking quick, steady breaths, she manages to compose herself, and the room stops shaking. "Please just let her go," she says calmly and stands again in an act of defiance.

Gigas' mad eyes bore into her, and an evil smile creeps across his sickly face. He glares at the girl with malice and brings his blade to Jessica's eye, which stares wildly at the dagger's edge.

"Oh shit, oh shit, oh shit," Jessica whispers between panicked shallow breaths.

Gigas tightens his grip on the dagger and forces Jessica's head closer to the pointy end. "Such pretty eyes too, what a—"

A guard storms into the room, flinging the door wide.

"What is the meaning of this interruption?!" the general shouts, then his hawkish eyes widen upon recognising the guard's strange shoes. "You!" he gasps.

Ed throws his helmet off and draws Remy's magic sword. "We don't want any trouble, so just let us walk out of here, and you'll never see us again." He feigns bravado while his knees tremble like jelly.

The general staggers forward and draws one of the halberds from above the hearth. "This is all your fault!"

As Gigas swings for Ed, the sword in his hand comes alive and shrieks, "Fight me!"

"What the fu—?!" Ed gasps as the sword swishes and spins on its own, tugging his arm wherever it needs to, to defend against Gigas' strikes.

Lauren leaps over the table to Jessica's side and wipes the mascara smudges from her cheeks. "We're getting out of here right now."

"Not without a little payback!" Jessica stands with a look of intent, grasps one of the metal candlesticks and hurls it at Gigas, striking his back and knocking him off balance.

The magic sword seizes the opening and hastily runs the general through. Ed looks mortified as he considers that he technically just murdered someone, but the general grins devilishly and steps closer to him, impaling himself on the blade until he's close enough to grab Ed by the throat and wrestle him to the ground. Gigas drops the halberd and draws the magic sword from his chest then inspects it while the weapon's monstrous eye inspects him right back.

"Strange blade," he mutters, turning it in his hand. "It'll make a fine trophy after I kill you with it."

Jessica prises the other halberd from the wall and brings it down on Gigas, severing his arm above the elbow. The general roars furiously and staggers away as his limb hits the floor before Ed, who doesn't hesitate to prise his sword from its grip. As he peels back the fingers he notices them twitch and wriggle, then the arm reaches for him, and it dawns on Ed that Gigas isn't as alive as he appears.

"You're undead!" he gasps.

The three of them watch Gigas stumble about, groaning as his humanity fades and the affliction begins to overpower his mind. He tears at his robes, revealing the gaping mortal wound Vincent had inflicted.

"Good!" Jessica pulls a wicked grin. "Then I won't lose any sleep over this!" she runs the halberd through the general and charges, pinning him to the wall.

The decrepit war hawk lets out a furious cry as he reaches out for her. "Look at what you've done!" he growls and spits as the last vestiges of his soul fester. "I'll t-tear your flesh f-f-from youuurghhh!" His slurred words dissolve into nothing but throaty rasps.

Ed swings his blade with both hands, decapitating the undead general and defeating him once and for all. The head hits the ground and rolls at Jessica's feet, with the jaw snapping and hissing at her, so she kicks it fiercely to the far end of the room where it hits the wall and – KABOOM!

The wall comes crashing down in a deafening shockwave, knocking everyone clean off their feet.

Jessica coughs and sits up amidst dust caking the air. "Jesus Christ, I didn't kick him that hard!" She rubs her eyes and sees Valentine charge over the rubble from outside with his sword drawn.

"You're late!" Ed cries.

"What?" Valentine lifts the visor on his helmet and lowers his weapon. He glances at Gigas' dismembered corpse pinned to the wall and then at his severed arm crawling on its fingers across the room. "... Oh."

*

Bengeo shuts his eyes and drowns out the jeers of mean-faced peasants, while an executioner fastens a noose around his neck. The chiming of the clock tower bell in the distance quiets the crowd. Seven tolls and the bandit looks to the setting sun.

The Runegard-appointed regent, Alphonsine Gifardus De Pfeffel Alabaster IV, watches from his private box on a tower overlooking the gallows. His rotund body is cloaked in crimson velvet with gold trim. Atop his balding head sits a dazzling crown decorated with jewels, shiny and immaculate. He's a glutton by all accounts, ramming cured meats into his mouth while he eagerly awaits the execution. After all, what sordid noble doesn't like dinner and a show?

George looks up at Bengeo next to him on the gallows. "Still think we're not gonna die?" he asks.

Bengeo winks at the boy and looks out at the mob, frothing at the mouth for the death to be dealt. "Gotta get bad before it gets good, right?"

"How much worse can it get?" George says fearfully as the crowd of angry, bloodthirsty peasants pelt him with cruel words and rotten fruit.

"On your mark!" From a platform beside the gallows Diamond raises her sword high but meets George's wide, fearful gaze and hesitates to give the order. She can't in good conscience condemn a child to death.

Remy shuffles past the peasants as she follows Regis through the crowd, and stands on tiptoes to get a better look at the stage.

"Wait, I don't see Jess and Lauren!" she gasps.

"The plan remains unchanged. We hold for the signal," Regis insists.

The faint boom of Valentine blowing the keg during his mistimed rescue echoes from above and people look warily about for the origin of the noise.

"Was that the distraction?" Remy panics. "I thought it would be bigger and louder!"

"No, something's wrong," Regis replies in a foreboding tone.

"Then we can't wait any longer." She tightens the strap of her shield arm and skulks through the crowd.

"Get on with it!" one of the peasants cries.

"Hang the bastards!" shouts another.

The executioner looks to Diamond for the go-ahead. She stares at George's innocent face and shakes her head. Her gut is telling her this isn't right, but the executioner grows impatient and kicks the block from beneath Bengeo's feet anyway.

He jolts down and flails as the life is choked out of him. Gritting his teeth, he forces out the last words he can muster: "Close your eyes, kid."

George shuts them tight as the executioner approaches his block, but Remy leaps onto the stage and tackles him with her shield. Both of them crash over the other side of the platform and hit the street with a thud as the crowd gasp all at once.

From her hidden vantage point in the upstairs window of a bakery overlooking the square, Astrid draws her arrow and debates whether to sever the rope choking Bengeo, but if she does it could ruin the element of surprise. She hesitates a moment, then purges herself of emotion and stays her bow, biding her time for the perfect moment to strike.

Regis leaps onto the gallows, draws his golden sword and severs the rope around Bengeo's neck in a flash. The bandit collapses in a heap and lets out a desperate gasp as he inhales as much air as he can.

"Cutting it bloody close!" he cries.

*

Ed and the others tread quickly through the palace's west wing to avoid the guards hunting them. As the pitter-patter of sabatons on hardwood resound through the corridor, Ed shoos the others through one of the many large white doors along the opulent corridor and shuts it behind him before the soldiers pass by.

"George and the others are in the dungeon," Lauren whispers to him, while he presses his ear to the door.

"Don't worry, Remy and Regis are taking care of it," he replies.

Lauren lights up with excitement. "Regis the Good?"

Ed rolls his eyes. "Oh alright, he's not *that* good."

Jessica looks over the room with wide, hungry eyes. "Jackpot." It looks like they're hiding in a trophy room of sorts, with tall glass cabinets spaced about displaying a variety of super rare enchanted items – magically infused weapons and armours, prophetic scriptures and tomes, a possessed boot and a haunted oil painting of a cat that leads to a demonic pocket dimension.

"Maybe that magic map I mentioned is in here?" Lauren swiftly traverses the hall, checking each glass cabinet for her prize.

"What does it look like?" Jessica asks.

"*What does it look like?*" Valentine frowns. "You've never seen a map?"

Jessica shrugs. "I use Google."

"Look for a scroll or a big piece of parchment!" Lauren says.

Ed wipes his clammy brow and calls to them, "Forget the map, if we don't get out of here now we're—!"

XVI

GRAND THEFT AIRSHIP

The nobles and peasants gawp at a flash of white light from on high. A colossal ball of varicoloured fire engulfs the grand palace, then comes a deafening boom. The crowd erupt and trample each other, fleeing in all directions, and despite their efforts to subdue the panic, the city guard is ignored and swept up in the chaos. An arrow soars over the square and hits the throne in the regent's private box, inches from his pompous head. He shrieks and wails as his bodyguards pull his royal arse behind cover.

"Coward," Astrid tuts, and leaps out of the bakery window in one fluid movement, drawing a pale glistening longsword from her belt as she soars towards the street below – the only token she has of her heritage, the legendary enchanted sword, Icerend. She flicks her wrist, spinning it elegantly as she cuts her way through the guards charging towards her. Each strike freezes them solid and a second shatters them to glittering dust.

Regis frees the captives from their bondage while Remy attacks the executioner with her shield until he passes out from head trauma.

"Told you we'd be alright," Bengeo laughs and throws off the noose from his neck then lifts George onto his broad shoulders. "This is gonna get rough, kid, so hold on tight."

The town guard surrounds them, and Bengeo hits a soldier so hard it dents his helmet and he collapses in a heap. Esmerelda's hands crackle with embers as she shapes a sphere of fire in her palms and hurls it at the others, setting them ablaze.

"Been a while since I did that," she smirks as the screaming men drop and roll.

From her platform, Diamond watches the pandemonium spiral as Astrid's loyal revolutionaries attack the town guard and burn the houses. A shimmer of light in the crowd catches her eye, and she spots the rogue princess herself, battling her way towards the cowering regent in his private box. In a flash Diamond leaps into the square and pushes her way through the crowd to confront Astrid. In an instant, their swords clash.

*

Ed rubs his stinging eyes, and chokes on the smoke. Ash flutters around him as the palace goes up in flames. Heaps of rubble collapse from the top of ivory spires and crash through the roof of the hall, scattering stone and glass everywhere. His vision clears in time to make out Tank's silhouette. The knight walks fearlessly through the flames with his broad sword in hand. It isn't long until the clang of clashing metal rings out over the crackling fire.

"Son of a bitch," Valentine spits and coughs as he rolls onto his back. He forces himself on his feet and exchanges a nod with Ed, each letting the other know they're alright.

"Jessica? Lauren?" the detective calls out.

"Fuck, that was loud!" Jessica rubs her ears with her fingers to stay the ringing in her head.

"Where's Lauren?" Ed scans the room but can't see her through the billowing smoke and dust.

"Over here!" Jessica spots her huddled by the wall, rocking back and forth with her hands covering her ears.

Tears stream down her face, her heart thuds like a stampede, her eyes dart wildly as the flames pour off the roof like water. The putrid stench of smoke brings her back to the worst moment of her life.

"I... can't... brea—!" she gasps, and clings onto Jessica for dear life.

Jessica has never really thrived in high-pressure situations, but she's all Lauren's got right now and so tries her best to say something helpful.

"Oh shit." Not helpful.

She pats down Lauren to check if she's wounded – thankfully nothing but cuts and scrapes.

"I think... I think you're just having a panic attack! Okay?"

She smacks the side of her head, wracking her brains until, eureka! The YouTube videos she'd watched to try and overcome her stage fright come flooding to her. The Zen voice of Jim Squits, the mind and wellbeing doctor in the tutorial, echoes sound advice in her mind.

"First thing we need to do is find a relaxing location." Jessica looks around her. One of the roof beams collapses into the fire on the far side of the room and bursts into flames. "Okay, we're gonna skip that part." Her cracking voice instils no confidence at all in Lauren, who looks at her with desperation.

"We've got company!" Ed cries as a party of soldiers scramble over the crumbled wall to apprehend them.

Lauren folds in on herself as the surrounding noise hails her like bullets, but Jessica takes her face in her hands and locks eyes with her.

"I know you're freaking out, but you gotta pull it together. Now inhale through your nose. One, two, three, four."

Lauren stares into her wide, caring eyes, shining through the hellfire and smoke. If she can lose herself in those eyes then maybe she can overcome the trauma surging through her body and mind.

Ed's sword springs to his defence, quickly dispatching the first of the soldiers to cross the rubble. Valentine grapples the second and unwittingly throws him into the haunted cat portrait, where the canvas swallows the man in an instant with a wailing meow. The third soldier charges at the girls, and Jessica turns as the sword comes at her face. It soars past between her eyes as she trips backwards to get away. The soldier then swings for Lauren who scrambles on all fours in a fit of panic over the splintered wood and shattered glass, until her hand lands on an iron staff which she brings up to defend herself. Before her attacker's blade makes contact, a burst of lightning erupts from the end and hurls him across the room. The air around her crackles and hisses. The fissure in her chest widens to a chasm and the staff rages.

Jessica shields her face and watches through her arms as reinforcements charge into the hall only to retreat as the lightning tears what's left of the room to shreds.

"How is she doing that?" she shrieks.

"It's the staff!" Ed replies. "She's out of control, we've gotta get it away from her!"

Jessica takes a deep breath and goes to rush in, but Valentine pulls her back. "Are you crazy? You can't go out there!"

Jessica defiantly tugs her arm from him. "Watch me." With unbridled determination she sprints into the open. Jolts of electricity arc across the hall like a Tesla coil tearing up the marble floor by her feet, and with a well-timed leap she reaches Lauren, then places her hand over the staff.

"Let it go," she cries over the crackle and wind as her hair stands on end. "I've got you!"

But the magic's exertion on Lauren's fragile body only brings more breathlessness. Her limbs tighten, her mouth runs dry and everything becomes a blur.

Jessica presses Lauren's head tightly against her chest – duh duhm, duh duhm, duh duhm. Lauren clings to its beat and draws deep heavy breaths while Jessica prises the staff from her iron grip. It topples to the floor and the lightning dissipates as instantaneously as it appeared.

"It's okay, you're okay." She cradles Lauren tightly. "Don't crowd her," she says as the others warily approach.

"S-sorry," Lauren heaves, and wipes her nose on her sleeve.

"Don't be," Ed grins, "you just saved our butts."

"Can you walk?" Jessica asks.

Lauren nods, and her legs tremble as she stands. She slips, but Valentine catches her and takes her in his arms. Ed leads them over the rubble and out of the burning hall, but Jessica runs back for the staff, rejoining them again quickly. They escape the palace just as the west side collapses entirely, shrouding the lush gardens in a haze of smoke which provides them with the cover they need to make it through the gate to the sky harbour unnoticed.

"Looks like they've barred the other gate!" Valentine points to the portcullis that leads into the merchant quarter.

"That means Remy and the others are trapped." Ed pours his frustration into his fist and clenches until his knuckles turn white.

"Heeeey!" a deep womanly voice cries, and Avarice leans over the deck of one of many docked gunships. "Scrawny boy, this way!"

"Who or what is that?" Jessica asks.

"It looks like a troll, a girl troll?" Lauren says as Valentine sets her down.

They board the gunship and Avarice leads them straight to the cockpit where Ozrune stands before the flight controls and two chairs at the prow of the ship.

"We need to pick everyone up," Ed says. "Can you fly this thing over the market?"

Ozrune tilts his head curiously. "Oh, I can't fly this thing," the wizard says plainly.

"Come again?" Ed gasps.

"I'm a scholar, not a pilot," the old crow replies.

Ed frowns. "What kind of wise man are you?"

"Perhaps I can offer some encouraging words?"

Ed scrunches his face in his hands and swallows his boiling temper.

"This is why I never play as a mage," he mutters and inspects the flight controls. "... Two seats mean two pilots," he mumbles, "but what do these do?" He jiggles one of the yokes mounted in front of the chairs, but they're unresponsive.

Lauren notices something familiar about the controls. Stepping backwards, she tilts her head and sees the bigger picture. The two adjoining consoles look like two sides of a game controller, and the steering yokes are like the thumb-sticks. Below each chair are two pedals, on the right and on the left, just like the shoulder buttons on a Game Station controller.

"Ed, look!" She waves him over. "What do you see?" she asks.

He takes a long hard look then his eyes snap wide as it comes together. "Oh my God, I think I know how to fly this thing."

He jumps in the left seat and grabs the yoke in front of him with two hands then looks back at Lauren. "Come on, I need a co-pilot with gaming experience."

Lauren shakes her head. "No! No, I can't!"

"Hey," Jessica stays her quaking hand, "you got this."

"Oh God." Lauren takes a deep breath and ties her hair back, then takes a seat beside Ed and places her feet on the pedals.

"Everyone, buckle up!" Ed gives Lauren a nod to power up the ship.

She jerks sideways and vomits all over the floor, and the others take a broad step away while Ed gently rubs her back until she gets it out. She sits up, wipes her chin and nods that she's ready. He hammers a triangular button between the adjoining consoles, and two colossal propellers roar to life on each side of the oblong hull.

"Okay, so if I'm left, and you're right, then I control altitude and you control direction?" Ed says.

Lauren nods. "So we have to work like two thumbs?"

"Yeah. Hive mind."

They exchange a foreboding look.

"Okay, hold on to your butts." He presses forward on the yoke, and the ship tilts down and shunts into the dock beneath them, throwing Jessica and the others violently forward.

"Sorry! Inverted controls! My bad." Composing himself, Ed gently pulls back this time, tilting the ship's nose high, then he presses on the pedals, and the gunship rises with a loud hum.

*

Streaks of bright azure encircle Astrid as she twirls her glowing sword with graceful ferocity, and the blade howls as it prangs against Diamond's unbreakable rapier, whose own enchantment makes it immune to the magical sword's lethal freeze. Turning on her heel and ducking low, the captain avoids Astrid's broad slash and unleashes a flurry of thrusts which the princess blocks, then with a flick of her wrist, Diamond spins her blade and disarms her foe, sending the Icerend flying across the courtyard. Astrid draws the silver bow off her back and fends off the captain's strikes, but every swipe cuts the bow to pieces until the only weapon she has left is herself.

"Give it up, you're hopelessly outmatched," Diamond says.

Over the captain's shoulder, Astrid spots a battalion of men rallying to the regent. If she's not quick she's going to miss her window. Her face blazes with hatred as she glares at her opponent. Leaping dexterously, she wraps her legs around

Diamond's sword arm as she thrusts it forward and in one fluid motion wrestles her shoulder from its socket. Diamond shrieks as Astrid throws her to the ground and takes up her rapier. The rogue princess recalls vividly the look of fear and despair on her mother's face as her head was cleaved from her body. She was weak then, shaking as she hid under the bed with her mother's blood flecked across her face, but she's not weak now, and during her exile, she's become far too accustomed to the sensation of blood.

"For my country! For my mother!" she howls. Summoning every modicum of strength in her petite frame, she hurls the rapier like a javelin. The sword soars towards the watch tower and pierces the regent through the heart. His lifeless body flops over the railing of his private box and crashes into the street with a bone-breaking wallop. Astrid quivers with relief. Bittersweet tears trickle from eyes aflame with rage. After fourteen years of plotting and training and suffering she has, at long last, avenged her family. She steps backwards, clutching her breathless chest as her act of vengeance sinks in. Her face darkens with malice and she vanishes amongst the crowd.

*

Two soldiers come at Remy from each side. The first's spear prangs against her shield, knocking her over as the second raises a musket and takes aim.

With a gasp Remy ducks behind her shield before the gunshot sparks against it.

"That's cheating!" she yells, scurrying to her feet with her shield held in front of her.

A second shot crackles through the air and the buckshot ricochets off the pauldron, knocking her down again. Even with her arm guard, it feels like she's been stung by wasps. A quick glance and she breathes a sigh of relief. The shot didn't pierce her armour, just put a nasty dent in it – why can't she have nice things?

A pale blue glimmer catches her eye. Lying discarded on the limestone street is Astrid's Icerend. Remy rolls for the sword, taking it up in her left hand, then spins around and rushes the guard before he can fire again, slicing at his rifle with the enchanted sword. The barrel freezes in his hand. He drops it and gasps as it shatters against the ground. Remy wallops him in the head with the sword's pommel, breaking his nose. She twirls the blade and points it daringly at the soldier with the spear, who hesitates to attack, partly because of the mad look in her eyes but mostly because this is his favourite spear and he doesn't want it to shatter into blocks of ice. Instead, he backs away from her, only to be clobbered from behind by Bengeo.

For a very short-lived moment it looks like they have the upper hand, but any hope of victory leaves Remy as waves of soldiers arrive from the palace. Armed with muskets and blades, they surround the square and fire warning shots into the air. The remaining peasants disperse immediately, leaving Remy, Bengeo, Regis, George and Esmerelda huddled in the centre clutching their weapons tightly as the guards close around them.

"What do we do?" Remy asks.

"If we give up we're dead for sure," Esmerelda growls, and her palms ignite with wizard fire. "Might as well give 'em hell first."

"Not the pep talk I was hoping for."

A burst of wind kicks her hair across her face. Remy glances upwards and sees a huge gunship descending over the merchant quarter. The bluster from the propellers rips the gallows apart and throws up enough dust to shroud them from the gunners. Her knees give way. She's certain the airship will unleash a barrage of gunfire that'll obliterate them all. She's already visualising what song she'd like played at her funeral when Avarice leans over the balcony with Jessica and uncoils three rope ladders, which flutter towards the street.

George cheers as Bengeo hoists him onto the ladder first. Then he lifts Esmerelda as Regis leaps onto another. Remy takes firm hold of the rope and the bandit climbs on behind her as the ship ascends.

Gunshots crackle from below, and the soldiers fire at will, but thankfully their rifles' range is too stunted. Remy struggles up the ladder one-handed until Avarice and Regis hoist her aboard just before the ship crashes through the roof of a clock tower, smashing it to splinters.

"Who the hell is flying this thing?" the bandit yelps as he watches the tower collapse into the street below. Avarice lets out a hearty laugh. She's having too much fun.

Jessica leads everyone to the cockpit where Ed and Lauren are fighting to keep the ship in the air.

Bengeo leans between them. "You're doing a bang-up job an' all, but mind if I—?"

"Oh, please do!" Lauren doesn't hesitate a second before unbuckling herself from her seat and passing over the controls.

"Gods, does it feel good to fly something with some oomph again!" The bandit grins like the Devil as he takes the helm.

"Where did you get this thing?" Remy looks impressed.

Avarice shrugs. "They were not using it."

"C'mon get us outta here," Bengeo barks at Ed. "We're going north."

"Aye aye, boss." Ed swallows his terror with a big gulp and helps Bengeo orient the ship north.

Remy gazes down at the city erupting in fire and chaos. Looks like Astrid's revolution is in full swing.

"We've got company!" She leans over the console and points out of the window at a fleet of Runegard gunships rising from the sky docks.

Bengeo shoos her back. "Alright, listen up, this thing

is a gunship, so it's gotta have guns. We need asses on those cannons."

"Yes, sir!" George sprints out of the cockpit.

"Wait!" Lauren calls to her brother, but he's already gone.

"We'll watch him," Regis assures her, and signals Valentine to follow him.

George remembers the layout from when his character had to sneak aboard one in the game. Internally he's geeking out at how it all looks so similar but doesn't show it of course, because above all else an eleven-year-old boy has to appear cool at all times.

"C'mon!" He waves them over to a bulk hatch at the end of the steel corridor and attempts to twist the wheel lock, but he's too weak to turn it. Regis does the honours. The hatch swings open and the boy scrambles down the ladder into the long metal room below. He gawks at the spherical turrets connected to each end, like an old World War II bomber.

Valentine points at the chairs and asks, "Are those—?"

"Guns!" George grins ear to ear as he jumps into one of the turrets. "This is gonna be legendary!"

"Why are these guys so much more technically advanced than anyone else?" Valentine looks bewildered at the machinery.

"Because they're the bad guys," George replies, "we're the underdog."

"The underdog?" The detective shakes his head as he climbs into the last turret. "So how does this work?"

"I must admit I'm not familiar myself," Regis replies.

George wastes no time. He grasps the joystick, and with the slightest movement the gun and his seat rotate. "Aim with the stick! See?"

"Yeah, looks easy." Valentine gently tilts his joystick and is almost thrown out of his chair as it jolts sharply left.

The stolen airship rumbles violently as it sustains fire from two enemy vessels flanking them. George squeezes his trigger, sending a burst of cannon fire roaring across the night sky.

"Whoa!" he gasps as the vibrations rattle his little hands. A few well-placed shots down one of the Runegard ships before it can even get above the city.

"Great shot, kid!" Regis cheers, but George is too in the zone to notice, he's busy blasting the enemy ships to scrap – who says video games don't teach useful life skills?

They're barely across the Great Lake before he downs another gunship on their starboard side. It drops out of the sky trailed by thick plumes of black smoke and plummets into the serene water below.

"Wooooo! I got another one!"

"I think mine's broken..." Valentine clumsily jerks left and right while firing pot shots into the sky.

"C'mon! You're gonna get us killed!" George yells. "Fire bursts, it's way more accurate!"

*

The ship rattles as it tears across the dark sky, soaring over forests and meadows. Ed and Bengeo steer it high into the clouds to provide some visual cover from the bombardment.

"Agh, she's tough, but she's got a heavy arse." Bengeo manoeuvres the ship evasively, but there's no shaking the enemy. "Hey, crow, anytime you wanna step in would be great!"

Ozrune, who is sitting cross-legged on the floor in a deep meditative state, blinks one eye open and, with a sigh, stands. He exits the cockpit and opens the bulk hatch leading outside, his robes fluttering in the shredding wind as he climbs onto the deck and fixes his beady eyes on the imperial gunships pursuing them – one behind and another on the port side. Raising one hand, he clenches it slowly, bringing it into his middle, centring himself while the night sky around him lights up like the fifth of November. Ed gawks from behind glass as the wizard conjures a tremendous blue sphere which engulfs the ship, shielding it from the barrage of cannon fire thrown their way.

"Wizards," Ed scoffs and pulls back on the yoke to keep them steady.

Each blast the barrier sustains weakens both it and Ozrune. The enemy is hot on their tail and has their sights locked. Bolts of white-hot energy ignite the sky, tearing through the clouds and into the stolen gunship. The barrier dissipates with a bang and a flash, and Ozrune drops to one knee to catch his breath.

"Magi-cannons?! Damn, there goes our trump card," Bengeo curses. "Hey, old woman, know any spells that'll get us out of this jam?"

Esmerelda shakes her head. "My magic is mostly good for patching things up, I'm afraid."

"How about we launch you out of a cannon at them?" Bengeo says to Avarice.

"I would tear their puny ship apart," the troll girl spits.

Remy leans over Ed like an overbearing backseat driver. "You're gonna get us killed, pull up!"

"Will you just let me fly this thing," he shouts.

"You're gonna fly it into the ground at this rate!"

"Oh yeah? Well, you wanna try it with one hand?"

Unable to concoct a biting retort, she slaps him upside the head.

"Ow!" he whines, and looks back at her aghast.

"Keep your eyes on the sky!" she yells, pointing at the window.

"Will you two behave like adults for once in yer goddamn lives?!" Bengeo shouts, but as usual all he does is incur Remy's wrath.

Jessica watches in disbelief while the three of them scream at each other like some dysfunctional family on a road trip. She looks at Lauren, standing beside her and notices her balling her fists.

"You okay?" she asks.

Lauren nods. "I guess, I just wish I wasn't so useless."

Jessica glances at the magic staff resting on one of the consoles and smiles. "You're anything but!" She takes Lauren by the hand, snatches the staff, and leads her out of the cockpit, stopping before the bulk hatch to the deck.

Jessica plants the staff firmly in Lauren's hands, swings open the hatch and points to the deck above the rest of the ship. "If we get you out there, reckon you can do that zappy thing?"

"Are you crazy?!" she yells over the shredding wind.

"I'll be with you every step, promise!"

"No… I can't!" Lauren tries to give back the staff, but Jessica pushes it towards her.

"You can do this!" Her eyes glimmer like a beacon on a bleak night – how can Lauren say no to that? It would be like letting down Bambi.

She hesitantly nods, and reluctantly follows Jessica up the ladder onto the deck.

The enemy ships release another burst of magi-cannon fire. Ozrune forces himself up and concentrates his energy. His hands pulse with a white plasma as he forces them together and the light swells into a glowing sphere which he hurls upwards before it explodes into a dozen magic missiles that soar outwards and clash with the oncoming projectiles, illuminating the sky.

"Hold on!" Jessica shouts to Lauren whose face flashes red, blue and green in the exploding light.

They shuffle along the deck, clinging tentatively to the safety railing and to each other as the brutal wind batters them. Once they reach the bow, Jessica ducks behind Lauren and takes hold of the guardrail with one hand and with the other grips her belt.

"Okay, here goes!" Lauren shakes the staff, but nothing happens.

"What's wrong?" Jessica yells.

"I don't know, it's not working!"

"Why n—?!" BOOM!

A direct hit from the enemy ship blows a gaping hole in the deck. Splinters scatter in all directions, and the girls are thrown away from each other.

Lauren covers her ringing ears tightly, and her vision tunnels as the stench of gunpowder floods her lungs. She picks herself up and tries to stay her long hair from flailing over her eyes. Sweeping it back, she sees Jessica lying deathly still.

"Get up!" she shrieks. "Please get up!" Tears stream from her bloodshot eyes, her mind flashes – glimpses of broken glass… the metallic tang of blood… the stench of hot tar on a sweltering August day… more flashes… everything shifts… a car overturned… she's calling to him, but he's not moving. She can't either. Cracked bones, split skull, she's never known suffering like this… but no, that's not now!

She claws her way to Jessica. *Never again*, she tells herself. She's not losing anyone ever again.

"Get up! Get up!" She shakes Jessica until she comes around.

"What the fuck was that?" Jessica coughs and looks up at Lauren's frightened face staring back at her. "Okay, this was a really dumb idea!" No kidding.

The air crackles around them as the staff works its magic. Black clouds swirl and lightning strobes from the staff's end, while the metallic hull conducts the arcing electricity and scatters it across the ship. An enemy gunship closes in on the port side, cannons booming. Lauren thrusts the staff at it and the lightning crackles across the sky and tears the ship to pieces.

Bengeo and the others look out at the sky baffled.

"Storm came out of nowhere!" the bandit says.

Ed scans the cockpit and notices Lauren and Jessica are missing. "Oh no." He shoots Remy a look that churns her stomach.

"What?" she asks, knowing she's not going to like the answer.

"Aim for the magi-cannon!" George cries over the rat-tat-tat of gunfire.

"What the hell is a magi-cannon?" Valentine replies.

"The big gun," Regis cries. His eyes grow wide as the cannon's charge disperses a bolt of energy right at them. The swordsman pulls George from his seat just before the blast strikes. With a head-splitting boom the gunnery is blown apart. Regis clings tightly to George with one arm and the ladder with the other as the G-force threatens to hurl them into the sky. Valentine frantically unbuckles himself and springs out of his seat before the whole module gets sucked into oblivion. His wrinkled hands grasp whatever they can find, and he skirts his way to the ladder and reaches out to Regis. As soon as they clear the hatch, George slams the bulk door shut, dispelling the violent wind. All three of them collapse against the walls with a sigh of relief. George lets out a nervous laugh, happy to be alive, while Valentine, whiter than white, tries not to empty the contents of his stomach.

*

Lauren's bounding pulse fuels her adrenaline, which in turn fuels the magic. The staff ignites a sudden sense of connection with the world around her. It comes all at once, a rush that overwhelms her senses. Her body shivers as the wind bites her face, she breathes with the tide thrashing against the land. Her ears quiver with the blaring drum of her friend's racing heart and with the beating heart of the world – a pulse, shared by all living things. She screams amidst an awakening deep inside herself, as though roused from a bad dream. Strobing arcs of wrath engulf the enemy gunships entirely. A head-splitting bang rings out across the sky as they break apart in a burst of fire and light. Her hands tremble as she snaps open her eyes – BOOM!

A blinding explosion scatters the enemy ship into chunks of burning debris that hail the deck.

"You can stop now!" Jessica cries.

But it's too late, the conjured storm feeds on Lauren's unprecedented panic attack and grows exponentially. Black clouds swirl and crackle around them as rain lashes down like needles, soaking them to the bone. As it dawns on Jessica how monumentally out of her depth she is, Ozrune comes to their aide. His billowing robes lift him up, and he glides gracefully towards them. With a flick of his wrist, the wizard disarms Lauren and summons the staff to him, then with it he redirects the lightning away from them, and launches it at the black sky.

He calls to Lauren. "Condition your mind, step into your fears and push through until you transcend yourself. Ride the emotion, do not shy away from it. Control it before it consumes you!"

"She's trying!" Jessica shrieks. Her worn soles slip and slide about the deck, and inch by inch she crawls towards the ladder, but the wind beats her back, and she grasps the railing tightly, hugging Lauren's waist and cursing her past self for this incomprehensibly stupid idea.

Then like an angel sent from heaven to save them – a grey, horned, snarling angel, tethered by rope to the inside of the ship – Avarice appears over the ladder. The troll girl looks in fear at the raging tempest. She's never seen anything like it. Such unimaginable destructive force is something a troll should revere, but she's inherited enough of her mother's sensibility to know that this is nothing to be desired.

"Come!" She throws Jessica the end of the rope.

Her dainty hands reach for it as it flaps violently in the wind. Avarice reels it in and throws it again. This time she catches it and quickly fastens it around herself and Lauren.

Lightning hammers the deck and the gunship jolts downwards, hurling both girls into the air. They flail in the squall, tumbling through the night, but the she-troll reels them in with all her might while Ozrune holds back the unforgiving force of nature. He thrusts the staff downwards, conjuring a gust of wind that pushes the girls onto the deck, before the wind sweeps him off the ship and hurls him into the clouds.

Lauren can't muster a scream. Panic possesses her like a twisted marionette, crushing her chest as the storm amps up, releasing an endless chain of lightning across the sky. Everything goes dark and with a wheeze she slips away.

The rope blows out of Jessica's hand and both girls slip across the waterlogged deck. She clings to Lauren's belt with one hand and spreads herself flat to stop them sliding.

To make matters worse, a barrage of lightning strikes the ship, killing the engines.

"No, no, no!" Bengeo turns pale as the gauges and dials on the consoles all drop to zero. "We're dead in the air!"

"How do we fix it? Turn it off and on again?" Ed asks.

"How would that help?" Bengeo snaps.

"Well, have you got any bright ideas?!"

"Yeah, buckle up and brace!"

Ed whimpers and pulls back on the yoke with all his strength to keep the hulking heap of metal they're riding straight enough for an emergency landing. The gunship descends at breakneck speed and bursts through the black clouds, revealing the snowy forests scattered between the frozen mountains.

The knot securing Avarice to the ship comes loose and she slips over on the deck. Remy catches it in her hand and winds it around her arm, while she screams for help at the top of her lungs, trying to keep them from being hurled into the tundra. Her desperate pleas fall on Valentine's ears on his way to the cockpit. He looks back while Regis and George continue on but hesitates to investigate until she screams again. He then races down the corridor and finds Remy practically upside down, with her feet pressed either side of the hatch and the rope wound tightly around her left arm and across her body. The gunship smashes treetops to splinters and pounds across the frozen tundra, hurling him against the ceiling. Remy loses her footing and slams into the door as she's sucked outside. The detective grasps her ankle, but the force pulls him with her, and both of them are hurled off the deck, along with Avarice who shields Lauren in her arms while Jessica clings tightly to her back.

Relentless snow blankets the ship in white, and what's left of the gunship collides with a towering spire of ice. Ed and Bengeo scramble from their seats and dive clear as it shears the cockpit in two until the ship grinds to a brutal halt and lies smouldering in the snow.

XVII

The Dread Knight

Droning gales give voice to a dead land, like the hollow remnants of 100,000 wailing souls. With one arm outstretched Vincent holds his blade, using its enchanted flame to guide him through the dark; the other clings to Domina slumped on his back. Inch by inch he pushes through the wind and ice. With only his thoughts to keep him sane on this perilous expedition across the darkest, most isolated region of all Pangea Ultima, he finds himself wondering why he didn't leave her on the ship, or even abandon her in the snow. She's slowing him down. It's unlikely the cold would affect a dark creature such as her. He reminds himself that she's not as human as she looks. It's just a shell, wearing the face of someone he cared about. Perhaps that's why then, he couldn't bring himself to abandon her again – or maybe he's just afraid of dying alone.

He recalls fondly the first time he had seen her. The first time he'd found himself physically transported into the game. She had a different name then and so did he…

*

It was late and Vincent had stayed longer than anyone to patch a particularly buggy questline involving a little backwater village called Hoarfrost in the northern part of the map. The quest, entitled Into the Necropolis, involved rescuing missing villagers who had been kidnapped by a clan of subterranean goblins. The bug was almost game-breaking, as it prevented the player from progressing to an essential part of the main questline. His work had yielded little reward and he was ready to call it quits when he noticed a chill in the air – which despite the flippant nature of English weather was utterly surreal for a summer night. When his breath fogged the air, he knew something strange was afoot, and when snowflakes fluttered into the room, and the faint howling wind pricked his ears, he was sure he was losing his mind. An ex-girlfriend had once warned him that spending too much time in fantastical lands would cause him to lose touch with reality. It looked like she might be right.

Vincent cautiously approached the seventy-inch screen mounted to the wall, and a biting wind sent a shiver tingling down his spine. He reached out to touch the television, and to his amazement, his hand passed right through, as though it were reaching through an open window. He was now certain that he was absolutely insane. His hand trembled at the snow's icy kiss, and he swiftly retracted it and rubbed his tired eyes. This had to be a dream. He had been working extremely hard so it wasn't crazy to consider he'd dozed off at his desk and had concocted some fantasy about the game coming to life, after all, it was the kind of thing he dreamed about on a daily basis. But he knew what dreaming felt like, and he was sure he was awake.

He picked up the game controller and threw it at the screen, but it passed right through and landed in the snow with a squelch. He hesitated a minute then climbed through after it, instantly feeling weightless. A dark abyss surrounded him. Slowly he glided towards the wintery scene in the distance before him – strange how it had seemed so close when he reached through.

A swelling pressure built up in his skull. He shut his eyes tight and squeezed his head until the splitting pain vanished. Then his feet felt cold. He opened his eyes and saw his shoes planted in the snow, which immediately soaked them through. He looked back at the screen-shaped tear in reality and through it, where the office was now filled with snow.

Taking his first steps into the game's world, he climbed the ridge and found the little village he had been coding that very night. He shuffled down the snowy slopes to investigate and admired the little wooden houses with profound wonder. They were real incarnations of the rendered models from the game – small huts made from chopped trees, five or six scattered about with sloped roofs. He spotted a couple of NPCs on the far side of the village, heading towards a large cabin in the centre. There was no mistaking it. It was the Hoarfrost Inn.

He hurried inside and immediately his nostrils were tickled by a mouth-watering aroma. He gawked at the beast roasting on the open fire in the middle of the tavern and cautiously approached the bar. His damp shoes squelched against the creaky wooden floorboards. All eyes were on him, and the townsfolk looked him up and down with intrigue.

"A stranger," they whispered.

"What's he doing here?"

"Strange clothes…" they muttered.

He pretended not to hear and took a seat at the bar, keeping his head down.

"Where are you from, stranger?" a girl asked him.

He lifted his eyes to meet hers, and stuttered at her familiar unblinking face.

His lingering stare made her uncomfortable, so she stepped backwards and crossed her arms. "Can I get you something?"

His mouth hung open. His eyes explored her ash-blonde hair and every freckle and blemish on her Nordic face. Like all the barmaids in the game, her figure was shapely in all the right places, and she wore a low-cut corset over a bunchy white blouse.

"You alright, Nef?" an old villager asked, seeing that Vincent was making her nervous.

She nodded. "Aye. Not sure about this one, though."

"S-sorry," Vincent said, "I'm a little lost."

"I'll say. We seldom get visitors in our little village. This is about as far from civilisation as you can get." She noticed his strange clothes, and asked, "Where are you from?"

"I'm not exactly sure," he replied.

He also wasn't sure whether or not she was real. She seemed just like him, capable of independent thought, and unlike an NPC, she wasn't spouting the same dialogue over and over again.

"You thirsty? Hungry?" she asked.

He nodded with enthusiasm. "Always hungry."

She gathered a bowl and spooned some of the stew bubbling on the stove behind her. He devoured it as soon as she placed the bowl before him. The flavours were rich and hearty. Every sip warmed him thoroughly.

"How long have you lived here?" he asked her.

"My whole rotten life," she smiled. "I dream of seeing the world but hardly have the coin for it. What brings you to Hoarfrost? There's nothing this far north but snow and more snow. I suppose we're plenty rich in misery too."

"Just exploring," he replied.

"You're an adventurer, then?" She leaned towards him, intrigued.

"Not really," he laughed. The idea of him plundering dungeons and wielding swords seemed utterly ridiculous.

"A wanderer, then. So what'll I call you, Wanderer?"

"Wanderer sounds good," he said. Better to keep it vague. Although it's not like she could've googled him or anything.

"Very mysterious." She smiled as she wiped the bar top with a damp rag. "Well, let me know if you need anything else,

Wanderer." She slinked away to deliver a tray of tankards to a table of village elders, who looked like they'd died a winter past but their bodies didn't get the memo – which in this world is entirely possible, although the undead probably have better table manners.

Vincent finished his stew, and watched Nef work a while before creeping outside, and back through the rift. He sat a moment in front of the screen just watching the snow flutter in, wondering how all of this was possible, and how he would explain it to everyone in the morning. His mind raced with questions. He was sure he was insane and the whole thing was the beginning of a psychotic break. Eventually he dozed off, and when he awoke in the early hours of the morning the screen appeared normal again. Perhaps it had been a dream, but sure enough every night around midnight he returned and spent more time in Hoarfrost, speaking with Nef, the barmaid. Over the passing weeks, they grew closer, and keeping up his moniker as the mysterious Wanderer, Vincent learned all he could of the game world, not that it was anything he didn't already know. This carried on for about six weeks until he had decided he needed to show Eric, if only to prove to himself that he wasn't mad.

*

His foot slips, tearing him from his past. Vincent tumbles down a rocky mountain pass and lands with a crunch in the deep snow. After a moment's respite he picks himself up and casts his eyes across the frigid expanse, searching for Domina. Her piercing eyes stare back at him as she sits up. She regards her icy surroundings with contempt.

Vincent climbs on his feet and picks up his sword, resting it on his shoulder. "We need to get out of this blizzard," he says.

She stands without even a shiver. "What happened to the ship?" she asks.

"Gone," he replies, "we're on our own now."

Together they scramble up the rugged ice and rock, and traverse the winding paths that weave through the mountains. Relentless snow shrouds the distance in a veil of white, slowing their advance. The cold seeps through the Dreadmail, chilling Vincent to the bone. It is unfortunate that it cannot shield him from the harsh unforgiving elements the way it resists the strike of a blade or hammer. *Fitting though*, Vincent thinks. His life has been nothing but misfortune since he came to this godforsaken place.

Domina stalks him closely, her expression as lifeless as the land they tread. It chills Vincent more so to see her like this, so inhuman, utterly immune to the blizzard's razor bite. His eyes narrow upon spotting a small cavity in the mountainside. He races inside and warms himself by the fire of his God Cleaver. The burning blade illuminates the cavern. Shadows dance back and forth across the glittering icy walls.

"Maybe this leads through the mountains," he says pointing ahead at a tunnel that stretches into utter darkness. "How are you feeling?" he asks.

Domina looks at her bandaged shoulder and frowns. "We should burn that forest to ash."

"It'll all burn soon enough," Vincent replies, looking sombre. "What troubles you?"

His eyes drift back to the fire. "It's nothing."

Domina kneels forward, placing her hand on his face, then gently brings his eyes to hers. "Tell me."

For a fleeting second, he sees the girl she used to be before the darkness took hold of her. "Don't." He moves her hand away. "You're not her."

"I'm better." She slinks towards him.

"You're useful."

"Then let me be."

"What do you see, when you look at me?" he asks.

A devious grin sweeps across her icy lips. "The Dread Knight, herald of the world's end."

He pulls her close. "What do you see?"

She gazes deep into his eyes, pitch dark like a starless night sky.

He releases her and bows his head shamefully. "I feel strange... my mind is cut loose. I'm tired, but I can't close my eyes." Vincent wipes his face up and down with both hands, but feels only cold steel not flesh.

The dour expression on his face and the nihilistic desperation in his voice evokes something in Domina – a flicker of a feeling, a remnant of her humanity. She holds him close and runs her fingers through his damp hair.

"This armour..." he sighs as she runs her hand across his cheek, again pulling his gaze to hers, "... am I wearing it or is it wearing me?" After a moment he musters a deep breath that looks more painful than anything else. "Eric's alive."

"Alive? But how?" she asks.

"The other players didn't end up here by chance." He grips the hilt of his blade and pulls himself onto his feet then inspects Remy's festering hand chained to his belt and frowns as its fingers twitch and writhe.

Is this all because of you? he wonders as his mind returns to where it all went so very wrong...

*

All the time he had spent traversing the game world with Nef saw him fall behind with his work. Eric had been on his case about fixing the bugged Hoarfrost questline, and he finally had to appease his friend, who had enough to worry about with the shareholders and the publisher breathing down his neck. But that wasn't the reason Vincent had called Eric in that day. He had decided it was time to share his discovery with the only person he could trust.

Eric stood impatiently behind him as he booted up the computers in the testing room.

"You're going to lose your mind," Vincent smiled.

"I don't think it's *my* mind we should be worrying about." Eric let out an impatient sigh.

"I'm not crazy," Vincent said, with a glint of crazy in his eyes.

The Ultimate Adventure VII remake in its beta version began to run and Vincent's avatar stood idle amongst the falling snow, which danced effervescently around it. He stared expectantly at the screen, but nothing happened.

"You fixed the bug?" Eric asked him.

"Yes, but this isn't about that."

"Because that bug is a game-breaker. If the goblins don't raid the town, then the whole story gets stuck. After the shitshow surrounding the launch of Ultimate Adventure XV, we can't afford to release another buggy game," Eric sighed. The memes would haunt him to his grave.

Vincent's eyes darted across the screen, and looking deeply disappointed he muttered, "Just give it a minute. I'm sure…"

Certain that Vincent was overworked, Eric patted him on the back. "Okay, buddy. Thanks for bringing me in on a Sunday night."

"It doesn't make any sense."

"Seriously, get outside for a bit, you've been in here all day every day for months. What did we used to do for fun?" Eric asked.

"Nothing," Vincent replied.

"Oh yeah, that's right."

Vincent followed Eric to the door. "Maybe I have been pushing it." He rubbed his eyes, which were marred by dark circles.

"We got you that intern to help lighten your load," Eric said, "isn't she pulling her weight?"

The way he casually referred to Lauren as though she were some inconsequential tool and not a person with hopes, dreams and talents made Vincent uncomfortable. "No, no, she's great..." he insisted.

"Really? Because these past couple of months you've seemed kind of distracted. Are you guys...?" Eric raised his eyebrows suggestively.

"Are you kidding?" Vincent laughed. "She's almost half my age and I'm pretty sure she's..."

"She's what?"

"I think she's gay."

"Huh... well, good, that would be a HR nightmare. Never shit where you eat," Eric said, like a sage spouting wise anecdotes.

"Didn't you sleep with Catherine, from design?"

"Learn from my mistakes."

"Yeah, you're a walking, talking cautionary tale."

Eric's eyes tightened with an ambitious glint, like some crook hatching a nefarious scheme. "A Chinese lesbian on our staff, that'll be great PR. We should get her to write a blog post or something."

"She's from north London," Vincent sighed. "You're a monster..." He trailed off, his eyes following a snowflake as it landed on Eric's shoulder.

Eric looked back and his jaw dropped as a flurry filled the room. He approached the monitor and hesitantly outstretched his hand, which, to his amazement, passed right through the television, just as Vincent's had before. After a second or two, he pulled it back, scrutinising it.

"Crazy, isn't it?" Vincent grinned.

"It's warm..." Eric rubbed the snow between his thumb and forefinger. "... It's ash."

Vincent looked ill as a horrible realisation hit him like a truck. He had fixed the bugged questline in the game, meaning that the inciting incident could've triggered in the game world. Without a moment's hesitation, he leapt through the screen.

"Whoa! Vince?!" Eric cried, but he was already gone.

Vincent raced over the ridge and sank to his knees as he beheld the village, laid to waste.

"What is going on?!" Eric yelled as he too came through into the world and caught up, but Vincent just sat in the snow and watched the horror unfold before him. Hideous lumpy-faced goblins with long pointed noses and sharp beady eyes dragged the townspeople from the burning houses, cutting down any who resisted.

"We need to go back!" Eric tugged on Vincent's jacket, and as he turned back towards the rift, a club struck his head and he collapsed in a heap.

A pack of goblins set upon Vincent, kicking and beating him until he stopped resisting. The monsters dragged the pair of them away deep below the mountains. That part was a blur. All Vincent can remember is the throbbing headache as he dipped in and out of consciousness.

He came to first, and by the time Eric awoke, they were shackled in a cage, forged of bone and scrap. He looked fearfully at his whereabouts, not a shred of natural light in sight.

"It's all connected..." Vincent's voice spoke from the shadows. Eric's eyes wandered until they found him sitting in a dark corner of their cell.

"What's going on? Where are we?!"

"Don't you recognise it?" Vincent asked.

He did. The bones protruding from the dirt, the arched rocks of the tunnel, the skeleton strung up next to them – it was all familiar.

"Why aren't you freaking out right now?" Eric asked.

"I am, but I'm trying to think of a way out of this mess."

Eric shook his head. "No, I mean you don't seem too surprised that we're locked in a cage that looks exactly like one from our game."

Vincent shied away. He was definitely hiding something. Eric could always tell and was undoubtedly the better liar of the two.

Vincent wondered how he could break it to him gently. "I don't want you to panic."

"Panic? I'm shackled in a bloody cave, a prisoner to monsters from a video game we created! I think I'm handling it pretty well, mate."

"Two months," he sighed. "I've been coming in and out of here for two months."

"Coming here? You mean we're really in—"

"Yes, keep your voice down, will you? Don't want to piss off the goblins."

"Fuck the goblins!" Eric pulled on his bonds. "I'm getting out of here!"

He writhed and wriggled and kicked against the bars until he worked his way upside down. There he hung, slowly rotating like a slaughtered carcass on a hook.

"Are you done?" Vincent asked.

Eric groaned. "I would very much like to not be here now."

"Agreed, but let's think about this logically. We're in a game, and not just any game but *our game*. We know it inside out, we can survive this, we just need to play to our advantage."

Eric wriggled his way upright. "Play to our advantage?"

"These creatures are stupid and have low hit points. We could probably take them as long as they don't gang up on us."

"You're insane. You want to role-play? Go right ahead, but leave me out of it."

"I'm serious, Eric, we're in real danger here. You know how this questline plays out, what they do with the townspeople?"

Eric shuddered. "Y-yeah, alright."

He relayed his plan, and Eric came around after a bit of convincing, then they lay in wait, haunted by the nerve-shredding screams that resounded throughout the dungeon.

A goblin finally came to retrieve them, and as soon as it unchained the cage door, Vincent conked it on the head with a bone he'd yanked from the skeleton sharing their cell. They quickly unshackled themselves using the monster's hatchet to break the chains. Eric looked both ways out of the cell as he stepped out, and both directions seemed equally eerie, stretching for miles into nothingness. The screams seemed to emanate from the right, so he decided their best bet was left and jogged a short way before he realised Vincent wasn't following. He stood looking towards the screams and clutched the goblin's hatchet in one hand.

"What the hell are you doing?" Eric called out in a hushed tone.

"I've got to find someone," he replied.

"Find someone? Who could you possibly need to find?"

"A friend."

"Oh no, we're not doing this, we're not adventurers, we're desk jockeys! When was the last time you set foot in the gym? You're gonna fight your way through this dungeon to rescue some NPC who isn't even real, with what? A blunt axe and a can-do attitude?"

"I can't leave her here. I understand if you don't want to come with me." Vincent smiled at his friend and took a deep breath. "If you follow that path it should lead back to the village, just watch out for low-level critters, nothing crazy, maybe a couple of giant spiders."

"Oh God. Why'd it have to be giant spiders?"

Vincent shrugged. "It's a trope."

"Someone else will come along," Eric said.

Vincent frowned. "Someone *has*."

"I meant someone with actual combat experience." He let out a deep sigh, and begrudgingly his conscience wouldn't allow him to abandon his friend. "Alright, we find this girl and we get out. That's it, right? I'm not dying for some hero fantasy of yours."

A grin crept across Vincent's face. "Agreed, no dying for either of us."

With that, they traversed the sprawling network of tunnels deeper into the mountain. The blueish cave walls, every cobweb, every bone that lay scattered in the dirt was like déjà vu. Vincent had spent months debugging and replaying this particular dungeon, and it was as familiar to him as his morning commute. They kept to the shadows to avoid any patrolling goblins and cut down any oversized bugs or rats with the hatchet they'd looted. Eventually, they came upon the dungeon's central chamber, which was lined with corpses grafted into the walls with a black mucus. Some had long rotted away, but others looked fresh, likely the poor villagers. Vincent scanned the bodies and desperately hoped that Nef wasn't among them. A shriek startled him. Peering through a hole in the ground, he saw her in a hollowed room below, shackled to a stone altar by those abominable creatures.

Vincent called to Eric who had wandered down a small tunnel, but he continued, his attention fixed on treasure ahead. He crawled through the stalagmites to reach a beaten chest and kneeled before it. Sliding his hands along the rough lid, Eric quietly opened it and lifted a grizzly looking battle axe which he gripped with both hands. Its handle was crafted from bone and the head adorned with a goblin skull. He felt its weight as he admired the onyx head. Eric grinned at Vincent. This wasn't an ordinary axe, he held 'Gobchopper'– a unique weapon capable of dealing high damage against subterranean hell-spawn.

As he made his way back, Eric caught his foot on a rock and fell face first into the dirt. The axe slid across the cave floor to the hole overlooking the altar. Vincent lunged and caught it in time, and Nef's wide eyes twinkled with hope as she spotted him. She screamed and he raised a finger to his lips as he pulled himself back up, and she nodded affirmatively.

"That's her?" Eric whispered.

"We've got to get her out before… Oh no." Vincent's face turned deathly pale as the goblins began to chant.

"Domina! Domina! Domina!"

From the shadows emerged a writhing tendril. Its needle tip oozed gooey black tar. Nef let loose a bloodcurdling scream as it rose above her, and two of the goblins prised her mouth wide as the tendril slithered its way down her throat and force fed her the foul liquid.

"We're too late, let's go before they see us!" Eric pleaded, but Vincent shot him a fierce glare. "Yeah, alright," he sighed.

"You've got my back, right?" Vincent handed Eric the Gobchopper.

Eric hesitated. "Y-yeah, but what are you—?"

Vincent leapt without a second thought into the chamber and landed on the altar. With a swing of his hatchet, he butchered the tendril and pulled it from Nef's throat. She puked and retched and violently choked, while Vincent fixed his attention on the abomination crawling from the shadows. A beautiful naked woman emerged with a twisted grimace across her face. Her wild matted hair writhed like snakes across her icy skin and she walked on six spindly stalks that protruded from her back like the legs of a spider. She curled her pale lips back across her razor teeth and opened her mouth wide as another tendril slithered from her throat and swayed in the air.

"Eric, help!" Vincent cried as the creature crept towards him. He could hardly believe he was staring down one of the most dangerous creatures in Ultimate Adventure lore – a corrupting hag.

The goblins backed away still chanting, "Domina! Domina! Domina!"

Against his better judgement, Eric leapt onto the creature from above and hacked ferociously with his axe. Foul monster blood splattered his face as he cleaved its neck, almost severing the head. The hag swatted him against the wall and pinned him with one of its stalks. He roared at the sharp sting in his side, and he squirmed on the end of its leg as it thrashed him about and threw him to the floor. He hit the dirt with a thud and his glasses went flying. Sweeping his hair from his eyes, Eric squinted as the blurred creature howled in agony, flailing its slender arms in a futile attempt to reattach its head, which was hanging sideways by only a few threads of tissue. Eric lifted his axe and buried it in the beast's abdomen, spilling its guts everywhere. The monster collapsed with a shriek and gurgled until it died. The chanting died down, and the goblins watched and whispered to each other. Eric fumbled around in the dark for his glasses while the hag's corpse festered and melted away, revealing a gleaming green jewel which shimmered like a beacon, illuminating Eric's face. He put on his cracked spectacles and looked hungrily upon the gem, which called to him with a soft whisper.

"Eric, wait!" Vincent cried, but it was too late, he had already gripped the crystal shard tightly in his hand, and in an instant it bored its way into him.

The shard had chosen him, but for what purpose was still unclear. Perhaps his fear, his desperation, his hunger for survival had enticed the crystal. Perhaps that's all nonsense, and he was simply a willing dope who all too quickly took the gem in hand. Either way, it became a part of him. The whites of Eric's wide eyes shone from his blood-soaked face as he examined his left hand with intrigue. But for the dull ache in his palm, there was no evidence the shard ever existed. It left no scar or blemish.

Vincent hacked away at Nef's brittle chains and freed her as the hiss of the goblins surrounding them became a chorus of fury. It seemed the creatures sought to avenge the death of their beloved mother. Eric got on his feet and doubled over in pain, pressing his hand against his soaked jacket. The beast's stalk had struck him hard, and its pointed end had torn a deep gash in his ribs. He was so full of adrenaline he hadn't noticed the wound, but his shirt now seeped red and he looked up at Vincent, trembling.

"I don't want to die," he whimpered.

"You're fine, it's just a scratch," Vincent assured him, but Eric was always the better liar of the two.

"Why aren't they attacking?" Nef cowered behind Vincent and coughed more of the foul liquid up while the goblins grew ravenous, savouring the scent of her fear like a fine perfume.

Vincent noticed their beady eyes were all fixed on Eric's hand. "The shard!" he cried. "They fear it!"

Eric worriedly examined his palm and held his arm out. Most of the goblins cowered, but braver ones began to step out of line and jerk towards the three of them as they backed into the tunnel the hag had emerged from.

"Stay back!" Eric tensed his whole body, trying desperately to wield the crystal shard somehow. The game had always been very vague about what could and couldn't be done with the shards, so he hadn't a clue how to use it.

One restless goblin jerked towards him and swung its blade, which nicked his outstretched hand. He retracted it sharply. Blood gushed down his arm and he poured all his fear and desperation into a mighty shout. In an instant, the shard flickered within him, and he clenched his fist as nerve-shredding pain lanced through his arm and crackled through his body. The goblins howled in fear at the jewel's unholy glow and tripped over each other long enough for the three of them to flee. Vincent pulled Nef and Eric through the winding tunnels as the creatures' evil roars echoed behind them. It sounded as if every goblin in the dungeon was amassing in pursuit.

In all the mayhem Vincent had got turned around and wasn't sure where he was going. A light at the end of the tunnel filled him with hope, and he hurtled towards it. The cave opened up into a vast chasm deep underground, where molten lava ran like a hellish river. A wide stone bridge connected both sides of the gorge – a remnant of the long extinct dwarves and their subterranean city. They sprinted across and snaked through desolate streets carved of black stone, past empty dwellings and dilapidated ruins. Vincent knew all too well what had become of the former residents – the crystal had warped them into the very creatures they were fleeing from. All roads led to a towering temple built into the chasm, and Vincent led them up the scarred broken steps. Gargantuan columns of rock that propped up the mountain were all that remained untarnished. The climb felt never-ending, like taking the stairs at Camden Town station, which Vincent often did when the escalators were bust. They reached the top and looked back. No goblins were in sight, but their screeching chorus resounded through the under-city. They certainly weren't far behind.

They scrambled through the temple until they reached the grand throne room. If the walls could talk, you'd cover your ears. Bones and body parts were strung up like morbid bunting, a celebration of lives lost, of agony inflicted. It was a dead end. The only passage out of the throne room was caved in.

"I don't like the look of this," Vincent said. "A big chamber, lots of bones, that usually means—"

"I don't feel good," Eric groaned as he stumbled towards the steps that led to a broken throne atop a plateau. He grew weaker by the minute and couldn't climb more than a few.

"You came for me, I thought you weren't an adventurer." Nef looked feverish. Her pale lips smiled before she coughed and fell to her knees, retching to expel the foulness from her body. Her eyes turned a cloudy white as she balled up on the floor, and Vincent held her as she convulsed.

"What's happening to her?" Eric cried. "Those things were chanting—"

"I know!"

"If she turns—"

"Just shut up a minute!" Vincent clutched the poor girl tightly. "She's ice cold." He looked worriedly at Eric who was distracted by something, and squinted at a shadowed figure that sat atop the throne. He couldn't quite make out who or what it was in the dark.

"I don't think we're alone in here!" he said as a shiver ran down his spine.

"It's just an old suit of armour. Probably the last poor bastard who found himself trapped in here," Vincent replied.

Eric was transfixed, and took off his specs to rub his eyes. He could've sworn the armour moved, but his vision was blurred, his mind was racing, and he was losing blood, so he knew he could be imagining things. He turned sharply towards the shrill war cries resounding through the ruin.

"They're coming," Vincent warned. Taking Nef in his arms, he hurried up the steps past Eric, frantically searching for a secret door or something, anything, to get them out. He looked at the rusty armour and at the skeleton wearing it. "Don't suppose you know an exit?"

The howls and hisses of the goblin horde grew louder with every passing second. Vincent knew there was no escape, but he laid Nef down atop the plateau and kept searching out of sheer blind desperation.

"Shit! It's a dead end, Eric." He threw his head in his hands.

"D-dead end?" Eric shuddered, and the garbled war cries of the goblins were deafening. "No, no, it can't be a dead end! There are always secret passages and trap doors and—"

Vincent shook his head. "Not here, friend."

Eric fell to his knees, and pressed against his wound. "I don't want to die," he whispered to himself over and over as he rocked back and forth and pictured his office in his mind – his comfy leather chair, his cabinet of awards. "I want to go back, I want to go back, I want to go back."

The horde burst into the chamber and charged towards them.

"I want to go back!"

Eric's despair ignited the crystal. Pale green light shone from his palm and he howled as the shard came to life. He shook, horrified at his flesh which rippled like water, and in a flash he was engulfed in light. "Vincent, save me!" he cried then imploded into nothingness.

A wave of fiery energy pulsed from where he stood, and knocked the horde back, sending Vincent tumbling down the steps. In an instant, the light dispersed, and Eric was gone. All that remained in his place was a small malformation in the air, like a glitch in reality, and the faint echo of his parting scream.

"E-Eric?!" Vincent trembled. "Oh God." He slumped on his knees, cradling his head in his hands as grief struck him like a hammer. He had no time to mourn, though, the horde were already on their feet again and thirsty for blood. Vincent hurled his hatchet into the crowd. "Get back!" he cried as tears welled in his bloodshot eyes. He stumbled up the steps, tripped backwards and fell at the armour's feet. The horde mauled him as he screamed, "I'll kill you all!" and then he felt a hand grip his wrist – cold, unforgiving metal.

He gazed in fear at the armour coming to life before him. It clambered piece by piece onto his body as if it were alive. The relic was rejuvenated by his life force and the rust fell off like a diminishing illusion, revealing its true form. By the time he realised what it was he had stumbled upon it was too late, it had attached itself to him like a parasite.

The goblins swarmed, beating him with their clubs and hatchets, but by some miracle their weapons bounced off the black armour like cheap plastic toys. An uncharacteristically intelligent goblin adapted and sliced its jagged knife across the bridge of Vincent's nose. He clasped the horned helmet and pulled it onto his head for protection as he screamed. With the final piece attached, the armour roared to life. He could feel each segment tighten around him, bolstering his bones and muscles. Unbridled strength flowed through him like a riptide, and from the darkest depths of the blackest void a magic blade appeared unto him. He gripped the hilt of the God Cleaver sword and fought his way onto his feet. He lifted the blade while the creatures relentlessly assaulted him, snarling, spitting, snorting. It was chaos like he'd never known. With a thundering cry, he swung wide, cleaving twenty goblins in half with a single blow. The blade erupted in a blaze of scorching hellfire and slid through them like soft butter, felling dozens at a time. More and more poured from the tunnel. Their bloodlust knew no bounds, but he killed every one that came at him. He could feel the armour encouraging him to smite them all and grew frenzied as body parts stacked up around him. He decimated every wave until finally, they stopped. The hall was splattered red. The sight of their kin's dismembered and smouldering body parts was enough to ensure their respect or at the very least, exacerbate their terror. The survivors huddled together by the entrance, grunting and squealing and one by one, they knelt before him. To them, he was the Dread Knight – bathed in the hellfire of the god-killing sword, a walking demon of legends long past, returned to rid the world of light and life.

Vincent clasped at every breath as he composed himself. Slowly the fire of his sword flickered out, and he sheathed it on his back. He examined his hands, clad in the pitch-black gauntlets. The armour had no seam, as though the plate mail had joined together into one chitinous exoskeleton. Recalling the game's lore in his mind, he shuddered. One who spills blood in the Dreadmail is doomed to wear it until they meet a bloody and violent end, and all who take up the Dread Knight's moniker meet such a fate. Such is the price to pay for unrivalled power. There was no going back. His life as Vincent Golbez was over.

In the chaos he had forgotten about Nef, who sat upright and looked at him with sunken eyes. She was changed too.

Most unsettling of all was her cold, vacuous expression, like a machine booting itself up. She knelt before him, for all creatures of the void owed allegiance to the Dread Knight Grimoirh. He was their saviour. He would herald the world's end, silence the song of life that had driven the demons and monsters so mad and in doing so, reclaim the world for them.

Together they ventured back to the smouldering remains of Hoarfrost. The blizzard had calmed, and the sun began to rise, but the rift into reality was gone. Vincent knelt on the ridge overlooking what was left of the village. It took all his might to prise the helmet from his head, and he tossed it into the snow. Attempts to remove any other piece of the armour proved utterly futile. It wasn't coming off. It was as much a part of him as he was it. Vincent, Wanderer, Grimoirh, it didn't matter what he called himself anymore...

*

It's fitting, Vincent supposes, that all of this will end right where it began – deep beneath the frigid, desolate wasteland. His only hope of respite is a quick death once he's cast this cursed world back into the void. He can't be certain what will happen to him after he plunges the shards into the heart of the world, corrupting it until it breaks apart, but truthfully he doesn't care. The armour has extracted a terrible price for keeping him alive on his perilous journey – his humanity. He feels as though he has become the armour itself – a cold, hard, empty shell. With every passing day, the last vestiges of himself slip away like melting snow.

The black tunnel gives way to blinding light. They emerge on the other side of the mountain and Vincent gazes ahead at a colossal storm stirring on the horizon, tearing the ice and snow into the air, as if the sky and the earth were at war.

"What is that?" Domina looks humbled by the tempest.

"The Scar is past that barrier," he replies. "When the crystal was forged, it bore a heavy price. They bled the world for its power, inflicting a deep wound that would never heal. This storm is like a scab, it's the world's last defence."

Domina trembles at the sight. To stand against Pangea Ultima itself seems like a mad feat.

"What makes you so sure this will work?" she asks.

He turns to her, his cold eyes brimming with confidence. "As the Dread Knight it is my destiny to destroy this world."

XVIII

FALSE EVIDENCE
APPEARING REAL

George picks himself off the floor and shuffles away from the frozen spikes piercing the cockpit. He sits back against the cold metal wall and crosses eyes with Esmerelda who is lying awkwardly opposite him. She lets out a feeble groan and his wide eyes dart to the shrapnel lodged in her stomach.

"H-help!" he gasps. "Someone help!"

Ed stumbles over his broken chair to investigate. The kid looks ashen as he points to Esmerelda.

"Oh no." Ed looks to Bengeo who, for the first time since they met, is noticeably shaken. He didn't think things would go to hell this fast. Boy, was he sorely mistaken.

The bandit carefully steps over the debris and kneels beside her.

"How am I looking, Ben?" Her wrinkled face grimaces as she copes with the pain.

"Better than I feel." He smiles, but the light in her eyes is fading.

Bengeo shares a foreboding look with Regis who shakes his

head. One glance at Esmerelda's wound is all it takes to assess the fatality of the situation.

"Are the others alright?" Ed asks.

"The old man was behind us," Regis replies, "but I didn't see anyone else."

"What about Lauren?" George croaks.

Regis shakes his head. "Didn't see her, the sisters, Ozrune or the troll either."

"Shit." Ed runs his hand through his hair and exhales his stress.

To add to it, the nose of the cockpit breaks apart with a thunderous creak and plummets into the snow.

*

Lauren's eyes flutter open to morning light, and the tang of blood lingers in her mouth as she lies in the snow amongst scattered debris. She wiggles her toes and sighs with relief that she can still move her legs. Her warm breath materialises as she sits up slowly and gets her bearings – nothing but snow, ice and Jessica's toothy grin.

"She's awake!"

"About time," Avarice grunts from atop a giant propeller blade that was torn off in the crash.

"Did we make it?" Lauren asks in a raspy voice.

Jessica nods. "Barely."

Avarice leaps off the propeller and frowns at Lauren. "Can you walk?"

She shifts her weight onto her legs and her calves tremble as she stands. "What happened? We were in the sky and then..." Recalling the storm she conjured, Lauren looks ashamed.

"Yes, a stupid and dangerous thing you did." Avarice casts a stern eye at Jessica, who shrinks with guilt too. "Magic is not to be trifled with."

"Magic…" Jessica looks worried, remembering that Ozrune was swept into the sky, "… Mr Bird Wizard, he got thrown off too, do you think he's okay?"

"Perhaps. Wizards like him often have tricks up their sleeve…" the troll scowls.

Jessica looks relieved.

Avarice continues, "… but it is more likely he is dead." And with that, whatever comfort Jessica briefly felt is banished.

"George?! Is he…?! Is he okay?" Lauren panics.

Jessica looks worried. "He's probably fine, he's with the others, they'll watch out for him."

Lauren looks terrified. She can't lose him too. A low howl, haunting and desperate, fills her with despair. She looks warily about the empty white expanse. "What is that?"

The other two look at her like she's crazy.

"You can't hear anything?"

"Hear what?" Jessica asks, wondering if Lauren has a concussion or something.

"It's sort of like whale song but it's everywhere and nowhere…"

Avarice perks up. "I hear something too!" She looks to the north and sees Remy and Valentine waving at them from atop a slope.

"Heeeeey!" Remy's voice carries across the frigid wastes as she races towards them.

"Hey!" At first Jessica looks relieved, then she notices Remy's disposition and backs away as her sister comes straight at her with a face of wrath. "What's your deal?"

"How could you be so stupid?!" Remy barks, shoving Jessica who staggers backwards. "So selfish?! So reckless?! What were you thinking? Huh?" She shoves again and again until Jessica snaps and pushes back. The sisters glare at one another for a moment, nostrils flared. Their harsh breath fogs the air between them.

"Uh, guys…" Lauren says meekly.

"You too! What if you didn't make it? What would we tell George?" Remy snaps.

Lauren bows her head. "I… I'm sorry."

"Don't apologise, you saved us," says Jessica.

"You almost killed us! Ed and the others, they could be hurt, or worse," Remy yells. "This is the problem with you, you never think about anyone but yourself!"

"No, that's you!" Jessica barks.

"Enough!" Lauren cries as Valentine comes trudging over the ridge, panting heavily.

"Why'd you run off like that?" he wheezes, completely oblivious to the tension that could rival the icy field they're standing in. He looks at the girls' stern faces and asks, "What's going on?"

"We can't be at each other's throats like this, we need to work together if we're going to survive," Lauren says.

Jessica and Remy exchange a bitter glance before both casting their eyes to the opposite horizons.

From the brow of the hill, Remy stares at the scattered airship parts trailing north towards the rugged mountains in the distance, where the sky darkens with a primeval rage.

"Of course this could only get worse." She shivers as she speaks, knowing well that no good awaits them there, but of course with her rotten luck that would be where the others are, *if* they survived the crash. Perish the thought.

The five set off along the trail of debris while the sun crawls over the horizon. The bitter wind is a burden to all. Even Avarice shivers as the breeze carries the snow against her. Lauren straggles behind the others, and as they press on the distance between them grows. Jessica lingers back also, wanting to be as far from Remy as possible.

She glances at Lauren with her arms wrapped around herself and her head tucked far into her raincoat, which is fastened all the way up. She clearly isn't coping with the unforgiving cold, and with her rail-thin figure who could blame her.

"You alright?" Jessica asks.

Lauren pokes her head up like a tortoise emerging from its shell, revealing her rosy freckled face. "So c-c-cold," she stutters.

When she was barely a child, Lauren's maternal grandmother had told her of how freckles were traditionally considered undesirable in China. This comment had rooted itself deep in her psyche despite her mother telling her "to hell with tradition". In her adolescence she tried to cover them with makeup but wasn't particularly adept at that sort of thing and couldn't be bothered to learn, so eventually she accepted that perhaps it was her lot in life to be 'undesirable'. Little does she know, the sight of those freckles on her reddening nose is anything but to Jessica.

"You don't need to worry about me, I'm fine," Lauren says, mistaking her lingering admiration for a look of pity.

Understanding of her desire not to be patronised, Jessica concocts a little white lie. "I know. I'm just sick of walking in silence. Those guys are boring."

"Oh." Lauren looks apologetic, and worries whether she sounded harsh a moment ago, but Jessica doesn't seem bothered. "You really think George is okay?" she asks.

Jessica nods resolutely. "No doubt."

Up ahead, Valentine sighs. "I can't take this anymore, we'll die from exposure if we stay out here."

"Not me," Avarice says, "trolls do not feel cold."

"Then why do you look as miserable as the rest of us?" he replies.

"Misery is all we trolls know," she says, stone-faced, and resolutely takes the lead beside Remy.

The snow flutters harder, faster, blanketing all in a white haze, while the wind drones in the distance as they slog across the plains and snake through the winding mountain pass which offers little respite from the blizzard. The pass ends at a clearing and the hollowed remains of some bygone village. Lauren stumbles over the remnants of a structure buried in the snow, which looks like the foundations of what was once a house.

"Look!" The others look back at her as she kneels down and dusts the ice off a wooden plaque. It reads 'Hoarfrost Inn'. Her face takes on a wan expression.

"Hoarfrost…" Dread gnaws at Remy as she recalls the town from the original game. "We should move on."

"Hold on," Valentine says, "we need shelter before it gets any colder. If we get turned around in this we're as good as dead."

"He's r-right, the sun's already going d-d-down, we won't find our w-way at night." Lauren clenches her jaw to stop her teeth chattering.

"How can it be dark already?" Avarice asks.

"We're probably far north," Valentine replies. "In the winter Iceland only gets five hours of light."

"Ice Land. A fitting name for this realm."

The detective shakes his head at the troll and tucks his blue hands under his arms to warm them.

A glint in the sky catches Jessica's eyes, and she shields them with her hand then squints. *Am I seeing shit?* she wonders, but the golden light glistens again. "What's that?"

They watch as it floats towards them and Avarice warily draws her knives.

"A wisp!" she cries.

"A what?" Jessica asks.

"My father told me stories about ghosts that lure travellers to grim deaths."

Jessica groans – why can't there be nice things in this world?

By contrast Remy looks hopeful at the glowing apparition as it shapeshifts into a bird of pure light, circling above – the very same one that appeared to her in the crypt.

"I think it wants us to follow it," she says.

"Then that is why we should not," Avarice insists.

"Trust me, I've seen it before!" Remy sprints after the spectre, which soars through the heavy snow, leading them away from the ruined village to a cavern hidden in the mountainside. The five stand hesitantly before the cave's tremendous maw, peering into the dark as the glowing apparition drifts further inside.

"Like I said. Grim death," Avarice grunts.

Remy breathes uneasily. The last dungeon nearly claimed her life, and she had hoped not to set foot in another – fat lot of good hope has got her so far.

Lauren notices the anxiety flaring up on Remy's face, a look she herself is all too familiar with, and presses her hand on Remy's shoulder. "Hey, we'll be alright if we stick together."

Remy gives a thankful smile before turning back to the gaping maw of darkness. She tells herself, *We'll be okay, if Ozrune's guiding us we'll be okay. It has to be him, must be.* With a sigh she draws Astrid's sword that she had taken during their escape from Parousia. Its pale glow illuminates the cavern as she cautiously steps inside.

*

Regis unfurls a map, looks out at the vista from atop the crashed airship and points to the mountains on the eastern horizon. "If those are the Iron Top mountains, and that's the Owl's Window then that puts us somewhere about here, on the Quiet Rise just south of the Violent Summit."

"Please tell me the Violent Summit is named ironically." Ed hops from one foot to the other to keep warm.

Regis shakes his head. "It's named for the storm over the mountain. Beyond that is the Scar. No man's land."

Fear smothers Ed like a pillow over his face, and he gazes at the vortex stretching from the heavens to the earth. A raging, swirling wall of snow and black cloud collide while booming thunder rolls over the rocky peaks.

"We got lucky," Regis says.

"Lucky?!" Ed snaps. "We're stranded, half of us are missing and Esmerelda is... well..."

Regis bows his head. "Forgive me, I misspoke. What I meant was, if the legends are to be believed, the Scar is where the crystal was forged. This must be Grimoirh's destination. He has at least two shards and he's days ahead of us. I know you're worried about your friends, but if we don't catch up to him soon, none of us will live long enough to see each other again."

Games are supposed to be fun, but these weighty moral decisions are enough to break Ed. He can't cope with the consequences when actual lives hang in the balance. He looks to Bengeo for reassurance, but the bandit is transfixed by something strange in the distance: a black mass growing on the southern horizon.

"What is that?" Ed asks.

He didn't believe it when Diamond told him, but now they're on his doorstep. Bengeo sighs. "The dead, marching."

*

George lays another blanket over Esmerelda to keep her warm where she lies in the upturned cargo hold, atop a bed made of crates and fur skins.

The crow's feet vanish from the corner of her eyes as she smiles tenderly at the worried boy who stokes the crackling fire Bengeo had lit in the centre of the room.

"Are you scared?" he asks.

She shakes her head. "There are worse fates than dying."

George looks downcast and croaks, "What do you think happens... after you die? Do you believe in the lofty realm?"

Despite doing his best to hide it, Esmerelda can see the boy is deeply distressed.

"I've lived a long life, rich with adventure and folk good and bad, but as I got older all I dreamed of was a simple life. Used what coin I saved to open an inn, wasn't much but it was mine, 'til it was gone. Warm beds, a roaring fire, good food and drink and loved ones lost, that's all I long for. I expect that's what I'll find. So don't be sad, little one, nothing lasts forever in this life and that's alright. We all find each other again."

He's unsure whether it's her words or the kind twinkle in her weary eyes that ease his worry, but either way he's grateful for her company.

Ed and the others return from outside, solemn and silent, but the grim expressions on their faces say a lot.

"What is it?" George asks.

Bengeo and Regis exchange a severe glance, then the bandit sighs, "Undead. Thousands of them are coming our way."

"Well, we can't leave without Lauren and the others," he replies.

"If we stay we'll die," says Regis.

"That's bullshit," George cries. "You and Bengeo can take 'em!"

Bengeo shakes his head. "Look, kid, I don't like it either, but right now we've got to make some hard choices. If your sister is out there then it's our job to keep you safe until you find her, and it ain't safe here."

"I don't care, I'm not leaving without her and you can't make me. I don't have to listen to you, you're not my dad." George looks stone-faced at the bandit, but Bengeo can see he's fighting back tears.

"Bengeo's right." Ed kneels beside George and rests a hand on his shoulder. "We need to make hard choices…"

George looks betrayed until a little smile crosses Ed's lips.

"… So I'm staying too. We go together or we don't go at all."

"If we don't go at all then we die," Bengeo sighs.

Ed nods. "Then we die together."

"Very well," Regis sighs. "The cold will slow the undead

down, but not for long." The swordsman stands up straight and adjusts the scabbard on his back. "I'll scout ahead, see if I can find a way past that storm that won't kill us." Before he leaves he holds a finger up to Ed. "I'd wager you have until dawn before they're at your door, so take only what you can carry. Let's just hope the others make their way here before then. I'll leave markers for you to follow."

Ed shakes the swordsman's hand. "Thank you."

With a sad smile Regis bids them farewell, slips through a hole in the cargo hold and begins the climb to the crater on the other side of the mountain.

*

The spectre floats a short way ahead of Remy and the others, casting its warm light across the gleaming walls of ice.

"Do you really think it knows a way out?" Lauren whispers to Remy, who nods.

"The last time I saw it, it led me to you and Mr Valentine."

"Well, I don't trust it." Avarice grips her knives tightly and keeps her eyes fixed sharply on the apparition.

"We know," Jessica sighs, "you haven't shut up about it. Grim death, we get it."

The troll sneers at her and strides ahead of them.

"What's with her?" Jessica asks.

"She's just… Avarice," Remy says.

Jessica pulls a shit-eating grin. "Reminds me of someone else I know."

Remy rolls her eyes. "Yeah well, she's only spent a day with you, shows you how patient I am."

Jessica pokes her tongue at the back of Remy's head and makes an ugly face.

"Very mature," Valentine remarks as he passes her.

Suddenly, like dwindling candlelight, the spectre shrinks

until the darkness snuffs it out entirely. The group stop dead in their tracks, their anxious faces lit only by the cold glow of Remy's enchanted sword.

"Now what?" Jessica panics.

"There's only one way, we keep going," Remy says.

"I say we go back," says Valentine.

"And risk the blizzard?" Remy scoffs. "We'll freeze before the sun comes up again."

"She's right," Lauren says, "if we're lucky this will lead us through the mountains."

Valentine lets out a condescending laugh. "If we were lucky we wouldn't be in this mess."

"Very mature," Jessica says still wearing that shit-eating grin of hers.

"It's got to lead somewhere," Remy says.

"And why's that?" Valentine asks.

"Because we're in a video game. Nothing is designed by accident. Dungeons, caves, they always lead to something important. Right?" Of course, they're also always filled with something awful, but right now she's trying to stay positive.

Remy looks to Lauren for reassurance and she nods earnestly. Holding her blade ahead to illuminate their path she guides them through the glittering tunnels.

"Grim death it is," Avarice sighs.

*

Bengeo, Ed and George pile as much junk as they can salvage outside of the ship. The bandit tosses the last wooden crate onto the heap then empties a barrel of oil over it. "Got a light?" he asks Ed who rummages through the items he bought in Parousia and pulls a small parcel wrapped in cloth from his bag. He throws it to George who unfurls the rag and a black lump of coal plops into his hand.

"What is it?" He notices an incantation scrawled on the rag. "Mind of fire, soul on fire, feeling hot, hot, hot." The stone glows red hot in his palm and he drops it with a yowl, then kicks it into the pile of wood which immediately ignites into a roaring bonfire. He plants his hand in the snow to cool it and looks impressed.

"Think they'll see it?" he asks.

"Well, there sure as shit ain't nothing else to see." Bengeo scans the dark, desolate wasteland and sighs. "If they're out there, they'll see it." He pats the boy on the head and returns inside to check on Esmerelda.

Ed warms himself by the fire, and upon stealing a glance, George notices Ed appears as worried as he feels.

"It's okay if you're scared," the boy says.

"Huh?"

"Just because you're scared, doesn't mean you're not brave."

Ed smiles. "You think so?"

George nods, and hesitates to ask, "Do you think the crystal can really get us home?"

"Well, they say it can do anything, right?"

"Is it true it can bring the dead back to life?"

"Yeah, it sure seems that way." Ed recalls the sight of the undead blackening the horizon. It chills him worse than the bitter cold, but George looks relieved, almost happy. He wonders what the boy is thinking, but decides, considering their dire predicament, to just let him enjoy whatever fleeting thought brings him comfort.

*

Around a long bend warm light flickers against the cavern walls, and Remy raises her shield defensively as a throaty wail resounds through the tunnel.

"What the F was that?" Jessica cowers behind Avarice.

A long humanoid shadow moves across the wall ahead and onto the floor, then a silhouette rounds the corner. The sound of creaking bone and breathy gasps grate their ears as it staggers towards them. Remy raises her sword, and its ethereal glow casts a light on the mysterious figure. It's a man, sort of – broken and bloody, but he doesn't quite look undead.

"Not me..." the figure croaks, "... should have been you..."

"Stay back!" Remy's cry rouses not even a glance from the man. "Come any closer and I'll run you through!" she warns.

"Should have been you!" the stranger hisses and raises a bony crooked finger at Lauren, who trembles as though his words bear some meaning. Remy thrusts her sword forward, and the figure hobbles back from whence it came.

"Well, that was nightmare fuel," Jessica whimpers, blood pumping, eyes wide with terror.

"Wait!" Lauren calls out as the stranger's murmurs carry through the tunnel. "Wait, please!" Without notice she sprints after him.

"Hey, what are you—?!" Remy calls to her, but she's already gone. "So much for sticking together."

They hurry after her and round the bend, where the cave widens out into a hollow chamber, and they find Lauren kneeling before a twisted burning car wreck.

"Is this real?" Remy notices tears streaming from Lauren's eyes as the firelight flickers on her grieving face.

"You see it too?" she whimpers.

"It's kind of hard to miss," Remy replies.

Lauren breathes a sigh of relief. She was certain she had lost her mind, but if they see it too then that's better, isn't it? Probably not considering the kind of things that lurk in this world.

"How the hell did this get down here?" Valentine asks. The familiar shape of the car brings him some solace. It feels like ages since he's seen anything normal, even though this is about as far from normal as a situation can get.

A foreboding creak reverberates from the wreck, and the shape of someone moves inside it.

"Should have been you!" the familiar voice calls out again. A charred arm stretches out from the flaming wreckage, pulls its mangled body from the car and crawls towards Lauren who bursts into tears.

"Stay back!" Remy warns, but the man pays her no mind. He extends his arms out wide, grasping air in Lauren's direction.

"D-Dad, I'm sorry!"

"It should have been you!" the man croaks as she cowers at his charred shoes.

"Christ almighty!" Valentine gasps. "That thing is your dad?"

"Not helping!" Jessica berates him and wraps her arms around Lauren, turning her away from the creature. "Get rid of it!" she cries.

Remy swings and severs his head with a single blow. The body collapses in a heap at her feet.

"Can someone explain what the hell is going on?" the detective barks.

A harsh cackle bounces around them. They fix their eyes on the dismembered head.

"Think you're tough, Remy Winters? I've seen you for what you are, a self-absorbed brat who's no use to anyone!" the mangled head shrieks as its shape contorts with a bone-crunching pop into that of Remy's career adviser, Norma, only with pale blank eyes.

"You've got no future, Remy. You're not fit for purpose." The head speaks in Norma's grating voice. "You're going nowhere, you should've died in that pit!"

Remy looks appalled as it shifts again into her mother. "You're a rotten, callous bitch, I was so relieved when you left. I'd been waiting eighteen years to get rid of you. The second you came back into our lives you made everyone miserable because

342

you poison everything. Your father had the right idea leaving, he could see what a vile girl you'd grow up to be!"

"It's not real, don't listen to it," Jessica cries. "Mum would never say those things!"

But the cruel whisper in Remy's ear returns, only louder – *hate you everyone hates you, loser good for nothing no future you'll die here.*

"Tell her how miserable she makes you. She should know what a burden she is to us all." The head speaks softly to Jessica, hoping to drive a wedge between the sisters.

Miserable burden no good to anyone. Remy shuts her eyes tight and spirals. Her feet feel leaden. She shudders as a hundred decrepit hands spring from the ground and drag her into the mud. Their raspy voices, sodden with contempt, drown her desperate pleas – *Die here you'll die here!*

"Shut up! Shut up! Shut up!" Remy screams as the others scramble to pull her free.

Avarice brings her foot down on Helen's severed head, splitting it like a melon, and in an instant the flaming car and the undead arms simply vanish, leaving the five of them in blackout darkness. The sound of their panicked breath echoes around the cavern as they huddle together.

"Daddy?" a little girl's voice calls out from the shadows.

"Who is that?" Remy raises her glowing sword to illuminate the voice's source.

"Daddy?"

Valentine feels a gentle tug on his coat tail.

"Where have you been, Daddy?"

His face drains of all colour. He shies away from his daughter's apparition.

"It's not real," Jessica assures him.

"Can we get out of this horror palace?!" Unwilling to face the daughter he abandoned, he snatches his coat away from the girl and storms away.

343

"You heartless old fool, you'll die here and no one will mourn you!" the girl hisses. Her voice deepens, becoming distorted. "Look at me!" she roars.

Jessica glances back and is startled by the child's face – devoid of features, save for a ringed maw, lined with razor teeth, identical to the creature that stole her away and brought her to the game world. In the blink of an eye, she finds herself on stage at the Underbelly. She tries to sing, but no words come, only muffled screams of terror as she realises her mouth is sewn shut. A bottle strikes her in the face, cutting her forehead, and she backs away fearfully, cupping her wound as the crowd grow wild and claw their way onto the stage wielding bar stools and broken bottles. Avarice's hand grasps her firmly and pulls her out of her hallucination and back into the moment.

Jessica frantically feels her lips, ensuring they are thankfully back to normal. "What's happening?!" she gasps.

"It's like our demons are coming to life," Lauren whimpers.

Valentine takes Lauren by the arm and leads her away. He treads quickly and blindly through the intersecting passages, ignoring the howls and shrieks echoing behind them until they reach an exit. Jessica drops to her knees on seeing the cave mouth completely frozen over.

"Oh God."

"It's just another illusion!" Valentine charges at the wall and crashes into it with a thud, falling flat on his arse. "Not an illusion," he groans.

"Something is coming!" Avarice draws her knives and stands ready for whatever approaches.

The thud of metal courses through the tunnel – a familiar noise that sends a visceral chill shooting down Remy's spine. Her chest tightens around her racing heart as she stares intently at the dark tunnel. The God Cleaver ignites, illuminating him in hellfire, and Remy lifts her shield arm as he strides towards her.

"Vincent?" Lauren calls out to him, but the Dread Knight pays her no heed.

"Back off!" Avarice swipes her knives.

Grimoirh lunges. His flaming blade comes down between them with a whomp.

"That felt pretty real." Jessica crawls backwards as he corners her and raises his sword to deliver a fatal blow. She releases a breathless gasp as the blade comes down.

Before it reaches her sister, Remy cleaves off Grimoirh's arm. The Icerend tears through his armour and it shatters like glass.

"Get away from her!" she shrieks.

Grimoirh faces her slowly and she realises there's no one beneath the armour – it's moving on its own. Regardless, she can sense a fierce presence peering at her from beneath the ebony helmet. Before he can make another move, she runs him through with her sword, and the armour falls to pieces and melts away, revealing a small ethereal orb, which hovers before her. She pokes it with her sword and the ball freezes solid and hits the ground with a resounding ca-thunk.

"I told you. Wisps." Avarice looks unimpressed.

"All that was because of this tiny thing?" Valentine asks.

"Are all other-worlders this dense?" the troll mutters.

"But the spirit that led us here looked just like the one Ozrune conjured to save me," Remy says.

"Wisps are tricksters. They twist your hopes and fears against you to lure you to—"

"A grim death?" Jessica says.

Avarice scowls and sheathes her knives while the others look uncomfortable at having their deepest insecurities laid bare before each other. Lauren shrinks into her coat and faces the wall of the cave. She doesn't want anyone to see her upset.

"False evidence appearing real," Valentine mutters.

"Huh?" She looks teary-eyed at the old man.

"Just something I used to tell Sophie. She never liked the dark. F.E.A.R, false evidence appearing real."

"You were with him when he died, weren't you?" asks Jessica.

Lauren looks downcast. Her tears splatter her trainers.

Valentine places his hand gently against her arm. "Look, if your dad ever had a choice between him or you walking away from that wreck, he'd pick you every time, that's the truth of it. What you think, what you saw, it's not real."

Avarice, Remy and Jessica watch silently as the old man consoles her. Every now and then he shows he's still got a heart.

"It's alright," he says, "cry if you want, none of us will think any less of you. We're barely holding it together ourselves."

Her eyes sting as she fights back the flood streaming down her cold face.

"*It should've been you*' – you can't think like that. What happened, it's not your fault and it's not fair, but sometimes shit, horrible shit, it just happens to people who don't deserve it."

Her eyes burn with anguish at the old man as he holds his arms out to her, and she balls her fists as he embraces her slowly. The stench of smoke and whisky hit her as her walls come crumbling down. Her cries of sorrow and fury at the world echo through the frozen cavern. She fights Valentine, and he clings to her, easing her onto her knees while she comes undone, picturing the accident in her mind. Only fl-ash-es. She awoke a week later, her body broken in all sorts of ways. Her baggy clothes hide the scars – washed-out evidence of surgeries that restored her ability to walk, serving as an outward voice to her inner torment that her father is but a dream fading with every passing day.

Jessica tears up at the sight of Lauren utterly falling to pieces, buried in Valentine's ratty coat. Her hand finds Remy's and squeezes it tightly – an unspoken gesture of sisterhood, long overdue, offered from one to the other as they both realise how lucky they are with what they have. Their family may be dysfunctional at the best of times, and they've both experienced loss in their own way, but miraculously through that loss, they were given each other. Remy looks lovingly at Jessica and smiles apologetically while she struggles to hold in tears of her own.

Avarice too is touched by Lauren's pain. Seeing this girl mourn the man that raised her resonates profoundly, and tears down her beliefs about trolls and humans. Perhaps they're not so different after all. They certainly are no strangers to suffering.

Holding Lauren in his arms makes Valentine wonder about all the heartache he's missed with his own daughter, all of the times she might have needed a shoulder to cry on but he wasn't there. He lets out a pained sigh, expressing grief and regret as only he knows how. Oh well, all he can do is try to be a better man.

Having emptied herself of the pent-up grief, Lauren sits up and dries her eyes.

Jessica goes to console her. She's always been good at that kind of thing. Good at seeing what people need and connecting with those around her. She wipes away her inky tears and sits next to Lauren, and the others give them room to talk. Valentine fumbles a cigarette out of his pocket and feels around for a lighter before he remembers yet again that he lost the damn thing, so he tosses the smoke away.

"That was a pretty good thing you just did," Remy whispers. "I think you'd have been a good dad if you'd given yourself a chance."

Valentine purses his lips, never one to wear his heart on his sleeve. He watches Jessica regale Lauren of how she threw up on stage at her last gig. The story lightens the mood and even elicits laughter as Lauren composes herself.

"It's time we got out of this hole," Valentine grumbles.

"Yes." Avarice taps her knife against the wall of ice blocking the mouth of the cave, using the sound to indicate its weakest point, then drives the blade into it with force and starts chipping away.

Inspired by her determination, Remy joins her and together they hack away until the ice falls in blocks. One by one they step out to the cold tundra, where the blizzard has calmed and the sun crawls once more over the eastern horizon. With the rugged mountains at their back, they trek over the northern ridge and survey the land. The faint glow of Bengeo's pyre twinkles in the distance like the northern star and banishes Remy's despair.

She turns to Avarice and wonders, "Strange, we didn't see what you're afraid of."

The troll looks sullen. "When you have lost everything, there is nothing to fear." She turns her gaze south, tightening her eyes at strange shapes moving over the foot of the slopes. A thousand walking corpses, living skeletons, vicious draugr and shrieking wights plough towards them. Among them walk the accursed – larger twisted horrors warped by the crystal's malevolent power. Hideous appendages have mutated and broken through their rotting flesh like a demonic cancer.

"Oh God." Remy turns whiter than the snow as she beholds the black march and covers her ears to muffle the monsters' ear-splitting cries. Death is coming for them.

XIX

ENDGAME

Lauren's dainty feet pound the snow like a deer fleeing a hunt. Her rasping throat burns, but she forces herself forward no matter what, taking long strides to keep up with Avarice's relentless pace. Seeing the troll run with grace and strength sparks an ember of hope that they might actually make it out of this alive, until she glances over her shoulder at the bloodcurdling horde gaining on them. The dead do not tire, but her muscles burn with lactic acid, she grits her teeth with each step and exhales hard to expunge the pain until her legs give way, and she tumbles into the snow with a breathless gasp.

The others swiftly halt and turn back, and only then does the hopelessness of their situation truly sink in. The frozen tundra is black with creatures.

"Climb on my back!" Avarice pulls Lauren onto her feet.

She wraps her arms around the troll's shoulders and binds Avarice's waist with her legs. They plough ahead, giving no heed to the spine-chilling horrors behind them.

Jessica glances over her shoulder and screams. A gangly abomination stalks her on two spindly legs and reaches out with grotesque malformed hands. She drops into a ball as the horror lunges and crashes in the snow with a howl, sweeping Avarice's legs. She throws Lauren from her back and they both tumble down a steep decline. Jessica turns back to help them, but Remy takes her arm.

"No, don't stop!" She pushes her sister towards Valentine. "Get her out of here!" she barks.

Valentine nods, taking Jessica by the wrist before Remy sprints, sword in hand, to Avarice's side.

Lauren tries to help her up, but Avarice sluggishly retracts her arm, draws her knives and stands on her own, ready to face the onslaught.

"My father was Terak the Troll, leader of the Boulder Clan. He slaughtered One Eye, the most ferocious of all boar beasts, he defeated the usurper Meldreth with only a single apple, he led the people of Trout safely through the Witched Wood after their town was burned by the Dread Knight and he died there, protecting them from the demons of the forest."

"What? Terak is—?!" Remy looks stunned. All this time she hadn't a moment to consider why Avarice had joined them but her father had not.

Avarice keeps her sight fixed on the ridge. "Most will remember him as a monster. Most do not think we feel, do not think we matter, but today, a troll will fight to defeat the Dread Knight and his hell-spawn. People will learn that trolls had a hand in shaping the future of this world. Word will spread that trolls can be heroes too. If a troll thinks he can be more than he is, he will do good and others will do good back. Then perhaps the world will not be such a dark place for us."

Lauren trembles, unable to conjure a word. Warm tears roll down her cheeks as her breath fogs the air between them. Avarice turns to her with prideful eyes and they exchange an unspoken understanding at having both lost the men who raised and nurtured them.

A haunting shriek heralds the first wave. Amongst the wights and corpses, a mutated horror lashes a barbed tail behind it and spits acid, which catches Lauren's shoulder and burns through her anorak. She throws it off and staggers backwards in the snow as the abomination towers over her, eager to peel her skin from her body. It rises, then lunges for the kill. She steals a breath, one she's sure will be her last. Her eyes lock on the razor tail as it hurtles toward her, and she hopes she'll at least see her father again. Fate has other plans. Avarice leaps over her and drives her knives into the beast's putrid flesh. She lops off its tail and black blood stains the crisp snow. In a blur she cuts the monster to ribbons, and it howls as she fells it.

"I am Avarice, last of the Boulder Clan, slayer of monsters and protector of bony, freckled girls, I will not die this day! Now flee!" She slashes in all directions to keep the creatures at bay while Remy drags Lauren away and struggles up the slopes ahead. Dozens of horrid wights charge after them. She swings her sword true and the magic blade shatters the dead to glittering dust. A hatchet comes at her, but she brings her shield to meet it in the nick of time, then another comes from her right and clashes with her blade. She pushes the dead back down the slippery slopes, but ten more take their place.

"Go! Go!" Remy ushers Lauren up the hill and turns back for the troll. "Avarice!" she screams. "Avarice!"

"Run!" Avarice cries. "Run and do not look back! Tell the world what you saw today! Tell them that Avarice, a troll, fought the hell-spawn and she felled a hundred alone! Tell them!"

A macabre horror splits her calf with its jagged claws. She tumbles to the ground and drags herself through the snow. Gripping her blades tight, she plunges them into the beast and slices it in half with two crossing strokes, then forces herself up on one leg and fells dozens more single-handedly. Her father taught her well.

"May the troll god Ubek grant me eternal glory in the lofty realm!" Her valiant cries echo across the barren land.

Remy watches on the edge of tears until Lauren pulls at her screaming, "Come on!"

They take off north across the plains towards Bengeo's beacon, until the airship wreckage rears on the horizon.

*

George looks wary as the sun kisses the mountain peak to the east and hangs his head.

Ed sighs and looks to the bandit, who nods. Time to move.

Bengeo gathers their weapons and a modicum of provisions salvaged from the gunship then kneels beside Esmerelda, who despite being bundled in blankets is blue from the cold. It was warmer inside, but she wanted to see the sky one last time.

"Look at you, boy, you've come a long way from that crying babe with skinned knees." She fights to keep her eyes open.

Bengeo swallows his pain. "I'm sor—"

"Shhhh," she whispers. "You've nothing to apologise for."

The bandit nods, and they exchange a look of love and respect. He stands and buries the heartache down deep, for he still has a job to do.

"I can't thank you enough for everything you've done for us," Ed croaks and looks downcast. "I… this is all our fault." He tries to hold himself together in the face of it all, but the poor guy is cracking.

The old woman caresses his face and brings his chin up. "You know when we first met, I thought you other-worlders thought only of yourselves, but you've shown an old woman that people can still surprise you. When you see the Dread Knight, give him hell for wrecking my tavern, will you? Now go, I'll buy you time if I can." She squeezes his hand tightly.

Ed bites his lip and swallows the bitter taste in his mouth.

"Come along now," Bengeo says to George, who looks broken-hearted that Lauren has not returned – what will he tell his mother? Will he ever see her again?

Bengeo hands Ed the magic sword Remy had gifted him and he slings it on his back and wonders too, if he'll see her again.

"We were eleven, now we're three with one capable fighter," Bengeo whispers as they begin their climb to the Violent Summit.

"Don't be silly, you're capable," Ed assures him.

The bandit frowns.

"Don't worry, as long as I've got 'Mr Slashy' here, I'll be fine." He gestures to the sword on his back.

"*Mr Slashy?*"

"All the best swords have names."

"You named it that?"

"What would you name it?"

"Not that." Bengeo shakes his head and walks on ahead.

"How're you doing?" Ed asks George, who walks quietly beside him.

"I'm fine," the boy replies, feigning bravery when really he's worried out of his wits about his sister. He glances back at the smoking airship wreckage at the foot of the mountain pass and prays that Lauren is safe and sound.

*

Esmerelda's heavy eyes flutter as she battles to stay present in the cold. Then she snaps forward as the horrors approach and she spies the three girls, and Valentine sprinting just ahead of them. Desperate to make her last act in this world count for something, she musters her strength. Her quivering hands crackle with embers as she shapes a flame in her palm.

"Fly true," she whispers, then lets loose a fireball, which swoops across the white expanse and explodes, blowing a cluster of monsters to ash. But it's not enough, there are thousands now, blackening the horizon as they swarm towards the wreckage.

Remy screams and swings her blade splitting a wight in two at the waist. She loses her footing as she draws the sword back and rolls over in the snow. A tight grip clenches her arm and Lauren pulls her onto her feet and keeps her moving.

Esmerelda shrieks as they approach, "Follow the path up to the crater. Don't stop for anything!"

Of course Remy does the exact opposite of what she asks, and stops.

"What about you?"

"Insolent 'til the end," Esmerelda laughs. "Go, hurry and you'll catch the others!" She shoos Remy away and sacrifices what life she has left to conjure a final spell. Taking a deep breath, she forces herself to stand, holds her feeble arms wide, closes her eyes and smiles as the dead charge towards her. She's always wanted to try this.

Her entire body glows brighter than the sun, her form becomes flame itself and, in an instant, bursts into a cleansing fire that erupts in all directions, engulfing the stampeding dead and the wreckage all at once. A blast of white-hot atonement scorches the land, incinerating hundreds of creatures in a baptism of holy fire.

The explosion knocks Remy off her feet as she scales the mountainside. She rolls on her back and the rising flame flickers brightly in her fearful eyes as she clings firmly to her sword. The little voice in the back of her head is telling her she's as good as dead, but today that voice can suck it, she's not stopping until she's home again.

*

The explosion crackles over the Quiet Rise. Bengeo looks over his shoulder at the searing fireball rising in the distance and hangs his head. A grave loss darkens this day. He watches the black mass gathering at the foot of the mountain and glances at the swirling twister ahead. His gut is telling him this is a one-way trip. The higher they climb the closer they edge to the swirling tempest surrounding the Scar, and the wind turns ferocious as the black clouds bleed into the sky, eclipsing the sun.

Mr Slashy jostles on Ed's back. He looks over his shoulder and the eye blinks open at him, heralding eminent danger.

"Guys!" He draws the blade and grips it with both hands.

Bengeo hurries George up the mountain pass as a chorus of nightmares rises with every harrowing second.

A glint catches the boy's eye. "Look!" He points above to a shimmering bird comprised of golden light. He remembers what Bengeo had told him when they were locked up, about his father looking over him from the lofty realm, and takes off like a shot after the spectre.

"Hey! Where are you going?!" Ed cries.

"That's my dad! He's leading me to her!" he calls back.

Ed looks confused at Bengeo who shakes his head.

"Ah shit." The bandit sprints after him. "That ain't your dad!" he yells at the top of his lungs.

"Sure it is and he's taking me to Lauren!"

"It's not what you think!" Bengeo skids down the slope and catches the boy. "Are you crazy?!"

"Look!" George rejoices as the bird circles above them, and over the hill comes Jessica followed by Valentine. Remy comes next, and finally Lauren stumbles behind. As soon as George sets eyes on her he wriggles from Bengeo's grasp and runs to his sister's embrace. Squeezing her tight, he buries his face into her jumper, and she smells like home.

Bengeo and Ed rally to defend their friends. The living and the dead clash on the mountainside. A tall creature shambles over the rugged terrain and springs at Remy, throwing back its ragged hood to reveal a circular maw flush with jagged teeth, ready to make her insides outsides. She immediately recognises the creature by the collection of game controllers strung on its belt, and concludes it's the reason she's in this world in the first place. A powerful swing and her magic blade lops off the monster's fingers as it reaches for her. The cursed chill spreads up its arm, and it swipes Remy clumsily and lifts her by the throat with its other hand. She drives her Icerend through its head silencing the creature's ear-splitting shrieks.

"Fall back! We'll lose 'em in the storm!" Bengeo's voice booms as he tears the undead to pieces with his bare hands, and his eyes dart wildly about. There are more creatures than he can possibly count ascending the mountain.

Holding her shield high, Remy thrusts her blade through the first corpse to reach her. The strike freezes it. It crumbles as she draws the sword back and huddles shoulder to shoulder with Ed and Bengeo who hack, chop and smash anything that comes at them. But the horde is an overwhelming force that shows no sign of slowing, and they can't hold back the tide for long.

The spectre circling overhead caws defiantly, drawing Remy's attention to it. Her heart flutters with hope – *It must be him. This time it has to be. Please God.*

It swoops and dive-bombs the horde, eviscerating fifty or so in a blast of holy light. After the flash, Ozrune then appears before them, clutching Lauren's staff in one hand. His robes billow in the raging wind as he conjures a protective barrier around the party.

"Darkness will never thrive where there is light to meet it," the wizard's voice booms, and drawing his hands in the air, he conjures a wave of fire, which cuts the creatures off from the party.

Remy turns away as the undead hurl themselves at the barrier only to disintegrate in a blinding flash. Slowly they battle their way towards the titanic vortex. The gusts lift George off his feet, but Lauren clings to his wrist and with Valentine's help keeps him grounded. The wind is a chaotic assault. Enormous chunks of ice are swept into the air and hurl past them at breakneck speeds.

"This is suicide!" The cold steals the breath from Remy's lungs, rendering her cries unheard.

The wizard summons blinding streaks of light that pierce the haze of sleet and hail. He moves his arms wide then thrusts the staff forward and parts the storm like the Red Sea. Bengeo leads the charge and guides the party, inch by gruelling inch, through the pass. The dead pour in after them. The frailer skeletons and corpses are torn apart or swept away in an instant, but the stronger creatures break through unscathed and flood the gap like a tidal wave of death.

"Go!" The wizard spins the staff with discipline, and it glows pale blue as he thrusts it above his head, conjuring enormous spikes of ice that rise from the ground and skewer the foul creatures. With a spin he lets the wind carry him into the air.

"Old man!" the bandit calls to the old crow, but he knows he must stay and bide them time.

"He's not coming!" Remy pulls Bengeo out of the twister just as Ozrune closes the gap behind them. Snow, ice and wind engulf everything. The black vortex ignites with strobing light. Within it the wizard makes his stand.

The party sprint into the megalithic crater, and into the scattered ruins of an ancient city ravaged by a magical cataclysm. The streets that long ago crawled with life are now ice and rubble. The city caves in on itself like a bowl. Its centre has been swallowed by the world. Gone are the children who played and laughed, the merchants who haggled and bartered; no flower graces the frigid soil, no critters of nature make their roost. This is a dead land by all accounts.

Jessica collapses panting and wheezing, but Remy grasps the collar of her jacket and drags her sister through the streets after Bengeo who leads them into the buried remnants of a cathedral, through a crumbling hole in the ice-encased wall. One after another they stumble down a heap of frozen rubble, and collapse inside it. Their breathy gasps bounce around the dilapidated walls.

Ed stares at the broken stained glass windows above, then jolts upright. "Avarice! Where's Avarice?!"

Remy looks teary-eyed at him and shakes her head. The remorse on her face says it all. She clutches her chest as it spikes, and a swell of sadness comes up from her stomach. She didn't get to say goodbye. Even worse, she never rightfully thanked Avarice for standing up to her father and her clan, nor Esmerelda for putting her back together after she'd lost her hand, or even Ozrune for guiding her out of that tomb. Now she'll never have that chance. She fights to keep the floodgates shut, but she's a dam that's about to burst. Desperate to conceal her grief she stumbles to the other side of the hall, takes a pew facing away from her friends and rests her head in her hand.

Bengeo dusts himself off and stands tall. "Catch your breath fast, rest ain't a luxury we can afford."

"How do we even know Grimoirh is here?" Jessica asks, wheezing.

"If video games taught me anything, it's that when you encounter enemies, you're going the right way," Ed replies.

Jessica pauses. "Whoa, that's deep."

"He's right," Remy says, panting from the back of the room, "we can't stop. Not now."

Bengeo gives her a nod. Despite his severe expression, she can tell he's relieved to see her.

He approaches the cathedral doors and forces them open, then looks back at the sorry lot before him.

"I don't know what's gonna happen when we step outside of here. Hell, I'm sure it'll be damned awful, and I know this ain't your world, but I appreciate you all trying to save it." The bandit clears his throat and sighs. "I give you my word, if we survive this I won't stop 'til we get you all home."

Ed stands. "We're with you."

"Esmerelda, Avarice, Ozrune. We fight for them. Honour their sacrifice." Bengeo takes the first step out of the cathedral. Valentine and George follow, then Lauren.

Remy looks down at her boots and blinks away the tears from her stinging eyes. She's never really known anybody to die before. Ed takes her hand in his to stop it from shaking.

"We're gonna make it," he says.

"Not all of us…" she whispers.

He looks at her with admiration and warmth while she trembles with fear, uncertainty and the weight of the world on her shoulders. Neither of them speak a word, but their gaze tells a tale worth hundreds. She leans into him, runs her hand from his jaw to his chest and feels his beating heart then presses her lips against his – a gentle kiss that provides comfort in a way that words couldn't.

"What was that for?" Ed tries to contain his delight as Remy pulls away.

"Just don't die." She slings her sword on her back and storms outside.

He looks to Jessica for an explanation, but she just smirks and raises her thumb.

*

Remy plants her feet in the snow and looks upon the frozen city surrounded by the monumental twister. The deafening drone of the wind howls around them, but the air is eerily still. They're in the eye of the storm now.

They trek over the ruined buildings encased in millennia of ice and snake through frozen streets and alleys until they reach the gaping maw in the centre. Valentine leans over the edge and gauges the drop. Craggy rock and remnants of an old palace descend into a deep chasm of glittering crystal.

"So how the hell do we get down there?" the detective asks.

"We climb," Bengeo replies.

"I was afraid you'd say that."

They descend miles deep into the vast hollow cavern, carefully edging down the jagged crystal that juts out of the rock like wild weed. Remy looks forlorn at the towering crater around her and shivers with despair as once more she's pulled deeper and farther from the sun.

The air grows thick and warm, and at the base huge bergs of crystal levitate above a bottomless lake of spirit energy. Jessica marvels at the crystallised walls refracting the shimmering teal light like a prismatic mirror, throwing vivid colours around them.

"What is that stuff?" she asks.

"You're looking at the lifeblood of Pangea Ultima," Bengeo replies, "but I've never seen a well this big."

"Is that bad?"

"Well, it explains why the north is so dead. It's like the world is drawing all the energy from the land here."

"It's trying to heal itself," Lauren says. "It's just a feeling. I can't explain how, but it's like I can hear the land crying out."

"Esmerelda once told me that magic was a power bestowed by the world, and those that wield it can commune with Pangea Ultima itself. Sounded like nothing but a story at the time, but when I saw her and Ozrune healing Remy it seemed anything but."

"What do you mean?" Remy asks.

"You were half dead, but they used a pocket of spirit energy to fix you up. It moved through them, like they were bending it to their will, and took away your pain."

"*All magic is just conjured spirit energy, channelled and redirected with intent*," George says, impersonating a deep tone of voice.

The others look shocked and amazed that a child could bestow such nuggets of wisdom.

"Where did you hear that?" Lauren asks.

"Ozrune said it," George replies. "Didn't any of you listen to the tutorials?"

Remy, Ed and Lauren collectively shake their heads.

*

The clash of metal echoes below, and Regis' golden longsword gleams as he unleashes a succession of slashes and swipes on Grimoirh and Domina. His skill with a blade far exceeds theirs, and despite being outnumbered he has the upper hand. Leaping and diving to avoid Grimoirh's hefty attacks, Regis brings the Dread Knight to his knees and swings to sever his head, but before his blow lands, Domina's snake sword constricts his blade and she disarms him. Grimoirh jolts to his feet, upper-cutting Regis with the hilt of his sword. He swings intently, but Regis backflips from harm's way as the others touch down on the floating crystal floor and run to his side.

"Vincent!" Lauren's cry bounces around the cavern walls.

He turns to her, sword in one hand and Remy's necrotic hand in the other. "This is the only place that can destroy these shards once and for all. I'll cast them into the light and the world will purify the evil."

"And crack into pieces!" Regis cries. "Just look at the destruction those jewels have wrought here!"

"Then so be it, this world should never have existed in the first place," Vincent replies.

"Is that my hand?!" Remy's eyes burn with hatred for what he did to her. She clenches her sword tightly. Every cell of her being hungers for revenge. She grinds her teeth, her blood boils and her thoughts scream, *Kill him annihilate him run him through take his hand take his life!*

"I needed a vessel to transport the shards here. You left me no choice after I learned you were dead set on using their power to return to reality. Carrying the shards myself was too dangerous. With this armour, you can't imagine what I'd become if the crystal's malevolent power overtook me."

"Looks to me like it already has," Remy scowls. She squeezes her sword's hilt until the wrapping digs into her palm and her knuckles turn white, and the voice in her head screams, *Liar bastard despicable monster!*

"Believe it or not, I have no desire to fight any of you. Surely you understand, this world is a grave threat. When you told me Eric was alive, I realised that he must have returned to reality with the shard he had, and ever since then players like all of you have been appearing across the continent. If things from this world crossed into ours it would be catastrophic." He meets Remy's scornful gaze. "Can't you see? If you take these crystals home there'll be nothing for you to go back to?"

"So you're gonna destroy the entire world?" Ed scoffs. "Don't you think that might be… oh, I don't know, completely crazy overkill?!"

Vincent's expression darkens. "Those shards are evil, it doesn't matter how pure your intentions are. They'll whisper in your ear, twist you up and drive you mad."

"Enough of this fantasy role-play bullshit, Vincent, we're going home." Remy's eyes stay fixed on him. She won't blink or flinch, or hesitate even for a second. Not again, he'll never hurt her again.

"You're being manipulated by forces you can't comprehend. None of you are here by accident, the crystal brought you here for a purpose. By taking it home you're playing into exactly what it wants."

"Look!" He holds out her severed hand. Its withering, pale flesh pulses as the fingers twitch and wriggle on their own. "Everything they touch they corrupt, the promise of a fresh new world to devour is too much to resist. So you can't return, or you'll doom everyone you ever knew. The only way to save them is to end it all, here and now."

"And what about us? We're all here too," Lauren says.

Vincent shakes his head. "It is what it is."

"We're not letting you destroy anything. These people are real enough for me, and they have a right to exist," Remy says. "We're saving this world and then we're going home. You can come with us or get out of our way."

"Vincent, please," Lauren pleads, "this isn't you."

Her tearful eyes make his chest swell with regret. "Lauren, don't look at me like that. The only difference between us is I accepted my fate and became what I needed to be to accomplish what is necessary."

She clasps her hands together, and begs, "Please. If we work together, we can find a different way back and stop the evil."

"One shard has already escaped, the last two grow more powerful with every second. If the crystal were to become whole again, it would be the end of everything. Its only purpose, its only goal, is to extinguish life."

"No, that's your only goal!" Remy raises her sword at him. "You took my hand. Give it back, or I'll take your life!"

Vincent looks resolute, then holds her necrotic hand over the edge and drops it.

"No!" Her wide, fearful eyes watch it plunge into the endless sea below. She erupts with a hoarse cry and swings her blade overhead, but Vincent raises his before it lands. Their swords clash in a cacophony of fire and ice. He wields the God Cleaver with savage might, cleaving the floating crystal on which they're standing in two, separating them from the others.

*

Domina extends her snake-sword and lashes in all directions. Ed's blade eyes her hungrily, eager to purge her black soul, but she constricts the magic blade. She pulls back, tightening her grip until the eye on Mr Slashy's hilt bulges and darts frantically about while Ed tries to wrestle it free. Regis then takes up his golden sword and severs the chain linking Domina's weapon. She staggers back, and stares at her snake-sword lying in pieces. Bengeo hurls his fists, but she evades them with inhuman speed. A mad grin crawls across her lips as she hunches over, shrieks, and six long stalks tear out of her back, lifting her up.

*

"Come on!" Jessica brazenly leaps from one hunk of crystal to another and without a thought, plunges her arm into the deep sea and fishes out her sister's necrotic hand which smoulders as though it were bathed in acid.

"Got it!" she cries.

"Wait!" Vincent's warning weighs heavy on Lauren's mind. "What if he's right? What if it would unleash those monsters into our world?"

"You want to see your mum again, don't you?" Jessica says.

Lauren nods. "Of course, but—"

"But nothing! We can't get home without this, we've fought so hard to get here!" As she holds up the hand, it then wriggles from her grasp and tightens its black, withered fingers around her throat.

*

Grimoirh's sword blazes wildly as he swings for Remy, and her Icerend flashes, every blow dousing his flaming sword with a chilling frost. She knows she doesn't have a hope in hell of matching his brute strength, especially one-handed, but weighted down in all that armour he's slower than her. His attacks are wild and sloppy, and if she's careful, she can win this. Left, right, duck, he's wide open. She lands an upward strike on his helmet, which he casts aside and watches in fear as it freezes over.

Nostrils flared, eyes ablaze, he howls, "Where did you get that sword?!"

He strikes with greater fury against her shield, and she grimaces as the force crackles through her forearm.

*

Domina weaves around Ed as he swipes left and right. She floors him with a hard kick and pins him down with two of her stalks until Bengeo takes hold of her from behind. But she slips from his grasp, slithers up his back, wraps her thighs around his neck and chokes the life from him.

"Get her off me!" The bandit gasps with shallow breaths and turns shades of red and purple, his vision tunnels and he drops to his knees.

Regis charges and ferociously runs Domina through from behind, and she lets out a groan as she falls from Bengeo's shoulders and slumps onto her side. As she lies dying, a glimmer of Nef returns. She drags herself to the edge of the crystal rock and gazes at the light shimmering below, and a passing smile graces her striking face. At last, she is free from the twisted entity that possessed her.

*

With all his strength Valentine prises the leathery fingers from Jessica's throat while Lauren and George pull at its charred wrist to free her. They fall backwards as its grip falters, and Lauren wrenches the unholy hand away from her brother. Holding the fate of the world and her friends in her hands, she hesitates and looks wide-eyed at the necrotic limb. Then she glances up at Vincent and Remy locked in battle.

"Do it!" Jessica pleads in a raspy voice. "Take us home, I'll do it!" Jessica reaches out, but Lauren hesitates and holds the hand over the stirring spirit energy, which branches out and snakes through the air, eager to purge it from existence and restore balance to the natural cycle of life and death.

"Stop!" George cries. "We can go home. With this, we can see Dad again!"

Lauren looks appalled. "What?"

"It can bring the dead back to life, we could use it to—"

She shakes her head. "He's gone, George, this won't bring him back."

The boy looks tearfully at his sister, then frowns with determination. "Why not? It brought those things back. Why not him?"

The desperate look on her brother's face breaks her heart.

"Don't!" he begs.

"Do it! Do it!" Vincent screams from above.

While he's distracted, Remy drives her blade into his ribs, and the Icerend sears through his cursed armour and pierces his flesh. He roars in agony and drops to his knees, then brings his arm down on the blade, breaking it in two, but the tip remains lodged in his side. Remy's whole body quakes as she comes to terms with what she's done. She's slain a fair few monsters, sure, but Vincent is a person under that demonic armour, and she might have just killed him.

But he deserves it, doesn't he?

George's eyes sting as he fights back tears. "What about Mum? If we don't go back, she'll be all by herself."

Lauren reluctantly brings the necrotic hand towards her, and George and the others breathe a sigh of relief. She can't do it. If saving the world means ending her brother's life and their mother living alone never knowing what happened to them, then she'll just have to live with whatever consequences going home brings.

She raises Remy's festering hand overhead and gazes at its blackened, rotting fingers as they wriggle. "Take us home," she cries, shutting her eyes tight, and pictures her life before the game. "Take us home!"

At her cry the sea of spirit energy swirls with unrest like a violent ocean. A sudden flash of wind emanates from the malignant hand and shimmers throughout the crater, knocking everyone off their feet. The shard's power awakens, and Lauren screams as a single ungodly eye blinks open from Remy's undead palm.

A cold disembodied voice speaks. "Let me see you, instrument of my reunion."

The eye bores into her. Its wicked consciousness creeps into her mind, slithers between her ears, and chills her to the bone.

"Home?" The voice lets out a booming laugh. "There is no home, only souls to devour, destruction to sow and corpses to reap."

Lauren clutches her neck tightly and screams as a mark scalds her skin. The others cry out too as a cursed brand burns itself onto each of them.

"Bear my sigil, and so you shall be forever mine." The disembodied voice shakes the crater. She releases the hand as it floats upwards, pulled by some unseen force. The pupil widens, then collapses in on itself, conjuring a spherical portal which slowly expands.

"My power knows no bounds. All existence, all realities, will bend to me..." The crystal's words thunder as it retreats into reality.

Vincent staggers to the edge overlooking the swelling void and gazes fearfully at it. "What have you done?"

The look of horror on his face makes Remy shiver with the crushing thought that he might have been right all along. She watches him leap into the rift and disappear through it. Then a haunting shriek from above steals her attention. She can see the sky, not one blackened by a violent tempest but clear and bright. The storm has dissipated and the undead creatures are drawn towards the black hole, like sharks to blood, as the crater collapses around them.

"We've got to go!" She leaps across the floating crystals to regroup with the others.

"Go where?!" Valentine cries.

She points at the spherical black hole. "I think that's our way home."

"*You think?*" he frets.

The crater quakes around them and the floating rocks begin to descend into the world core.

"Go on, we'll hold back as many of those things as we can," Bengeo exclaims.

"No way, we're not leaving you here!" Ed says.

"This is the end, kid, once you go through, there's no coming back."

"It's up to all of you to stop that thing from your side. We've done all we can," Regis says. "We'll hold the line, cut down any that come. Now go before this whole place comes undone!"

Remy silently beholds the chaos around her. Deep fissures snake up the crystalline walls and heaps of rubble come tumbling down and plunge into the spirit energy.

What have we done? She trembles as a tide of hideous beasts make for the portal, desperate to infest a thriving new world.

"Go!" Bengeo pushes Remy and cracks his knuckles as he turns towards the onslaught.

Regis twirls his blade and takes a defensive stance at the bandit's side.

The 'players' race towards the rift, leaping between hunks of crystal across the widening chasms of pale green light. Being the shortest, Jessica and George lag behind the others, and as they ready themselves to clear another jump, the rock beneath their feet sharply drops.

"What do we do?!" The boy retreats from the edge as they sink.

368

"George! Jess!" Lauren screams, alerting the others who turn back.

"Come here." Jessica lifts George and with all her strength, throws him to Lauren who catches him.

"Jess, you have to jump!" Remy cries.

Jessica looks over her shoulder at Bengeo and Regis valiantly fighting the horde. Too many abominable creatures have slipped past them and are heading her way. She gulps and looks at Remy with eyes that say farewell.

"No! I'm not leaving without you!"

"You can still make it," Jessica sniffs and puts on a brave face. "Please, you gotta go!"

"Shut up! There has to be some way we can reach you! What if—?"

"There's nothing you can do. Just go." She gazes down at the endless sea, and her heart sinks. She always loved the bright stage lights, mostly because they shielded her from the watchful crowd – a barrier that lulled her fear into a deep sleep. It's fitting then that she'll meet her end bathed in light.

*

Festering bodies pile up around the two warriors as they slay one horror after another. The swordsman severs a behemoth's head with a broad strike, and as he balances atop its shoulders he spots Jessica trapped on a rock rapidly descending into the core.

"We got a problem." He points at the stranded teenager.

Bengeo looks over his shoulder at her and frowns. "Damn fools can't do anything by 'emselves." He wipes the sweat and blood from his brow. "You got this?"

"I'll kill as many as I can." Regis twirls his blade with grace and smirks. "If I don't see you..."

"Yeah. It's been one hell of a ride," Bengeo nods.

"Give 'em hell on the other side, Bandit." Regis turns and cuts down another monster in one swift motion as it lunges past him.

Bengeo takes off towards Jessica, and covers the floating rocks with great lolloping strides. A loud squawk echoes above. Casting his eyes up, Bengeo lets out a raucous laugh at the glowing apparition soaring overhead. A golden crow swoops and rains hellfire upon their foes like a mythical dragon.

"You sly old crow! Wahoooooooo!" Bengeo yells with glee as he leaps onto the rock beside Jessica. She shines with hope anew as he lands, and throws her arms around him.

"Come on, blondie, time to go." He tosses her effortlessly to Ed and Valentine who pull her up safely.

"Come on!" Ed yells to the bandit.

Bengeo sizes the distance, and luckily he's got at least two feet on Jessica – four with his arms outstretched. He leaps and catches Ed's hand.

"Holy fu—!" Ed squeals as the force of the bandit's weight is thrust on him, and he screams as his shoulder starts to separate from its socket. "You're too heavy!"

"I told you, muscle weighs more than fat." Bengeo grips Ed tightly as he dangles above the maelstrom of teal light, which snakes past him in wisps and solidifies into gleaming jagged crystal spikes.

Another hand grabs Bengeo's arm and then another. Lauren and Valentine cling to him while Remy, George and Jessica pull them from behind. All together they drag the 280-pound bandit to safety.

Ed winds his shoulder, and his fingers tingle as the feeling returns to his arm.

Bengeo laughs. "Looks like I owe you all one."

"I think we still owe you, like, forty." Jessica hugs him gratefully and they look back at Ozrune as he lifts Regis out of the crater while hundreds of undead creatures rain down and desperately hurl themselves across the crumbling platforms.

Remy leads them to the rift and peers into it – into the very absence of matter.

"Together." She offers her hand to Ed, who takes it and offers his to Lauren, who plants hers in Jessica's, who takes George's, who grabs Bengeo's, who holds his out to Valentine, who sighs before taking it.

Together they take a broad step into the void, and as they're engulfed by the seemingly endless abyss, deafening silence drowns out the chaos behind them.

Her hand slips from Ed's grasp, and Remy clings to thoughts of home, her mother, her stepfather, her crappy little futon on her sister's bedroom floor and her boxes of stuff stacked everywhere. She prays that the rift will lead her there and not somewhere worse.

XX

BACK TO REALITY

Remy drifts through the space between worlds. This place reminds her of the bugs that games sometimes experience when an avatar glitches outside of the constructed level and falls into infinity.

Is that where I am? she wonders. *Have I clipped out of bounds? Am I going to die here? How long would that take?*

She curls up alone in the dark recesses of nowhere – no, not alone. The whisperer in her ear, the demon on her back, her smiling shadow, is always with her, always flooding her mind with disjointed thoughts.

Alone, all alone, we're going to die here.

You again. Why are you always so scared? Remy asks herself.

Not me, you, we. They're all gone. Gone like Avarice, like Esmerelda. You're alone again with nothing. Nothing to go back to. Nothing to go back for.

No, that's a lie. Maybe my life is a mess, but it's mine. I can turn it around. If I can survive this, I can survive anything.

The voice sneers in her head. *You barely survived and it cost you an arm. You're broken, you'll never be whole.*

She looks at the prosthetic shield strapped to her right arm, beaten, scarred, worn, just like her, and smiles. *It doesn't matter, I've got this far without it. You drag me down like those corpses and I'm sick of you. Sick of me. I can change it. If I get back, I'm going to change it.*

A glint catches her eye – a lone star in the abyss. As she floats towards it a ringing tingles her ears, faint at first but it grows to head-melting loudness. She presses her hand against her throbbing skull and releases a hellish scream. Her eyes snap wide as the pressure stops as suddenly as it came and the pull of gravity weighs her down.

"Remy?" She hears Ed's voice, but she can't see him.

"Ed?!"

She runs her palms across the ground to gauge where she is. It feels smooth – some sort of stone maybe, but coated in a thick layer of God knows what.

A gentle breeze brushes her face, but the air feels sticky, unbearably humid and stale, and the smell of scorched dust offends her nostrils. *Another dungeon?* she wonders.

"Ed?" she calls to him again.

"I'm here," he replies.

Her fumbling hands find him in the dark. She pats his shoulders and throws her arms around him.

"You're alright?" he asks.

"I was drifting, lost, confused, alone. It sucked." Nothing a floundering twenty-something hasn't experienced already. "I didn't think I'd ever see anyone again."

"It was five minutes." Valentine's grouchy voice resounds from the dark. Remy can barely make out his shape in front of her.

"Is Jess—?"

"Yeah, I'm fine, I made it," Jessica replies.

"George?" Lauren calls out.

"You're sitting on me!" he groans.

She feels about, and cups his head in her hands.

"Sorry." She stands to free him and bashes her head on something hard. "Agh, what the f—?!"

"Where are we?" Jessica asks.

"Hell if I know," Bengeo says. "At least we all made it."

Lauren draws her phone from her pocket and switches it on, hoping the two per cent of battery will last enough to activate the flashlight app. She illuminates the dark, featureless tunnel that surrounds her and a familiar racket thunders in the distance. She casts the light on the rail suspended above, and it dawns on her where they are.

"Run!" she screams.

"What's wrong?" Jessica asks.

"Just run!" She takes George's hand and bolts towards the light at the far end of the tunnel. The sound of her trainers slapping the concrete is quickly muted by the roar of whatever calamity is stalking them. The noise is monotonous, repetitive and evokes unprecedented misery. The light draws nearer until they can see clearly, and the seven of them emerge from the tunnel and scramble onto the platform of Highgate underground station, only to be met by the confused and bewildered stares of people occupying the platform. They gawk and video the ragtag party who look out of place, dressed in a mishmash of fantastical clothing, caked in blood, sweat, tears and filth.

Bengeo looks amazed at the station. It's like nothing he's ever seen – the yellowing tiles, the huge tatty billboards opposite the platform advertising package holidays and a cure for erectile dysfunction. He peers at the numbing fluorescent lights hanging above, bathing everything in a sickly yellow hue, and jolts, startled by the train pulling in behind him.

"Get back!" He raises his fists defensively as the doors beep.

"It's just a train," Ed wheezes.

"*That's* a train?" The bandit looks dumbstruck as the doors slide open by themselves and people disembark and board. He looks curiously about to ascertain the source of the announcement telling him to 'mind the gap'.

A young couple exit the carriage, look Bengeo up and down and smile. "You look awesome!" the man exclaims. "Can we get a selfie?" he asks.

"A what?"

"Actually, would you mind? It'd be cool if we were both in it." The young man hands his phone to Lauren who, in a daze, politely takes it and frames the photo while the couple poses either side of Bengeo, who looks utterly unimpressed. Click, click, click.

"Thanks!" The man grins as Lauren passes back his phone.

"You guys going to the con?" his girlfriend asks.

"Uh, what?" Lauren's mind is occupied with a million thoughts – *How did we get back? What about what the crystal said? What are these brands on our skin? Did Vincent make it through too?*

"The game convention, at the ExCel centre?" the girl asks.

"Oh, sure…" she replies absentmindedly.

"Well, have a good one."

"The hell was that about?" Bengeo asks, eyeballing the couple with suspicion as they exit the platform.

Lauren shrugs. She's still pretty disorientated. Her eyes wander to the tube station sign and a little smile creeps across her lips.

We're back. We're home.

Never in a million years did she imagine she'd be happy to be standing on the platform of Highgate tube station.

Jessica throws her arms around Lauren and jumps up and down excitedly. "We made it! We made it!" She's so happy she'd kiss the floor if it weren't so filthy it might kill her.

"So that's it? It's over?" Ed asks.

"What? It wasn't thrilling enough for you?" Valentine leans against the wall and lets out a thankful sigh. Maybe with years of therapy and alcohol he can put this whole ordeal behind him.

"But what about all that stuff the voice said?" Ed lifts his sleeve, revealing the blistering brand on his forearm. "What are these marks?"

Valentine scoffs, "Consider it an ugly reminder that this wasn't all a psychotic break."

The doors bleep before shutting, and the train departs as usual, then violently shunts to a halt. The party stare with dreaded anticipation while the passengers inside look about in confusion as they pick themselves up. Remy wonders if it's just a run-of-the-mill train fault, happens all the time. Her gut tells her no, but her heart tells her, also no. Her worst fears are confirmed. Colossal tentacles emerge from the tunnel and slither around the rear carriages.

"Well, that didn't take long," she sighs.

"Oh God, I, like, can't even with this game," Jessica whimpers. The trauma of her time spent petrified in stone comes flooding back. Perhaps most torturous of all was the inability to scratch her nose or go to the toilet. She couldn't see or speak in her condition, but she could feel, and being petrified when you need to pee is without a doubt the Worst. Experience. Ever.

"Hey, Muscles, gimme a hand with this!" Valentine says to Bengeo, and together they prise the rear set of doors open, allowing the passengers to flee before the creature drags the end carriage back into the tunnel and crushes it like an empty soda can.

More tentacles writhe onto the platform in search of the 'players' who are caught up in the rush of passengers fleeing the station, which only incites fear into the people walking by the entrance, who start to panic as well.

"They probably think it's a bomb or something," Ed says as people push past him in a frenzy.

"That's not a bad thing right now, long as it keeps them out of the tube station," Valentine cries.

"Yeah but the police aren't going to have any idea how to deal with that thing." Lauren pushes her way up the stairs and clings to George's hand, making sure they don't get separated.

"That's why we gotta warn 'em. All of you, come with me." Valentine forces the ticket barriers open and once outside, glances at the foreboding overcast sky. A biting chill lingers in the air and snow starts falling all over the city.

*

Helen sits in her car, parked on the street outside the police station. The worry on her face ages her horribly. She's hardly slept a wink this past week. She's been parked here for hours because she doesn't know what else to do with herself. She gnaws her fingernails to the cuticles while staring absentmindedly at a strange group of people bickering with each other as they jog across the road towards the police station entrance. It takes a moment to recognise Jessica and Remy covered in all that muck, but the second she does, she jolts forward, headbutts the window and spills her coffee everywhere. By the time she's scrambled out of the car, they're gone.

*

Valentine bursts into the police station, darts past the reception desk and into the backrooms with the others following closely behind.

"Hey, you can't go back there!" the receptionist cries, but they pay him no heed, and he sits down in a huff.

Valentine marches everyone through the holding area and up flights of stairs to the offices, where Constable Alapati is trying to explain to Lauren and George's mother that there's no new information on her missing children, without giving away that, not only is she out of her depth, but the lead detective has

377

disappeared also. She spots Valentine through the blinds of the meeting room and excuses herself immediately.

"Scott?!" she shouts across the office, drawing the stares of her colleagues who regard the group curiously.

"Nitya!" Valentine smiles like he's welcoming her to a dinner party.

She looks him up and down and grimaces. He smells like he's been wading through sewage.

"Where the hell have you been?!" She prods him in the chest. "You disappear in the middle of a bloody investigation, you don't answer your phone, you don't check in! We had half the station out looking for you, diverting valuable time and resources from finding those missing people!" She points at Lin sitting in the office on the far side of the room. "Everyone said you were a waste of space, but I defended you, and now I'm the dickhead that has to—"

"Mum?" Lauren's meek voice interrupts her rant.

"Mum?" Alapati lights up, recognising Lauren from the picture her mother had shown her. "You...? You found them?" she gasps.

Valentine grins. "Yeah, I found them. So maybe soften your tone, eh?"

"Everything. I want to know everything right now." She grabs a passing constable and tells him, "Put 'em in the break room, we'll interview them one by one. Who's this?" She gives Bengeo a sharp eyeballing as Valentine takes her aside.

"Listen, something utterly insane is happening, and it's going to sound unbelievable," he whispers.

Knowing he doesn't take much seriously, she assumes by his severe expression that whatever he has to say must be important.

"In here." She leads him into one of the interrogation rooms for a quiet word while the others are escorted into the break room.

Lauren breaks the line and bursts into the office her mother is sitting in.

"Mum!" She flings her arms wide.

"Lauren?!" Lin catches her daughter, pulls her close and sobs with joy. "Are you alright? Are you hurt? Is George with you?! Where have you been?!"

"I'm okay, Mum." Tears stream down Lauren's cheeks. She shuts her eyes with a smile. "We're okay."

Lin spots her son standing in the doorway and waves for him to come. George runs to his mother, and she embraces him too.

"Mum, it was crazy! There were monsters and airships, and Grimoirh was real! Only he wasn't really Grimoirh, but he still had this sword that explodes with fire, and I shot down an airship when we got chased through the sky and crashed into this big crater and underneath..." The boy barely stops for air while Lin tries to keep up, but she hasn't the foggiest idea what he's talking about.

Through the window in the break room the others watch the Bakers' reunion.

"That wouldn't be happening without you." Ed nudges the bandit. "You're a real hero, you know."

Bengeo shrugs it off, the tough guy act, after all, is hardwired in him.

*

"Trapped inside a video game?" Alapati is a picture of scepticism as she perches on the desk in the interrogation room.

"Believe me, if you'd seen the shit I've seen, you'd question your own sanity too," Valentine laughs.

"Scott, this is—"

"I know how it sounds, I mean, hell if it were the other way around... but c'mon, Nitya, you think I'm making this up? You know I'm not that creative."

"You're telling me monsters, actual monsters, from a video game are crawling out of Highgate tube station."

He nods emphatically.

She breathes a long sigh and folds her arms. "I'm sorry, I can't… I don't even—"

Valentine wipes his hand down his face and sighs too. "Terrorists then. Armed terrorists have seized the underground."

She glares at him and shakes her head.

*

Ed watches Jessica struggle to unwrap a chocolate bar the policeman had given her from the vending machine in the corner of the break room.

"You okay?" he asks.

She shrugs, then bites off more than she can chew but tries anyway. The poor girl looks like she's been dragged through a series of thorny hedges, mauled by wild animals and kicked down a mountain. No filter on earth could fix her.

He glances at Remy sitting opposite. They exchange a fleeting smile before she lets out a brooding sigh and runs her hand through her tangled, matted hair.

She's happy to be back, but an undercurrent of dread is sweeping her out to sea. It's not over yet, and that's scarier than any monster could ever be. She looks worriedly at Bengeo who's sitting against the wall, his mind a million miles away. He's always been a wayfarer, but he loved his world, and now it's lost to him.

Sensing the dour mood, Ed raises his little plastic cup of water. "To fallen friends."

The others look tenderly at him, and raise their cups in solidarity.

"May the great spirit guide them to infinity." Bengeo sips his drink then pours the rest on the carpet to commemorate them.

A ruckus outside the room disturbs their memorial silence. A familiar voice pricks Jessica's ear.

She looks at Remy, on the edge of a smile and asks, "Do you hear that?"

Remy nods. That brash voice is all too familiar and chills her to her core like nothing else can. She exits the break room to find her mother screaming at several police officers, who try in vain to calm her down and usher her downstairs.

"Hey," Remy shouts, "that's my mum!"

Helen pushes her way through and squeezes Remy and Jessica tightly.

"Where in God's name have you two been? What the hell are you wearing? What is this thing on your arm?" she shouts, somewhere between fury and rapture.

"It's a long bizarre story," Remy replies.

"Why didn't you call? Jess, you never go anywhere without your phone! Are you in trouble? Did someone—?"

"Mum, we'll tell you everything, but you're going to want to sit down." Jessica escorts Helen to a chair. Remy perches on the desk beside it, and regales her mother with their adventure.

*

"Bum a smoke?" Valentine leans his head back against the wall.

Alapati rolls her eyes and pulls a pack from her breast pocket. She knows you're not allowed to smoke inside, but good lord, he looks like he needs it. Valentine takes the cigarette and holds it in his mouth while he fumbles around for a lighter. Alapati pitying him, offers hers. He leans over the flame and his eyes roll back as a wash of nicotine floods his body with euphoria.

Alapati places her hand on the door handle but hesitates before opening it. "I'll bring them in one at a time, get to the bottom of all this. Sarge will want a full debrief. If I were you, I'd drop the crazy schtick."

"Yeah… maybe," he sighs, exhaling a cloud of smoke.

As Alapati steps into the hallway two uniformed policemen sprint past her down the corridor.

"Hey, watch it!" she cries, but they pay her no mind. Moving into the main office, she notices everyone is mobilising from their desks, and grabs another uniform passing her by. "What's going on?" she asks.

"Something is happening on the underground."

"What do you mean '*something*'?"

The policeman pulls out his phone and shows her a shaky video of a tube train being ripped apart on the platform. It's difficult to make out what exactly is happening, but it looks like something hurled the carriage.

"This is a joke, right?"

"I've seen four other videos just like it, and the phones are lit up." The policeman shoves his phone back in his pocket and sprints out the door.

"Can't be..." She looks down the hall at the room Valentine is in and weighs up whether or not to humour his story. After a moment of hating herself, she begrudgingly returns to him.

"Alright, say I believe you. What the hell is going on?"

Valentine grins like the Devil, clenching the cigarette between his teeth. "Shut the door."

*

Remy isn't having much luck explaining it either. She tells her mother of the monster in their living room, how Jessica was petrified, Bengeo's daring rescue, the man-eating forest, the trolls, the crypts, the crystals, everything. Helen listens with a pinch of salt until Remy hesitantly unbuckles her prosthetic shield and shows her mother her bandaged stump.

Helen clutches her stomach and turns ghastly white at her daughter's dismembered limb. Jessica's efforts to comfort her prove futile. She pushes the girls away and retreats to the other side of the room where she leans over, drawing slow breaths to quell her nausea.

"Oh Jesus," she sniffs. "Who did this to you? What are you going to...? How could...? Oh God."

Remy and Jessica, recalling their earlier predictions on how Helen would take the news, share a smirk at her expense.

"Why on earth are you two smiling?!" Helen snaps.

"N-no reason." Remy sucks her lips between her teeth.

"Ray is going to go spare." Helen clutches her head as the room spins.

"Calm down, Mum."

"Calm down?!" She looks furious at Remy. "You disappear for over a week without so much as a word and show up with a bloody hand missing and you're telling me to calm down?! Remy Meredith Winters, you tell me right now who did this to you! No more nonsense about games and monsters!"

"Mum, she's telling the truth," Jessica insists.

"Not you," Helen gasps, "you've always been the sensible one." Her anger quickly turns inward as she spirals down into a dark abyss. "This is my fault. I shouldn't have been so hard on you, I drove you away, but you just kept pushing..." She leans her head against the wall and slides down it onto her knees. "I... I've failed you."

Throughout all their arguments over the years, never has Helen shown a flicker of weakness or self-criticism, which usually drives Remy mad, but hearing her mother say those words hurts in a way she never expected.

"Mum..." Remy kneels beside her, "... I know I'm difficult. I push you all away and act like I don't care, but I do. I felt so alone all the time, and I didn't know what to do. I'm just so sick of feeling like... like I don't belong anywhere... I'm sorry that I'm not the daughter you wanted."

Helen looks at Remy, raw and ragged before her, and hugs her tightly without a word, then she takes Remy's face in her hands and looks her dead in the eye. "No matter what you think, you have been and always will be my whole world."

Remy trembles in her mother's hands. The look in her teary eyes says everything she can't.

A blaring alarm cuts short their embrace. Any police left in the building hurry downstairs, and Alapati and Valentine tear out of the interrogation room and regroup with the others in the main office.

"What's going on?" Lauren asks.

"Not sure." Valentine stubs his cigarette out on a desk.

"All of you wait here," Alapati exclaims, "I'll find—"

The air is torn by shattering glass. A rabid winged feline bursts through the office window and crashes into a desk. Alapati watches speechless as its humanoid face shrieks while it scrambles on its razor paws. Bengeo wastes no time and leaps at the creature, which swats him aside with its sprawling wings. Remy draws her broken sword and drives it through the beast's head freezing it solid before it shatters. She turns to her mother, who looks absolutely stupefied.

"Got it."

"What in God's name was that?" Helen yelps.

"I... uh, I think it was a manticore." Remy's explanation brings no comfort to her mother who looks just as terrified if not more so.

Ed peers through the broken window at a dozen more game monsters striding through the snowfall towards the police station.

"I count fourteen!" He draws Mr Slashy from his back.

"There are more of those things?" Alapati asks.

"A lot more and a lot worse!" he replies.

"We need to lock this place down," Valentine says. "Go to the locker and sign out something with stopping power."

But Alapati is too busy tapping a frozen chunk of the monster with her toe to pay him any attention.

"Nitya!" he shouts, pulling her back to the moment at hand. "Guns?"

She composes herself and races to fetch them.

Jessica stares at the brand on Lauren's neck and recalls the evil entity's words. "They're coming for us," she says.

"No kidding," Remy replies.

"I mean they're hunting us!" She hikes up her jeans, revealing the brand on her calf. "The voice, it said we belong to it."

Ed looks worriedly at the blistering sigil on his forearm then at Remy who shares his concerns.

She looks at her mother and at Lin. "We can't stay here. We're endangering everyone."

"Where can we go?" Jessica asks.

"We could drive into the country. Maybe they wouldn't follow us that far, at least that would buy us time," Ed suggests.

Remy shakes her head. "Those monsters will keep flooding the city, and my sword froze that thing, which means magic somehow works in reality, and that can't be good. We need to find Vincent. As much as I hate to admit it, he said this would happen."

"But we don't know where he is. Again," George says.

"Maybe, maybe not." Everyone looks at Lauren expectantly. "Today is the London video game convention."

"So?" Remy asks.

"So, Eric's unveiling the DLC, announcing patch updates and doing a whole bunch of promotion. When I saw Vincent in the game, he looked shocked to hear Eric was alive, and in the crater he mentioned how that made him realise one of the shards had already escaped the game. I'd bet my life that if we find Eric, we find Vincent and your hand."

"Did she just say '*your hand*'?" Helen looks visibly disturbed.

Remy purses her lips. She regrets stabbing Vincent but shudders to think that he might have had even a shred of justification for his horrible actions.

"They're at the doors!" Ed yelps.

"Let's go!" Valentine says.

"Excuse me!" Helen cries. "Can someone please explain what on earth is going on?"

"I second that," Bengeo says.

Helen points her finger at the bandit. "And who the hell are you?" She looks to Lin for backup, but she shrugs.

"Mum, you're embarrassing us," Jessica whispers.

A crash and then screams ring out from downstairs.

"This way!" Valentine leads them through a fire exit to an emergency stairwell.

Remy grabs her prosthetic from the desk as she passes, and manages to fasten it on before an undead rhinotaur bursts through the wall and tackles her. Bengeo rushes to her defence and wrestles the creature's horns, twisting its head away from her. It snaps its jaws and hurls him into the wall with a jolt of its head, then fixes its attention to the others. Remy puts herself between them and slashes the beast as it charges. The thing releases a quaking roar and Helen shrieks as it grips Remy's broken blade in its hands. BOOM! A gunshot crackles through the corridor, and the creature collapses in a gory heap at Helen's feet. All colour drains from her face as she stares at the guts and debris scattered across the carpet.

Alapati cocks the smoking pump-action shotgun in her shaking hands.

"What the fuck was that?!" she gasps.

Ed gently lowers the barrel towards the ground. "Nice shot."

They descend the stairs and follow Alapati through a heavy fire door into an underground car park.

"So what's the plan?" she asks, deferring to Valentine, who looks surprised that she's actually on board for this crazy rollercoaster.

"Where's this convention held?" he asks.

"The ExCel centre," Lauren replies.

"That's the other side of the city," Alapati says.

A chorus of spine-chilling wails draws their attention to the exit ramp, and the hell-spawn pouring down it. Alapati tosses Valentine the shotgun and arms herself with the carbine rifle slung on her shoulder. They open fire on the monsters, but the hail of red-hot lead and buckshot isn't enough to keep them back for long, and walking dead overrun the car park in a matter of minutes.

"Mrs Winters, stay back!" Mr Slashy vibrates in Ed's hand as it springs to life and in one swoop, lops off three festering heads.

"Dirty undead bastards!" the blade chants, slicing another in half at the waist.

Helen turns green at the decapitated legs stumbling about while the top half crawls towards her, trailing its rancid guts behind it.

Bengeo brings his boot down, smashing its skull, then hurls the body like a rag doll into the horde. Jessica pulls George away and they scramble beneath a parked car as the corpses swarm them.

*

Ed's voice croaks with fear. "If we don't make it—"

"Oh shut up, we're going to make it." Remy pushes back the living dead with her shield, but they pile on and drag her to the floor with clawing, bony arms. She drives her sword through a wight's face, which shatters as she retracts the blade then stabs another. Her bounding heart fuels her with adrenaline, and she lets out a bloodcurdling scream as the dead pull her in every direction. Memories of the pit come rushing back, sending her tumbling down a well of panic. A scream, desperate, determined, human, tears through them like a chainsaw. From within, she summons the strength to push back with her shield as the corpses clamber over her and sink their rotting teeth into her flesh.

With all his might, Ed brings Mr Slashy down, cleaving a wight's head above the jaw. His hand finds Remy's amongst the struggle, and he pulls her free.

"Go!" He helps her onto the bonnet of a police car and she pulls him up after, then they hop across the parked vehicles and climb atop a police van which is tall enough to keep them from harm.

Helen and Lin clamber into the back of the same van while Alapati and Valentine cover them.

"Hurry!" Lin shouts and stretches out her arm, but before Lauren can reach her mother's hand, a wight grasps a fistful of her long hair and drags her away kicking and screaming. Lin shrieks as her daughter is engulfed in a tide of withered flesh and bone.

Lauren struggles and writhes until her hand finds Remy's discarded sword, and with one swipe she lops off her hair, freeing herself from the creature's iron grasp, and wastes no time scrambling back towards the van while Valentine fights his way to her. BLAM! Limbs and guts fly everywhere as he fires into the crowd while she crawls on her hands and knees to him. He pulls her onto her feet and keeps the dead back until they reach the van. Remy and Ed quickly hoist her onto the roof with them, and Valentine turns to join them but flinches suddenly at a sharp sting below his ribs and staggers backwards. Looking down, he sees a splintered bone protruding from his stomach and with a groan he slumps to the floor, gasping. His wrinkled hand trembles as he pulls the bloodied photo of his daughter from his pocket.

XXI

SUICIDE RUN

Remy and Ed leap off the van and into the horde, bashing, slashing and smashing, to keep the monsters away from Valentine as he drags himself on one arm across the icy concrete, the other firmly clasping his wound.

Lauren slides off the roof and pulls open the back doors. "Help!" she cries over the chorus of raspy hisses, struggling to lift Valentine into the van until Helen and Lin clamber out and help.

"There's too many!" Alapati winces with each thunderous round she fires. The bullets do little to slow the dead, even their dismembered parts continue to draw on their prey.

Once inside Lauren slides the side door open and waves the others over. "Get in!"

Remy, Ed, Bengeo and Alapati pile inside and slam the door behind them before the undead surround the van and rock it violently. Remy sweeps her hair off her face and looks at Valentine – deathly pale and gasping with each ragged shallow breath. She notices the scrunched picture clutched in his quaking hand.

"That's your daughter, right?"

The detective nods.

"You wanna see her again, don't you? So hold on."

His hand squeezes the picture tighter.

"Give me some room!" Lin pushes everyone back, then strips open Valentine's shirt to assess the damage.

Lauren trembles at the tide of red gushing from his abdomen. She hasn't seen this much blood since... *No, can't think about that now.* She staves off the panic and banishes fragments of the accident that took her father from creeping into her thoughts.

"M-Mum, what can I do?!"

"Towels, a shirt, anything to stop the bleeding!" Valentine groans as Lin gently rolls him over and checks the entry point. "Through and through."

"Is that bad?" Helen asks. "That's bad, isn't it?"

"Mum," Remy snaps, encouraging Helen to try and pull it together, but her nerves are shot to hell.

Lin mops the sweat from her brow with the back of her bloodied hand, smearing flecks of red across her forehead. "I think it's a clean puncture, but he's losing a lot of blood."

Remy raids the glove box and tosses a first aid kit to Lauren who lays it out beside Valentine while Lin bunches her jacket around his wound and applies pressure.

"If we don't get him to a hospital he's going to die." Lin looks wide-eyed at the others. "The Whittington isn't far."

Remy looks to Alapati, who recoils in the driver's seat as the corpses press their nightmarish faces against the glass. "We need to draw those things away, so you can get him to the hospital."

Alapati freezes over. She's beyond out of her depth.

Remy grabs her arm and pulls her back to the crisis. "I get this is insane, but we need you. So save the nervous breakdown for when we're out of this shitstorm."

The determination with which Remy carries herself inspires Alapati to pull it together. She nods affirmatively and passes the assault rifle to Bengeo.

"You know how to use this thing?"

He takes the gun and holds it sort of correctly.

She points to various parts of the rifle. "Finger here, squeeze the trigger to fire, safety on, safety off. Only got one clip, so I hope you're a good shot."

"I know what a blunderbuss is." The bandit examines the rifle with bravado, hoping to mask that he has no idea how to use it.

"Blunderbuss?" Alapati frowns. "Maybe you are out of this world."

*

"What are we gonna do?" George whispers from beneath a car.

Jessica's eyes light up as she spots the shotgun Valentine dropped lying in a bloody puddle on the floor. "Maybe we can lure them away from the van?"

"And then what?"

"I don't know." Her voice cracks with worry, but she steels herself and looks at George with eyes that mean business. "Right now, we're their only hope."

"Y-yeah. Okay." George nods resolutely. "I'll get them away from the van, you get the gun."

Jessica smiles and raises her fist. "Be careful."

George bumps it, hastily crawls out from beneath the car and scurries on all fours unnoticed – he is, after all, a level thirty-three assassin – past the undead until he reaches the next car. He tugs the door handle, but it's locked, so he looks for something to break the window and finds Remy's shimmering sword lodged in a slain corpse. Gripping the hilt with both hands, he wrestles it from the corpse's face with a mighty tug and strikes the passenger window, which shatters immediately. He climbs inside and presses on the horn, releasing an explosive honk, which lures the dead away from the police van, giving Jessica a window to pick up the shotgun, which she promptly aims at the swarm surrounding George. BLAM! The kick knocks her over.

"Ouch!" she whines.

"What was that?" Remy presses her nose at the side window and sees her sister fumbling the shotgun. "Jess, are you crazy?" she hisses.

"They've got George surrounded!" Ed presses his face beside her and fogs the glass with his breath.

"Everybody hold on!" Alapati starts the engine, throws the van into drive and ploughs into the corpses like traffic cones.

Bengeo slides the side door open and pulls Jessica in by her waist while Remy kicks open the passenger door and calls to George.

"Get in!"

George leaps out of the parked car and sprints towards the van dragging Remy's broken sword behind him. She pulls him in before Alapati floors it. The tyres screech as the van peels away and bulldozes through the undead blocking the exit ramp.

"Get Valentine to the hospital, and we'll take care of the rest." Remy looks back at her mother. "Did you drive here?" she asks.

"What?" Helen looks shaken.

"Mum." Remy frowns. "Your car."

"My car? But you're not insured and how're you going to drive with one hand?"

Remy looks to Ed. "You can drive, right?"

"S-sure." He nods hesitantly.

"This is absurd, Remy," Helen says. "You're not gallivanting off into the city with these people, you're coming with me to the hospital and we're getting you looked at!"

"Mum, I've got to go. The world might literally depend on it. More monsters are crawling out of the underground as we speak. Give me the keys!" She shoots Helen that trademark scowl.

With an exasperated sigh, she reluctantly passes Ed her car keys. "It's parked on the street outside the little Tesco. Don't scratch it!" Helen warns.

"Y-yeah, of course," he nods. "Could you call my dad and let him know I'm alright?"

Helen's expression softens. "Keep her safe, and I don't mean the car."

Ed smiles and takes the keys as Alapati drives them to the little Tesco.

"There!" Remy points at the red Volkswagen Golf parked on the street, and Alapati pulls up beside it. "We're going!"

"Wait!" George offers Remy her sword, which she accepts with a grateful smile, then strides towards her mother's car and climbs into the passenger seat beside Ed, who buckles up behind the wheel.

Lauren presses her hand softly against Valentine's cheek and whispers, "Please be okay." He's out cold, but she tells herself he heard it. "Wait, I'm going too!"

Lin looks at her as if to say absolutely not.

"You said Dad always thought I was going to do something great, well maybe he was right." She kisses Lin on the forehead and hugs her brother. "Look after Mum until I get back, alright?"

"Is this all because of us?" The guilt ages George far beyond his years. His shoulders are too small to bear the weight of the world like this.

Taking his head in her hands Lauren brings her brother's eyes to hers. "None of this is your fault. Protect Mum and Mr Valentine, leave the rest to me, okay?" She kisses him on the forehead then climbs into the back seat of Helen's Volkswagen beside Bengeo.

After a moment's deliberation, Jessica leaps out of the van too. "Wait up!"

"Don't even think about it!" Helen gasps.

"Mum, this is real life and death stuff," she says sliding the door shut.

Alapati winds down her window and leans out. "Hey, please make all this crazy go away."

Jessica nods emphatically. "He'll be okay, right?"

Alapati hesitates to reply and glances at Valentine lying in the back. Honestly, she doesn't know.

Jessica clutches the shotgun firmly as she climbs into the back seat, forcing Bengeo to shove over into the middle. The police van pulls away as Remy turns back to her sister with a foreboding look.

"Jess, this is more or less a suicide run."

"I know," Jessica replies, "but I'm not letting you go alone." She feigns a cocksure grin to hide that her guts feel like writhing worms and her legs are shaking like jelly.

"Everyone buckled up?" Ed adjusts the rear view mirror and locks eyes with a disgruntled Bengeo, who's squashed shoulder to shoulder between Lauren and Jessica. "Okay then. Here we go…" With a deep breath he starts the car and grips the steering wheel at ten and two, then backs slowly out of the space, and stalls immediately.

"Ed, you *can* drive, right?" Remy looks worried as a couple of walking corpses stumble towards the car and bang against the hood.

"Sure, I mean… I've had plenty of lessons," he mumbles.

"Lessons?" She buries her face in her hand.

"Wouldn't this be a lot faster if we just took an airship?" Bengeo asks.

"Yeah, except we don't have those here," Lauren replies.

"Can everyone just calm down, I can't drive under pressure," Ed scolds them.

"You can't drive at all," Remy mutters under her breath.

"Excuse me?" He looks at her aghast.

"Floor it!" she barks as a wight takes a running shot at the car and crashes against her window.

He throws it in gear and stomps the pedal. The tyres skid in the quickly settling snow and the corpses tumble over the bonnet and hit the road as he peels away.

Remy watches through the glass as all manner of game critters continue to pour out of the underground stations across the snow-swept city and wreak havoc. A glint in the wing mirror catches her eye. She winds down her window and peers out. A large winged creature is tailing them in the distance.

"Uh oh!" she gasps.

Ed glances at her. "*Uh oh?* What's *uh oh*?!"

"Just worry about the road," she tells him right before a loud ca-thunk! Dark red sprays the windshield and Ed looks mortified.

"He was already dead, right?!" He tightens his grip on the steering wheel then flicks on the wipers, which smear the blood and guts across the window until it thins out enough for him to see the road.

Remy nods supportively then cranes her neck out of her window to get a look at the dismembered carcass strewn across the asphalt. She's ninety per cent sure it was already dead or undead or – whatever.

Lauren stares up at the foreboding sky. The blizzard is ramping up and blanketing the city in white.

"You think the snow is just a coincidence?" she asks.

"Probably not," Bengeo says, looking amazed and dumbfounded at the high-rise buildings out of the back seat window.

"This is all my fault," she sighs.

"How do you figure that?" the bandit asks.

"When I wished for it to take us home I thought about standing on the station platform. I couldn't believe I missed it, how boring and mundane it was. In that moment I'd have given anything to just be back there, to be bored and safe, and that's exactly where we ended up. So it's my fault. I brought those things here." She looks downcast and miserable until a soft hand takes hers.

"You brought us home. You saved us." Jessica leans over Bengeo to comfort Lauren. "None of this is your fault," she says with a stern look that doesn't suit her cherubic face.

"*In 500 yards, turn left*," the sat nav on the dash blurts out. Ed makes the turn only to be stopped dead in bumper-to-bumper traffic.

"No, no, no!" Remy sticks her head out of the window at the long line of cars. "Back up, find a way around."

He shifts the car into reverse and shunts into a van pulling up behind them. The van driver approaches Ed's window. He winds it down, and the man leans his head into the car as Remy leans over Ed, brandishing eyes of fury.

"We don't have time for this, piss off," she says.

"You 'aving a laugh? You hit me!" The man scrunches his face at her strange attire and glances at the back seat where the muscle-bound Bengeo clutches an assault rifle next to Jessica, who's resting a shotgun on her lap. "Forget it, s-sorry to bother you!" He backs away, with his arms held high and climbs back into his van.

Remy watches as the van U-turns and speeds away, then notices people flocking past her window. She steps out of the car to get a look at what they're running from and her vision narrows to a pinprick at a creature blocking the road on two towering legs, with arms of all sizes protruding from the cluster of fused corpses that comprise its torso. Its many heads release a haunting roar as soon as they spot her. It strides towards their car, tossing others aside like a child throws toys.

"Ed, go! Go! Go! Go!" She jumps back in and slams the door.

"We're stuck!" He leans out of the window to get a glimpse of whatever is up ahead, and one look is all it takes for him to frantically mount the curb and back out.

He weaves through the pavement pressing his hand firmly on the horn. People leap out of his way as he tears through a newspaper stand and spins the car around. He clocks the creature coming up behind them in the rear view mirror, and laughs nervously because the whole thing reminds him of that scene from *Jurassic Park* where the T-Rex chases after the car – although he'd welcome a dinosaur over this abomination any day. The monster rams into Ed's door, and tries to flip them over.

"Ben, take it out!" Ed yelps.

Recalling Alapati's instructions, Bengeo leans over Jessica who covers her face as he smashes the back window with the stock. Taking aim, he squeezes the trigger and pumps hot lead into the beast until it crashes lifelessly into a parked car.

"Damn, this thing's got some kick!" the bandit grins.

Another creature swoops overhead. Two sets of razor claws burst through the roof of the car.

Lauren shrieks as they narrowly miss her, and she ducks down in her seat while Jessica fumbles the shotgun in her lap, aiming it upwards. She blows what's left of the roof to shrapnel and clips the creature's wings.

"I think I got it!" she cries as the beast lunges back onto the car, snapping its jaws while Jessica cowers in the footwell.

Remy draws her Icerend and stands up on her seat, getting a proper look at the beast – *Shit shit shit!* Half lion, half eagle, patches of plumed feathers give way to decomposing flesh and bone – the dreaded undead griffin. It beats its black wings against the snow. Its cloudy eyes lock on her and it parts its bloodstained beak with a screech.

"Just piss off, you rotten piece of—!" She lops off the griffin's talons with hearty strikes. It shrieks and lashes the sword out of her hand with its thick hind paws as it retreats.

"Shit!" Remy gasps as the blade clangs against the road, and slumps back in the passenger seat.

"What? What?!" Ed glances at her out of the corner of his eye.

"Remember the undead griffin, the one boss I could never beat?"

His face becomes a picture of dread. He knows what she's about to say but really hopes that she's not going to say it.

"It's behind us." She said it.

Clasping the wheel tightly, he turns his attention back to the road, swallows his panic and makes the turn onto the overpass above. He presses the pedal to the floor and overtakes the other cars as the heavy snow flutters past.

With a quaking squawk, the griffin dive-bombs the car, and latches its claws into Ed's shoulder.

He lets out a piping scream and swerves left and right. "Get it off me! Get it off!"

"Stay still!" Bengeo takes aim and shreds the creature with a shower of bullets.

Defiantly, the griffin flutters harder, and Ed's seat belt tightens across his other shoulder as he's lifted out of his seat. He releases the wheel and grabs hold of its talons to prise himself free while Jessica and Lauren lunge over the seat to weigh him down and Remy steadies the wheel with one hand, desperate to keep them from veering off the bridge.

Passengers in other cars watch in disbelief as Helen's banged-up Volkswagen Golf skids across the icy carriageway while the winged terror struggles to fling poor shrieking Ed into the air. A sharp lane change shakes off the griffin and it prepares for another pass. Ed clutches his shoulder tightly as he flops back into his seat and takes the wheel from Remy.

"You okay?" she asks.

"Mmm," he nods. "Just a scratch." Honestly, it stings like a bitch, and he thinks he might have peed a little, but goddamn he'll die before he lets her know that. He grimaces as Bengeo pats his shoulder from behind.

"Hang in there, tough—"

The griffin crashes into the car, tears off Remy's door with its lion paws and snaps its beak.

"Get rid of this thing already!" Jessica shrieks as Ed swerves to avoid a car.

"I'm trying!" Remy howls, relentlessly kicking the monster's head. "Shoot it!"

Bengeo pulls the trigger – click, click, click, he's out of ammo. "It's not working!" He smacks the gun impatiently.

"Freeze it! Use your sword!" Ed shouts.

"I lost it!"

"*You lost it?!*" He looks at Remy like a parent scolding a naughty child.

"Don't judge me!" she screams, thumping the creature again and again with her boot.

Ed swerves into the inside lane along the hard shoulder and pins the griffin between the car and the stone barrier. Remy scrambles into the back seat on top of Lauren as the friction tears the griffin apart. Bones crunch, flesh rips until Ed pulls away, and the mangled carcass tumbles across the road with a thud.

"Ha! Not this time, you ugly bastard!" Remy shakes her fist at its broken corpse as they speed down the A12 towards Stratford. "How far?" She shuffles off Lauren's lap and back into the front passenger seat.

"Not very." Glancing at the sat nav, Ed takes the next exit off the A road. "Oh God," he whimpers at a mass of wights clawing their way out of Canning Town tube station.

"There's so many," Jessica gulps.

"Everyone, hold on!" Ed guns it through the horde, and undead bounce off the car like rubber balls, limbs flying.

"That one's big!" Lauren points at the colossal giganeye terrorising the streets about forty metres ahead.

"Not again," Jessica quivers as the creature spots them.

Its malignant pupil looks right at her, and she shudders as its gigantic jaws part, releasing a cloud of toxic breath.

The smog floods the street, rendering the hysterical crowd petrified in stone.

"Everyone get down as low as you can!" Ed cries, and at his word the others scramble into the footwells and curl themselves into a ball.

Leaning forward he tucks himself in tight behind the steering wheel and guns it into the smog, which breezes over the car as it speeds through.

The wights petrify as they blindly pursue the car through the haze, then the Volkswagen itself begins to transmute. Ed loses control as the wheels turn to stone and skid along the frozen road at breakneck speed.

"Hold on!" He pulls the handbrake, and the car spins out of the toxic cloud. The others sit up in their seats and brace themselves for the worst. Patrons flee in terror as the Volkswagen slams through the glass window of an Italian restaurant and smashes into the bar.

After a moment, Remy climbs out of the smouldering heap, rubbing her head, and slumps against the hood until everything stops spinning.

"Everyone okay?" Ed fights with the airbag as he staggers out.

"Any landing you walk away from, right?" Bengeo laughs and climbs out of the car through the gaping hole in the roof. Winding his shoulder, he picks up a bottle of whisky from behind the smashed bar and takes a hearty swig before tossing it aside.

"How far?" Remy asks.

"Not very, ten, twenty minutes if we hoof it," Ed replies, thumbing the map on the cracked sat nav screen.

The horrified restaurant manager approaches them and looks thunderstruck at the smoking wreck in the middle of his eatery.

"Are you alright?" he asks, while the crowd of diners slowly gather round to film and snap pictures with their smartphones. Jessica leans into the car and pulls the shotgun from the back seat.

"Whoa!" The restaurant manager ducks away.

"S-sorry!" Jessica lowers the gun. "It's for the monsters."

The bewildered manager turns to one of his customers. "Did she say monsters?"

Jessica finds Lauren sitting on the floor amongst the rubble with her head between her knees. She kneels at her side and places a hand on her shoulder.

"You with us?"

Her bright eyes shine at Lauren and, like a soothing spell, quell her anxiety. Lauren nods affirmatively and breathes slowly.

Jessica smirks at her hacked hair, which is now considerably longer on one side than the other. "That's a bold look." She offers her hand and pulls Lauren onto her feet.

Remy looks at the wreck that was her mother's car and massages her temples with her thumb and forefinger.

"It'll be alright," Ed vainly tries to reassure her. "A lick of paint, a new door, fix the holes in the roof, bang out the dents, replace the wheels and she's good as new."

The car bursts into flames before their eyes. He looks downcast and takes a quiet step backwards.

"If I survive this, my mum is going to murder me," Remy sighs as she fans smoke away from her face.

They step through the shattered restaurant window onto the frigid streets, leaving the crowd inside utterly baffled. The roar of the giganeye rolls like thunder in the distance, but they can barely make out its shape through the full-blown whiteout.

"This is c-c-crazy!" Jessica groans through chattering teeth and stares at the river Thames, which is completely frozen over.

The imposing shadows of roaming tentacles sweep through the blizzard, crushing parked cars and street lamps. Ducking behind cars, the five sneak unseen to the end of the street until they run out of cover.

"We can't outrun that thing," Ed whispers.

"What choice do we have?" Remy replies.

He looks out at the Thames a moment and then back at Remy, and takes in her exhausted face – scarred and bruised and her blue lips cracked from the cold.

"Why are you looking at me like tha—?"

He kisses her unexpectedly and for a brief instant, it obliterates every thought – the what-ifs, the worries, the world on her shoulders – but she quickly comes to her senses and pulls away. "What the hell are you doing?"

"I just want you to know that whatever happens, I'm glad I got to have this adventure with you."

"Why are you telling me this?" she asks wearing a scowl he's come to find endearing by now.

"Because I'm about to do something dangerous and stupid but maybe a little bit heroic. At least I hope you see it that way." He clutches the silver ring on a chain around his neck – a token of bravery awarded to him by the barmaid from Trout. God knows he could use a little of that right now. He plants Mr Slashy back in her hands. "He's a good sword, but he belongs to you. Don't die, okay?"

"Whatever you're about to do, don't," Bengeo growls.

"I hate to say it, but you were right."

"About what?"

"About being a hero. The pay sucks, and it doesn't end well." With a smirk, Ed bolts into the open, screaming at the top of his lungs. "Over here, you ugly one-eyed son of a bitch!"

The giganeye slithers after him as he leaps over the railings and onto the Thames. His Converse sneakers skid about. He sprints like an Olympic champion, clutching the ring in his sweaty palm, avoiding as best he can the creature's sweeping tentacles that smash the brittle ice as they plunge in and out of the water. The ice buckles beneath the giganeye and it plummets into the river with a whopping splash. Like his childhood hero Crash Bandicoot, Ed clumsily leaps from iceberg to iceberg while the creature writhes and drowns.

"Oh God!" Jessica gasps as the tentacles plummet in front of him, and in an instant, he's gone under too, swallowed by the frigid river.

Remy waits on tenterhooks for him to emerge. She scans the murky water for signs of life, but there are none.

"No," she whispers, and with every passing second her heart cracks with the ice. She drops to her knees. The thought of losing him rips her asunder. Winning without him doesn't seem possible, or even worth it. This isn't how it's supposed to be.

Bengeo watches the water settle. "Come on, Ed, come up already, quit messing around." He looks over at Lauren holding Jessica while she sobs. His heart sinks at their red eyes burning in the cold and their tears freezing on their faces. "I don't think he's—"

"Don't say it!" Remy scolds him and prepares to dive in herself, but Bengeo stops her.

"You won't make it five feet in this cold. We still got a job to do."

He holds her tightly to keep her from doing something stupid, and her fist pounds his chest as she pushes and fights against him, but she's no match for his overwhelming strength. The raspy inhuman groans of more horrors carry on the blustering wind, and Bengeo spots their horrid silhouettes shambling closer.

"Come on." He shakes Remy to her senses. "We can mourn when the job's done."

Her eyes burn raw while she tries to hold it all in, but the walls that hold her up inside are crumbling. She wants to scream, but she can't. Her lips tingle with warmth from where Ed kissed her. Everything around her fades into the background as she holds onto Mr Slashy, his parting gift.

XXII

COMIC CON

Eric's hand tremors as he adjusts his glasses. His footsteps clack against the floor while he paces backstage in the auditorium of the London Game Expo. He's on in five and despite his calm demeanour, has barely slept a wink. He rubs his tired eyes and adjusts his frames again, then a stage assistant passes him a wireless mic which he clips around his ear. She gives him a nod, and he steps through the curtain onto the stage as music booms over the cacophony of cheering, clapping and whooping while colour pulses from the lighting rigs surrounding him. Time to put on a show.

"Look at this! This is amazing! Let me just take you all in." He pauses to soak in the audience's palpable excitement. "It's great to see all of us here care so deeply about video games. I think that's because video games can do things that no other form of entertainment can. They transport us to incredible new worlds and put us in unreal adventures, and at 4D Games we live for adventure."

The word adventure sends the crowd into a frenzy, and he waits for the raucous applause to die down, then smiles.

"Well, let's just get to what you all came here to see. For the last five years, we have been working extremely hard to create something extraordinary. As I'm sure you all know the Ultimate Adventure VII remake has been out for about a week now..."

The Ultimate Adventure VII logo fades in on the jumbo screens to more roaring fanfare.

"Thank you," he says. "You know, the reason I got into games was because I never quite felt at home in the real world. Growing up I would often imagine my own worlds, but only recently have I come to realise that just playing a game is no longer enough..."

The crowd whisper amongst themselves while he paces back and forth on the stage.

"... What do you guys think about virtual reality?"

Some of the audience hollers, expecting him to announce a VR port of the game.

"Okay, alright..." he waves his hands to quiet them, "... but the thing about virtual reality is, it still *isn't* reality." Eric pulls a wry smile. "So, we've gone further than any games dev ever has, and created a living, breathing RPG experience. Ultimate Adventure VII everywhere you go, all the time and it's completely free to play. No micro-transactions, no subscriptions, no servers."

He watches the crowd talk feverishly amongst themselves, then glances back at his colleagues who look utterly baffled.

"This isn't a gimmick, I'm talking about something you can touch, something you can smell, something as real as you or I, and it's available to all of you as of right now."

He kneels and presses his left hand on the stage. Pale green light shimmers beneath his skin, and crystal sprouts like brittle grass across the stage and spreads throughout the auditorium. The audience look amazed at the shards and geodes which extend from nowhere. It isn't until the first rows of spectators are consumed, encased or impaled by the crystal that they panic, but by then it's too late, the exits are blocked by towering crystal obelisks. The light gleams off Eric's glasses, and he relishes the chaos unfolding around him.

"What the fuck is happening?" his assistant shrieks.

"The world's always changing. If we want to thrive we must do more than simply change with it, we must change it ourselves." He recedes into the shadow as the last survivors claw desperately at the exits. Their gut-wrenching screams go unheard by the people enjoying the rest of the convention outside, until one by one, they fall silent.

*

The police van skids to a halt outside the hospital. Alapati throws open the back doors and helps Helen and Lin lift Valentine inside. George sticks close behind them, warily keeping an eye out for monsters. A herd of walking corpses shambles down the road, and he gasps as a taxi swerves to miss them then skids into a bush. After one look at the creatures, the taxi driver takes off screaming in the opposite direction.

George shivers, not from the cold, but from an overwhelming sense of pity. He gazes at the corpses' morose eyes, devoid of love or life, and supposes that Esmerelda was right – there are fates worse than death. He realises how foolish he was to think the crystal could bring his father back to him and wipes a tear from his eye as he parts with the notion that he'll ever see his dad again. But there's no time to feel sorry for himself now, not when there are people counting on him. Determined to atone for his foolishness, he sprints back towards the van and climbs into the driver's seat.

"Hey!" Lin calls to him. "What do you think you're doing?"

George starts the engine and slams his foot on the pedal so the van jolts onto the road and mows down some of the undead.

One of the monsters smashes the driver's side window with its club, thrusts its bony arm into the vehicle and grabs him. George panics and presses his weight on the accelerator. The van judders forward into a parked car and rips the corpse's arm from its socket. He shakes off the dismembered limb clasping his shoulder, tosses it out of the window and watches it scurry under the van. Before he can think, Alapati pulls him out of the passenger side and drags him into the hospital, where Lin is briefing a nurse on Valentine's condition, while two more frantically lift the detective onto a gurney and whisk him away.

Lin wipes her bloodied hands across her jeans and lets out an exhausted sigh.

"Thank you," Alapati says. "If it weren't for you, well, he wouldn't have made it this far. Thank you."

Lin nods appreciatively as she takes a seat on the floor and rests her head against the wall. "This is all so—"

"Crazy?" Helen's smile comforts the weary nurse. "That was your daughter? The girl with the long hair?" she asks.

Lin nods. "Lauren. She's been through a lot these past couple of years. I can't believe she's caught up in this."

Helen bites her nails, and her worries about what her own daughters are heading into escalate.

"Those were your girls, then? They seemed like they could handle themselves," Lin says.

The corner of Helen's mouth creeps upwards. The sight of Remy decapitating that manticore filled her with pride... well, mostly horror but a little bit of pride. To her, Remy will always be that little girl with scuffed knees and a scowl on her face. Now she's wielding enchanted swords and slaying beasts. They grow up so fast. Still got the scowl though.

"I can completely believe my girls are caught up in this," she laughs.

Alapati stares out at the car park and counts the approaching wights in her head. At least thirty, but through the blizzard, it's hard to tell.

"We need to build a barricade," George suggests, "just like in State of Decay!"

"Barricade? Good idea." Alapati runs to the hospital desk and points at the automatic doors. "Do these lock?"

The receptionist clearly doesn't share her sense of urgency.

"Listen to me, some really freaky shit is about to come down on us. We need to secure the doors and windows, I need people moving cars and ambulances to block the entrances now!"

The receptionist frowns. "Is this some kind of joke?"

"No. We've got five maybe ten minutes so just humour me, will you?"

The receptionist gives a patronising smile as she lifts the telephone to call security and have the crazy-eyed constable escorted from the building, but she stops dialling and her eyes snap wide. One of the wights hurls itself through the automatic doors and crashes into the A&E waiting room, the occupants of which promptly scatter in floods of panic.

George snatches hold of an old man's walking cane and bashes the creature's legs until it falls over, then he prises the rusty sword from its bony fingers and cleaves off its head with three frantic strikes while everyone watches in shock and awe.

The receptionist leans over the counter and turns pale as she looks down at the snapping severed head. She hurriedly puts her ear to the phone and dials security, then immediately relays Alapati's instructions verbatim.

The hospital staff, and some of the more able patients in the waiting area, swiftly mobilise. Under Alapati's command they reverse ambulances against the doors and windows and barricade the inside with whatever they can find – chairs, vending machines, desks, benches, anything. Everyone huddles back from the full-length windows as the dead approach.

"Please God, let it hold," Alapati whispers, and tightens her fist so hard her nails dig into her palms.

Further into the hospital, nurses and doctors cut Valentine's clothes off him and prepare to operate. His finger twitches defiantly as he holds on to the promise he made. He clings to the distorted echoes of machines beeping and the indecipherable murmurs of the doctors as they pump him with anaesthetic. His eyes roll shut, and then darkness. They get to work immediately.

*

Remy covers her frozen nose with her hand and breathes warm air into her palm to regain some feeling in her face. No one has spoken since they lost Ed. The wind drones across the silent courtyard outside the ExCel centre, which is empty save for a few cosplayers taking pictures in the snow.

Bengeo stares up at the massive glass pyramid which serves as an entrance into the sprawling concrete convention halls. "What is this place?"

"It's like a celebration of video games," Lauren replies.

"Video games. There's that word again. Never explained what the hell it is."

Bengeo's attention is stolen by two girls in scanty craft foam armour hurrying past them into the warm convention hall. They eye him up as they pass and giggle to themselves.

Jessica nudges the bandit. "Put your eyes back in your head."

Beyond the tall glass doors they find themselves faced with a heaving crowd of gamers, cosplayers and vendors buzzing around the restaurants and coffee shops in the foyer. Spacious hangar-like halls offshoot at either side and are separated from the foyer by large metal shutters, but only the halls on the right side are open and flooded with even more people moving in all directions.

"There!" Bengeo points at Grimoirh queuing at a noodle bar.

"Wait! That's not—!" Lauren's cries fall on deaf ears as he fights through the crowd to the Dread Knight and pulls off his helmet to reveal a pimply teenage boy, who looks back at him, frightened.

"Wha—?!" Bengeo lowers his balled fist.

"C-can I help you?" the boy stutters.

"Sorry, thought you were someone else." Bengeo pokes his craft foam armour to see what it's made of.

The boy lights up. "Oh! Bengeo the Bandit!" He taps his friend on the shoulder and points at Bengeo. "Get a pic of us."

Before Bengeo can protest, the cosplayer is posing beside him while his friend snaps away.

"I tried to tell you, that's not him." Lauren bows her head apologetically. "Sorry, we gotta go." Taking his arm she leads poor confused Bengeo away.

"Why is he dressed like Grimoirh?" he asks.

"It's cosplay. People dress up and pretend for fun."

Bengeo scoffs at the idea of anyone revering the Dread Knight. They regroup with Remy and Jessica beside a hulking six-wheeled jeep, parked in the centre of the foyer, next to a huge banner advertising the newest Tank Racer game.

Jessica marvels at the armoured vehicle. "Coulda used that earlier…" she sighs at the people climbing in and out of it taking photos, all of them blissfully unaware of the danger fast approaching. "When those things get here it'll be like a geek buffet," she mutters.

"Let's try the playtest area or one of the stages? Eric is supposed to be giving a presentation," Lauren says.

Remy snatches a map from a passing couple. Her severe expression silences their protests and scares them away. She looks over the map for the stage when a familiar voice calls out from behind her.

"Remy?"

Her blood runs cold. She glances up, her face a picture of disdain.

"Remy, thought that was you!"

Simon. Her former boss, who killed her spirit and ruined her life – not that she's still sore about it or anything – greets her with a limp hug which she most certainly does not reciprocate.

"As if this day couldn't get any worse." She pushes him away.

She had thought long and hard about the day when they would again meet, only she imagined she'd look flawless and successful and exude a kind of charming confidence that would crush him and make him realise what a terrible mistake it was to mistreat her. But here she is, beaten to shit and on the verge of an emotional breakdown. Yay.

He looks her up and down, and winces. "Jesus, Remy, you look awful, and you smell like... Are you alright?"

She wipes the muck off her face with her arm, shakes her head disapprovingly and pushes past him.

Lauren follows her and nods politely as she passes, while Bengeo and Jessica eyeball him threateningly. Remy storms through the crowd, doing her utmost to keep it together. Losing Ed has her second guessing everything. Lauren corners her as she rests her forehead against the wall.

"Hey, who was that?"

"Nobody." Remy's voice cracks. She toils and labours with each breath and wonders if her thudding heart will burst.

Lauren all too easily recognises her symptoms so takes Remy by the hand and leads her to a quiet corner inside the main hall. "I didn't know him well, but he made all of us smile. That was no small thing."

Remy sinks. Her eyes burn. She blinks away tears and balls her fist tightly, as though she were channelling all her rage and heartache there. "Screw all of this," she says, gritting her teeth. "It's not right."

"I know," Lauren sniffs, "but we have to finish this. Maybe it shouldn't be on us, but it is. Avarice, Esmerelda, Ed, they all faced their fate with unshakable courage. All of them are an inspiration for the ways I wish I was... and so are you."

Remy softens, and looks at Lauren who radiates warmth and reverence. "Me?"

Lauren nods. "You're fearless."

Remy shakes her head. "I'm terrified."

"Maybe, but you don't let it swallow you and that's what counts. When we met you'd lost a piece of yourself, but you never let it slow you down, never let it stop you. You made me realise I don't want to be the girl whose dad died, I want to be everything he wanted me to be and more. I've come to realise that I'm not weaker for losing him, I'm stronger for the time we had. My dad, Ed, Avarice, Esmerelda... they live on through us, in our hearts, our memories and our actions."

A hurricane of emotion stirs in Remy. Her face turns red as she bites her bottom lip and pictures Ed's messy hair and the way he'd always play with it; the goofy smile that he wore even when all seemed hopeless. Esmerelda's nurturing eyes, wrinkled with years of wisdom she would kindly impart, and Avarice's scowl, her ferocity and unwavering heart; against all opposition she stood for what she believed in. She was relentless until her final breath.

Remy holds her head high, determined. If this is a game, she's playing to win.

*

Having lost the girls amongst the heaving crowd, Jessica and Bengeo are swept into the main hall. The bandit regards everything with childlike wonder. The people in costumes, the stalls selling action figures, T-shirts and memorabilia, the banks of game consoles that people are queuing to play and the giant screens looping trailers and adverts blow him away.

"What is this?" He examines a monitor playing footage of a new first-person wartime shooter. "Some kind of magic mirror?" He prods the screen, which draws the attention of the man working at the stand.

"Pretty sweet, right?" He leans against the display and tries to plug a sale. "Dedicated GeForce RTX graphics card, more cores and higher clocks, making it twenty-five per cent faster than the old series." He taps the PC lovingly. "It'll feel like you're in the game."

Bengeo shrugs. He knows the man is speaking a language he understands, but not a lick of what he just said made any sense. Before he can ask, Jessica urgently drags him away, much to the salesman's disfavour.

"I know being in another world is, like, overwhelming, but you gotta stop wandering off. We've got to find Vincent!" she says.

"Maybe I didn't cut you all enough slack, this is… a little much." Bengeo rubs the back of his neck and looks at the electronics around him with unease. A stand selling Ultimate Adventure merchandise catches his eye, particularly the life-size statuettes of Grimoirh and Ozrune erected either side of it. He notices a figurine of himself and pushes through the other customers perusing the merchandise.

"Is this supposed to be me?" He picks up the box, inspecting the toy closely.

"I guess you're kind of a big deal here," Jessica smiles.

Bengeo tears the figure from the box much to her dismay. "Is that what they think this is?" he grunts, turning its little head with his brutish fingers until it snaps off. "A toy? A game? My pain, my loss, it's real! And soon a world of pain is gonna be coming down on all our heads. Then they'll see this ain't no game!"

"They don't know any better. Magic worlds, monsters – that stuff is just fantasy here." She prises the figure from his hand, places it on the counter and whisks him into the central aisle.

She hops up and down, hoping to spot Remy or Lauren who are now most definitely lost somewhere in the crowded hall.

"Great." Unable to jump to even half the bandit's height, she sighs. Being short has few advantages. "Just stick by me. No more distractions."

Bengeo holds his hands up in the air. "Yeah, sure," he nods as another fan approaches him asking for a picture.

Clutching the shotgun in her hand, which thankfully blends in amongst the dozens of cosplayers carrying realistic-looking props, Jessica shoos them away and drags Bengeo along behind her until she finds a thin spot in the mass of people milling about. She wonders why this particular patch is so empty. The answer almost deafens her.

Blaring music erupts from behind. She jolts around and looks up at the small rainbow-coloured stage before her, branded with the upcoming Karaoke Star: Sing Your Heart Out logo. She quickly plugs her ears with her fingers to quiet the bloodcurdling racket of the girls on stage murdering 'Bohemian Rhapsody'.

*

Having circled back to the foyer to find Bengeo and Jessica, Remy struggles to make sense of the map she swiped, when Mr Slashy starts to jostle on her back. She scans the foyer with foreboding eyes and sees nothing but people. The hairs on the back of her neck prickle on edge. She lifts her head up and spots a winged creature circling the skies above the glass ceiling.

"Oh God."

Lauren wanders into the main hall to locate the others, and lights up on seeing a stall selling replica weapons and air-soft guns.

"Excuse me!" she calls to the middle-aged bloke behind the stand, wearing a retro Boba Fett T-shirt tucked into his blue jeans.

"How can I help, miss?"

"I need a weapon," she says impatiently, "something really sharp!"

"Well, we have a couple of 'live blades'. You gotta be over twenty-five to purchase one though."

"Yeah, yeah, sure. Lemme see."

The man fetches a katana from the shelf behind him and places it on the counter between them, then unsheathes it.

"So this is actually a replica of the sword wielded by the Samurai Heishiro Mitsurugi in the Soul series of fighting games." The steel gleams as he turns it in his hands.

"Mind if I—?" Lauren eagerly reaches out. The shopkeeper hesitates to let go, but she practically snatches it.

"So this won't break or anything?"

The sword salesman shakes his head. "Our replicas are handmade, folded steel just like the ones crafted in feudal Japan," he insists.

"Oh my God, what about that one?!" She points behind him and he glances over his shoulder. By the time he turns back to her she's taken off.

"Oi! Get back here!" he yells after her, but she slips through the horde of people and back into the foyer.

Growing impatient with the crowd, she climbs onto a table by a sandwich bar to spot Remy, and incurs the wrath of the people eating their lunch as she stumbles over their food. Lauren notices her staring up just as the glass ceiling shatters and rains onto the crowd, who scatter in a panic as a shrieking cockatrice crashes into a KFC. People gawk as the creature regains its footing, towering above them on its tall chicken legs. They cautiously close round, camera phones fixed in front of their faces. It isn't until the monster sinks its beak into a man dressed as Ken from Street Fighter and flings him across the hall that people realise this isn't a publicity stunt.

Remy charges with her shield as it lunges for the bystanders. She cleaves its leg with extreme prejudice then does her best not to end up between the creature's jaws as it hops after her. Lauren fights her way through the screaming flood of people fleeing the foyer and strikes the cockatrice with the katana she stole. The blade immediately shatters on impact and cuts her hand.

415

"Folded steel my arse!" She tosses the broken sword aside and the creature swats her into a table with its ratty tail.

"What are you waiting for?! Kill it!" Remy yells at her sword.

"Yes, ma'am!" Mr Slashy replies, then cuts the beast to ribbons in a whirl until it collapses with a shrill cry.

*

On the steps outside, two friends enjoy lunch and each other's company while revelling at the snow fluttering around them. A woman dressed as Jinx from League of Legends sprints past screaming.

"Don't you hate it when women cosplay outside of their body type?" asks the one dressed as Spider-Man, blissfully ignorant of his own gut poking out of his Zentai suit.

"Yeah," Kratos laughs, spitting food all over himself and his buddy.

The foyer doors burst open behind them. A surge of people spill out of the convention centre amidst a symphony of terror followed by a surly two-headed death dog that crashes through a window and flops down the stairs in a heap. It picks itself up and hungrily eyes the two men, licking its ravenous jaws. They cower as the hellhound leaps to devour them, when a flaming blade explodes from its chest and cleaves it in half. The terrified men look up. Their blood-soaked faces stare agape at Vincent, blazing sword in hand.

"Run," he grunts and rests the God Cleaver on his shoulder before pushing on into the convention hall as people push past him.

He smites wights, lizard men, ogres and anything else that crosses his path through the foyer, biding time for as many to flee as possible.

Inside the main hall, Lauren ducks and weaves through a maze of demo exhibits, pursued by a slithering basilisk. She throws anything she can to fend off the serpent, but it cuts her off with a whip of its tail, sending her crashing into a row of chairs set up for a press junket. Vincent rushes in and flanks the giant snake, drawing its attention away from Lauren while she picks herself up. A shadow from above her catches her eye, and a giant spindly-legged spider descends from the ceiling. She edges backwards then... vroooosh! Vincent's sword hums as he brings it down, cleaving the insect in two. He turns to face the basilisk behind him.

"Come at me, you rotting filth!" he taunts the beast, which dives at him, fangs dripping with poison, but his sword tears through the air, and he decapitates its leathery head in one fell swoop.

He turns to Lauren warning her, "You should leave while you still can."

"Not a chance," she says.

Something about the way her sweet, trusting eyes behold him sparks an ember of emotion.

"I've done awful things, I'm not excusing any of it, but I just want you to understand I only wanted to prevent this. I always liked you. I'm sorry you got dragged into this."

"I'm not," she says sincerely.

"Drop the sword!" Jessica cries. Her trembling hands grip the shotgun aimed at Vincent's back.

"Jess, wait! He's not going to hurt us," Lauren insists.

Vincent turns and grips the gun barrel, slowly lowering it towards the floor. "Don't let her get herself killed," he says, staring at Jessica coldly.

His concern for Lauren's wellbeing shocks her, but there's no time to question it. Bengeo and Remy sprint towards them with a heap of trouble hot on their heels. A pack of wild ghouls chase them, slobbering and shrieking as they run on all fours like deranged apes.

"Move it!" Remy howls.

Vincent puts himself in front of the girls and raises his sword. With a sweeping strike he slays the first two that come at him, then three more set upon him and drag him to the floor. He kicks one across the room, while Bengeo prises the other two off him and beats them back with his bare hands. The bandit lifts one over his head and throws it at Remy who brings Mr Slashy up, cutting the beast through the waist. Vincent kills the last, crushing its skull between his hands. He pushes its limp carcass off him and stands, resting his gigantic blade on his shoulder.

"If you've come to finish me off, it'll have to wait," he says, looking warily at Remy and Bengeo.

"We're not here to fight you," she replies, "we just want all this crazy to go back in the box. Same as you."

"Is that right?"

She nods resolutely.

He knows he doesn't deserve her help, but he's certain he'll need it. The dregs of his conscience gnaw at him. Nothing he could say would make amends for what he did to her, so he says nothing and leads them to the auditorium where Eric should be, stopping before the set of double doors.

Turning to Remy he warns, "Whatever is through here is likely to be worse than anything you've faced thus far."

"Is that supposed to be a pep talk?" she frowns.

Holding her head high, she enters the darkened auditorium with an unwavering heart, sword and shield in hand, beaten to a pulp and hopelessly outmatched. She is Remy Winters, twenty-seven, unemployed and ready to save the world.

XXIII

Final Form

Remy's sword hand trembles as she scans the walls of the silent auditorium. Webs of ebony crystal render the space totally unrecognisable – more akin to a cavern from the game than an expo hall. Most disturbing of all, fused within the rugged geodes are the contorted bodies of the audience, all their faces frozen in a bloodcurdling scream. She senses a presence watching them and runs her eyes across the room until she clocks something scurrying across the ceiling. Her gaze tightens on her necrotic hand as it races towards the stage, which flickers in the glow of a strobing light dangling from the damaged rig overhead.

Clack, clack, clack. Hard footsteps resound through the crystal tomb. A figure emerges from the shadow and pauses at the edge of the stage. Its eyes gleam with the flashing light – not eyes, a pair of round lenses.

"Look at you here, I thought you fancied yourself a hero, but black does suit you, friend." Eric pulls a wry grin.

Vincent looks betrayed. "I thought you were dead. I mourned you, but when Lauren confirmed you were alive, I knew somehow you must be responsible for all the others appearing in the game. What happened to you after you disappeared?"

"I was so pathetic then," Eric replies, "pleading, begging for deliverance from that hell hole, but my prayers didn't fall on deaf ears. In the blink of an eye I found myself bleeding all over the floor of my office. A few days passed and I started to hear whispers. That shard was still in me, showing me glimpses of things I never thought possible. A violent, irrepressible miracle."

"What are you saying?" Vincent asks.

"It's more than a gem, it's alive. Incomplete and yearning to be whole. I could feel the other shards calling to me from beyond the abyss, faint whispers that grew louder with every moment someone played Ultimate Adventure VII. The game was like a conduit, strengthening our bond and our power. Maybe it was never just a game at all."

"Then why drag them into it? Why not go back and get the shards yourself?"

"Far too dangerous. I couldn't risk anything happening to me again. Without all of the shards I was still vulnerable, still just flesh and bone. Their sacrifices were an unfortunate but necessary evil."

"Coward. Disgusting coward," Lauren growls under her breath, then erupts, "you thought you could just throw our lives away for some sick fantasy?"

Eric's eyes dart towards her. His sharp gaze still gives her the creeps. "I thought you of all people would be eager to escape your miserable existence," he says.

Lauren gasps, at first stunned by the cruelty his voice carries, but her expression quickly turns fierce. "It was you, wasn't it? You started the fire in Vincent's apartment."

His trademark wry smile creeps across his face. "I didn't think you'd last a day in the game, but *it* saw something in you that I apparently overlooked, something beyond weakness. It knew the love for your brother and your determination to find

Vincent could be exploited, and that all your choices would lead you here, back to me."

Remy looks sceptical, and whispers to Bengeo, "All of this is because of him?"

Bengeo shrugs. "I expected something much more... well, just more."

Eric laughs. "You expected what? A demonic knight carrying a flaming sword?"

As Eric sweeps his hair behind his ear Vincent notices strange blemishes on his hand. His flesh is turning necrotic – the crystal's mark.

"That shard is rotting you to the core," he warns.

Eric shakes his head. "I thought Grimoirh's aim was to harness the crystal's power and bend it to his will, but here you are dead set on destroying it. A futile quest, what's done cannot be undone. You've all played your part in the dawn of this new age."

Vincent pleads, "No, it's not too late, we can still stop this, together."

"Why, Vincent? Why develop fantasy when we can shape reality? We can mould this world into something we've always dreamt of. I left you in that dungeon with nothing but the clothes on your back and here you are. The Dread Knight, who transcended dimensions. Now that's a world of possibility!" Eric cheers.

"People have suffered and died just so you can live out some twisted delusion?" Lauren's eyes burn as she reels from the loss of Ed, Avarice, Esmerelda and, for all she knows, Valentine. "This is just a game to you?"

"What do you think this place is?" Eric replies. "It's like a mass. People flock to this convention like zealots. They dress up, pretend to be someone else and buy into fiction and fantasy to escape their mediocrity."

"Is that really how you see your fans?" Jessica snaps. "People dream of having what you have, loyal fans that cherish your work, how dare you belittle them!"

"People are fickle!" Eric sneers. "Their ever-escalating sense of entitlement disgusts me. Thanks to the internet every nobody who can fumble a controller believes their opinion means something. Do you have any idea how hard it is to make a successful single-player game in today's market? It's absurd, there's no creativity anymore, we're just pandering to a horde of toxic, entitled brats while publishers racketeer your game, fleecing players with micro-transactions and loot crates. For years I poured everything I had into each game I worked on, but every new release was mired by past successes. Nobody wants anything new, they want what they know, but they don't understand that you can never recapture that nostalgia."

"Boo hoo," Remy says, glaring. "Take it from someone who's spent the last week stuck in your game. Reality isn't that bad."

"I disagree," Eric replies. "I won't live another second in this putrid world."

Bengeo cracks his knuckles. "Well, that's one thing we can agree on."

Eric regards the bandit coldly, then looks to Vincent. "Stand with me. It'll be just like old times. No pressure, no crunch, just pure uninhibited creation. The crystal chose me, I can feel it, control it!"

Eric turns his left hand. Pale green light shimmers in Vincent's eyes as he seemingly mulls the offer over in his mind.

"We've always been a team. I only abandoned you because I was weak and afraid. I was certain you had died in that dungeon, but when you took possession of the shards I sensed your unrepentant will. I realised then that we both had to endure all of this suffering. It was our baptism. We have to let our old selves die to become what we need to be."

Vincent recalls saying something of the sort to Remy and shudders. "What we need to be?" he asks.

Eric grins madly. "The Dread Knight and the Game Master. This is it, Vincent, the greatest game ever made. We'll reshape this world into the ultimate role-playing experience. Only the strongest players will survive."

"He always did have a complex," Lauren mutters as Vincent hesitantly takes a step towards Eric. "Don't!" she pleads. "Please don't."

He looks downcast and climbs onto the stage taking position at Eric's side.

"So you're just a villain after all?" Remy raises her sword defiantly.

Eric extends his arm and from behind his back, Remy's malevolent hand scuttles on its fingers over his shoulders, down his arm and rests its palm against his. His eyes look starved of power as he interlaces his fingers with Remy's, and a blinding light swells between them.

In a flash Vincent's God Cleaver ignites with a swift tune. He brings it up to cleave Eric's arm from his body, but a wall of crystal springs up from the stage, and the God Cleaver strikes against it. Eric looks coldly at his life-long friend.

"You always were too sentimental, Vincent."

More geodes sprout between them and engulf Eric in a gleaming suit of crystal armour. He leaps from the stage in a swift motion, summoning a long emerald blade seemingly from nowhere. Its green hilt materialises in his left hand with a shimmer of pale light before he lands between Remy and the others.

She wastes no time and swings for his head. He blocks her strike effortlessly, then Bengeo lunges fists swinging, but Eric barely breaks a sweat as the crystal fights for him – or through him. He deals a flurry of counterattacks that floor Remy and send Bengeo skidding across the auditorium. His emerald blade flies at Lauren's throat, and she gasps as he stops just shy of nicking her artery.

He looks her up and down callously. "You're as useless to them as you were to us."

Vincent lets out a deafening war cry and leaps off the stage, bringing his sword down on Eric with almighty force. Their weapons clash, again and again. Vincent swings with savage ferocity, but Eric deflects blow after blow with calculated precision until Jessica clips him with the shotgun. The blast shatters his crystal pauldron, stealing his breath as Bengeo comes back swinging, along with Remy too, twirling and slashing with rage. Eric's composure breaks. He can barely hold his own against all three of them at once. Crack! Bengeo's fist slams into his nose. His glasses clatter across the hall. He swings blindly in retribution, but Remy's sword clashes against his and Vincent's slams his back, knocking him clean off his feet. Jessica aims again, but Eric weaves the crystal's magic, and with a push of his hand and a clench of his fist, manipulates the webbing lining the hall and sweeps her feet from under her. She shrieks as cold, hard crystal encases her foot and crawls up her calf.

Lauren rushes to break her loose and beats the webbing with the stock of the shotgun, while the self-proclaimed 'Game Master' lifts his blade, spits blood and grins with spite.

"Five against one is hardly fair."

A rising croak commands their attention, and the party look on in horror as the contorted remains of the audience reanimate and break free of their crystal cocoon.

"Don't come any closer!" Lauren's hands quake as she clutches the gun.

The corpses clamber manically towards her, hurling themselves over the chairs – BLAM! The recoil knocks her back into Jessica who props her up while she picks them off as they come.

"Stop this, Eric!" Vincent cries. His chest tightens and his breath grows heavy as the sword tip still lodged in his ribs slowly drains him of life. Were it not for the magical properties of the Dreadmail he'd be a popsicle already.

The undead pile on him like a rugby scrum and wrestle him to his knees. Eric charges, and a lofty blow hurls Vincent across the hall. His plate mail crashes through the geodes. He tumbles and skids to a halt then lifts himself on all fours, but more undead pin him down and hold him in their punishing grasp as Eric approaches. Red clouds his vision, and Vincent roars as a creature gouges his right eye with its jagged fingertip. Struggle as he might he can't quite reach his sword.

His screams draw Remy's attention, and she brings her sword overhead, winds her arm back then hurls Mr Slashy at Eric. The magic blade twirls through the air with the grace of God and skewers him through the forearm as he brings his sword to Vincent's head.

With a roar Vincent wrestles his arm free, clasps his God Cleaver and swings broadly. The blade sears through the undead like butter. His Dreadmail imbues him with the strength of ten men, and he rises to his feet, driving his weapon into Eric. The wicked flame torches his crystal cuirass. He writhes on the edge of Vincent's blade as Remy rushes in and grips the hilt of Mr Slashy, impaled through his arm. Throwing all her weight forward she twists the sword, tearing flesh and crystal. Eric's limb hits the floor with a mighty thud. He lets out a hoarse cry and convulses as his unravelling mind comprehends what has happened, then with a haunting scream he prises himself off Vincent's sword and collapses in a gory heap.

Vincent falls to one knee, clutching his bloodied eye. He can feel the chill in his bones as with every second lassitude poisons his body. He staggers towards Eric, who crawls away on his belly and cradles his severed arm.

His sunken eyes tremble as he foolishly tries to reattach it. "My flesh feels wrong. My mind is coming loose... Dozens of worlds, I can see them all..." His voice reverberates with a deep undertone as though something else is speaking through him. "I thought I was a man, now I'm not sure..."

His detached arm ripples like liquid and sprouts fleshy vines that latch onto his torn elbow. The fingers grow spindly and long like spiders' legs, and the arm races towards Remy dragging Eric behind it.

She looks disturbed as his flesh expands like baking bread, his eyes roll back into his head, showing only the whites, and his jaw unhinges as spires of black crystal protrude from his throat.

Would this have happened to me? Remy shudders, and her eyes bulge as the crystal contorts him into something unspeakable. "What's happening?!" she shrieks.

Vincent shivers, lost for words. He edges away from Eric's flesh bleeding across the auditorium like gelatine. It engulfs the stage in a matter of seconds, assimilating all it touches, melding, shifting, like wet sand. The undead in the auditorium grow frenzied and hurl themselves into the gibbering mass, which swallows each one into its being. Bone, crystal, metal, flesh, all recycled into something new, something blasphemous. Dozens of eyes flutter open and dart wildly about while jaws of all sizes breathe through the surface and wail like newborn children.

"The hell is it doing?" Bengeo cries.

"Feeding." Vincent's reply chills him to the bone.

The morbid living structure expands, buckling the roof. The ceiling cracks and caves inwards and the lighting rigs come crashing down.

"Get me out of here!" Jessica desperately tries to wrestle her leg free of the crystal grasping it, while gelatinous tendrils ooze from the foul form and snake towards her. Vincent severs them with a broad slash, but more spring out in place like living vines, lashing and flailing.

With every furious swing Remy chips away at the crystal, hacking relentlessly until it cracks like an eggshell and Lauren and Bengeo pull Jessica free.

A damning voice crackles around them. "Instruments of my

reunion, weathered and weary, cast your struggle away and take solace in my form."

More ghastly living branches sprout from the central mass, whooshing through the air, and latch onto Remy's armguard with a thud. The flesh softens, quickly turning to spongy globules, which expand, engulfing her shield. She frantically unfastens the straps across her chest while Bengeo clings to her waist. They trip backwards as the last buckle comes loose, and she watches the abomination swallow her trusty prosthetic into its hideous mass. All she can think is, *In a few minutes, that'll be me.*

The brand on her thigh glows hot as the voice booms again, "Rudimentary creatures, you cannot shirk your fate. You are marked."

A rising horn resounds from beyond the walls. The burly armoured Tank Racer from the main hall bursts through the blockade, throwing hunks of crystal across the auditorium.

"Get in!" Ed, sopping wet and almost blue, leans out of the driver's side window and looks aghast at the titanic horror. "What the f—?!"

"Drive!" Remy cries, shocked that Ed's still kicking, as she and the others pile into the hulking all-terrain vehicle.

Ed shifts the jeep into reverse and peels out of the auditorium. The abominable blob lets out a thunderous roar through its hundred salivating mouths. The tendrils snake through the convention centre after the 'players', who blow through display stands and stalls.

"Buckle up!" Ed yells as he steers the car towards the foyer. Thank God it's an automatic.

"You're alive?!" Remy leans over from the back seat and punches him in the arm. "You stupid, selfish—" The others hold her back as she tries to kill him herself.

"Don't obstruct the driver!" he barks while Jessica wrestles her raging sister back into her seat.

The tendrils constrict the vehicle and flip the car, so that it skids on the roof through the foyer, smashes through the metal shutters on the opposite side, and grinds to a halt.

"We can't let it be," Vincent growls as he forces open the door and staggers out.

Remy crawls out of the back seat after him and peers over the car as the tendrils plant themselves in the ground like malevolent roots while a shroud of dark cloud descends from the sky, enveloping the convention centre in a dark mist.

"Seriously, what is that?" Ed asks. "I don't remember a giant blob monster in the original game!"

"We changed a few elements of the story," Vincent sighs. "Now it's whole again, it'll consume the world and spread like cancer throughout the universe."

"I could just about tolerate the midgey merchants, but this?! Why change what wasn't broken?!" Remy snaps.

"It doesn't matter, we just have to beat its final form," Lauren says.

"Final what?" Jessica asks.

"All of these big bosses have a final form, something harder to beat than the last, it's a trope," she explains.

"I'm sorry, can we just circle back to *you're not dead?!*" Remy looks at Ed, unsure whether to kiss him or kick his ass.

"I got a magic water-breathing ring, turns out it wasn't a gyp," he replies.

"You... what? Why didn't you say so before you plunged into the river?"

"Well, I didn't think it would actually work. Are you seriously mad at me right now?"

"Yes!" she scowls. "I thought you were... I can't even say it."

Though ecstatic that she cares for him, he suppresses his smile, reasoning she'd probably smack it off him if he did. "That water was freezing, I mean, I could still get pneumonia." He tries to appease her. As usual, he only makes matters worse.

428

"Can you put a pin in your drama!" Jessica cries, looking apprehensively at the ground. "Does anyone feel that?" Her feet tingle through the soles of her boots.

The hall quakes. A low rumble rises from beneath and the tendrils rupture the convention centre floor, then retreat into the auditorium. Bengeo is the first to cautiously approach the gaping holes left in their wake and peers into the seemingly bottomless caverns. A choir of hissing, roaring, bellowing, shrieking rises, then a horde of undead beasts and giants, wyverns, ravenous wights, cackling harpies and living skeletons claw their way up from the underground.

The party scatter as the monsters tear the foyer apart, and they fight back where they can.

"Bengeo!" Remy screams as a colossal tendril comes crashing through the wall and sweeps through the hall. He jumps clear before it whips itself up and out of the building. "It's getting bigger," she groans.

"How do we kill it?" Bengeo asks.

"We don't." Vincent wipes the blood trickling from his eye and draws a small stone from a pouch on his belt.

"A rock?" Bengeo looks sceptical as he and Remy gather around Vincent.

"It's not a rock," Remy says, examining it with wide eyes. "Is that the ferry stone?"

Vincent nods. "Good for one trip to anywhere you've ever been."

"You want to send that thing back?" Remy asks.

Vincent tightens his grip on the stone. "If we cast it back into the crater maybe we can destroy it."

"Or it could corrupt the whole damn world!" Bengeo yells. "Last time it swallowed a whole city and reduced the north to a wasteland," he squares up to Vincent, "who's to say it won't do worse this time?"

The tendril sweeps back, blowing through another wall and

assimilating a tide of monsters before it retreats into the sky.

Vincent exchanges an uncertain look with Bengeo. "It has a physical form now, and that much spirit energy could destroy it. Imagine a droplet of blood in a limitless ocean, the water dilutes it until it fades entirely. Honestly, I can't be sure what will happen, but that thing will not stop until everything in this world is dead or a part of it. None of us can kill it on our own." He holds up the stone. "This is our only shot."

"Are you telling me we could have used that ferry stone to warp back to reality this whole time?" Remy asks.

"No—" A wight charges and crashes into Vincent.

Mr Slashy springs to Remy's defence and cleaves it in half. Two more come charging, weapons in hand, but Bengeo catches one and pulls it apart like a child tearing the wings from a fly. Vincent runs the other through and looks back at Remy.

"This might only work because that calamity has bridged the veil between reality and the game. You didn't just open a rift into reality, it's like both worlds are crashing together."

She shrinks with guilt. "You mean—"

"It's only a matter of time before our reality and the game world collide. The blizzard was just the start. Soon it'll be landmarks, mountains, cities, all melding together at once. So if we don't banish it now, we're all dead anyway."

Remy looks worriedly at Bengeo, who, after a deep breath, gives a reluctant nod.

*

Footsteps race through the foyer, crunching broken glass and debris. Lauren and Ed flee the onslaught of raving dead and leap behind the counter of a burger bar. The wights come sprinting after them, and Ed throws one over him then pushes it back into the kitchen while Lauren pulls down the shutters and locks them in. She trips backwards as dozens more bald, festering horrors pile up against it and shove their arms through the gaps in the metal, frantically clawing after her.

From behind a staircase, Jessica watches the monsters rush the barrier to the burger bar, and panics. She saw Ed and Lauren go in and knows they're as good as dead unless someone comes to their rescue. She smacks the side of her head and breathes deeply to compose her racing thoughts.

Distraction. Need a distraction. Her eyes light up, and without a second thought she sprints from behind cover into the convention hall. A trio of harpies swoop down on her, cackling and shrieking, then lift her into the air kicking and screaming. Jessica slips out of her jacket and crashes to the floor with a wallop. The harpies set on her like a pack of drunken yobs, biting, scratching and pulling her hair. She crawls towards the karaoke stage she'd spotted earlier, enduring the savage beating through gritted teeth. The darkest of the harpies pulls her head back and looks at her with cruel eyes, cackling.

Memories of a seaside holiday come flooding back – rain lashing the window, scent of cheap pine air freshener, a dozen faces staring at her. She was small then, usually bright-eyed and full of energy, but not that time. Her throat dried up, she stuttered on the small stage, and the mocking laughter of other children was all she could hear. She took it hard, swore she'd never sing again. That night Remy – in an uncharacteristic act – had told her something she'd never forgotten: *'Never give up and never let them see you cry.'*

A berserk strength rises from her stomach and she forces herself up and takes hold of the cackling harpy, which shrieks and thrusts into the air to throw her off. She claws at its wings, tearing out feathers by the handful until they crash into the karaoke stage and tumble. She glances up and jolts as a hefty blade slams into the harpy and bursts aflame. The wicked creature dies with a shrill cry and the other two scurry away in fear of the Dread Knight, who draws his sword and winces at the pain shooting through his side.

Remy picks Jessica up. "You alright?" she asks.

Jessica wipes the blood from her split lip and nods. "I gotta get this thing working, Lauren and Ed are trapped!" She peers behind the velvet curtain and inspects the soundboard to check it still has power. Lights are a good sign.

"Where?!" Bengeo asks.

"We don't have time, we need to get back to the auditorium before that thing gets any bigger," Vincent says.

"You're gonna kill it?" Jessica asks.

"Not exactly," Remy replies, "but we think we can get rid of it. Maybe."

"Then go, I've got this," Jessica says.

"You sure?"

She nods. "Yeah. Maybe."

The hall quakes again, with a thunderous roar from on high. Vincent looks worried as he rests his sword on his shoulder. "Come on."

"Wait!" Jessica leaps off stage and launches herself at Remy, squeezing her tightly as years of animosity melt away.

Despite the new-found respect and admiration Remy holds for Jessica, she cradles her like a child. After all, no matter what, she'll always be her little sister. "Be careful!" she says.

"You too," Jessica smiles, and races back onto the stage. She picks up the microphone, then slides all the dials on the sound board to max.

*

Lauren and Ed do their best to hold up the shutters while the undead horde pile on the pressure until an enormous reptilian foot crashes down, smushing the wights and scattering their bones. A wicked wyvern casts its eye on them. Ed pulls Lauren behind the grill as the creature parts its slender jaws, conjuring a stream of fire that melts the shutters to molten goop.

432

A silky voice echoes through the convention centre and the tune it carries drives the creature into a frenzy. It whips around and stalks through fire after the source.

Ed looks amazed. "Is that singing?" he asks.

Lauren's eyes snap wide with dread. "Jessica!" She bolts out of the kitchen, hops over the counter and sprints through the foyer.

"… Tear me up inside, her heart had buried a diamond, eyes are open wide, okay I'm looking to find you…"

Swells of power roll off Jessica's tongue. Her voice is music, brought about by the heartfelt determination to protect the ones she loves. Her melody blares to every corner of the convention centre sending the game monsters into a fit of hysteria. They charge the stage desperate to silence her. Jessica opens her eyes and sees the wyvern barrelling through a horde of undead right at her.

"Oh shit!" She dives off the stage as the beast summons a stream of fire from its throat and burns the karaoke stand to ash.

Jessica's distraction clears the way for Remy and the others, who creep over the crystal rubble and skirt along the back wall of the auditorium. They peek over the seats, peering through the sleet enveloping the room. The pale light from the hole in the roof illuminates the snow-covered stage, but there's no sign of the living mass anywhere.

"It's gone," Remy whispers.

"Not gone." Vincent points above, and cloaked in the blizzard, amidst flashes of lightning, a colossal, baleful eye blinks open. Enormous fleshy tendrils emerge from the dark clouds and crash into the sides of the building like thunder.

Remy scrunches her face with unprecedented dread. "How do we get close to that?"

"Did you ever play Shadow of the Colossus?" Vincent asks.

Remy nods, but her eyes protest as his mad plan dawns on her. "Climb it? Are you crazy?"

Vincent plants the ferry stone in Bengeo's hand. "We'll cover you," he says.

"Bah, you're half dead, and she's got one arm, you'll only slow me down."

"We go together." Remy gives him a stern eyeballing, and he knows by now there's no use in putting up a fight.

"Fine, but you ain't getting far on yer own." He kneels and Remy climbs onto his back, wraps her arm around his shoulders and cinches his waist with her legs.

"Get ready." Vincent forces himself up, and his sword erupts in hellfire. The blaze garners the eye's attention, and it casts its unholy gaze upon him as he walks into the open.

"What is your purpose here, Dread Knight? You had only to retreat if you sought to prolong what life you have left." The calamity's voice booms like the wrath of a vengeful god, but Vincent lifts his sword high in defiance. "So it is oblivion you seek? Very well, I will grant thy wish." The voice cackles, and the calamity brings a gargantuan tendril down on him.

Vincent draws long breaths to gather strength as the tendril barrels towards him, crashing into the auditorium floor like the trunk of a falling oak tree. The abomination slithers its appendage aside and snaps its eye wide, searching for Vincent's remains, but the creature sees no sign of him, until he leaps through the sleet and drives his sword through its tendril, pinning it to the floor.

"Go!" he calls to Bengeo, who sprints from cover, flings his arms wide and leaps.

He grabs hold of its lumpy flesh with both hands and scales the creature with Remy on his back. Vincent clings tightly to his sword lodged in the calamity's flesh and hurtles into the air as the creature raises its limb into the heavens.

The sky is an assault on all senses as a devastating storm cloaks the ungodly orb. Quaking thunder and howling wind is all Remy can hear, and she gasps as the frigid air fills her lungs and struggles to keep her eyes open against the bitter sleet and snow.

The biting wind cuts through her like a thousand knives. She shakes on Bengeo's back while he climbs the beast further, and watches the shadows of lofty tentacles sweep through the clouds.

The calamity's flesh shifts like quicksand between Bengeo's fingers. Malformed arms sprout from the tendril and grab at him with globby, misshapen hands. Remy quickly hacks them off, but more shoot up like malicious weeds and grapple them. Bengeo tears them off himself with one hand, but his grip falters and they both tumble downward, before more arms spring out and latch hold of him, pulling in different directions.

"I can't reach them!" Remy cries, swinging her sword overhead.

"Go on!" Bengeo yells as a dozen more emerge from the trunk of flesh and pull him in. "Keep climbing!"

"Not without you!"

"Damnit, girl, for once just do as I ask!" and with all his might he tears one arm free, draws the ferry stone from his pocket and shoves it in her mouth.

She clenches it between her teeth and shuffles up his body. Standing on his broad shoulders she drives her sword into the tendril and clings to the hilt.

"Make it count, kid!" Bengeo's arms sink into the creature's flesh, and he writhes and struggles as it drives to absorb him into its form. Summoning every ounce of strength he possesses, Bengeo tears himself free in one broad swoop and then plummets.

Remy watches on the edge of despair as his tank of a body crashes into the auditorium below with a whomp. She stares through the blustering snow and prays.

Get up. Please get up, but he lies still amongst the rubble.

She clenches the ferry stone in her jaw, and wraps her legs and right arm around the tendril. Inch by gruelling inch, she jabs her sword higher and higher, using it as a hold to pull herself further.

435

"Fuuuuuck!" she cries as the creature raises its tendril high.

She spots Vincent hurtling towards her. Like her, he's using his sword to cling to the beast and he holds out a hand as they pass each other. Remy shakes her head violently. There's no way in hell she's jumping.

"Come on!" Vincent cries over the raging tempest and leans out to catch her.

She shudders at a cold, wet sensation washing over her hand as the creature absorbs her sword and pulls her into its flesh. Against her better judgement she reaches out and takes Vincent's hand. He pulls her free and they cling to each other with all they've got.

*

Jessica races up the stairs to the mezzanine overlooking the hall and with a shrill roar, the wyvern thrusts itself into the air, crashes through the balcony and tears through a wall. She doubles back for the stairs, only to see Ed and Lauren sprinting towards her with fearful faces, behind them a stream of gnashing violent wights.

Ed takes her arm as he passes and leads the girls through snaking corridors between various conference rooms. The wyvern comes bursting through the plaster walls after them, snapping and roaring, clumsily treading over the undead until it wedges itself in a narrow bend.

Ed and the girls skid to a halt as a blue amorphous blob rears up at the far end of the corridor. Two big round eyes blink open from the goo and stare at them.

"Aww," Jessica swoons. It kind of looks like the emojis on her phone.

The blobkin parts its gooey maw and swallows her in one bite. She floats inside its gelatine body and chokes until Ed and Lauren plunge through the ooze and pull her to safety. All three of them tumble out the other side, coughing and wheezing as their skin burns like nettle rash all over. Jessica staggers to her feet and screams as the blobkin's eyes shift inside its body and pop out of its back. Now she knows those adorable buttons herald a painful demise.

The goo expands, filling the width and height of the corridor, then advances like a boobytrapped wall. They flee but are cut off by a trio of skeleton warriors, who charge at them. Thinking fast, Lauren pulls Ed and Jessica into a conference room and slams the door behind her.

"Help me with this!" Ed drags a long wooden table in the centre of the room against the door before the undead come bursting through. Clawing. Swinging. Screaming.

Lauren scans the room. *We're trapped! Shit, we're trapped! No no no! There's always a way out!* She glances up and gets an idea.

"Over here!" she cries. Climbing a cabinet in the far corner, she forces her way through the ceiling tiles into the crawl space above.

Ed boosts Jessica as the dead ram the door off its hinges until it caves inwards and burst into the room after them. A hand grabs Ed's heel, but he kicks it free, pulls himself into the crawl space and shuffles on all fours after the girls.

"Are we gonna die?" Jessica whimpers as she crawls behind Lauren.

Lauren looks back and vehemently shakes her head, "Not a chan—!"

The wyvern bursts through the tiles beside her, and she shrieks as it beats and claps its razor wings then tumbles back into the corridor below. The ceiling gives way and the three of them crash on top of the snarling lizard, which spins and kicks, trying in vain to fling them off while they cling to the spines running down its back. With a roar it dives off the mezzanine and soars into the hall that hosted the convention.

The beast snaps over its shoulder as a searing fireball hurtles past, then another explodes in the wyvern's face and it violently crashes through the demo area, scattering the monitors and games consoles across the hall.

Lauren lands awkwardly on her wrist and something that definitely shouldn't pop, pops. Throttling pain lances through her forearm. She bites her lip to stop herself from crying out and watches her wrist swell. The wyvern rises behind her as another fireball comes soaring overhead. Ed and Jessica pull her onto her feet and they sprint across the convention hall. Fire explodes at Ed's feet, hurling him back into the girls like a bowling ball. A hissing skeleton mage thrusts its bone staff forward, letting loose a chain of lightning that arcs straight at them. The wyvern crashes down between them, shielding them from the brunt of the spell, giving the girls an opening to get Ed to safety.

Jessica glimpses the vile undead mage, which hovers without legs, while two malevolent flames burn where its eyes should be. Behind it, more ravenous undead foot soldiers rally with weapons held high.

"We're screwed," she whimpers.

"Don't say that!" Lauren scolds her. "We've been in bad spots before, but something always came along!"

Pearly tears roll down Jessica's cheeks and she looks lovingly at Lauren. "I gotta tell you something."

"We're not gonna die!" Lauren cries, cradling her swollen wrist in her chest.

The building quakes and trembles, dislodging parts of the ceiling, which come crashing down around them.

Jessica looks at Lauren then quickly shies away. "I'm trying to—!"

The floor suddenly tears up in a circle. A long segmented worm tunnels around their feet and with a piercing shriek, rears its bulbous head. Great globs of phlegm ooze from its circular contracting mouth, filled with razor teeth that line its fleshy throat.

"What the fuck is that?!" Jessica screams.

"Death worm! Run!" Lauren sprints towards the toilets on the east side of the hall and pushes a dazed Ed into the men's room while dragon fire erupts with a bang behind them, scattering the skeleton mage's bones wide. Lauren watches the staff clatter across the floor and skid into the rubble. She lifts Ed's arm from around her shoulder, shifting his weight on Jessica who gasps as Lauren takes off and makes a brazen play for the staff. Her racing panic crushes her chest as her feet thud the floor. She can feel the violent rumble of something big stirring beneath her and leaps onto her belly before a stream of dragon fire soars overhead. The death worm blasts out of the floor beside her and ploughs into the wyvern, knocking it on its side. Lauren tumbles across the floor, and slams into a broken game station stand. She lifts herself onto her knees and lurches forward, heaving from the adrenaline and pain shooting through her wrist. Crawling on her elbows, propelling herself with her knees, she reaches out and grasps the staff tightly as the death worm and the wyvern battle behind her like the climax to a Godzilla movie.

"Please work!" she prays as she points the staff at the beasts and tries to conjure something – anything – that'll get them out of this mess. "Come on! Come on!" she cries, shaking it violently.

A hand lands on her shoulder. She jerks her head back and sees Jessica looking stern at her.

"Move your arse, Baker!" She drags Lauren into the men's room and Ed slams the weighty fire door behind them then presses himself against it. It shunts open, but the three of them pile their weight against it, forcing it shut. It bursts open again with greater force, throwing them against the stalls. The death worm jerks forward. Its salivating maw huffs while it desperately tries to contract itself enough to squeeze through the doorway while the wyvern sinks its teeth into the worm's tail.

Lauren looks at the evil creature then back at Jessica and takes a deep breath. If this is where their story ends, then she might as well come clean.

"I… I've felt pretty lost and numb these past couple of years, but somehow, it's like you lift that burden off me. Despite everything we've been through, I'm lucky that I got to meet you… I wish I hadn't waited until we're literally about to die to tell you that."

Jessica, thrilled beyond words to be the recipient of her affection, presses her lips against Lauren's, and for a fleeting moment time stands still. All the chaos and suffering and strife melts away. There's no more flesh-eating monsters or world-ending abominations, just the two of them. Lauren shivers and closes her eyes, but not to darkness. Instead she sees vibrant bursts of light. She's always wondered what it meant to lose yourself in a kiss. Now she knows as she disappears with Jessica.

Ed smiles while the girls share their first – and probably last – kiss. After a deep breath, the worm flops into the bathroom, tearing part of the wall down with it.

They tremble as it rises before them like a cobra ready to strike. Splitting pain crackles through Lauren's chest like a burgeoning panic attack, but she's sure this is something different, yet not unfamiliar to her. Her senses go haywire. She feels the swell of despair coursing through Jessica and Ed, and the worm's malicious intent. She can hear the wailing sky in the distance, and feel the heat of the fire coursing through the wyvern's throat. Ozrune's orotone voice resonates deep in the recesses of her mind.

"… *Step into your fears and push through until you transcend yourself, ride the emotion…*"

If her fear granted her power to tear the sky asunder, then surely her compassion could be the most effective way to banish the darkness. Kindness, selflessness, sacrifice – what evil could stand against that?

She throws the staff up in defence as the worm pounces, and releases a visceral scream that encompasses her entire being – her struggles, her pain, her hopes, her dreams. The staff shimmers with golden light as she clutches it steadfastly, illuminating her like some holy goddess. Warm tears spill down her cheeks as a wave, an awesome wave, swells from her chest and shivers to her fingertips, bestowing a powerful urge to nurture and protect – a love and light within that will not be threatened.

Jessica watches in awe as light engulfs the room. The thought that her life might be snuffed out before she had the chance to really live fills her with desolation, but the soft yellow glow quickly soothes her pain. The light must be – she thinks to herself – the prelude to some kind of afterlife, but no. In a flash, the light cuts them off from the death worm, which rages against an ethereal wall born of Lauren's unyielding will to save her friends, until a surge of dragon fire floods the bathroom, scorching it, and everything else, to blackened charcoal. Varicoloured flame dances against Lauren's barrier. She clenches the bone staff tightly in her hand and the tiny cracks that scar it splinter up and down as the spell takes its toll. The sweltering heat kisses her face as the barrier falters against the wyvern's primal ferocity. She feeds the barrier her life force like an IV drip. Jessica and Ed prop her up assuring her she's not alone, while the magic drains her already weary body.

*

Against the bitter rage of the calamity, Vincent battles his way towards the colossal eye. Every movement is a struggle as he bears the weight of his armour and Remy on his back. Jabbing his sword into its flesh, he forces himself across the jagged crystal spikes that jut out across its central mass. He bides his time and brazenly leaps onto a tendril as it sweeps by.

441

"Face me!" he cries over the thunderous tempest. "Let me look into the eye of the world-ender! Eric, if you're in there let me see you!"

Somewhere in the darkest recesses of consciousness a flicker of Eric remains, aware of the malevolent force trying to erode his being – his memories, all he ever was. He can feel the pull of the evil, feeding on the tormented souls of hundreds, if not thousands, of undead that wail in despair amidst the cycle of energy coursing through its veins. To give in, to disappear amongst the tide would be the end of him – a fate that Eric cannot bear. The crystal was to be his tool to reshape the world. He created it. To become a mere part of it would be too cruel and too ironic. His hubris was always one of his most defining traits. Even in the face of utter annihilation his ego doesn't shrink.

"*M-y ar-m, i-t's m-y a-rm.*"

The calamity raises them before its gargantuan eye, and the unholy pupil bores into their souls, chilling their minds with unspeakable terror. Some say the eyes are the window to the soul, but this window gives way to no such thing, only darkness devoid of love, of light, of anything good and pure. If death is defined as the absence of life then they are certainly looking into the eye of the reaper. Ed was right, this is evil incarnate.

"Most run from death, cower before it, but the two of you stand in its presence, audacious. Others have tried, all have perished and risen again as my boon," the voice thunders. Every word conjures a disturbing sense of wrongness that churns Remy's stomach and makes her skin crawl.

Vincent collapses on his knees as it stares them both down and clutches the broken sword tip lodged in his side. "I'm done," he groans.

"Not yet! We're not done yet! So get up!" Remy pulls him on his feet. "We've still got the stone, we can end this!"

He struggles to focus on her and slips back onto one knee.

He can feel death's icy touch lingering over his shoulder. His blood runs cold, his limbs stiffen.

"I'm done."

"I know..." Remy looks woeful at his ice-white face. The frost has him in its grasp.

"Finish it," he coughs and collapses onto all fours as his body starts to shut down.

If I do this, there's no coming back – a thought that breaks her bounding heart.

The violent wind scatters her hair across her face while she gazes at the ferry stone. Tears spill like water from a crumbling dam. Funny, she despised that bedroom – the pastel paint, the lumpy futon, the view of Ed's house from the window – but right now she'd give anything to be back there, snuggled in her duvet, warm and comfortable, a far cry from the spite she's enduring now. Her muscles quiver like a child taking their first steps, but she glares at the eye with utter fury and thrusts the ferry stone into the air.

"Darkness will never thrive where there is light to meet it!" she screams.

The eye tightens its gaze on her. "Foolish girl, I dwell in the shadows and extinguish the light. Hear me now, this world shall never see another dawn!"

Its pitch-black pupil expands, engulfing her field of vision. She glimpses a universe devoid of stars, of light, of life. A cold hopelessness washes over her, weakening her resolve – how can she stand against this?

She releases a rebellious cry imbued by love for her family and new-found friends. The stone glistens in her hand. She closes her eyes, accepting her fate.

Her unrelenting determination to persevere and sacrifice herself touches Vincent who, on death's doorstep, forces himself on his feet one final time. The Dreadmail tightens around his muscles, bolstering the splinter of life he has left.

Remy pictures the crater and its holy light in her mind. The air dances around her and magic swells from the stone as it begins to transport them all back into the Scar. Cold metal grasps her wrist. She opens her eyes and Vincent snatches the stone from her.

"Remy... thank you... for playing my game." A parting smile graces his gaunt face, and he pushes her off the calamity as it releases a cacophonous roar that shatters glass for miles. Rays of blinding light break through the black clouds like the grace of God. The calamity and the Dread Knight disappear in a flash.

*

Across the city Lin, Helen, Alapati and George watch from the barricaded hospital as the undead fall apart. With the evil vanquished from reality, the monsters fester and crumble to dust. Now the power that animated them is gone, perhaps their corrupted souls are finally free to make their journey to the lofty realm.

Helen looks ever so relieved that the madness appears to be over, but her heart is burdened with thoughts of her children's safety. She looks worriedly at Lin, who hugs George tightly, and prays that Lauren is okay too.

*

Jessica, Lauren and Ed stare slack-jawed as the wyvern coils up before them and dissolves like sand in the wind. The dead too lay down their arms and fall away.

"Is it over?" Ed asks, picking himself off the floor of the wrecked bathroom.

He limps into the crumbling remains of the expo hall and sees nothing but ash and carnage. Lauren breathes a sigh of deep relief as she props herself up against the battered wall. The ExCel centre has been laid to waste.

Jessica races through the hall towards the decimated remnants of the auditorium and scans the rubble for any sign of the others. She finds Bengeo lying in a heap on his side and shakes him.

"Hey! Hey! Wake up!" she cries, fighting back tears.

"Stop…" he groans.

"Wha…? What did you say?!" She holds her ear over his mouth.

"I said, stop. You're pushing on broken bones…" He rolls slowly onto his back, grimacing. "… Did we win?"

"Looks like," she smiles, barely believing it herself.

"Good." With a harsh breath he rests his eyes.

Lauren looks for signs of Remy and Vincent. Her heart sinks as she fears the worst. "I don't see them."

"Remy?" Jessica calls out while sifting through piles of rubble. "Remy?!"

No answer and no sign of her either.

"Did she—" Ed drops to his knees, unwilling to even consider that she got sent back into the game. Fury bubbles and he erupts. "Fuck! Shit! No!" he cries, beating his fists against the rubble until he can't swing anymore.

"Ed…" Lauren says softly. He looks at her with reddening eyes.

"It can't be…." He leans on his knees. His stomach twists in knots.

Jessica sobs as the thought of never seeing her sister again begins to sink in, but as the wind dies down a faint murmur catches her ear. She listens intently. It sounds like one of those groaning corpses.

"What was that?" she asks.

They fan out across the auditorium searching for the origin. Ed climbs over the crumbling wall and trudges outside, turning his head slowly to pinpoint the source.

"There!" He spots Remy lying in the crisp white snow and runs to her. Pressing his ear to her chest, he rejoices at the faint beat of her heart.

Her eyes flutter open to the sight of his head buried in her bosom.

"Get off me, perv," she mutters groggily.

He looks at her, elated. "Yes! Yes! We did it!" He slumps back and laughs.

Jessica comes running and skids to her knees. Burying her head in Remy's shoulder, she sobs, "I swear I'll never complain about sharing my room with you again!"

"Same," Remy smiles. Shifting her weight onto her elbows, she casts her eyes over the destroyed convention hall – which somehow looks worse on the outside than it does inside.

She jolts suddenly. "Bengeo! He fell and—!"

"Bengeo's fine!" Lauren calls out as she hobbles over the rubble, leaning against the bandit for support.

"Bengeo's alive. Fine doesn't quite cut it," he groans.

"W-what about Vincent?" Lauren asks in a meek voice. Deep down she already knows he's gone.

Remy shakes her head. "He... he saved me."

Lauren lets out a solemn breath. Another loss darkens this day.

Battered and bruised the friends embrace each other amidst the ruin and wreckage as the faltering snow flutters over them. The evil lies defeated, and the rift supposedly closed. It seems their adventure has finally reached its end. Game over.

POSTLUDE

Valentine casts his tired eyes over the drab hospital room he's come to know as home these past few weeks. Magnolia walls with yellowing trim; the curtains too have faded from their original blue and yellow floral pattern to dull shades of beige. He tuts in disgust at the news playing on the boxy television in the corner, and shakes his head as the report downplays the unreal events of last month as a severe weather storm that decimated the London ExCel centre and cost millions in property damage across the city. He reaches for the remote on the edge of the table at his bedside and grimaces at the sharp pain in his gut. Abandoning the remote, he lies back slowly as the door to his room creaks open, and a mass of scruffy red hair emerges from behind it.

Ed skulks into the room and pulls up a chair. "How's the hole today?" he asks.

"It's not a hole. How many times do I...! Bah," Valentine scoffs. "Don't you have anything better to do than pester an old man?"

"You're not *that* old," Ed replies.

"Ha!" the detective laughs. "So you're getting out, huh?"

Ed shrugs. "You make it sound like prison."

"Feels like prison." Valentine frowns at the unsightly pudding cup on the table while Ed wanders to the window and looks over the get well soon cards on the windowsill. Five in total, one sagging helium balloon and a stuffed bear – undoubtedly from Jessica. He picks up a card, opens it gently and smiles at Remy's chicken scratch writing.

Valentine knows just whose card he's looking at. "She came by last week, was getting her arm checked."

"Yeah, I kind of remember seeing her, but I was so out of it I wasn't sure if it was just a morphine fever dream. Did she seem okay?"

"Sure…" Valentine says, recalling the lost look in her eyes, hidden behind a smile that wasn't disingenuous but more a courtesy than anything else, "… I expect she just needs a little time to adjust, eh?"

Ed sets the card down with a loving sigh. "Hole in your gut aside, how're you coping? Speak to your daughter?"

"She doesn't want to see an old man on his death bed."

"You're not on your death bed." Ed rolls his eyes. "You did call her though?" he asks.

Valentine lets out a long sigh, bracing himself as he forces out words he can't bear to hear. "She… she didn't want to see me."

"Oh."

They both look downcast.

"Women, am I right?" Ed's attempt at lightening the mood falls flat. They sit rapt in silence, and Valentine looks a sorry sight pitying himself in that polka-dot hospital gown.

"Well, these pills they're giving me are taking their toll," the detective grumbles, "I better get some rest."

"Yeah, I'll leave you to it." Ed approaches the door and turns the handle.

"Hey uh…" Valentine clears his throat, "… you don't all have to stop by every day."

"Yeah, I know. Catch you tomorrow?" he smiles.

Valentine tries not to let on that these visits actually mean a lot to him, but a creeping smirk gives him away. "Yeah, tomorrow."

With that, Ed pulls the door to and peers through the crack at the tired old man while he stares longingly at the tattered picture of the daughter he misses so dearly.

*

Jessica leans against the bar, anxiously biting her nails to the cuticles while she stares at the stage, recalling the last time she graced it and the audience with the contents of her stomach. What a night that turned out to be. She looks fondly at the venue – the brick walls painted black, the spotlights illuminating the stage which overlooks the concrete dance area surrounded by tables and chairs spaced about. It all feels so much smaller now. Still smells like piss and beer though. At least some things never change.

A hand takes her wrist and gently rests it by her side, sparing what's left of the chipped black nail polish she's wearing.

"You shouldn't bite your nails, I read that it can make your voice deeper."

Jessica looks with dread at Lauren's face beaming back at her.

"I'm kidding," she grins.

"Don't do that, I'm bricking it enough already."

Lauren chuckles. "Surely this is nothing compared to your last gig."

"Is it wrong that I wish we were playing to flesh-eating zombies?" Jessica laughs. "How's your wrist?"

"Itches like crazy." Lauren looks at her cast, decorated with doodles and scribbles, most prominently a sketch of Avarice the troll, drawn in black marker like a pin-up you'd see on the side of an old war plane.

"Reckon you could cast a spell or something? Make it heal quicker?" Jessica asks.

"Doubt it," Lauren sighs. "Think I lost my mojo after Remy sent that thing back to hell. Guess I'm not special anymore."

"You're special to me." With a loving smile, her eyes meet Lauren's and they lean into each other.

Helen's jaw hangs open. She stutters, watching the girls kiss and embrace each other.

"Relax, Mum. I'm happy for them." Remy tries to subdue her shit-eating grin as it all clicks into place for her mother.

"They're at it again," George sighs, staring over his shoulder at his sister until his mother nudges him.

"What did we talk about?" Lin asks in a foreboding tone.

He rolls his eyes. "Privacy, yeah, yeah…" He slumps back in his chair, sips his Diet Coke and turns his attention back to the video game he's playing on his handheld console.

"So all this time they've been spending together…" Helen trails off, but her eyes stay fixed on the girls. "… Ray, did you know Jessica and Lauren are—?"

"Mmm," he mumbles and sips his lager while he scrolls through the news on his phone.

Remy glimpses the article over his shoulder. The residual energy blast from the ferry stone banishing the colossal eye in the sky had caused a city-wide power outage, which had to some extent helped slow the exchange of information about the incident while it unfolded. Because of the whiteout most of the pictures and video evidence were just shaky images of faint silhouettes in the snow – the stuff of conspiracy theorists and crackpots. Call it a cover-up, and maybe it is, but chatter still permeates online. Entire sub-reddits and forums are dedicated to debunking the truth behind the 'Beast from the East', as the storm was dubbed by the mainstream media. But only a few truly know the reality of it all. Perhaps reality is a poor choice of word.

Remy spots Bengeo leaning against the back wall, happily devouring a cheeseburger and relishing every bite. Despite his best efforts to blend in, his herculean stature makes him look wildly out of place.

"Not as strong as the stuff you're used to, but it's not bad." Remy approaches and hands him a beer.

"It all goes down the same."

"It's not easy being stuck in an alien world, but I hope it's not been too difficult for you."

"It ain't all bad, this world certainly has its perks," he says, licking ketchup off his fingers.

"Yeah, it's not so bad." She glances tentatively at the door.

Bengeo laughs. "Waiting for anyone in particular?"

She breaks into a smile and quickly deflects the conversation. "Jessica show you how to use the internet yet?"

"The magic window thingy? I think I'm getting the hang of it." He brandishes an old smartphone Jessica had given him and shows her his Instagram profile, which has thousands of followers.

Remy gasps. "How'd you get so many?" She takes the phone and thumbs through his gallery of shirtless pictures and videos of himself lifting inhuman amounts of weight. The latest shows him deadlifting Jessica and Lauren like dumbbells.

"Of course," Remy laughs, "been in this world less than a month and you're an influencer." She notices Bengeo turn his gaze towards the door.

Following his eye line, she sees Constable Alapati looking all dolled up. She scans the room and looks relieved when she spots them.

Remy asks, "Is that—?"

"Yeah," Bengeo replies.

"She's coming over."

"We've been… What is it Jessica says? Snapping?"

"*Snapping?*" Remy looks visibly unsettled. Like a child of divorce whose father is dating someone they disapprove of.

"Hi." Alapati greets Bengeo with a timid smile while Remy stares at her in utter disbelief. "Remy." She nods politely.

Remy continues to stare like she's seen a ghost. "You're... here?"

"Believe it or not, I'm actually a person under all that stress and paperwork," Alapati replies.

Remy snaps out of her trance. "Yeah, of course, I just... I mean, I never in a million years thought... because he's... and you're... well, you know."

The three of them stand uncomfortably for a good minute before Remy takes the hint and excuses herself.

Pushing her way through the growing crowd, she steps outside to process Bengeo, not only assimilating into society more successfully than her, but dating the woman who'd spent hours interviewing and cross-examining them about what had really happened while they were missing. It was all an act, sure. She knew the truth, and so did they, but they had to get their story straight – *'invent a more suitable narrative'* as Valentine had put it. After all, Alapati had to put on a show for her superiors, and there were too many questions that needed answering. But after the game world was gone, the monsters had all festered away and other than some shaky video footage and scrambled statements from panicked convention attendees there wasn't any concrete evidence that any of it had really happened. Officially the deaths and disappearances of all those at the convention were explained as a tragic loss of life sustained in the building's collapse. So back to a life of obscurity it is.

The cold night air is a refreshing change from the stench of stale beer permeating the bar. Taking a deep breath to calm her nerves, she casts her eyes at the starry sky. Over the past weeks she had spent a great deal of time staring at the silver moon, reflecting on the trials she had endured and the people that had played such a vital role in it all. She found herself missing them all – Avarice the troll, Regis and the crow-headed wizard Ozrune, Marcus, Cleo and Esmerelda, the townsfolk of Trout, even Astrid and Tank. She often wondered what had become of Pangea Ultima. Had it survived the great calamity? Was it ever just a game or was it always as real as the world around her now? Most of all she thought of Vincent and what had become of him. Had he died, nobly sacrificing himself as he cast Eric's abominable form into the Scar, or by some miracle clung to life and survived in that place? She wrestled with accepting she would probably never know the answer but liked to believe that they had at least saved the game world from ruin, whatever the nature of its reality was. Strangely she would often picture the look on Vincent's face as he pushed her off the creature right before casting it into the void – the little smile that graced his lips, the glint in his eye. She doesn't think she could ever forgive him for all that he'd done, but to some extent, he had redeemed himself in her eyes, if only a little. Her breath materialises in the winter air as she lets out a frustrated sigh, her mind weary from treading in circles.

Ed spies her as he walks the street approaching the bar and stops to watch her through the trees as she lingers in the car park, lost in deep thought. Her dark hair glows at the edges under the hazy yellow streetlight. His heart flutters as she turns, and he ducks, worried that she'll spot him. He hasn't the faintest idea what to say, and he's desperate not to put his foot in it this time. A deep breath brings composure. He peeks again. Her face sends a shiver through him. She's the most beautiful thing he's ever seen.

"Hey, you," he calls to her as he crosses the street, hands tucked into his jacket pockets. His footsteps crunch on the remnants of snow, which had mostly thawed since closing the rift but some still remained, tucked in the nooks of the city.

"Hey." She greets him with a shy smile.

He looks her up and down, savouring every detail. It feels like a lifetime since they last saw each other properly. He admires her hair tucked behind one ear as it falls onto her face, which is marked by a dozen cuts and scrapes that fade with each passing day, and a sweep of mascara lines her amber eyes which look on him fondly.

"Aren't you cold?" he asks her.

"I just needed some air."

He notices the doleful look on her face. "Dwelling on the past?"

"That obvious?" she sighs. "I just… How are we supposed to go back after all of that?"

"Maybe one day it'll seem like more of a dream than a memory."

The very notion seems impossible to her. "Do you think you'll play it again? The game?" she asks.

He shakes his head. "I don't know, it feels too soon. Maybe someday."

"Yeah, I get it." She tucks her loose hair back behind her ear and looks downcast. "Doesn't it drive you mad? Wondering how… why it all happened? Sometimes I feel like, are we crazy?"

"No," Ed replies. "I think we've just been through some stuff."

Remy offers a smile at his attempt to comfort her, but the not knowing is gnawing away at her, like an itch that can't be scratched, and Ed can see it too.

He clears his throat. "Have you ever heard of fictional realism?"

She shakes her head.

"I read about it when I was in the hospital. The theory is that if an infinite number of universes exist, then somewhere a sequence of events has led to things playing out exactly as they do in a video game or a movie or a book. So I'm thinking maybe we weren't actually in the game at all, but trapped in an alternate universe where the game is reality?"

"So what? We're all just a work of fiction in someone else's world?" she asks, her face a picture of scepticism.

Ed shrugs. "Maybe it was all just a big cosmic glitch. That's my top theory anyway. Others include a secret government experiment gone awry or a tear in the space–time continuum. Honestly I try not to dwell on it too much, or I'll lose my mind."

"Yeah…" Remy sighs. "Still, I can't believe we're back."

"How is it? I mean, got any idea what you're gonna do now?"

She shrugs. "Not really, but I'm okay with that. I decided I'm just going to take some time to figure stuff out, unscramble the egg that is me. I'm realising that who I am isn't what I do, I still have worth. Besides, Mum has been surprisingly non-confrontational about the whole no job thing, so no pressure there. Guess I'll be across the road for a little while."

"That's good. Awesome actually." He feigns cool composure, but inside he's dancing the boogaloo.

"Yeah, I've even got an actual bed now," she laughs.

"Look at you," he smiles. "You look good. I mean… you seem happier in some way, not that you don't look good, you do. Great actually! I'm not used to seeing you pretty but… Oh God, not that you weren't pretty before, I just meant like… you know. But you looked great without makeup too, even with muck and blood all over your face. It was a bold look, but you worked it…" Internally he's screaming at himself to shut up. He's faced monsters, undead generals, driven through central London in a blizzard, why is this still so difficult? Chalk it up to some things never change.

Remy finds a smile creeping across her face as he nervously babbles and realises that she kind of missed it. "I'm sorry I've been so—"

"Distant?"

She shuffles awkwardly on her feet. "I just needed some time to process everything. The way everything went down, losing Esmerelda and Avarice, well, I needed to get my head right."

"It's okay, I get it. It was probably for the best anyway, I got pretty sick from swallowing all that river water."

"Yeah, I know," she chuckles. "When I came to see you, you shared every excruciating detail."

He combs his hand through his hair, dreading to think what he said. "Oh. So that was real? I was pretty out of it."

She leans towards him. "When you plunged into the Thames, and we thought you were... well, it occurred to me that I'd got pretty used to having you around and recently I realised that I like having you around."

Her eyes meet his for a fleeting second before absconding to the far reaches of the night, but she caught the smile creeping across his face.

"I think I was a little scared that if we weren't running for our lives or saving the world then it wouldn't be the same or we wouldn't feel... I mean, *if* you feel the same. Lately, I've been thinking about you a lot and well, I really would like it if you were in my life." She rubs her forehead, looking frustrated. "Am I making any sense?"

He's been thinking about this moment for the better part of the last month, hopelessly waiting and wondering about her, but now the words are lost. Her eyes are begging him to say something, anything to put her out of her misery. He knows he should kiss her now, but before he can make his move, Helen's shrill cry carries from the doorway of the bar.

"They're starting, hurry up and come in!"

"Guess we better..." Remy sighs and nods to the door.

Ed leads her inside, nodding politely at Helen as he passes her. "S-sorry again, about your car," he mumbles guiltily.

"Thanks, Mum," Remy's eyes scream, but Helen's oblivious as to why.

*

Berserk Statement step onto the stage. Ziggy, Tyler and Scuzz ready their instruments as Jessica adjusts the mic stand to her height. She looks back, giving Scuzz a nod. The music starts, the room falls silent, and all eyes turn to the stage as the spotlights go up. Jessica's golden hair falls at her shoulders, and her makeup hides her blushing beneath a blanket of white. For a moment, fear seizes her as she presses her lips to the mic, but a deep breath softens the tightness in her chest. She looks out into the crowd, at Lauren, at Remy, at her friends and family, and closes her eyes. She breaks into a smile as she pictures the horde of flesh-eating horrors, which oddly brings her confidence, and as the applause dies down, she parts her cherry lips.

"Is it reality that shapes us, or us who shape reality? Is any of this real or not?" The lyrics roll off her tongue, melting her fear away. Oohs and ahhs roll over the room like waves spilling on sand. Her silvery voice transfixes the crowd as she sings the words only she knows well.

Bengeo smirks as he bobs his head at the back of the room. Watching Jessica sing, and the others dance, makes him feel like it all was for something. His world is gone, and he's sure he'll never see it again, but they're his crew now. His family.

Remy looks proudly at her sister glistening in the spotlights on stage. She stands with Ed amidst the crowd, stealing glances and choking her words while they tremble beside one another. Her hand grazes his, and her heart spikes as he takes hold of it. For a moment, she forgets her troubles and rests easy. Even though her adventure is over she knows this is the beginning of so many things.